The Arcadian Path

The Arcadian Path

Jeff Taylor

ISBN 978-0-578-30295-9

First edition

I dedicate this book to my wonderful wife Elvira for her love, support, and encouragement. I couldn't have done it without you. I also thank my good friend Jan for reading and commenting on the manuscript. You could always make me laugh.

Table of Contents

Introduction to the United Worlds History Series

A button click can take you across town or across the galaxy. It can also strip away every shred of human privacy, safety, and security.

The year 2070 CE marked the beginning of the Age of Enlightened Expansion. RingTech portal technology allowed human expansion into the universe, while the Arcadian Path philosophy enlightened and united humanity in a shared dream for a better future.

Part one, The Arcadian Path.

Miles Finerty was the first person to breathe the air of an alien world, the first person to experience the profound, mind-altering effects of planet Arcadia. His journey in 2070 CE inspired the Arcadian Path—the philosophy that has shaped civilization on all of the United Worlds.

But, not even a good philosophy can change human nature. Without strict control, a RingTech portal is the ultimate weapon. It allows the corrupt to peer into a neighbor's bedroom, empty a bank vault, or drop raw sewage directly into the President's office.

Part two, Beryl Awakening

By 434 EE, RingTech portals are everywhere, in every home, office, pocket, and purse. Cromen and Nava are two young lovers from opposite ends of society, that get pulled innocently into the center of a terrifying, galaxy-spanning conspiracy, orchestrated by the corrupt leaders of the Church of Seven Apostles, commonly called WARU. The Orthodox Waru clergy hold their non-orthodox congregation to very strict moral codes. Do they really live by the same standards they impose on the congregation?

Nava and Cromen only wanted to be together and have a little adventure—but now, the fate of civilization rests in their hands.

From the utopian heights of advanced civilization to the dark frontiers of bootleg planets Heaven and Hell, Nava and Cromen fight to survive while revealing dark secrets along the way.

Can they stop the ultimate galactic threat and find their way back to each other? Or is the age of enlightenment about to burn?

"...sanity is a rather rare phenomenon, I am convinced that it can be achieved and I would like to see more of it."

- Aldous Huxley

Part 1 – The Arcadian Path

Chapter 1 Paradise

By the time humans reached the stars, there were more than eleven billion people on Planet Earth. As the population had grown, so had science and production to meet their growing needs. But production, always a step behind the needs, left many millions in poverty and misery. And production was always at the expense of the beautiful natural environment.

The development of practical space travel (fast, easy, and cheap) opened new worlds to colonize for the ever-expanding human race. New worlds that provided opportunity and hope for the future.

But the emigration to other planets brought Planet Earth to a crossroads. Would Earth be abandon like trash and humans move on to places more pristine? Or would Planet Earth be made into the human paradise of our dreams?

The physical and spiritual paradise available to everyone today on Earth and on all of the United Worlds was unimaginable in the mid-twenty-first century. This paradise is largely due to the Arcadian Path, the path to a more civilized society, the path to a happy fulfilling life for all people.

Earth's natural environment has been restored to provide sufficient food and resources to meet the need of everyone. The Earth has been nurtured, molded, and engineered to create ideal living conditions for her people; the people have learned to love their beautiful home and appreciate existence in harmony.

During the great expansion of the 22nd and 23rd centuries CE the United Worlds encouraged the governments on all the newly formed worlds to use the Arcadian Path as a way to promote healthy new civilizations. And most of the 222 new human worlds terraformed using RingTech did use the Arcadian Path to guide them. Most, but not all.

One man's experience on another planet, with the encouragement of his loving wife, led to creation of the Arcadian Path. This is their story, the story of two dreamers in love, devoted to helping others appreciate the beauty of human existence.

Chapter 2 Dreams

Miles Finerty was the first person to set foot on planet Arcadia, the first person to breathe the air of an alien world.

But on returning to Earth, Miles had dreams, waking him early in the morning, his heart racing, his body filled with excitement, his mind alive with an intense feeling of joy. In his dreams he was back on Arcadia, walking in the beautiful green landscape of that alien world, breathing the rich sweet air, feeling again the elation which planet Arcadia demanded of you, feeling that sense of beautiful joy Arcadia could impose on your mind.

One common dream began with Miles walking up the green slope of a hill near their ship with the crew's computer linguist. The hilltop had a comfortable shady place to relax and enjoy the view. Puffy white clouds drifted through a deep turquoise sky above a sparkling blue sea. Clouds drifted on, over green coastal plains and mountain foothills, then piled up against jagged mountain peaks. Miles had walked up the hill many times during the exploration of Arcadia, it helped him relax and enjoy the strange reality this planet presented.

But in his dream, he raced up the hill with a friend, like two children drunk with the energy and exhilaration of youth, arriving at the top gasping, panting, and laughing, in almost hysterical joy. Their emotions overwhelmed them as though the sky and Earth harmonized to a point of perfect resonance and then exploded in waves of ecstasy. Not romantic or erotic, just overpowering joy. It felt so good that Miles woke up emotionally excited and smiling.

These powerful dreams came to him often, even years after returning to Earth. In some dreams he was a child running and playing with other children, filled with the happy excitement to be alive. In other dreams he was just standing in the beautiful green landscape of Arcadia, observing and feeling what he described to others as: "a sense of profound mental clarity that made you feel perfect."

Doctors suspected Miles might be infected with an alien organism, either this, or he was losing his grip on reality. But the myriad of tests and observations showed no physical or mental problems. The other crew members had similar dreams, maybe not as often or as intense, but similar in nature. And all three were mentally and physically healthy, so concern about Miles' dreams had faded over time.

The doctors no longer worried, but Arcadia had changed Miles. The dreams seemed to drive him with a positive energy to a new purpose in life, a new passion.

Miles didn't worry about the dreams, he loved them; they felt good. They felt good all day!

Chapter 3 Miles

Miles hadn't aspired to be a space explorer, he just happened to be what NASA needed at the time.

As a boy, he had a passion for observing nature; he would spend hours following a lizard to understand how it lived; spend the whole day watching a flower to discover what insects came to visit. Miles was the quiet kid in the back of the classroom staring out the window, the one that seemed bright but failed all his classes. He liked people and had a few good friends, but had trouble fitting-in to most social situations.

His passion for observing nature was strong enough to overcome his early social and academic failure. This passion led him to a career where his intellect and powers of observation were valued. His talents in field biology brought him academic success and a position as Professor of Biology specializing in ecosystem field research at the California Institute of Technology (CALTECH), located in Pasadena California, just north of Los Angeles.

The biology fieldwork Miles conducted around the world had brought him face to face with people living in poverty and misery. He was overwhelmed by the contrast of these countries, between the rich and the poor, between the misery of the people and the beauty of the rich natural environment. Miles' thoughts were haunted by these people abandoned by their government, uneducated, and without opportunity or hope.

To understand how Miles developed his ideas for the Arcadian Path, we need to go back about 6 months before he visited Planet Arcadia. Back to a warm fall afternoon on the CALTECH campus.

A dry Santa Anna wind blew yellow and brown Sycamore leaves across the green well-kept lawn. The day was clear and bright, but too hot for late October. Students were relaxing on the grass when Professor Miles Finerty, walking back to his office after finishing a Field Biology lecture, ran into Carl Phillips.

Carl was a master of proposal writing and obtaining important research funding for the university, but Carl never did the work himself, not even the management. He always left the research work to others. Miles didn't mind. Carl was a nervous flake but a very nice guy and Miles had received some interesting and well-funded projects from Carl.

"I've been looking for you Miles."

Miles smiled. "Nice to see you, Carl. What do you have?"

Carl was excited about a new NASA project. He had funding and needed to build an organization to conduct the research. He needed people to do the work.

"Here's the project information," He said, handing Miles a messy folder full of papers. "There's a meeting on it tomorrow morning at 9:00, they're in a big rush."

"Wow. They're in a rush and I don't have time," Miles replied, not wanting to look too eager or available. "But I'll give it a quick glance. How about meeting at the Dulzura Tavern at about 5:30. We can talk about it over dinner?"

"Thanks, Miles, I'll see you then."

Miles was sitting in a booth grading examination papers and sipping a nice hoppy IPA when Carl rushed into the busy tavern.

"So what do you think, Miles?" He queried before even sitting down.

"Carl, have you looked at what you gave me? It's really low resolution. They want maps made without sufficient data. Half the information is classified and not shown. The data they do show isn't believable, it looks like they made it up. Where'd they get it? And what do they want me to do with it? I just can't make much sense of it."

"You know the NASA guys Miles. They give you incredible stuff, but don't always show their full hand. I need you on this one, you're the only man with the qualifications and security clearance for the job."

"Oh, come on, Carl. You know Bob Meyers could do it!"

"Bob's not the field biologist that you are, Miles. He's a great lab and theory guy but you're the master of ecosystem field investigation."

"Field investigation!" exclaimed Miles in surprise. "Where did it say anything about field investigation?"

"I promise you, Miles, this is just down your alley. It'll look a whole lot better once you see the complete package."

The enthusiasm in Carl's face told Miles that there must be something interesting. "Okay, if the data is real, I'd like to know where they got it. And, if it's bogus, well, I'll give the NASA guys a hard time about it. Where's the meeting?" responded Miles, feeling a little skeptical but committed to giving it a chance.

Carl knew Miles was hooked and smiled confidently as he got up to go. "See you tomorrow at 9:00 am in the JPL 231B conference room. You know the one."

The Jet Propulsion Laboratory (JPL) is a NASA research facility managed by CALTECH and located a few miles away from the CALTECH campus. Only seven people were in the meeting. Miles was surprised and knew it was something big when he saw Dr. John Watkins, the head of NASA JPL. He recognized Carlos Jones from the CALTECH Geology department and the other NASA staff member. There were two people he didn't know.

The doors were locked and Dr. Watkins gave a standard security brief. "The information I am about to tell you is Top Secret, it stays in this room. Don't talk among yourselves, nor your family or friends, nobody, no exceptions. This is very serious business."

Dr. Watkins paused, looked around the room, then stunned them all with the first words of his formal briefing.

"NASA has developed an inter-dimensional portal that allows virtually instantaneous travel from point to point anywhere in the universe. I'm not joking with you!" he paused to observe the audience before continuing.

"This is the most exciting technological advancement in human history and it will have a profound impact on everything, absolutely everything in our society."

He paused again and looked around the room at the dazed faces of the distinguished scientists.

"Take a deep breath," he smiled. "May I proceed?"

"The official name of this technology is the Directional Quasi Singularity Portal or DQSP, but you will hear it referred to most often as the Portal. It is just what the name implies, a portal or door, it acts something like a Black Hole singularity but in two dimensions. It bypasses the space between two locations within the area of a control ring. The DQSP creates an opening to another location anywhere in the universe and allows you, or a ship, to pass safely through to the other location."

"Whether it's flattened two-dimensional space or an opening thru the fifth or sixth dimension is debatable. Call it a worm-hole, warped space, quantum distortion, or whatever you like, it works and NASA has been using it for almost 16 months. The science behind the generation of the DQSP field is classified beyond the level of this audience. You don't have a need to know, so don't ask."

"What I can tell you is that the size of the portal opening is determined by the size of the control ring which generates the DQSP field. The bigger the ring the more power is needed to maintain the field. The distance you travel is determined by the frequency of the applied power. You align the ring perpendicular to the location you want to go (like pointing a telescope) and provide the power level and frequency to obtain the correct distance."

"It is safe, inexpensive to operate, and will change our world quickly and in who knows how many ways. Instantaneous transfer of people and material from one point to another will eliminate numerous forms of transportation; shipping of goods and materials around the country and world, business and tourist travel, and," he paused again before continuing, "of most significance for us at NASA is space travel."

"It should be obvious to you that this technology needs very tight control to avoid abuse. You could use a portal to look into your neighbor's bedroom or to empty a bank vault. It could be used to spy on another country or for business espionage. You could step into the office of the President of the United States and... well, use your imagination."

"Our government is currently talking with the United Nations about cooperation and regulation. We are hopeful that regulatory plans will be finalized before this technology is disclosed to the general public. But we can't keep the lid on this much longer. It will go public within a few months – sooner if too much information leaks out and NASA is forced to address it."

"But NASA is not waiting for the bureaucrats and politicians to come to an agreement. We have congressional and presidential approval to continue with research and development, and our funding is almost unlimited. Most of our older projects are obsolete. We don't need to send rockets to explore our solar system, or to deliver satellites into orbit. Who needs a two-year mission to Mars when we can make the trip in a day and at a small fraction of the cost and under much safer conditions."

"We have operational systems already in regular use between the Earth and the far side of the Moon, where a lunar facility is operational and growing rapidly. NASA's Houston facility has multiple large transfer portals sending a steady stream of shipping containers filled with construction supplies and equipment. We can actually drive a cement truck to the lunar facility, deliver the cement and drive the truck back to Earth in less than two hours. Water, electricity, and air are being supplied directly from the Earth to the Moon through pipe and conduit connections passing through utility portals."

"There is a portal here in this building which I use regularly to inspect mission progress on the lunar base. It's almost like going down the hall into another office. You can see the lunar base on the other side of the portal before you go through."

"Transfers are complicated, however, by the constantly changing relative position of the Earth and Moon. Sometimes their up is our sideways or down. But these are only engineering problems that have been worked out to make the transfer safe and comfortable."

"NASA has already sent a series of unmanned exploration probes to exoplanets which might be habitable. The strange data you looked at is a sample from these probes. We showed you a glimpse of the data from the project we want you to work on."

"NASA is growing and will continue to grow fast. We need people, highly skilled professionals like yourselves to work on these projects. You were all chosen for your unique and specialized talents and we want you to join our team. If you are interested in participating..."

He knew the impact his words were having and paused again, smiling as he looked around the room, obviously enjoying himself. He had seen it before. They were still stunned, so he went on.

"If you are interested in participating, we would like to bring you in full time on the project. But I have another surprise for you before we finish up," he said, with eyes sparkling.

"NASA is in the planning stages for several manned missions to the most interesting of the exoplanets and we are looking for volunteers. We are confident that we can get a team of scientists safely to another planet and back. You're the kind of scientist that could make the most of the first observations on another world. This is purely a scientific mission and you are the best scientists in your fields. Please give it careful consideration and join us if you can. We would like your participation in the program whether you volunteer for a manned mission or not."

Dr. Watkins finished the briefing with a bold statement.

"This is not your old NASA. We are no longer flying rockets with daredevil pilots strapped on top. Our mission is the same, but our methods have been completely revolutionized."

"That's all I intended to say at this time and I'm open for questions."

Most of the questions were about safety and logistics of the missions.

"How safe is the transfer?"

"There have been many thousands of human transfers with no ill effect ever observed. I visit the Moon at least weekly."

"How long is the journey to another planet?"

"Approximately 24 hours each way. We cannot at this time open a portal directly to another star system due to the difficulties of tracking objects at these extreme distances. The trip will be conducted in steps using deployable portal rings carried by the ship. Most of the time spent traveling to another planet is for deploying the portal rings and calculating DQSP settings for the next transfer step."

"When will the missions begin?"

"The mission we want you to man is the New Frontier 3 (NF-3 for short). It is on schedule to leave the Lunar base approximately six months from now. The NF-1 mission begins in about two months and NF-2 Missions in about four months."

"How much time would be spent on the planet?"

"You can expect to be on the planet between a few days and a month depending on what you find."

"Will we continue in our regular teaching and research responsibilities?"

"NASA will help transition in qualified professors to cover your teaching and research responsibilities."

"When can we start?"

"Today, if you like. But you can have a week, at least, to think about it."

The meeting broke up with a lot of dazed smiles. What can a person say when hit by a bomb like this? They introduced themselves and shook hands with each other before departing, each coping with this new reality in their own way.

Miles learned that the two unknowns were: Doctor Erin Colle a Medical researcher from MIT specializing in DNA theory and analysis, and Keri Wong a CALTECH professor of computer linguistics who had developed a universal translation program capable of interpreting almost anything.

Miles talked with Carl as they were leaving. "Did you know about this Carl?"

"Yeah, I'm NASA's primary scientific recruiter for these projects. The proposal and contract I showed you were just to tempt you into this meeting. You're one of the best field biologists in the world, so you fit the bill. And besides, you like an adventure."

Miles smiled big, "Thanks Carl, I owe you one."

"We can count you in?"

"You know me too well, Carl," replied Miles with a smile, nodding his head in affirmation.

Miles called JPL that afternoon with his acceptance and was told to report the next morning at 08:00 to building 321 room D27. He then went in person to talk with Professor

Alden, his biology department chairman, about the change. It went much easier than he expected.

"I heard it coming Miles," Dr. Alden told Miles. "Dr. Watkins called me last week to prepare me for your leaving. I hate to see you go, but it's important and you shouldn't pass up the opportunity. NASA projects can be both demanding and dangerous. So be careful, take care of yourself, and remember, Miles," he concluded warmly, "you always have a job here at CALTECH when you're ready to return.

Chapter 4 Sarah

Miles sat down on the well-kept CALTECH lawn in the shade of a Sycamore tree. He felt emotionally drained, in fact, he felt a little weak and shaky. After taking a few deep breaths, he closed his eyes, leaned back against the trunk and dozed off to sleep with his head resting on the tree trunk. The short afternoon nap was a ritual for Miles that cleared and energized his mind. But today he awoke with a start from a tense dream. Someone was sitting next to him.

"Hi Sarah, what are you up to?" he said with a drowsy smile.

"Watching you sleep," she said giving him a little kiss, but then scolded, "You've been too busy for me lately."

"I'm sorry, sweetheart. My head's in a spin right now. I've been really busy and this morning I joined NASA for a special project. It looks exciting, but will take a lot of time and energy."

"I've missed you," he added.

"I understand about being busy, my schedule is packed. I've missed you too," she replied, giving him another kiss. "What kind of project is it?"

"It's classified, but I'll tell you what I can over dinner if you like."

"That sounds nice," she responded, "but only if you're not working tonight. I don't want half your attention."

"I cleared my schedule just for you. Dr. Alden gave my work to an assistant. So, I'm free until tomorrow morning."

"Well, I'm all yours until then, Miles. Let's make the most of it."

Miles always liked Sarah and was dazzled by her beauty, but it took almost two years before they actually connected. Their friends knew, long before they did, that they were right for each other. Did their careers blind them to the emotional connection, or were they frightened by someone too obviously right?

Sarah was a young professor of social science whose work had exposed her to the human suffering of poverty-stricken countries. The shared dream of making the world a better place was a part of the bond between Sarah and Miles.

She wasn't tall but about right for Miles. Her dark hair and eyes reflected her Mexican heritage and was in sharp contrast to Miles' freckled red skin and reddish hair. They both looked strong and healthy, almost athletic. When together, people noticed them; they glowed with an obvious passion for life. It was Sarah's ideas about improving human happiness through education and training that added human psychology to the Arcadian Path.

Over dinner at Filippe's, Miles told Sarah what little he could about his new project with NASA JPL.

"Why is fieldwork to validate sensor data secret?" she asked. "Are you working for the CIA or something? Is there any danger?"

"It's definitely something new," he replied, "but no, I'm not a spy. You'll understand in a few months, so stop probing. You know I can't say much. And don't worry, Sarah, it's not dangerous," Miles added, hoping she didn't notice his doubt.

"I don't want you to go away for weeks at a time. Are there women going with you?"

"You are the most beautiful woman in the world," Miles said smiling sincerely. "How could I look at another? You are the perfect woman for me, my dream come true, I love you very much," he said, looking into her eyes and moving closer.

They kissed and then grew quiet, Miles went back to enjoying his spinach lasagna and IPA, while Sarah fidgeted with her Salmon Linguine and Cabernet.

"Well, I like that NASA is focusing on the ecosystems here on Earth," Sarah offered. "They should focus more on fixing our world and less on dreaming about the universe."

"The universe is beautiful and worth studying; it might someday offer new homes for humanity," Miles replied. "But I agree, our own world is most important. I hope my new work can help solve some of the problems facing us here on Earth."

"How is your fieldwork going to save us?" exclaimed Sarah, feeling a little negative about Miles being away from her. "Too many young people are having too many babies for the environment to keep up. The only thing that can heal our planet is to stop destroying and polluting the natural environment, and there are just too many people who don't believe in or understand the problem."

"Okay, maybe I am daydreaming a little," Miles replied. “But imagine how beautiful our world could be if people all got along and helped each other."

"You're right Miles, hold on to your positive vision of the future, it helps keep your hopes and dreams alive. So, tell me your latest vision of paradise."

"I'll read you my recent thoughts on the perfect society," he said, taking out his tablet and reading:

"One – All people are free to live their lives as they wish as longs as they don't harm others."

"Two – We all live in harmony with each other. All people of all cultures, ages, races, countries, religions, sexes or sexual orientations, physical characteristics (and...?) are respected equally. Diversity is not only respected but is appreciated."

"Three – No one lives in fear of other people."

"Four – Hard work, innovation, and creativity add great value to society and should be appreciated and rewarded fairly.

"Five – All people have opportunities for improving their lives and living conditions."

"Six – People live with harmony and respect for nature, and the environment is clean and well maintained."

"Seven – Everyone deserves, and should have a good education that is not corrupted by government, religion, or private interests."

"Eight – Governments are at peace and their primary work is to improve the lives of their citizens."

"And Nine – Laws are just and applied equally to all people."

"That sounds like a constitution for the human race, Miles. I was expecting a vision of some beautiful fantasy world where everything is perfect."

"If these conditions were met," he said, "Earth would be a beautiful perfect world. But how do we get there?"

"I don't know Miles, a lot of things would have to change."

"Sometimes I think we're just primitive animals," continued Miles, "driving around in cars and talking on cell phones. With all our science and technology and culture, why can't we act rationally to take care of each other and our planet?"

"Good question," Sarah answered, feeling a little sad. "But something is missing from your list, you need to add happiness. Because without being happy, you cannot appreciate the paradise around you."

"You're probably right, but happiness is complicated and different for each person. How can society help people be happy?"

"Your list is a good first step. It provides the perfect conditions for people to find happiness."

"It's your turn now. Give me your vision of paradise?" Miles said with a smile, trying to lighten the mood.

"Okay, how's this?" Sarah replied, smiling back with a little twinkle in her eye. "You and I spend our days walking in a beautiful forest, swimming in pools of warm sparkling stream water, making love whenever we like. There's plenty of healthy food to eat and a safe comfortable place to live in the forest. We have nothing to fear from people, the environment, or our health."

"Making love in the forest does sounds perfect," Miles said with a grin. "But aren't there always bugs and snakes and spiders in the forest? Could we modify thc cnvironment enough to make it perfect?"

"It's a fantasy Miles!" she replied smiling but a little serious. "Everything is possible in a fantasy. Your fantasies have power. If you believe it can come true, you'll work hard to achieve it."

"Okay, Sarah, I believe in your fantasy. If we work together, we can make part of your dream come true. Will you be okay without the forest tonight?"

Miles and Sarah clearly loved each other, but passion for their work interfered, far too often, with their passion for each other. They had talked of marriage and children, but just never got around to it.

Chapter 5 JPL

The 8:00 am meeting at JPL started with the same cast of people as the previous day. Dr. Watkins began. "Thank you all for joining our team and especially for your interest in a manned mission. You are our first choices to man the New Frontier 3 mission to planet Kepler 2356d. This will be your planet, you can name it when you're ready."

"Observations of Kepler 2356d show a planet perfect for exploration and possible colonization. There are four continents spread out around the globe with 60% of the surface covered in water. Green plant forms cover all but the high mountain peaks, there is a high-level atmospheric oxygen. Humans can breathe the atmosphere unless there are dangerous organisms."

"Finding a world with life outside our solar system is an extremely exciting discovery, but Kepler 2356d has another surprise for us. There are radio signals, weak low frequency signals only detectable within about 100 kilometers of the planet's surface, and radiating from multiple sources. We have not been able to determine whether the signals indicate an advanced technology, or some unknown geologic or atmospheric phenomena? We suspect it to be communication but we need more data."

"Understanding these radio signals is the first priority of the NF-3 mission. Keri, your advanced language translation software and knowledge of primitive forms of communication provide unique qualifications for interpreting these signals. Does the assignment meet with your approval?"

"Dr. Watkins," she replied, "it's the most exciting opportunity of my life. I can't believe it's real. Thank you."

"It is real, and you earned your place here by hard work and dedication. Thank you."

"But I have one hesitation," added Keri. "If it has intelligent life, isn't it dangerous? Will we have security?"

"I understand and share your concern. NASA will not ask you to go into a dangerous situation. From everything we've seen, we are confident of your safety."

Keri looked less than satisfied but didn't pursue the subject.

"The second mission priority," continued Dr. Watkins, "is to understand the biology. Is it safe? Are we a threat to it? Can we live in harmony with it? Miles and Erin will be leading this effort."

"Erin's research on biologic pathogens and toxin interactions on a cellular level, and her advance knowledge of DNA structures will help to determine if the air is safe to breathe and the water safe to drink."

"Miles is going to tell us how the ecosystems work. Top to bottom, what is the food chain like? What kind of plants and animals live there and how do they interact? How do humans fit into this ecosystem? Are they dangerous to us? Are we dangerous to them?"

"Does this sound good to you two, Erin and Miles?"

"You bet," Miles replied smiling.

"I'm all yours," replied Erin.

"Understanding the Geology is the third major mission priority," continued Dr. Watkins, "Carlos is going to tell us what if any geologic hazards exist, and where the valuable mineral deposits are located? What do you think, Carlos?"

"I'm excited and wouldn't miss it for the world," replied Carlos. "But I share Keri's concern about safety. How do we know if it's safe? This is an unknown world, there could be creatures or organisms that we can't even imagine."

"NASA will take every precaution and not allow exposure to significant risks," Dr. Watkins replied. "Your ship will first orbit the planet to investigate remotely. You will each participate in every decision that might affect your safety and you will always have the opportunity to withdraw from a situation you're not comfortable with."

"Thank you," replied Carlos.

"Your ship is currently in the final stages of construction. We expect you to dedicate yourselves completely to preparation for this mission. If you're not up to it, there are others, more than happy to take your place. Let me know if there is anything that could prevent you from giving your full attention to this project."

Chapter 6 Preparation

The daily work began at JPL, mornings in the lab and afternoons training on ship and equipment simulators. Within the first week, Erin suggested a new name for the planet.

"I don't like Kepler 2356d, it's too cold and feels awkward," She said. "The name Arcadia represents a place of pastoral peace, beauty,and tranquility. Can we call it Arcadia, at least until we have more information. This planet is a beautiful green and blue living world that looks so peaceful, and I want it to be peaceful. I want it to be Arcadia."

No one objected and the name stuck. It was Arcadia and would remain Arcadia after they had visited the planet and felt the profound peace which Arcadia imposed on the mind of all who visited. The name Arcadia suits the planet well.

Miles was disappointed with the laboratory even though it had the latest equipment. "I thought we'd have some super-secret new stuff to work with. There's no magic in the equipment, but at least we have magic data."

They created maps of topography, geology, ecosystems, and weather patterns that would help decide the most valuable areas for study.

Carlos and Miles worked together because geology and biology are interrelated, some plants grow better in one soil or rock type than another type.

"The change in geology is affecting the plant life in this area," was a common observation from Carlos to which Miles might reply. "I think you're right, Carlos. It doesn't look related to environmental conditions. It must be a change of soil type."

Together Carlos and Miles made the first detailed maps of this new world.

Keri Wong was clearly the computer geek of the group, always excited to learn new technology. Very quiet until asked how something works, she took pleasure in ensuring you understand an idea completely. In fact, she only seemed happy when she was either teaching, or conducting research.

"How does your translation program work?" Miles asked her during an afternoon break.

"This computer is a little faster than what I have back in my CALTECH lab, but still just a powerful computer with a lot of fast memory. It's only special because my translation software is loaded on it," she said with obvious pride.

"It's a little funny," she continued, "my program can use almost any kind of data: sound, light, electromagnetic radiation. It will find patterns in the data. Give the program forest noises and it separates and categorizes each sound. It doesn't know what they are, but it finds patterns and gives statistics about each one. To understand the meaning, it needs information, something to relate sounds to events. The more information you give it the better it can translate. With enough information, it can tell you what the forest is saying."

"What about speech?" asked Miles.

"With an unknown human language, it will find significant patterns related to other human languages and with enough information, it will provide a good translation of the new language"

"And alien communications?"

"Alien speech is more like the forest sounds. The program needs information about the sound, or in the case of Arcadia, radio signals. The signals from Arcadia appear random at this time. If it is communication, we can't translate it until we have data related to the signals."

Miles found that Keri's intense passion was limited to technology. Her brain seemed to freeze up when talking about natural science, confusion showed in her eyes. Miles showed her some remote images of Arcadia one day in the lab.

"Look Keri, you can see that the ground is covered almost everywhere with very low growing green plants, almost like grass or moss. You can see occasional small trees or big bushes. The images aren't good enough to give us details, but it appears to be a fairly simple ecosystem without much diversity."

"It's very pretty. Can the images be enhanced?"

"They've been enhanced as much as possible."

Keri looked surprised and disappointed.

"Here Keri, take a look at the ecosystem map I've been working on."

"Wow Miles, look at all the tools you have," she said taking control of the computer, quickly learning how to overlay the various images and apply different filters.

"This is great, but where's the back button, Miles?"

"Back button?"

"Yeah, are we in the dark ages here? Software needs a back button to undo your last step. What, do you have to select and delete or just start all over fresh? Needs a back button."

Miles didn't talk to her anymore about the ecosystems, they just weren't her thing.

Erin Colle, the medical officer, had responsibility for understanding the biological interaction between humans and the life forms on Arcadia. She couldn't do much without samples from the planet, so her days were spent in the lab with Miles and Carlos.

Erin was bright and intense, she liked to have everything in order. Organizing her workspace was something she needed before she could get her head in gear. Only when everything was in its place could work begin.

She often exclaimed after organizing her desk, "Where are my pens? I had several here when I left last night. Has someone been taking my pens?"

Miles suspected that she was inadvertently taking them home in her purse and forgetting them. He also suspected that her organized desk might be necessary to make up for a somewhat unorganized mind.

"There are lots of pens Erin, they're free," Miles would respond. "Nobody is taking your pens."

Miles grew tired of this routine and eventually, he began taking Erin's pens at every opportunity.

Every week they had a group therapy session and an individual visit with a NASA psychologist. There were obvious signs of growing tension. Carlos and Miles were the least affected, probably because of their experience in doing field research where they would be out of touch with the outside world for extended periods of time.

Everyone grew more nervous. Staying focused on work was the best therapy. Erin was the only one that expressed emotions openly, often exclaiming; "Holy shit, we're going to another planet," sometimes stated with excitement, like she was happy to announce it proudly to the world, but at other times you could clearly hear the nervous misgivings in her voice.

Chapter 7 The Lunar Base

After six weeks of lab work and training at JPL, the NF-3 crew members were excited and a little nervous with the approach of their first lunar visit.

The transfer portal room was on the 4th floor of the JPL building 231B.

"It works well for the Moon," the technician told them. "because the Moon is relatively close to the Earth and positioning information is sufficiently accurate. For more distant bodies within our solar system or exoplanets around other stars, we first transfer to space near the objective, then open another portal to transfer closer, or to the surface of the planet."

"It looks a bit different than I imagined," Keri observed. "Dr. Watkins made it sound like we would walk through a door into an office on the Moon. It's obviously more complicated."

In the center of the room was a large spherical cage, it looked like something from a carnival. A ring, about eight feet in diameter, was fixed on one side of the cage. A metal rail connected the top of the ring to the other side of the cage and a chair hung from the rail. The spherical cage could rotate allowing positioning of the ring to any direction or angle. The complicated structure allowed alignment of the ring and chair to the angle of the Moon which changes continuously throughout the day and month. On this day and time, the Moon was below the horizon and the ring and rail were pointed down at an angle of about thirty degrees.

Keri went first, climbing into the chair and buckling in. The portal ring was activated by the technician and the space within the portal ring became a window into a similar room with a technician on the other side. Only the angle was all wrong: the floor on the other side was tilted sideways and down from this side.

A hydraulic ram system controlling the chair pushed Keri's chair through the ring. As soon as she reached the other side, the Moon's gravity swung the chair slightly to match the angle of the floor on the Moon.

Keri Stepped out and smiled. "Nothing to it. The angle feels weird at first," she gave a little hop and continued, "but now all I feel is bouncy from the low gravity."

Miles and the others followed Keri and they soon found themselves touring the lunar facilities. Most of the buildings were large inflatable structures divided into offices, laboratories, and living spaces.

"The inflatable structures are first sealed to a foundation that forms the perimeter of the building," their guide told them. "Then a portal is opened to the Earth's atmosphere and the differential pressure between the Earth and the near-vacuum of the Moon draws air in and inflates the dome."

The tour included other projects being conducted at the Lunar Facility. One was a telescope with a DQSP ring attached to the end, it was being used for very deep space exploration. The scientists pick a place of interest anywhere in the universe and then send the telescope through the Universe Portal (UP). The telescope obtains close-up high-quality images by activating the portal on the front of the telescope. The images are sent back to JPL over a broadband radio connection through the open portals.

The New Frontier spacecraft each had its own building. Each ship sat on a hydraulic lift platform that could push the ship up through a large DSQP ring centered above the ship.

Miles found Rob, the biologist on NF-1, inside his ship going over some routine check-out procedures.

"Hi Rob, how's everything going?"

"Good Miles. NF-1 is almost ready, there are only a few technicians coming and going now. It's nice to see you out of the simulator and practicing with the real thing."

Miles looked around. The mock-up at JPL was mostly for instrumentation training, and this was his first look at a complete ship with living space, beds, bathroom, and food prep area.

"Hey Rob, you know, this thing reminds me of a big motor home without the cheesy carpet and fake wood paneling."

"I think it's actually a converted Airstream trailer," Rob joked with a smile. "One of those shiny rounded things that retired people haul around."

Miles laughed and thought about vacation movies. He decided on "Holiday Road" as his theme music for the trip. The music cheered him up and helped him think of the journey ahead as a crazy vacation.

Chapter 8 Portal Training

Portal operation training was given by Eldon Rye, the NF-1 computer geek. He began with some general information.

"As you already know, the portal system cannot be used for direct transfer to distant planets because the relative motion is too great and the exact position not sufficiently well known."

"Distance no longer matters in travel, only the accuracy of the position is important," he continued. "For distant objects, we travel in several steps. First, to space nearby our objective, then, from the new location, we determine the location of our target planet and use another portal to transfer into orbit. And from orbit around the planet, we can determine a landing point with sufficient accuracy to use another portal to transfer to the surface. Our journeys aren't limited by fuel or supplies, they're limited by the number of portal rings we carry with us."

"Each portal has a radio transmitter-receiver attached to the ring that keeps us connected to home. They create a G20 broadband connection over incredible distances with almost no transmission delay."

"Okay," Eldon continued, "before I show you how to operate a portal I need to caution you about potential dangers. It is very dangerous to zoom in on a star, hot planet, the vacuum of space, or planets with a significant atmosphere. If you are in the room with the portal you will be immediately subject to the conditions of the region that the portal opens on. Intense heat, pressure, and dangerous gases or liquids will pass right through. Safeguards have not yet been perfected. That's one reason we're training with a portal located in space rather than one located in this room."

"Now let's get started," he continued. "The controls are the same for all the portals. We are going to use the large Universe Portal (UP) for training. That's the portal you will use when you transfer to the Arcadia planetary system. The UP is located at the L2 Lagrangian Point just outside lunar orbit because this point is stable relative to the Moon. The UP has video cameras attached which are displayed here on the large screen so we can see what's on the other side of the opened portal."

"Where would you like to go?"

"Venus," responded Keri.

"Venus it is. But we don't want to enter the atmosphere because we would vent the Venus atmosphere into the space near the UP. The controls are simple, moving the joystick right and left, and forward and back controls the direction. The thumbwheel on top is used to zoom in or out. We need to give it a starting point because it's difficult to find Venus visually. Venus is one of the thousands of locations programmed into the system. For these locations, you just use the mouse to find and select the location you want."

"Here Keri, you sit down and take us to Venus."

Keri smiled, quickly found and selected Venus from the pull-down list. The Universe Portal repositioned and zoomed in until a large white crescent filled the screen.

"The UP system is now tracking Venus, so it will stay in view," said Eldon. "But if we try something farther away it's not as stable. Here, let's see what we get with Arcadia."

Eldon selected K2356d and the system took several minutes to find the position and then zoom in. A planet was visible but moving quickly across the screen. The system adjusted constantly to keep it in view. Eldon tried to zoom in but lost the image and it took another few minutes to find it again.

"When you zoom in to see any details of a distant object the velocity of that object relative to us is just too great for the tracking system to keep up. You can see why we need to travel in several stages. We just can't track distant objects with enough precision to transfer to the planet in one step."

"I'll finish by telling you about another interesting problem with using the portal," said Eldon. "Distant objects are not where we see them from here. If the object was 10,000 light-years away from Earth, then we see the position as it was 10,000 years in the past. The computer needs to first predict where the object is now, open the portal to that location, and then adjust for inaccuracies in our knowledge about the object's movement."

Chapter 9 Going Public

On December 3, 2070, two days after the departure of NF-1, the Washington Post ran an article revealing the new technology. It had very little detail and did not get much attention. Many people thought it was a fake news story.

A NASA spokesperson responded by saying, "NASA has dreamed of and investigated technology like this. But NASA is not prepared at this time to disclose the level of research and development conducted on this type of technology."

Several media outlets took this as an admission by NASA that the technology does exist. Media sources around the world became flooded with speculation about the possibilities.

The United States government responded to the rumors by accelerating the UN negotiations. On December 21 the President of the United States of America, Yolanda Espinoza, announced to the world the existence of the new technology.

"A very good afternoon my fellow Americans and all citizens of the world. I am excited, very excited, and happy to announce today the existence of a new technology developed by the scientists at our NASA JPL laboratory."

"It sounds like something straight out of a science fiction novel, a dream or fantasy. NASA calls it the Directional Quasi Singularity Portal. I like to call it the New World Portal because it opens the door to rapid space exploration and the colonization of other worlds. It opens the door to our dreams, the door to unlimited human expansion into the universe. The New Worlds Portal provides instantaneous travel between any two points, it can be opened on any location in the universe. It sounds too good to be true. But let me assure you that it is very real and we are actively using it today, at this time."

"This world-changing discovery brings opportunity and hope for humanity. My dream, my greatest desire, and the focus of my attention is that this technology benefits all of mankind."

"We no longer need fossil fuels, we can use the heat of the sun directly for electrical generation."

"We don't need air travel. Shipping of goods and materials by truck, train, and ship will be obsolete in the very near future."

"There will be an explosion of new technology and I want that technology used for the prosperity of all mankind. I want this to be the event that unifies the human race in love and appreciation of the beautiful varied cultures of man. I want this used first of all to unite the people of Earth in peace, harmony, and prosperity."

"With this goal in mind, the member states of the United Nations have developed plans and regulations for sharing this technology equitably with all peoples of the Earth. We have developed a strategy of control that allows participation by all nations while protecting the world from the significant abuse which could be conducted with uncontrolled use of the portal."

"Before I turn the meeting over to my NASA JPL Chief for questions, I would like to give a brief description of how we are using the Portal and some of our near-term plans."

"First, we have constructed a lunar base and are expanding it every day. We welcome all scientists of the world to use the base, it will be shared with everyone who has a legitimate use."

"Second, we have people on Mars right now investigating how to use the portals to make Mars habitable. It is so promising that I firmly believe some of you will live on Mars one day soon."

"And third, we have people currently on a planet outside our solar system investigating the potential for human colonization. That planet will need work before we can use it, but has the potential to be another world in the image of Earth."

"I invite you all to celebrate this as a new day dawning on the human race, celebrate the bright new future it will bring to all our lives in the years ahead."

"Now, here is Dr. Watkins of NASA JPL for questions."

The reporters were obviously having trouble coping with the new information and some actually looked sick. But the questions came.

"How will the portals be regulated?"

"A new international agency," responded Dr. Watkins, "called the DQS Portal Authority, will license each portal for a specific use. Each portal will be operated by employees of the Portal Authority and be set to make transfers only between the points it is licensed for. Video of every transfer will be automatically transmitted to the Portal Authority. And each of the secret field generation units will be enclosed in a tamper-proof container that self-destructs on unauthorized opening."

"Where will they be made?"

"NASA will make each control unit at a secret location that is not on this planet."

"How are you going to make Mars habitable?"

"We are investigating the use of large Portals to bring atmosphere and water to Mars from various locations throughout the Solar System. Yes, we are talking about terraforming. We can open a portal to one of the moons of

Saturn and allow the water to flow directly to the Martian surface. No pumps are needed because the water on the moon is at a higher pressure than the surface of Mars. The same with atmosphere, we just need to find the right places to open the portals. Mars will be a habitable planet within our lifetimes."

"Can you tell us more about the mission to an exoplanet?"

"Our New Frontier one spacecraft with a crew of four scientists is currently conducting research on planet Kepler 3208c, located 536 light-years from Earth. It is a planet similar in size to Earth and circles a G class star like our own sun. They have found no signs of life, but the temperature is favorable for habitation. If we can bring up the oxygen levels in the atmosphere it will be an excellent candidate for colonization."

"Are there missions planned for other exoplanets?"

"We have two similar missions, NF-2 and NF-3, scheduled for departure within the next few months. And we continue to search for planets that look promising."

"Where do people sign up to be colonists?"

"It will be some time before there are habitable planets to colonize. Discussions at the United Nations will decide just these questions."

Then the NASA chief said: "I could not answer all of your questions even if we had a month together. NASA has created a website with all the information we can release at this time. I ask that you visit the site for additional information." He then gave the web address and thanked the audience.

Chapter 10 Who's in Control?

The morning after the presidential announcement, Carlos came into the lab complaining. "Why share it with the world? It's ours, we developed it and we should control it."

"Don't you think something this important should benefit everyone?" responded Miles.

"Sure Miles, share it with the world, but we should control it. Once other governments get involved everything becomes more complicated. They shouldn't have a say in how we use our technology."

Miles didn't like to talk politics much but couldn't help responding. "So it's us against them. Why not all for one and one for all? Let's advance civilization a little bit."

"I hear you, Miles. But why give it away? We developed it and we should reap the benefits."

"What if another country had developed this technology? asked Miles. "Wouldn't the USA do everything in their power to obtain it? We'd use political pressure, espionage, and everything we could think of to get it."

"But we developed it, not some other country with twisted morals. We could use it to fix all the bad governments of the world."

"Maybe we could Carlos, but that doesn't mean it's a good idea. We could use it to wipe out everyone on the planet that we didn't like, but is it the right thing to do?"

"The right thing to do is to help our country first," replied Carlos, getting a little hot. "I don't want big brother looking into my house and bedroom. Giving control to countries we don't trust will cause paranoia and loss of personal freedom."

"You're being a little extreme Carlos. Don't you dream of a world where everyone lives in harmony and respect for their neighbor? Don't you want the Earth to be more civilized?"

"These are nice dreams, Miles, but only that. I don't think sharing control of the portal technology will bring us any closer to your perfect world. I don't trust other countries to play fair. The corrupt politicians and governments will take advantage in any way they can to gain power and control."

"Okay, I agree, the technology needs strong controls, but it should come from a multinational organization so that countries don't blame the United States for any perceived misuse or unfair practices."

"It will just be a big mess!"

Miles let it drop, but could not stop thinking about it. He continued a slow long-term conversation with Carlos, each bringing new thoughts to the conversation daily, to bounce against the other. They didn't come to many agreements, but their talks did help Miles develop his feelings about sharing the world with everyone.

The discussion also brought them closer together and distracted them from the nervous tension building about the mission, tension that was always there, lurking in the back of their minds and the pit of their stomachs.

Chapter 11 The Work-Up

The NF-3 didn't look like a typical spaceship. The pressure hull was a long cylinder, four meters in diameter, lying horizontal with an outer hull of stainless steel that made it look rather boxy. Sets of portal rings, each folded in half, lay on the flat top, a complicated cradle with wheeled landing gear supported it from below.

Their first ship training had been on simulators back at JPL, Pasadena, but on the Moon, they had their own ship to train with while it was still under construction. They used the onboard computers to perform mock exercises and routine system diagnostics.

The control room, at the front of the ship, had computer workstations for each crew member facing a large screen where they could share anything of interest with the others.

The laboratory was behind the control room, the kitchen next behind the laboratory, and then the crew quarters. A storage area at the back held equipment, food, and general supplies.

The crew was a little on edge as they worked up to their departure date. The lunar gym helped relieve stress as did the NASA-required therapist sessions. But the long hours and nervous anticipation were taking their toll. You could see the strain in their tired eyes but not in their work, their preparation continued with dedicated intensity.

The ship was completed ahead of schedule and the crew moved onboard for a two-week practice run, intended to prepare them for living and working together in the cramped spaceship and to function in weightlessness.

"Getting rid of us so soon?" Miles joked to mission control as they were being pushed up through the portal above the NF-3 and into space near the Universe Portal.

"Exactly, Miles," responded mission control. "We're sending you away to sit in the corner of the solar system until you learn to behave like good little scientists."

"You still haven't told us where we're going?"

"It's a surprise, Miles. Have a nice vacation," they responded and then broadcast "Holiday Road" over the NF-3 sound system.

The hydraulic lift pushed NF-3 up through the energized portal ring above the ship. Darkness and stars filled the front view screen until the ship rotated and the Universe Portal came into view. Thrusters pushed the ship into position and through the UP where the bright light of Saturn came into view on the port side. It was enormous, and looming very close.

"Mission control," Miles called. "Are we safe here?"

"Yes... Well, as safe as you are in a spacecraft sitting in space. You're in a stable orbit around Saturn at a distance that is outside Saturn's radiation belt. So, we believe you to be quite safe. We will monitor continuously while you're out there, and we are here for you 24 hours a day. Hope you brought a good book. Enjoy the view. Mission control out."

The bunks and chairs were comfortable and the food was good. There was no weight restriction on the ship. Anything they could fit in was okay. NASA wanted them to have a good experience and did what they could. They had plenty of fresh fruit and vegetables, eggs, milk, cheese, yogurt, cereal, bread, tortillas, and a big variety of meat and seafood.

Reviewing Arcadia data and practicing both routine and emergency shipboard procedures took most of their time.

"Ship Ring one" or SR-1, mounted on the roof, was deployed, operated, and retrieved many times for training and practice.

The crew took turns making regular reports to NASA, mostly descriptions of the work performed during that period.

Miles made a regular call to NASA after a few days. "Mission Control, NF-3."

"Good afternoon Miles. How are things going?"

"Everything is going well and there is nothing new to report. But I can't find the food replicator," he joked.

"Trying to create an IPA, no doubt," responded mission control with laughter in the background. Everyone knew Miles' favorite beer was a strong hoppy IPA.

"Don't be cruel," Miles responded. "But if there's no replicator, can I open a small portal to my refrigerator back home?"

"Nice idea Miles. We can't help with the food replicator or the portal to your home supply, but the IPA is stored in the back of the medical refrigerator. We're all surprised you haven't found it yet."

"Really! Hey, I love you guys. And I am terribly sorry, but I can't chat right now, there's some urgent business to attend to. NF-3 out."

The two weeks passed quickly and NF-3 returned to the Moon without problems. The crew was happy to be back and they were given two weeks vacation Earth-side to relax and prepare mentally for their journey ahead.

Miles and Sarah spent most of this time at a guest ranch near the San Pedro Martir National Park in Northern Baja

California, Mexico. There was no TV, no radio, no telephone, just a quiet little cabin in the beautiful isolated mountains with a swimming pool and great food.

In this quiet, private place, Miles told Sarah the true destination of his trip.

"I had a strong suspicion that you were on one of the NASA missions," Sarah told him with a worried smile. "Good for you Miles. Do you feel safe?"

"I think it is safe, Sarah. NASA has everything planned out pretty well. We should even have telephone and email while on the mission; I won't be completely out of touch."

"I'm proud of you, worried a little but very proud."

Miles proposed to Sarah the day before they returned home.

"I think it's about time Miles," she said smiling. "When should we do it?"

"As soon as I return from my mission," he replied, "let's go somewhere and escape for a while."

"Okay, sweetie. Wherever you'd like."

Chapter 12 The Journey

There was no blast-off, no high-g acceleration. The ship was pushed up gently through the overhead portal and into space near the Universe Portal. The NF-3 crew waited nervously while NASA mission control adjusted the UP to open on the Arcadia planetary system.

"How is everything on board?" asked mission control.

"Everything looks good from here," replied Miles. "Going to Saturn had felt somehow easier, just part of the training. Leaving the solar system is something else altogether."

"The UP is configured for the Arcadian planetary system," announced mission control. "Are you ready NF-3?"

"We're as ready as we'll ever be," replied Miles.

The ship's computer guidance system coordinated with the Universe Portal to safely maneuver the NF-3 through the open portal.

"You are now in Arcadia's planetary system, 357 light-years from Earth," announced mission control. "Deploy SR-1."

Keri activated the ship's ring deployment system. "Ship ring one is ready," she announced after SR-1 was deployed and operational in space close to the ship.

"We are adjusting SR-1 to put you into orbit around Arcadia," replied NASA. "The destination is set and we are guiding NF-3 through the portal now," NASA added after a few minutes.

The ship passed through the open SR-1 portal and into orbit around Arcadia. Scientists had not yet learned how to get a ring to pass through itself so SR-1 remained in space to be used for the return voyage.

NF-3 orbited Arcadia in a configuration designed for mapping, scanning, and visual analysis. Small robotic probes were deployed to sample the atmosphere, geology, and biology. Other probes were deployed to sample seawater and collect data on marine biology. Radio signals from Arcadia were monitored continuously and fed into Keri's translation computer for analysis. All data collected was transmitted back to NASA for analysis and storage.

The new radio signal data had Keri excited. "There's more detail. The signals come from all landmasses, changing a little from place to place, but they are completely absent from the mountains and oceans."

"Does transmitting a radio signal from the ship have any effect on the signal?" asked Carlos.

"There seems to be a slight change but it's complicated by the number of sources and the normal variation that I see. The computer is running through a series of signal variations to get a more complete picture. We should have better information soon."

"Do you see anything in the ocean, Miles?" asked Erin, watching Miles as he began looking at the new probe data.

"It's a little less salty than Earth's oceans," Miles responded. "And it's filled with things like plankton. But I need a sample to see what they are. There are also numerous "clicks" and "squeaks" that indicate a variety of marine life, and the sonar indicates some swimming objects the size of large fish. It would be interesting to see what's down there."

I see no construction of any type on the planet's surface," commented Carlos, "no roads, no houses, and no buildings."

"And no animals large enough to be detected," added Miles. "The vegetation consists of small low growing plants and occasional small trees or shrubs."

"Does anyone have information that might influence our landing site?" asked Erin.

"I see a lot of geothermal activity and would like to be close to one of these areas," Carlos replied. "Would anyone object to a landing site on the northwest coast of the largest continent? That would put us close to some mountains and very close to a strong active geothermal area."

"That's fine with me," said Miles. "How about you, Keri? Any objection?"

"It's good with me, the radio emissions are about the same everywhere."

"Erin, is it good with you?"

"Looks fine."

So, after a day in orbit, they decided on a landing site on the Northwest Coast of the largest continent. The second of three ship rings (SR-2) was deployed from the ship and prepared for transfer to the surface. A position beacon was sent through so they could fix the landing position exactly.

One significant danger in this form of space travel is that, if the portal ring shuts down when you are partway through, you are left half here, and half there. Hard contact between the ship and the ring could damage and shut down the ring. So the NF-3's front landing gear passed through, unfolded, and touched down quickly to insure the planet's gravity didn't tilt the ship enough to make contact and damage the ring.

There was no bumpy fiery nerve-racking descent through the atmosphere to a dangerous hard landing, which people of the time expected. It was more like driving out of a dark garage into a beautiful green sunny landscape. There was just a little bump as they came out: no alarms, not beeping equipment, no smoke or smells, only quiet.

Chapter 13 Arcadia

They came out of their seats in an instant to look through the small thick glass windows, each crew member was stuck to a window – each with a big smile on their face. The first words spoken were from NASA.

"Congratulations NF-3, is everyone alright?"

Pause.

"NF-3?"

Miles broke away from the window to respond. "We're great! Everything is great!"

He went back to the window, his heart racing with the excitement of a kid playing tag with his friends on a grassy lawn in the evening twilight. It took a good hour before the crew was really functional. They laughed, cried, smiled, and hugged each other, there were many exclamations; "Wow!", "I can't believe we're here!", "We did it, we did it!", and they looked again and again out the windows. NASA gave them time to adjust.

When they came to their senses, Miles placed a caged mouse into the airlock and exposed it to the alien atmosphere. The mouse didn't react when the airlock was flooded with outside air, but when the outer door was opened, the mouse stopped, very still, sniffed the air, and gave a funny shake like a wet dog shaking off water. It looked very excited, rolled over a few times, and began pacing around the cage. An hour later, there were no obvious changes. It looked energetic, maybe excited, but healthy.

"The odd behavior might be caused by the elevated oxygen levels," speculated Erin, "Maybe it took some time to show an effect."

The mouse was brought back inside in a quarantine cell for further observation.

Erin began her analysis of the environment to determine if there were any hazards in the air or soil.

"Take a look at these air samples, Miles," Erin said, directing him to the electron microscope display.

"It's loaded with microorganisms," Miles observed. "What are they?"

"Alien microorganisms of course," she replied with a funny smile.

"Is that all you can say?" responded Miles, unsure if she was teasing him or just elated with the idea of alien organisms.

"They look a lot like spores or pollen," she said, "but with a different cellular makeup than we find on Earth. I'm working on DNA sequencing and will have something more in a few minutes. Can you get me some samples of dirt and plant matter?"

Miles controlled robotic arms and placed both soil and plant material into a sample tray and then into an isolation box. With gloves and special tools, he prepared the samples for various forms of analysis.

It took two days of studying samples before Erin made her decision and reported to NASA and the crew.

"The first mouse exposed is still healthy and we have been feeding alien plant material to another mouse who shows no ill effects. I've cultured and studied every organism we've found and none of them display characteristics of harmful pathogens we find on Earth. If there is anything harmful, either we haven't encountered it or it's very slow acting. I believe we can safely breathe the air and conduct our studies without environmental suits."

"We agree with your analysis," NASA replied. "We have also concluded that not only are humans unaffected by the alien organisms, but the alien organisms are unaffected by contact with Earth organisms. The two forms of biology are too different from each other to interact negatively. It is safe for you to go outside and breathe the air."

Miles volunteered to go first. He put on a full spacesuit and stepped into the airlock, closed the inner door, equalized pressure, and opened the outer door. He had confidence in the scientific conclusions but was still nervous.

"Funny-looking plants," Miles commented as he stepped out of the airlock door and looked around. There was a small hiss from the equalizing pressure when he unlocked the faceplate of his suit.

"It smells nice and fresh. I am taking off my helmet now."

The video of his face showed something like a happy surprise. He put his helmet on quickly.

"I felt something strange," he said. "I don't know how to describe it, there is a strong pleasant smell of cool damp earth like from a rain forest of the Pacific Northwest. I felt good. I felt REALLY GOOD! There was a feeling of elation like something wonderful had just happened to me, something thrillingly good like just getting off a roller coaster or just after the bungee jump ends."

"How do you feel now Miles?" asked Erin.

"I feel normal. The feeling subsided soon after I put my helmet on. Maybe I should come back in and think about this a little," Miles stepped back into the airlock, closed the outer door.

Erin was concerned, she checked the mouse again. "The mouse is fine and acting normal," she reported. "There are no more tests to run. Are you sure you're not just nervous and excited, Miles?"

"Maybe some, but there was something more. I'm sure of it."

"NASA agrees with me that it is safe, but it's your call if you want to try again or not."

"Sweet euphoria sounds good to me. I'll go!" Keri chimed in.

"Okay! Okay," said Miles. "I'll give it another try."

He again opened the outer door of the airlock.

"Okay Guys, here we go again. I am taking several deep breaths and removing my helmet now."

He held his breath but found that holding it made no difference. He smiled at the camera, exhaled, and laughed, breathing in deeply the sweet fresh air.

"Wow! I have never felt better in my life: my mind feels clear, I don't feel drunk or stupid, just very comfortable and intensely alive. Give me a minute to adapt and see if it changes."

After a minute, Miles said, "Oh, what the heck! I'm going outside," and he stepped onto the alien soil and walked around the ship looking at plants and terrain.

"Limit his time to ten minutes," NASA ordered.

Miles returned after ten minutes, "Wow," he exclaimed, stepping out of the airlock into the control room, smiling and excited. "I am overwhelmed. There is definitely something strange happening out there."

"Take a break before venturing outside again," NASA commanded after Miles returned.

"How are the signals going," Miles asked Keri who had been quietly monitoring the radio signals while he was outside.

"There have been numerous changes to the signals related to our activity. On landing, they changed but then settled back to the pattern seen before landing. They changed when Miles was taking samples with the robotic arm, and again when he stepped outside. They always settle back quickly to the same common pattern."

"What does it sound like?" asked Carlos.

"The signals are below the frequency range of human hearing, so I haven't tried to listen."

"Have you checked their response to music?"

"Again there is the problem of the frequency difference. Most of our music is at a much higher frequency than what they broadcast. I could translate our music into lower frequency and see if I get a response."

Keri dug out a pair of earphones. She was busy for a few minutes and then exclaimed, "Wow, I never listened before."

She took off the headphones, "I was setting up the music and accidentally listened to the alien broadcast. It's the radio waves that make you feel good Miles. Listen to this!"

Miles listened and smiled. He didn't hear anything, but he felt it, not as strong as outside, but it made him feel good.

NASA came over the radio, "We're listening to it here now also. It is extraordinary, they are manipulating our brains with radio signals. The signals from the probe must have been too weak and distorted to have an effect."

"Listen to this," Keri said, looking around at the other crew members.

"Turn it off, I feel sick," said Carlos.

"That's the signal when we first landed. It didn't last long and then returned to the happy signal."

NASA came over the radio. "We suspect there is something intelligent broadcasting these signals. Is it welcoming us or luring us into a trap? Maybe they're underground. Carlos, could you use the Small Exploratory Portal to look for tunnels or caverns nearby. I want you all to begin your investigations close to the ship and work in pairs until we know what this is."

"I'm on it," Carlos replied to NASA. "Who's coming outside with me?"

"I am," said Miles and Erin at the same time.

"I'm not suiting up," said Miles. "Just going out in my coveralls."

Erin agreed with Miles but Carlos stuck with his spacesuit.

"You coming Keri?" asked Miles.

"No, the data is getting exciting and I want to monitor the radio while you're working outside."

It took only a few minutes for Miles and Carlos to get the SEP set up near the ship. The Small Exploratory Portal or SEP is used to make observations, including the subsurface. A person can step through the portal or reach through to take samples directly at any location of interest.

Carlos began with a limit of one hundred meters so they could not accidentally experience the heat of the planet's interior or the vacuum of space. He conducted a systematic sweep of the ground beneath and around the ship and then expanded the range to five hundred meters after finding no evidence of caverns or tunnels. There was still nothing.

Carlos reported back to NASA. "There are no caverns or tunnels nearby."

"Could they be watching us from a distance?" suggested Erin.

"Who knows," answered Keri on the radio, "but I won't feel safe until we understand where the signals are coming from."

"Let's get the radio signal locator out and find the source," suggested Miles. "But remember, I saw no animal trails outside. So I doubt anything is out there lurking about on the surface spying on us."

"Okay, Miles," said Keri, "I'll get the signal locator ready, but I don't want to be outside at night."

"Agreed. Let's use what light we have left to set up infrared cameras around the ship."

The night was calm but a gentle rain began falling as Miles and Carlos finished setting cameras outside. Keri was working with the radio signal data when the others went to sleep, and she was still working in the morning when the others got up.

"I stayed up all night guys," Keri told them in the morning. "The signal strength increased after dark, but almost disappeared for a while in the early morning. It gradually returned with the sunrise. I can't sleep until I know where it's coming from, so let's get going with the signal locator."

"Shouldn't we look at the camera data first?" said Carlos sitting down at his workstation and bringing up the camera video.

"There were no big events in the night," he commented after reviewing the video. "The cameras triggered three times on patches of soil near the plants. When I zoom in there appears to be some movement as if something small is churning the soil. But that's all."

"Who's coming with me?" Keri asked as she stepped into the airlock. The whole crew joined her.

"Wow, this is way better than the headphones," Keri exclaimed taking a deep breath of the clear damp morning air. "I feel like I slept all night and could work all day."

She scanned the area for radio signals while Miles investigated the ground where the cameras showed movement in the night.

"The soil has been disturbed, as if something came out of the ground in the night. It ate the older decaying part of these plants," said Miles, digging with his hands in the loose soil.

"There are radio signals from the ground all around us," Keri said, "but the strongest signal is in the direction of that small tree. Somebody come with me to have a look."

The group converged on her as she started walking towards the tree about 50 meters away. As they passed the tree, Keri said, "Wait a minute."

She turned around looking puzzled, circled the tree, bent down under it, then reached up with her instrument as high as she could. She scrunched up her face. "This tree is the strongest radio source I've seen. Everywhere else the signal comes from the ground."

Miles had been looking closely at the tree and responded to her words by tearing off a small leaf. When he did so, they all felt a change. The happy, exhilarating mood vanished immediately, replaced by nervous worry and a lack of energy.

"That doesn't feel good," exclaimed Erin. "Are the trees and plants modifying our feelings?"

"It looks that way," replied Miles. He put the leaf in a sample bag and got down on his hands and knees to look closely at the trunk and roots of the tree. He cut off a small branch and was rewarded by a feeling of intense dread.

"Let's go back inside and see what we can discover from these samples. It's not much fun out here anymore."

Everyone was relieved to feel normal again inside the ship. Miles and Erin examined the plant material while Keri laid down on her bunk and fell asleep. Carlos checked in with NASA and began a more detailed review of his SEP data.

"It's hard to believe," said Miles, "but there are undoubtedly filaments of elemental copper in the bark of this tree. I don't know why it's not corroded, I guess it's coated in something like natural rubber. But how did it get here? Carlos, is there copper in the soil?"

"There are copper-bearing minerals in the soil," Carlos answered, "but I can't imagine a little tree is processing it to make wire."

"This planet needs a mood report more than a weather report," Carlos added before opening the outer door and reporting back. "Hey guys, we're happy again. Who wants to go out for more samples?"

There wasn't much more they could do with the samples they had, so Carlos, Miles, and Erin went outside, leaving Keri to recover from the long night. They walked happily up the little hill with the tree on top, collecting a few soil and rock samples along the way.

"I've only seen three different plant species, and we know of the one possible ground animal," Miles observed. "Where is the diversity? It's like evolution stopped or everything else died out leaving only these few species. Or was there never much diversity to begin with?"

"Look at the ground cover," Miles went on. "There are two versions. Both look like big tongues growing flat on the ground, the older parts decay quickly. The two plants look very similar except one is a foot wide and light green while the other is four inches wide and darker green with slightly purple edges. The creatures in the ground feed on them, but they only eat the decaying ends."

"And the trees, if you look carefully, the leaves are a small version of the ground cover, like little tongues. I have seen nothing like an insect, nothing flying in the air. I hate to say it, but this is a boring ecosystem. It's beautiful and feels great, but it's really boring."

"What's that tell you?" asked Erin.

"Are you talking evolution?" asked Miles.

"No, more like philosophy. I just thought that we don't need much to make us happy. It's just a matter of the right brain waves."

"I get your point, Erin. It's strange that something we can't see is sophisticated enough to change how we feel," Carlos observed.

"And where are they?" asked Miles. "What's doing this? Is there some planetary consciousness controlling the radio signals? Are all the plants connected by a copper network to make a giant community brain? I just don't get it. I would feel confused and frustrated right now if that emotion was possible."

"And where is the dead material from the trees?" Erin observed. "The ground looks manicured, not a dead leaf or twig anywhere, as if the gardeners just left. Is it the ground creatures? What would happen if we left some food out overnight?"

"Let's try it, Miles," she continued." We can focus a camera on the spot and record any activity."

"Lettuce looks the most similar to their food," Miles commented. "Let's put out a variety of vegetables and see what they like."

In the late afternoon, several lettuce leaves, a carrot, a tomato, and a slice of bread were set out as bait and target for the video camera that night.

"Nothing has changed," Miles observed the following morning.

"Nothing came near it in the night," added Carlos looking at the video system. "At least nothing came close enough to trigger a recording."

"They don't seem to like our food," Miles suggested. "We could put out the leaf and twigs that we collected earlier."

"But then we don't have samples," said Erin. "And we need more samples. We should dig up some plants for study and some to use as bait tonight?"

"If breaking a twig make them angry, digging up plants might really piss them off," Miles replied, "but I think it's our best option. We would need to wear spacesuits while collecting. Or does someone like being tortured?"

"No masochists here," Erin replied with a grin.

Miles went out in a full spacesuit with a shovel and collecting bags in hand. He selected an area with healthy-looking specimens of both ground cover plants. He took off his helmet before beginning.

"I'm going to start without my helmet. I want to feel the reaction. If it gets too bad I'll put the helmet on," he reported and began to use the shovel to extract one of the large green tongue-like plants.

Keri was monitoring the radio signals and everyone was watching his image on the view screen. He first disturbed an area of bare dirt near the plant and there was no response. He then rather aggressively pushed the shovel down deep into the soil under the plant he wanted. They all saw him grimace and reach for his helmet exclaiming, "Ugh!"

"Oh my," he said after securing his helmet and sitting down. "That was fast and intense. It felt horrible to be exact. Almost knocked me over. It seemed to coincided with me cutting some roots. But I feel okay now, just a little trembling and shaky."

Miles dug out several specimens and placed them into collection bags. He took another whole plant and put it in front of the camera where the human food had been set out the night before. "They seem to eat the dead parts, so we'll let the plants sit in the sun all day to let them decay a little."

When he reentered the ship, Keri spoke up. "They are trying to train us, Miles. The negative signals spiked when you were digging and began to decrease when you stopped. Now it's back to the normal pleasant signal again."

Miles and Erin spent the day examining the plant samples. "These dark spots on the bottom might produce spores," Miles told Erin.

"Take a sample from those spots," she replied. "We'll see how they compare to spores floating around in the air. Get me some from both plant species."

Carlos spent the day exploring nearby mountains with the SEP, collecting samples of every rock type he could find. Keri continued her analysis of the radio waves.

"The plants are gone," Erin exclaimed early the following morning, looking out the window. "There's only a little patch of disturbed ground to marked the spot."

"I'll check the video," Carlos stated sleepily. Everyone watched in excitement as Carlos put the video on the big screen.

"Here they are!" he exclaimed.

"They look like snakes," Erin observed.

Three snakelike creatures come out of the ground within a foot of the plants. They were light gray in color, between two and five feet long, and an inch to two inches in diameter. There were four black spots in the area where you would expect eyes, and the large mouth was full of pointy teeth. They ate quickly without chewing the plants much before swallowing. It took fifteen minutes to consume everything. They seemed to elongate and get thinner as they reentered the ground, their pointed and armored nose penetrated the soil with ease.

"Wow, I need to examine one of those," exclaimed Miles. "The way they stretch out and deform suggests an invertebrate, like giant earthworms. Maybe we can catch one with the SEP?"

Miles got busy with the SEP while Erin helped Carlos deploy his seismic monitoring equipment.

"You can tell the planet is active geologically," Carlos told Erin as they walked. "The high mountains and numerous volcanoes indicate that the planet is pushing up rock material faster than erosion can wear it down. A less geologically active planet would be worn down flat by erosion, maybe even covered by ocean."

"So, what are we setting up today?"

"It's a seismograph for measuring earthquakes or should I say Arcadia quakes? It measures and records the vibration of the ground. The vibrations is generated by internal planetary forces moving the crustal plates of the planet. It tells us many things about the internal structure of the planet. We need to mount it on solid rock to get the best measurement. Let's go up that hill over there with the big exposed rock slabs."

Carlos and Erin made their way across a small stream and up a rocky slope to the top of a hill where there were very few plants and mostly bare rock.

"This looks perfect," said Carlos. "Good solid granite."

Erin explored the rocky surface nearby as Carlos drilled a hole and mounted the cylindrical sensor to the rock with a special epoxy.

"There's something strange here," Erin said on returning to where Carlos was working.

"What's strange? I haven't noticed anything special."

"Exactly," said Erin, "I feel almost normal. We're not being manipulated here."

"You're right, I feel sort of deflated. Is it only this place or has it changed everywhere. Call the ship and see if they noticed a change."

"Keri, Miles, this is Erin. Do you hear me?"

"Hi Erin, I hear you fine," responded Miles. "What's up?"

"Have you noticed any change in your mental adjustment down there?"

"I'm just outside the ship working on the SEP and I feel really good."

"We're not being modified here," Erin replied. "At least much less. I'm on a hill about two kilometers to your Northeast."

"Try to define the boundary of the area where you are not modified. It might help us understand what's happening. And look for trees."

"Okay Miles, see you in a little while," replied Erin.

Miles was about to start looking for the snake creatures with the SEP when Erin and Carlos returned. He looked up. "Did you find anything interesting?"

"We only feel the effect when we're within about 100 meters from the edge of the rocky outcrop," Erin replied. "There are trees and plants up there in the cracks of the rocks, but not any deep soil. As we get closer to areas of deep soil, the manipulation returns."

Chapter 14 Ground-Snake Surprise

Miles was able to locate the creatures using the SEP, but they moved so fast in their small underground burrows that they were difficult to catch. Searching with the SEP caused such terrible pain and depression that everyone outside the ship needed a spacesuit. Eventually one of the creatures ran the wrong way, passing through the SEP portal and right into a waiting metal cage.

"There are Ground Snakes in small tunnels all around us with groups congregating in larger pockets," Miles said coming into the airlock with the caged Ground Snake. "We were looking for something bigger and completely overlooked them when we first surveyed the area with the SEP."

"You're not bringing that thing inside?" asked Keri. "It gives me the creeps. And capturing it caused the most negative radio signals we've seen," she added as Miles entered the ship.

"But I feel okay now," Keri observed as Miles entered with the caged creature in hand. "I thought maybe it was these snake things that were affecting us. But there was no signal when you were in the airlock with it."

"I thought so too," Miles responded. "but maybe they're not the cause. I'll keep it in the storage room for now."

Miles spent the next six hours investigating the Ground Snake by direct visual observation and by various scanning techniques. "Their internal anatomy is somewhat similar to primitive Earth animals," he reported to NASA and the crew. "They have dense bony cartilage in their head with shark-like teeth in front but no other hard or bony structures in their body. They have a large brain for their size, and primitive eyes that only distinguish light or dark."

When Miles opened the storage area door the next morning, their fourth on the planet, horrible pain forced him to close it immediately. "I think it is the ground snake after all," he exclaimed, shaking his head to clear the momentary intense pain.

"I thought it was those snake things," Keri said. "Don't open that door again until we have our suits on."

Everyone put on their spacesuits and Miles reentered the storage room.

"The Ground Snake has somehow attached itself to the metal cage by a sticky gray patch on its lower jaw," Miles shared, coming out of the storage room and closing the door. "I think it's broadcasting negative emotion using the metal cage as an antenna. The Ground Snakes are definitely generating the radio signals."

"Why didn't we feel it when you brought the snake inside?" Erin asked.

"The metal cage must have blocked the emanations yesterday when I brought it in. But now the snake has attached itself to the metal of the cage and is using it for a transmitter. These primitive-looking little creatures living in the soil are controlling our minds."

"It doesn't make any since Miles," said Carlos. "How can these little blind creatures broadcast radio signals that affect our brains."

"If Eels and Rays can generate electricity," responded Miles, "and a silver cavity filling in your tooth can pick up radio stations, is it really so astonishing that a creature could broadcast radio signals for protection?"

"It's sort of beautiful in a way," Miles continued. "Instead of shocking or destroying their enemies, they worry them away without harm."

"But why then project the positive signals?" asked Erin.

"Maybe feeling good keeps them healthier and provides an evolutionary advantage," said Miles. "Or maybe they are always broadcasting their feelings, good or bad."

"Like chanting or singing together provides a heightened sense of happiness to the participants. They help each other feel good," suggested Keri.

"Or maybe just because they can, and they like it," Erin said with a playful grin. "And stop calling them Ground Snakes, these things are Mind-Snakes"

"Right you are Erin," Keri agreed. "They are definitely Mind-Snakes."

Chapter 15 Exploring Arcadia

In the weeks that followed, the crew of the NF-3 worked tirelessly. Keri worked to translate the rudimentary language of the radio signals. Erin continued to monitor the crew's health and to collect and study every living organism they could find. They all participated in exploring the many habitats and geologic domains of planet Arcadia.

From vast fertile planes to the high mountain peaks, from marshes to deserts, they explored. The SEP allowed them to make observations anywhere on the planet and to step through the portal to examine or collect examples of anything interesting. They took samples, made video and radio signal recordings, and made observational notes at every location.

Carlos investigated the active geothermal area near the ship during the first week on Arcadia. "I found an amazing hot spring," Carlos informed them with happy excitement. "Very hot water bubbles up in the middle of a cold stream. The hot water mixes in a large natural pool where you can drift into really hot water or really cold water. But most of the pool is just right."

"Sounds great. Let's go," Miles suggested.

They all walked through the SEP onto a large granite slab that bordered a large rocky stream with pools and boulders lining it's path. Steam rose from one side of the large pool which formed below a cascading waterfall.

"Wow," Erin exclaimed, soaking in the hot water. "Good Mind-Snake vibes while floating in this beautiful hot spring. Could we get any closer to perfection?"

"This is way better than the shower onboard ship," observed Keri with a tranquil smile. "I'm coming back here every day."

The crew used the hot spring often to relax and recover from the hard work of examining planet Arcadia.

When investigating an area devastated by recent flood water, they found a dead Mind-Snake hanging from a small tree. Miles's performed a biopsy and found that the digestive system extracts copper from the plants they eat and stores it as a colloidal solution for use. Like a spider creates web, the Mind-Snakes secrete coated copper filaments, leaving trails of them in the soil. A special internal organ has circuitry that generates the mind-altering signals. The copper filaments in the soil and trees act as broadcast antennae, increasing the strength of the broadcast.

They found other plants and animals in the rocky mountainous areas where the Mind-Snakes do not live. Streams contained eel-like creatures feeding on water plants. Larger trees covered steep slopes, and numerous varieties of the tongue plants, some like mosses, some grass-like, filled in everywhere there was soil.

A larger version of the Mind-Snake was found in these rocky mountainous regions, but it had no mind-altering ability. It was carnivores, feeding on other small version of the Mind-Snake which also had no mind altering ability.

“Nothing else we've seen is big enough to eat the Mind-Snake,” Miles concluded. “This is probably this bigger animal which caused the Mind-Snakes to evolve their protective mind-altering radio signals. The Mind-Snake has forced it to live in rocky areas that are uninhabitable for the Mind-Snake.”

During these explorations, the crew spent many hours talking about the strange Arcadian ecosystems.

"It looks like the perfect society to me," said Carlos to Miles. "Everything is under perfect control and the whole planet works together in harmony."

"You're right in some ways, Carlos. They have an incredibly stable population working in harmony with the ecosystem. But the cost is obvious; they are not changing, there is no progress, no evolution, and no diversification. They are an evolutionary dead-end. It is perfect and beautiful in a way, but sad and lost in another."

"Is paradise a 'dead-end' Miles? The fossil evidence indicates that for millions of years Mind-Snakes have dominated the planet."

"Yeah, I suppose you're right. It's just such a strange advantage," Miles replied thoughtfully. "Most successful creatures kill, eat, or out-compete their rivals, but these guys just mess with their enemy's heads and scare them away."

"Aren't they like humans in a way, Miles? We use our brains to dominate and control our planet."

"Could we learn to harmonize our emotions like the Mind-Snakes?" replied Miles. "Imagine all the people of Earth working together to improve society and the environment."

"What a dreamer you are Miles," commented Carlos. "Doesn't our competitive greedy human nature make working together difficult?"

"Probably. Humans do seem to compete better than they cooperate," answered Miles. "Our modern civilization suffers for it. Earth's beautiful natural environment suffers for it."

"It's because people are compelled by their needs and desires," Carlos stated. "If someone depends on cutting a tree to feed their family, they will cut the tree, no matter how much they love the forest and the trees. Laws and regulation can help, but only if the consequences are worse than not feeding their family."

"We need a world where people don't need to trade the trees to support their family," responded Miles. "I just want there to be another way, a way that encourages stability and prosperity without stifling creativity and real progress, a way that encourages man to become more civilized and cooperate with nature and each other."

"I like your heart, Miles," Keri said. "It's in the right place, but your ideas seem unrealistic to me. Try to see the world from my point of view. I'm a small, vulnerable woman. I try to be assertive, but I am afraid of people I don't know. I want protection from mean aggressive people that would take advantage of me. Those people exist and they need to be controlled. Most people see the world as I do. You're a strong independent adventurous man, and that alone allows you to feel like the world is a safe, friendly place."

"I'll stand with Keri," Erin began. "I'll take a bungee jump off a bridge, but I won't walk alone in many places late at night. Most people are good and trustworthy, but not all. There are people out there who will rob me and rape me if they think they can get away with it."

"I know you're right," responded Miles. "I think humans have become more peaceful and civilized over time. Most people manage to control their more negative primitive characteristics. But there are always problems; some people never learn to control themselves."

"You will need to change human nature in a big way, to make the perfect world you dream of," said Carlos. "How will you do that Miles?"

"Can education change humanity enough?" asked Miles. "Is it possible that improved education could solve many of our problems?"

"It might help," replied Carlos, "But there are billions of people. You're asking the impossible."

Chapter 16 Mind-Snakes Speak

Keri was a little frustrated in her quest to discover the first alien language. "The Mind-Snakes do actually communicate," she insisted, "but on a very low level. Their rudimentary language is limited to shared emotions, good vibes, and bad vibes. All they say is happy, happy, happy unless there is some danger and then it's sick, sick, sick, pain, pain, pain. I think the negative vibes don't continue for long because the animals feel the pain they project, and so, unless the danger continues, they quickly revert to the happy vibes."

"How they evolved to make copper wire is a real mystery," Miles mused. "They probably developed the radio signal capability as a defensive tactic that at first only worked at very close range. Then over millions of years, the broadcasting part of their anatomy improved from copper nubs on their chin to copper wires that amplify their signal. From there it was a relatively simple evolutionary step to being able to detach the wires and reattach when wanted. The most recent advance is probably the symbiosis with small trees that acts as an antenna, allowing the Mind-Snake to increase the range of the broadcast."

Chapter 17 Homecoming

It was a somber NF-3 crew that packed up, after a little more than three weeks, for the journey home. They gathered at the hot spring one last time, soaking in silence looking up at the stars. Each one fully aware that they may never feel this good again.

The return to Earth went smoothly. The landing cradle rolled the ship through the portal opened by Ship Ring 2, and back into orbit around Arcadia, leaving the landing gear behind with monitoring and tracking equipment.

SR-2 was recovered and stowed on top of the ship. SR-1, waiting where they had left it, opened a portal. Rocket thrusters propelled the ship through the portal to the outer Arcadia planetary system, where they stowed SR-1. NASA then opened the Universe Portal and the ship navigated through to space near Earth's Moon. In less than a day, they were back at the lunar base.

A crowd of workers gathered around to welcome them home. Dr. Watkins greeted them first. "Congratulations and welcome home," he said as they opened the door of NF-3 and stepped out into the Moonbase hanger. "The doctors want to check you over, but I would like a few words with you all first."

He led them to a small Moonbase conference room. "You will be in quarantine here on the moon before I can let you return home. It is only a precaution. Everything we've learned indicates that there are no dangerous organisms on planet Arcadia. The quarantine is only a precaution."

"Some details of your expedition are classified as Secret or Top Secret," he continued. "You are not to give details of the lifeforms on planet Arcadia. You may discuss the fact that there is life and that it is not dangerous to us. Specifically, the fact that Mind-Snake exists and anything about their mood-altering ability is highly classified for now."

"How long will it be classified?" Miles asked. "It is a significant detail that affects any plans for colonization."

"It should be soon," he replied. "We would like this to be a controlled release of information. If people begin to hear about this from different sources, it could cause people to worry. When the time comes, I would like you, Miles, as the lead biologist, to describe the true nature of life on Arcadia."

"When can we go home," asked Carlos.

"The doctors want you here in quarantine for two weeks," replied Dr. Watkins. "Just to be sure that you are not carrying some alien organism back to Earth."

After two weeks of quarantine and lots of testing, NASA doctors permitted the NF-3 crew to return to Earth. When they arrived back at JPL Pasadena, Dr. Watkins escorted them directly onto the stage of a small auditorium filled with reporters. "This will only be a photo op," he told the crew as they lined up on the stage. "You won't be answering questions today."

"Good afternoons ladies and gentlemen," began Dr. Watkins. "As you know the crew of NASA's New Frontier three spacecraft discovered life on planet Arcadia. The first life discovered on a planet beyond Earth. The life forms on Arcadia can not eat humans or other Earth lifeforms: their cellular biology is too different from our own. It is a planet with large oceans, rich fertile continents, and a very comfortable climate. Humans can safely breathe the air and drink the water. Arcadia is a good candidate for human occupation," Dr. Watkins went on to introduce and thank each

NF-3 crew member before directing the audience to a NASA website for complete details.

Cool rain sprinkled his face as Miles left the NASA JPL building. Sarah greeted him with a big hug and many kisses. "I missed you, Miles," she said with a happy but serious face, tears creeping down her cheeks.

"I missed you too. I feel like I am waking up from a dream Sarah," holding her happily in his arms. "I'm waking up from a dream to find my dream come true waiting for me."

"It's difficult to believe what's happened," Sarah said, smiling at the words of love. "The whole world is talking about moving to Arcadia. And they all want to talk with you," she added as they approached the JPL security gate.

A small crowd of sightseers and reporters, trying to get pictures or a look at the NF-3 crew, slowed their progress leaving the gate.

"Arcadia is already occupied," Miles told Sarah. "People will need to live with the inhabitants if they colonize the planet."

"And you and I will need a new place to live if this keeps up," observed Sara, as they turned into the driveway. Several reporters were standing outside the gate of Miles' apartment building. "They've been here for the past few days."

"I can't tell them much," Miles replied smiling and waving at them.

"You might need to say something. Not right now, but eventually."

"I suppose you're right. Maybe tomorrow morning."

Sarah and Miles spent the first night at home talking about Miles's experience. "You look so happy Miles," Sarah observed. "I was worried that you would be tired and distracted from your trip."

"I feel great, Sarah. There is something special about Arcadia that I can't share yet."

Miles was up early the next morning. Sarah was just waking when he brought fresh hot coffee and climbed back into bed.

"Thank you, sweetheart," Sarah said as she sat up and greeted his kiss.

"It feels so good to be here with you in my arms," Mile said, smiling, holding her close, kissing her tenderly.

The coffee grew cold while passion consumed them.

It was mid-morning when Miles walked to the front gate of the apartment compound. Half a dozen reporters stood outside waiting for him. They bombarded him with questions about the new planet. "Can people live on planet Arcadia," "Are there dangerous animals?"

Mile greeted them with a friendly smile and read a prepared statement through the gate. "Planet Arcadia is occupied, it is inhabited by complex living organisms which have an extremely stable population. The planet is almost entirely covered by one simple ecosystem. These living organisms exist in near-complete harmony with their environment. The animals have a low level of intelligence but have evolved a system of protection that is incompatible with human occupation. People can live on Arcadia, but some animals will need to be removed. Human occupation will be at the expense of the natives."

"How dangerous are they?" "Do you worry about the native creatures?" "Are they more important than human needs?"

Miles didn't answer their questions.

Officially, NASA said that the planet was habitable and contained vast agricultural land with rich deep topsoil, plenty of water, and mineral wealth comparable to Earth. Plans for colonization were in progress and limited emigration would begin within the year. NASA portrayed the Mind-Snakes as interesting primitive creatures which would be easy for humans to live with.

A few days after his return, Dr. Watkins asked Miles to visit him at his office. "You've already told me that you are not interested in further planet exploration, Miles. Would you be interested in another position? We're developing a research station on Arcadia to prepare the planet for human occupation. You could be in charge of the Arcadian research facility if that appeals to you."

"It sounds very interesting," Miles replied with some hesitation. "I assume it would involve living on Arcadia."

"You would need to spend a lot of time there," replied Dr. Watkins. "But with our tracking systems in place soon, portal transportation to Arcadia will be an easy commute."

"I am working on a social program with Sarah," Miles told Dr Watkins, "and I want to focus on this for now."

"I respect your passion and ideas for improving civilization, Miles. But you could do great things for humanity by continuing here at NASA. You could create the environmental habitats on new worlds where people will live."

Miles sat in silent conflict, weighing the options in his mind. "New worlds?"

"We are terraforming," Dr. Watkins said enthusiastically to Miles, "starting with Mars. We're using what we call redirect portals, consisting of two DQSP portal rings set together back to back. If you are not interested in research on Arcadia, would you consider being a Chief Terraform Biologist for the introduction of living organisms, plants and animals, for one of the newly terraformed planets."

"These are amazing opportunities, Dr. Watkins," said Miles with a sincere smile. "Thank you very much, but right now I feel compelled to work on social reform ideas with Sarah."

"I respect your passion for this," replied Dr. Watkins with some disappointment on his face. "There's nothing better for a person to pursue their passion. But if you change your mind, I would like you to work for me."

"Thank you, Sir," Miles said. "It has been an honor to work for you and I appreciate your offer. I will keep it in mind, but I can not accept it at this time."

Sarah was happy with Miles' decision. "You did the right thing Miles."

She could see his ideas pushing him. But pushing him where, she wasn't sure. At least he would be on the same planet with her. "Dr. Alden will want you back at CALTECH."

"I'll go see him this afternoon," said Miles. "But my interests are a little outside of research biology now."

After breakfast and a relaxing morning with Sarah, Miles went to see Dr Alden.

"Welcome home Miles," Dr. Alden said, greeting Miles with a friendly handshake. "What an amazing field trip that was."

"Thank you, sir. It is still a little hard to believe."

"Is this a friendly visit Miles?" questioned Dr. Alden, knowing Miles wasn't the type for friendly visits. "Don't tell me you're not continuing with NASA."

"I'm leaving NASA," Miles stated with a happy smile. "I have other interests that I would like to work on."

"You're always welcome here," Dr. Alden replied. "Would you like your old job back?"

"I would like to work on some ideas I have about improving human society," Miles told Dr. Alden. "I am afraid that planet

Arcadia will only be extra space for human plunder. If human society can't improve its character, then humanity is destined to destroy Arcadia and any other planet we inhabit. We need a society where people learn to appreciate life and live together in peace, a society where we all care about the welfare of the others."

"You're talking about changing human behavior Miles. Doesn't this belong in the Psychology or Sociology department?" replied Dr. Alden, "Or are you suggesting a biological approach to behavior modification?"

"It would require a multi-discipline approach," Miles responded, "biology, sociology, nutrition, medicine, psychology, neuroscience, and others. Anything I can find that will help all people live happy fulfilling lives and live together peacefully."

"Well Miles, you're famous now," replied Dr. Alden. "Your notoriety will bring funding for any research you are interested in. Welcome back to CALTECH. Just give me your proposals and I am sure we can get them funded. I'd like you to provide lectures on the biology of Arcadia to the advanced biology classes if you can. Other than that, you have free reign to work on whatever you like."

Chapter 18 Truth

A small group of demonstrators holding signs and chanting were outside when Miles left the Biology administration building. The group recognized Miles and approached him. "Arcadian contamination will destroy us all," they chanted.

"That's not true," Miles stated walking around the group.

"Arcadian contamination will destroy us all," they continued chanting as Miles walked away.

"Who are these demonstrators?" Miles asked Sarah when he arrive at her office.

"That's the Church of Seven Apostles. They call themselves Waru. They've been demonstrating ever since the announcement was made about life on Arcadia."

"They're going to scare people," Miles said. "And what they say is just not true."

"They want to scare people," Sarah replied. "It's part of their methodology."

"What about reality and truth. Can't people tell truth from fiction?"

"The truth terrifies some people, Miles. War, starvation, global warming, ecosystem collapse, people deny the truth when it scares them."

"Can't they believe in their religion without denying scientific truth?"

"It gets complicated here. Their religion comes with an easy button - a way out," Sarah replied with a twisted smile. "Their God relieves them of guilt and responsibility, forgives their irresponsible behavior. Scientific truth questions and jeopardizes their ability to feel forgiveness."

"But forgiveness come from within your own heart and mined," Miles replied. "If they can't forgive themselves without permission from their church, then they don't understand human nature, they don't understand who they are."

"Reality is frightening for those who don't understand it," added Sarah, "and the church wants them to be frightened so they seek the protection of God."

"Reality is beautiful," Miles responded, "but also frightening. An asteroid or a supernova could kill us all in a flash. Reality is ugly if you focus on the negative ugly possibilities."

"Most people don't appreciate nature the way that we do," said Sarah. "They never learn enough science to see the beauty of it. It scares them."

"Could we use the Mind-Snakes to help change people, Sarah? The snakes had a beneficial effect on me. Could the snakes show other people the possibilities for feeling happy?"

"Miles, are you saying that these creatures affected your mind?"

"Oops! That is the part I can't tell you yet, but yes, the Mind-Snakes of Arcadia have the unique ability to alter your mood."

"Well," said Sarah looking at Miles with some concern, "if it helps everyone to be as happy as you have been since returning, then it is worth studying."

"It might be useful," continued Miles. "But the emotional well-being people feel from the Mind-snakes may not always be appropriate to how a person should feel. It might distract people from the realities of life."

"Yeah, like a happy pill, it can't actually make your life better. It only makes you feel good for a time."

“But the Mind-Snakes have changed me, Sarah. Like I have an addiction to happiness, the more I have the more I crave and the happier I feel"

"That makes sense to me, the more happiness and love in a person's life, the easier it is to feel love and be happy. Could you bring Mind-Snakes here?"

"Probably not," Miles replied. "Are you coming to the parade with me on Saturday? I would appreciate your company. The Mayor will be there. And I'll be expected to speak."

"Of course Miles. It sounds fun to me."

Miles and Sarah sat in the back of a baby blue 1952 Lincoln Convertible as the parade moved slowly West on Santa Monica Boulevard. The morning coastal clouds were thinning and the April sun warm. Thousands of spectators watched the floats and bands marching past, they cheered and waved as Miles and Sarah drove by.

Waru demonstrators chanted across the street from West Hollywood park where the parade ended. Police struggled to keep the entrance clear for parade dignitaries to enter through the crowd.

Miles and Sarah followed Dr. Watkins and the other NF-3 crew members onto the stage. Various government and science officials were informally greeting and chatting with each other.

Dr. Watkins spoke briefly to the crowd before introducing the NF-3 crew member and asking Miles to speak.

"The planet Arcadia was so named because it is beautiful and peaceful," began Miles. "The animals on planet Arcadia live harmoniously with each other, harmoniously because one species completely dominates most of the land surface. Dr. Watkins has given me permission to tell you about this animal. We call it the Arcadian Mind-Snake. This animal lives underground and looks similar to a snake or large earthworm. It is called the Mind-Snake because this extraordinary creature has evolved the ability to affect the mood of other animals near them. It is not very intelligent, but its mood-altering defense mechanism is very effective against animals that might steal their food or try to eat them. These mood-altering emanations are shared and amplified by communities of Mind-Snakes. They create a universal mood which can be very good, or very bad."

"The Mind-Snakes live underground and are rarely visible on the surface. When walking on Arcadia without a protective helmet, a person will be strongly affected by the emanations of the Mind-Snake. If the snakes are happy, you will feel amazingly good, it is a beautifully, unique experience. But if you uproot one of their food plants the angry Mind-Snakes cause your mind to explode with terror, pain, and depression. It is unbearable. For this reason, people cannot live close to them."

"With proper management to protect the Mind-Snake, NASA estimates that 60% of the usable land on Planet Arcadia can be populated by humans."

"But, with or without new planets to live on, humanity needs to learn to live together. To improve society, we need to conquer ourselves, not the universe or our neighbors. We need a common dream for the future of humanity, a shared vision of a future we can all work for. We need to be better people for ourselves and our civilization. We need to stop ignoring the importance of the human character in making a good society."

Waru protesters began chanting across the street as Miles ended. "Don't forget God." "Trust God." "Happiness is Love of God." "Evolution is God's Work."

"They seem so irrational," stated Sarah as they were leaving the ceremony. "They are afraid of the truth."

"Scientific truth is what makes existence beautiful," Miles replied with a smile. "The truth about who we are and how we fit into the universe is by far the most beautiful enlightening knowledge that man possesses. Why does scientific truth scare people so much? Does it threaten their faith in God?"

"Only if their religion denies science," answered Sarah. "They are probably taught as children to mistrust science."

"If they're afraid of scientific truth then they don't believe in reality," Miles answered. "They live in a fantasy world created by those who manipulate them."

"It is who we are Miles, humans evolved this character as part of being civilized. You believe what your neighbors believe. It reinforces everyone's beliefs, makes us feel more secure."

"The Waru belief system isn't very civilized. Do they have the wrong God?" Miles joked.

"You know I believe in God," Sarah responded. "I see God and biblical teachings as metaphors, not scientific reality. I believe in God and science."

"Science does make some biblical stories a little hard to believe," replied Miles. "But science cannot yet tell us if God exists or not."

"But it can tell us what a person needs to have a happy life," replied Sarah. "For one, it tells us that it's hard to be happy when you live in fear."

"I don't know if God exists or not," Miles stated. "But science allows us to manage our fear with rational knowledge. It gives us more control of our destiny."

"You are unique Miles. Many people, including me, feel better believing God is watching over us and that there is life after death."

"You're in the majority," Miles replied. "Many people find comfort in faith. I think it's a psychological replacement for their parents? At birth, your parents are like God. They feed, protect, and care for you, give you love, and calm your fears."

"There is some logic to that, Miles. Religion provides a mental support system that's not available to people without religion. Many people never learn to take care of their own mental health."

"Modern society needs a better replacement for God and family," replied Miles. "We need a support system that uses true scientific knowledge to improve the mental health and well-being of everyone."

"Psychotherapists can improve the lives of most people," Sarah responded, "but they're typically used only during some crises."

"We need a system that teaches everyone to become responsible for their mental health," Miles replied, "supporting them throughout their lives. How does Scientific Spirituality sound as a name of this new field of knowledge?"

"Sounds perfect Miles. A scientific approach to improve mental health and help all people have a good life."

Keri Wong visited Miles at his office after the Los Angeles parade. "I like your ideas, Miles," she told him enthusiastically. "But you need a bigger audience. I want to support your effort by creating a website for you. It will help get your message out."

"Do you have some ideas?" queried Miles.

"Well, if people want to learn and benefit from your ideas, they need to understand them," she replied. "Your speeches aren't enough. How will they learn without access to your information?"

"What do you want to call the website?" Keri asked.

"I been thinking of 'The Arcadian Path,'" Miles answered. "Like we are on a path to a more beautiful existence. What do you think?"

"I like it, you'll have an Arcadian Path website within a week," answered Keri. "You better get your thoughts together. You're going to be showing this to the public."

"Wow, Keri, this is a big help. Thank you."

Chapter 19 More Parades

In mid-summer, the crew of NF-3 was invited to Washington DC by the President of the United States.

"I'm not comfortable with all this attention," Miles told Sarah. "I like the system we are creating, but I am not a good salesman. It'll be another parade and speech. And this Waru Church of Seven Apostles will be protesting again."

"Don't worry about the Waru," Sarah replied. "There will be lots of security. This is your opportunity to tell people about the Arcadian Path."

President Yolanda Espinoza rode with Miles and Sarah in the Washington DC parade down Pennsylvania Avenue. The large crowd cheered and waved as they approached and stopped at the steps of the capitol building.

Groups of Waru waving signs and chanting slogans were visible in the crowd. As Miles and Sarah ascended the capital steps, one group of Waru forced their way through the thick crowd until reaching the barrier of policemen. They yelled their slogans, pushed police and spectators, disrupting the event until enough police arrive to chase them off or take them to jail.

"These are unique and historic times," began President Espinoza after the disturbance had died down. "Humanity is on the verge of expansion into the cosmos. We will soon be living on Mars and Arcadia. There are an unlimited number of planets we can terraform, unlimited possibilities for the expansion of the human race."

"We celebrate today four brave scientists that helped bring this dream to reality."

Madam President then presented each New Frontier 3 crew member with the Medal of Freedom Award and allowed them to speak to the nation.

"We need to improve and unify humanity," Miles began. "We are going to the stars, we are on our way. As humanity expands to live on these new worlds, let this be our opportunity to create a more civilized society. Let this unite us all behind a common vision for the future, a vision of a better civilization for all people. Let us join together in a common dream, a dream that includes all people equally and promotes well-being in every individual."

Waru protesters shouted and held signs along Pennsylvania Avenue as Miles and Sarah left the Capital building. "No atheist morals," "Scientists out of God's truth."

"Look at this sign Miles, it says: 'If God wanted you to be happy, you would already be happy.'"

"What bitter, frustrated people," Miles commented to Sarah. "They don't seem to understand what I say."

"You can't expect everyone to like your ideas, Miles. But your ideas are spreading throughout the world. Your Arcadian Path website is getting more attention all the time. People are talking about your ideas."

Six months after the Washington DC event, Miles was asked to speak to the United Nations general assembly in New York City. It was the inauguration event to celebrate the formation of the United Worlds (UW) as a new department of the United Nations. The UW had responsible for terraforming new planets and emigration to the new worlds that were created. The UN general assembly approved of and promoted the Arcadian Path philosophy as a way to create more civilized human societies.

"The police look outnumbered," Sarah observed as they drove down New York City's First Avenue towards the United Nations Headquarters. Their limousine moved slowly past the large crowd of spectators lining the street.

"What do they come to see?" Miles wondered. "They can't go inside."

"I see a lot of different national flags in their hands. Maybe they're excited and want to show support for the United Worlds and the Arcadian Path."

A volley of eggs and bottles hit their car as they approached the main gate. Some of the crowd pushed into the street and quickly surrounded their car.

"No Mind control!" "The end is near!" they shouted. The angry Waru demonstrators began rocking the large limousine side to side while others swung hammers at the window closest to Miles.

"It's bulletproof," said the driver. "Don't worry about a thing."

The car couldn't move and two men with sledgehammers took turns hitting the window. "Are you sure this will hold?" asked Miles, moving away from the window.

"It should," replied the driver with obvious concern.

Fractures formed with the first few blows on the polycarbonate glass window, but it did not shatter. Sarah and Miles held each other close, watching the angry mob outside with mutual horror. Again and again, the hammers struck without penetrating the glass.

The crowd surrounding the car backed away as police and security guards rushed to the scene. The WARU disappeared quickly into the larger crowd of peaceful onlookers.

Their car was then surrounded by police who escorted them to the UN main gate.

As the car passed through the gate, the violent demonstrators reappeared. With vastly increased numbers, they quickly pushed aside police and gate security guards. Miles and Sarah watched as the mob streamed through the gate, running in pursuit of their car. "I'll go to the far entrance," said the driver, accelerating past the main building entrance, where vastly outnumbered guards were preparing to meet the mob.

Their car sped around the side of the building and down a ramp where a door opened to let them enter.

"Please follow me," requested a UN security officer. "The mob outside will take some time to control, all dignitaries are being moved to an underground strongroom for their safety."

Two hours later, Miles was escorted into the General Assembly chamber and onto the podium where the Secretary-General introduced him to the full assembly.

"Miles Finerty," began the Secretary-General, "for your work in promoting concepts of a better society for all humanity, the United Nations awards you the highest level of recognition and honor which we can bestow. Let it be known to all that Miles Finerty is hereby awarded the United Nations Public Service Award."

There was a standing ovation before Miles began to speak.

"Thank you, madam secretary," began Miles. "There is tremendous hope for humanity now that we have other worlds to live on. But other worlds to occupy will not fix human society. We need another way to treat ourselves, a new way of looking at ourselves and our civilization. Humanity needs to love themselves and each other. We need to unite behind a vision of a better future for human civilization."

"I propose a vision for all humanity," Miles continued. "A set of ideals that help each of us have a good life. Ideals that make sense to all people of all cultures. Ideals that will unify and improve all human societies. Ideals that will unite the entire human race."

"I call this set of ideals the Arcadian Path because its goal is to provide a path to a more perfect and peaceful human society. I submit this concept in the hope of making the Earth and any new human worlds a paradise for all."

"The Arcadian Path provides a vision of a perfect civilization and a path to a fulfilling life for everyone. The three foundations of the Arcadian Path are: the Goals of Civilization, the Principle of Humanity, and Scientific Spirituality."

"The Goals of Civilization – These eight goals provide a vision of a perfect civilization, they are:

Freedom. All people have the freedom to live their lives as they wish as long as they do not hurt other people.

Harmony. No one lives in fear of another. All people of all cultures, ages, races, countries, religions, sexes, sexual orientations, or physical characteristics are respected equally. Diversity is not only respected but is appreciated.

Value. Hard work, innovation, and creativity add great value to society and should be appreciated and rewarded fairly.

Opportunity. All people have opportunities for improving their lives and living conditions. Without opportunity, people have no hope, no dreams, no inspiration, their creativity is lost.

Harmony with Nature. A healthy natural environment is what allows us to live. We need to protect it.

Education. Everyone has access to good education uncorrupted by government, religion, or private interests. Education gives each person the knowledge and ability that they need to succeed in pursuing their version of happiness.

Peace. Governments are at peace with each other and their primary work is to improve the lives of their citizens.

Justice. Laws are just and applied equally to all people."

"It may be human destiny to populate other planets, but without solving humanity's personality problems, these new worlds will devolve into the typical human societies where political, business, and religious interests thrive at the expense of the less well born of the society."

"Every living human being is a survivor of the entire evolution of life on Earth. Hatred, racism, fear, worry, greed, selfishness, jealousy, etc...., are natural normal evolutionary traits acquired to help us survive the primitive past."

"But these evolutionary emotions are often counterproductive in modern society."

The second foundation of the Arcadian Path is the Principle of Humanity which together with Scientific Spirituality (the third foundation) can help people understand who they are and to find happiness.

The Principle of Humanity tells us that: "A person's first responsibility in life is to be happy and love themselves. And their second responsibility in life is to love others and wish them happiness."

"Being happy and following the Goals of Civilization require education and training provided by third foundation:

Scientific Spirituality is a developing academic field of study and practice focused on improving the lives of individuals. It helps people find their path to happiness and achieve their dreams and aspirations. Scientific Spirituality can help a person understand their negative emotions, control their demons, find meaning in life, and live their dreams."

"Without dreams, people live without purpose, only reacting to the problems life presents to us all."

"Without a vision of the perfect civilization, Governments have no direction, only reacting to the emergencies they all face.

"Let the Arcadian Path guide us to a better future. A future where all people share meaningful lives. Let us dream big, let us dream together as one people of Earth. Let us guide the human spirit in the right direction, towards a more peaceful unified humanity."

"Thank you."

Chapter 20 Epilogue

Millions of people now live on planet Arcadia in harmony with the Mind-Snakes. Hot spring resorts cater to tourists from distant worlds who come to relax in the springs and enjoy the Mind-Snake's powerful mood-altering effects.

Most people today have found paradise in their lives by following the Arcadian Path. There are no wars and very little crime. Peoples needs are met, most are happy and satisfied with life. They have meaningful work, and opportunities for improvement, education, and change. People have freedom, and time to pursue intellectual growth and self-improvement.

The United Worlds has promoted the Arcadian Path on all 222 planets terraformed with RingTech redirect portals. Every country and every religion of old Earth now has its own planet or country. There is unlimited space and opportunity for all to grow.

Most of humanity lives today in peaceful, happy harmony with each other and their environment, each person discovering the paradise within themselves.

But there are those worlds that haven't done as well for their people, worlds where opportunities are limited, freedom restricted. Those worlds are plagued by the age-old human problems of greed, corruption, and poverty. Those are worlds that failed to follow the Arcadian Path.

End Part 1

Part 2 – Beryl Awakening

Chapter 1 Beryl

Large sections of terraform ring emerged one at a time from the open RingTech portal as if materializing from empty space. A fleet of space tugs guided each ring section into position and connected one to another, forming a single ring of one kilometer diameter in orbit around a lifeless planet. When completed, this atmosphere redirect portal opened a direct path between this dry rocky planet and the high-pressure nitrogen-rich atmosphere of a gas giant planet within the same planetary system. The gas giant's high-pressure atmosphere forced gases through the open portal directly at the rocky world below.

A second RingTech redirect portal completed two months later opened a portal to liquid water trapped beneath the frozen surface of one of the gas giant's large moons. When this ring opened, a powerful stream of water rained down through the thickening atmosphere to the surface of the planet. It was an Earth-sized planet, orbiting in the habitable zone of a single G class star similar to Earth's Sun.

Engineers on Earth's Moon, 1327 light-years distant, remotely monitored and adjusted the large RingTech portals to achieve the specified atmosphere and water levels.

After 17 months of monitoring by the United Worlds Planetary Maintenance Directorate, the correct environmental conditions on the planet were met. The RingTech portals shifted into maintenance mode, automatically adjusting atmosphere and water content to maintain ideal conditions; the right conditions for the trillions of lifeforms required to build a global ecosystem suitable for human habitation.

Teams of Bioengineers then began their work, introducing bacteria, fungus, plankton, and plant spores over the entire surface of the planet. Grasses, trees, shrubs, animals, and insects were introduced into the areas that matched their living conditions on Earth, with with priority given to lifeforms most beneficial to humanity.

This fresh new world was designed and created to provide a good home for the growing human population. A mild and comfortable climate covered 90 percent of the landmass. That dry rocky planet is a green world now, thriving with life.

Bioengineers named the planet Beryl because of the magnificent gem crystals of Emerald and Aquamarine which formed from the abundance of beryllium occurring in the planet's continental crust.

Planet Beryl spins slower than Earth with a daily rotation of 27.3 Earth hours. One complete orbit around Beryl's star takes 321 Earth days but only 281 Beryl days.

RingTech redirect portals are the technology that made terraforming practical. A standard RingTech portal opens a door between itself and anywhere in the universe. The redirect portal has two rings constructed back to back. They open simultaneously in opposite directions to allow material to pass from one remote point directly to another remote point without the portal being physically located at either point. Redirect portals made terraforming a reality, they allowed the human race to expand out from Mother Earth into the far reaches of the universe.

The Directional Quasi Singularity Portal (DQSP), what we now call RingTech was developed by the National Air and Space Administration (NASA) in the year 2068 CE. Call it what you like: a worm-whole, warped space, or a Quantum door through another dimension, it works and allows the human race to cross the vast distances of space in the blink of an eye. RingTech created not only cheap instantaneous space travel, but a myriad of benefits to humanity: unlimited inexpensive electrical power, instantaneous transportation and communication anywhere in the universe, and the ability to rapidly terraform planets.

The first interplanetary use of RingTech spurred the development of the Arcadian Path philosophy which guides most governments today in maintaining truly civilized societies. The connection of these two events led to the creation of a new calendar in the year 2070 CE to celebrate the age of Enlightened Expansion (EE). It was the year humans began expanding out from Earth physically, while at the same time embracing a more enlightened human society.

RingTech portals at the time of this history were common and relatively inexpensive throughout the United Worlds. Most people on Beryl had the old-style PersPort, physically located in their homes and offices, which allowed them to instantaneously travel anywhere on planet Beryl quickly and cheaply.

The United Worlds (UW) government promotes the Arcadian Path on all 222 human-occupied worlds to encourage the healthiest governments and civilizations. And most world governments do use the Arcadian Path for guidance in maintaining a healthy civilized society. Most, but not all

There are worlds that do not follow the Arcadian Path, worlds that fail to provide a healthy civilized society. Societies similar to ancient Earth where wealthy families, businesses, or religions rule without sufficient respect for the common man. These are societies where many humans struggle while a small number of rich and powerful live in luxury and control the government.

Beryl is one of those worlds. A world governed for over three centuries by the cruel hand of the Orthodox members of the Waru Church of Seven Apostles. It is here on this world of Beryl that our story begins. The year is EE 434 (2504 CE), and 598 million people now inhabit this lush comfortable planet, a planet with an environment created by humans for humans, a planet with vast resources of land, water, and minerals.

The natural riches of planet Beryl provide security and physical comfort, but the common members of Beryl's Waru congregation suffer. They suffer not from a lack of basic needs, but from the mental cruelty of shame and guilt. They suffer from the repression of their natural human character. They suffer from the strict control of the Orthodox Waru leadership. They suffer because suffering is what the Orthodox Waru want them to do.

Chapter 2 The Forest

Nava followed her shadow as it scramble up the rocky path, her back warming with the rising sun, the gray granite sparkling in her light brown eyes. A brisk east wind played in her long dark hair.

The sunrise was as perfect as her heart had imagined, dark pastels of blue, purple, pink, and orange of early dawn gave way to bright reds, oranges, and yellows of the sunrise.

Personal demons drove her up the dark rocky trail. Her mind was filled with frustration, anger, and worry about her troubled life. Frustration with existence pushed her up the mountain, hoping to clear her mind and shake off the dark feelings that plagued her.

The strenuous predawn hike and meditation on the sunrise had calmed her mind. Nava breathed deeply, she felt good now, felt more focused and prepared, ready to return home to face the challenges of her life. "The hell them, the hell with what they think!" she said out loud to herself. "I know what's right for me."

She was angry still, but her mind was clear, her thoughts focused on being strong and not submitting blindly to what the Waru church and society expected of her.

The forested western slope came into view as she crested the bare East side of the Tikla Mountains. The bright purple flowers of the Karo trees were fading with the dry late summer weather but still displayed a soft purple hue across mountain and foothill. Thick smoke was visible coming from the North and moving Southwest toward her trail. The coastal city of Saint Carmen could be seen through the drifting smoke.

Nava walked quickly down two kilometers of trail before she realized the fire was moving in her direction, it might not be safe to continue.

"I'd better open a portal to home," she said, taking off her pack to get her ComPort, intending to open a portal into the family living room and safety. It should only take a moment.

"Oh, Crap! Where's my ComPort. Did I leave it on top?" she said frantically in the thickening smoke. "Here it is."

Nava called home repeatedly to open the family PersPort into her own living room and safety.

The ComPort powered up okay but it failed to connect. It couldn't connect. "I should have stayed up on top," she thought to herself with growing desperation. "But I can't go back now."

The fire wasn't visible, but the thickening smoke crossing her path told Nava she must hurry. Jogging down the steep trail was dangerous but necessary. A black column of smoke rose dramatically blocking the sun and casting an eerie orange light on the ground and vegetation around her. Thicker smoke began blowing across her trail, stinging her eyes and choking her lungs. Watery burning eyes forced her to slow down now to maintain her footing. The smoke grew thicker and she could see not just ash, but glowing embers blowing past her in the thick noxious smoke.

With teary burning eyes and choking painful breath, she made her way as fast as she could. Flames in the brush about half a kilometer distant gave her real panic. She could feel the heat of the fire. Gasping and stumbling in complete despair through thickening smoke, her eyes stinging and blurry with tears, she ran into a man coming up the trail.

"Come with me," he exclaimed coughing and grimacing. Without a moment's hesitation, he grabbed her by the arm and pulled her back up the trail. She followed him a short distance up the almost invisible trail, when he directed them off the side toward the fire, down a brushy narrow path. Nava couldn't help wondering if he was crazy, but he seemed to know where he was going and she couldn't think of an alternative. He was the only hope she had.

The heat became intense and painful, embers stung her skin, and the flames seemed almost on top of them as he helped her down a steep embankment and into the entrance of an old mine tunnel.

It was cooler almost immediately inside and the smoke grew less as they receded farther into the mine. The young man stopped, took a flashlight from his backpack, then continued leading them deeper into the tunnel. Nava felt occasional water puddles splashing under her feet and the man found a dry area for them to sit down. Still coughing with red swollen eyes, they sat silently for some time. He dampened a cloth, handed it to her, and with trembling arms she wiped her face and eyes.

"I thought I was going to die," she said, crying into the damp cloth.

"Me too," he replied.

"Thank you. I've never been saved before. I don't know what to say."

"It's okay," he responded, coughing, and trembling still. "I'm glad I found you when I did, the fire was almost on us. We're lucky to be alive."

They sat in silence for several minutes wiping their faces, calming down, slowly recovering themselves from the horror outside.

"How long should we wait in here?" Nava broke the silence.

"I don't know, maybe a couple of hours. My name's Cromen."

"I'm Nava."

"There's plenty of water and I have a little food. Are you hungry?"

"A little. I have some nuts and fruit in my bag."

"I've got some dried fruit and cheese."

The wet cloth soothed their eyes as they enjoyed their snack in the darkness broken only by Cromen's flashlight, recovering slowly from the panic of flame and smoke pf the fire raging outside. Only the slight smell of smoke reached their cool damp resting place deep in the ground.

"What is this place?" asked Nava, her trembling slowly giving way to a feeling of relaxed nervousness.

"It's an old gem mine," answered Cromen. "They found some beautiful pink, green, and blue tourmaline, and some aquamarine in this mine about 100 years ago. That's why I'm here this morning. I came up early to avoid the heat and spend the day digging for crystals. What brings you up here so early?"

"I came to meditate on the sunrise and adjust my head a little, sort of a spiritual quest I suppose. It worked great, I felt really focused and positive about who I am and how to deal with life. But now I'm in shock," she said with a doubtful smile. "It's strange how fast things can change."

"Well, you're safe and unharmed, so maybe the experience will help. They say a brush with death can make a person appreciate existence even more."

"I hope so. Why is there a tunnel here? I thought mining was all done remotely by RingTech portal."

"We Alton don't have RingTech," he replied. "This tunnel was dug by hand over many years by Alton people seeking gemstones to use and to sell. Your people aren't allowed personal adornment, so they don't value the gems at all. Sometimes I sell the crystals I find here to other Alton, but mostly I keep them."

"Don't you have a ComPort and PersPort at home?" asked Cromen. "Most Waru your age have a ComPort. It would have made your escape from the fire simple."

"I do, but it's a cheap model that doesn't always work right. Maybe I stepped on it in the dark this morning," said Nava with a bit of anger. "Anyway, it didn't work. Imagine if I had connected at the last moment with a friend. They might only have time to watch me screaming and gasping for air through the open ComPort portal while my body burned."

"Morbid thought," said Cromen sadly.

"My parents won't get me a good phone because we don't have that much money. But the fact that I dropped out of college to live with a guitar player for two years hasn't helped my case much since I moved back in with them," Nava finished with a twisted smile, reflecting on the man she no longer loved.

"I'm sorry things aren't going well. Any plan for improvement?" Cromen asked cheerfully.

"That 's why I came up here this morning before dawn," Nava continued. "Since I've been back home, I've been angry with myself and the world. I want to be more than just somebody's wife or girlfriend. I want to have control of my life and do something. I just don't know what to do. And I make so many bad decisions."

"Well, you look human to me," smiled Cromen. "And I've never known a human that didn't make bad decisions sometimes."

Nava's eye twinkled and she smiled a little.

"They don't approve of your boyfriend then?" continued Cromen.

"They think he's too wild and rebellious. Like a cheap phone would really keep us apart. They are so stupid sometimes. Maybe they suspect him of being Alton."

"Parents never know how to help," Cromen began. "How will they feel about you being rescued by an Alton and spending the day with him in a dark tunnel?"

"Maybe I should leave that part out of the story. But with any luck, this experience will encourage them to get me a better ComPort."

"So, is he Alton?" asked Cromen, looking into her face for her reaction. He would never speak this openly to a Waru under normal circumstances, but he could feel that the situation made the discussion acceptable. He had saved her life, and her eyes told him she wasn't offended by his question.

"I don't think so and I don't care. Besides, he's not my boyfriend anymore," stated Nava firmly with frustration punctuating her face.

"Don't care if he's Alton?" Cromen said in surprise. "Saying that could get you into trouble with many Waru, especially the Orthodox."

"Many Waru, but not all. I think the Orthodox Waru are insane and I'm not a fan of our divided society," Nava responded questioning him with her eyes. "We are both human, aren't we?"

"I like to think so, but that's not the opinion of many Waru. Your words aren't something I hear them say. Many see the Alton as primitive subhumans incapable of learning anything complicated."

"Do you think that about your people?" asked Nava. "You may not have the same education that I have, but you seem rational and intelligent to me," she added, feeling confused by her growing comfort sitting here in the dark cave with this young Alton man whom she knew nothing about.

"We have a different way of looking at life," Cromen replied. "My people teach many things that your schools don't or maybe cannot teach. I think we're happier and have less stressful lives than the Waru. I think we enjoy ourselves more. So by that measure, we are more intelligent. But are we different at all? I think it's only the culture." Cromen noticed a serious, worried look on Nava's face as he finished speaking.

Nava sat silently, feeling ashamed of her own people and wanting to apologize for the oppression they impose upon the Alton. She knew she couldn't change anything, but said: "I'm sorry," firmly after a long silence.

"Oh, so it's your fault. I've been wondering who to blame," joked Cromen. "Apology accepted," he continued with a big happy smile. "Now we're friends and can forget all about it."

Nava couldn't help but smile, and she thought how easy it was to like Cromen. The Alton people were a mystery to her, she wondered who they were and why the two societies were separate. Feeling completely safe sitting here in the dark with this strange young man of another culture; she was fascinated.

"You don't believe in God do you?" she asked, believing that the Alton have no true religion.

"I would like to believe in God," replied Cromen, "but just can't quite do it."

"I grew up believing in God," said Nava, "But I have big doubts. They say we're ruled by the authority of God. Why would God give me human desires but punish me for satisfying those desires?"

"I don't know. You make it sound cruel."

"I think it is cruel. Everyone goes along without questioning because they have a house and food and an easy life, but they're all angry frustrated assholes."

"There are Waru living in the Alton communities who seem like very nice people," offered Cromen. "And there are many Alton who believe in a God, but it is not my way. I follow the Arcadian Path," Cromen stated softly, his knowledge of the Waru religion was poor and he hesitated, thinking that he might offend Nava.

"Isn't that a religion?"

"In a way, it uses science as a guide to a better life. It's a system designed to make a better life and society for everyone. It offers the Goals of Civilization as a vision of a truly civilized society."

"If you're suggesting that the Waru aren't civilized, I get your point," laughed Nava in reply.

"I didn't mean it that way," Cromen replied, smiling back at her, "The perfect civilization doesn't exist. The Goals of Civilization are goals for a society to strive for. It's hard for a society to improve without some idea of what an improved society looks like."

"The Waru society is all screwed up," replied Nava. "Our religion controls everything in our lives. I feel trapped with no possible escape."

"Maybe all societies are screwed up in some ways," Cromen said. "The Arcadian Path can help people to have a happier life in whatever society they live."

"Do you live by the Arcadian Path?" she asked.

"I try to, but I'm lazy and don't study and practice enough," he replied, "I'm skeptical about everything. Mom says that I'm distracted and sort of a late bloomer."

"Do you believe in it?" asked Nava.

"Yes, I believe that if you want a good life, you should pursue the Principle of Humanity which is part of the Arcadian Path," said Cromen cheerfully. "If your God and religion help you live by the Principle of Humanity, that's great. But embracing the Principle of Humanity will help you, with or without God and religion. It's a principle that leads to a happier, healthier life."

"So, what is this Principle of Humanity?" asked Nava with interest.

"It's simple," said Cromen. "The principle is this: A person's first responsibility in life is to be happy and love themselves. And their second responsibility in life is to love others and wish the same for them."

"It sounds a little stupid," Nava replied skeptically "Everyone wants love and happiness. But I can't just turn on a switch and love myself, can I?"

"No, you can't wish yourself into love and happiness. But you can do things to help. Your happiness is entirely your own personal responsibility, and you need to work at it. Scientific Spirituality provides tools and resources that help you understand yourself and have more love and happiness in your life."

"Scientific Spirituality?" Queried Nava.

"It's part of the Arcadian Path. It is science and psychology that helps guide you in your pursuit of love and happiness," responded Cromen.

"Sounds great if it works," responded Nava. "I'm not sure I even know how to love and be happy. Like, I feel happy sometimes, but not mostly."

"It's something you need to work for and find for yourself," replied Cromen. "This is what Scientific Spirituality and the Principle of Humanity are about. Love and happiness take work. Work to understand who you are and what you need to be happy, work to help you accomplish the changes you want in your life."

"Do you feel happy, Cromen? Do you love yourself?"

"I'm generally pretty happy," responded Cromen with a questioning frown. "but I don't work at it much. Why should I spend my time trying to be happy if I'm already happy?"

Nava could see guilt in his justification and understood that he wasn't as happy and full of love as he'd like to be.

"If the Alton are peaceful and happy, and they don't reject God and religion, then why are the Waru so critical and unaccepting of them?" asked Nava. "Why do we have a divided society?"

"It pisses me off!" Cromen replied with a little anger in his voice. "I wish I knew. Your people are so serious and worried. Maybe they feel threatened by our happiness?"

Nava gave a nervous laugh and looked questioningly at Cromen.

"I'm sorry. I shouldn't react like that," said Cromen, self critically. "You see, I don't practice Scientific Spirituality enough."

Nava saw the frustration in his face and let the conversation die. It had become too complicated and would take too much energy to continue. They walked to the tunnel entrance and found that the fire had passed enough that it was safe to leave the mine tunnel. Nava felt rising emotions of affection and appreciation for Cromen and just before they stepped out of the mine tunnel she pulled him to her and kissed him on the lips, saying nothing.

It was only midday when Nava and Cromen came out of the old gem mine and into the smoky burned forest, a forest starkly different from the morning. The large underbrush was reduced to ash, the land looked bare and gray. Small fires were burning all around them on the remnants of bushes and old logs. The Karo trees were charred at the base, but the tops still held purple flowers.

"This forest is adapted for fire," said Cromen as they walked. "In a year or two it will look almost as if it never happened. A few trees will die, but most will survive and benefit from the nutrients provided by the burned underbrush. And most of the brush will sprout quickly from the roots. They're not dead, just going through another phase of life."

"Like the Phoenix bird rising from the ashes," observed Nava.

"Yes, and like the human spirit," countered Cromen, "If not burned too badly, time will bring your spirit back stronger and healthier than before."

Ash blew and swirled all around them, sticking to their sweaty skin and stinging their eyes. The light smoke continued to irritate their lungs. Using the damp cloth helped, but after an hour of walking down the trail, they were coughing, their eyes were red, and their skin was covered in ash. They could see fire control portals in the distance protecting houses near the edge of the forest. Like fire hoses spraying water down from above, but without the hose.

"Whatever happens, Cromen," Nava said with emotion, "I'll never forget what you did for me. Thank you for sharing things about your culture. Can we stay in touch?" Nava didn't want it to end. She liked Cromen, wanted to talk more with him and know more about his people.

"Thank you, Nava, you're very sweet, and I like you. It was special to spend this time with you. But it's not safe for us to be together," He responded with a fixed and worried stare. "I would like to know you better, you are beautiful and I appreciate your open mind," he continued with a worried smile. "But your people won't understand and it could be dangerous for both of us. It's probably better if we stay away from each other."

It was a cold answer that Nava wanted to reject. But Cromen spoke the simple truth of the divide between the Waru and Alton cultures, Nava could only respond with sadness.

Their conversation ended as fire control coordinators spotted them and opened a portal on the trail in front of them. Nava and Cromen stepped through the open portal directly from the dusty smokey trail into the cool clean air of a medical emergency waiting room.

Chapter 3 RingTech

From the earliest DQSP portals to the advanced RingTech redirect portals, the use of this technology has been tightly controlled. An unregulated portal could be used to spy into a neighbor's bedroom or empty a bank vault. In the wrong hands, a portal could deliver a nuclear bomb to the middle of a city, or send a stream of sewage into the chambers of congress.

The invention of portal blocking technology made these kinds of activities very rare if not impossible. The portal blocking field is an invisible spherical electromagnetic shell that prevents a portal outside the blocking field from opening inside the protected area. All homes and places that need to be protected from intrusion have blocking technology.

RingTech Portal and Portal Blocking technologies are still tightly guarded secrets, but advances in security and production have made them widely available to the general public. At the time of this story, anyone with a modest income could afford a RingTech PersPort, including ComPort control and communication system, for all their transportation and communication needs.

The ComPort personal communication system opens a small portal next to the person you want to speak with. You talk directly, through the open portal, face to face with that person. There is no signal, so there is no possibility of signal interception. You can shake hands, kiss, or pass things through the open portal as long as it fits through.

The ComPort also functions as your remote control for your PersPort, personal portal system. It controls your PersPort from anyplace that you have ComPort connectivity, allowing immediate portal passage to and from your home. People walk directly from their PersPort (generally mounted around the front door of the home) into any store or restaurant on their planet and then return directly into their home.

Online purchases from anywhere, on or off-world, are delivered a few minutes later through a portal. Dinner can be delivered hot from the kitchen to your table from any restaurant on the planet.

PersPort systems are not generally authorized for off-world travel. Official United Worlds Off-World RingTech Transit stations provide service 24 hours a day every day on all human-occupied worlds free of charge. The United Worlds monitors travel between planets, but there are very few restrictions.

The BroadPort G90 broadband network provided positioning and connectivity throughout the inhabited worlds at the time of this story.

Chapter 4 A World Divided

The immediate transition, from a hot smokey trail to the cool fresh air of the hospital emergency waiting room made Nava feel weak and she had to sit down. Nurses and police officers greeted them and provided water, oxygen, and damp wash clothes to wipe their faces. Nurses checked vital signs, asked them how they felt, and if they had any injuries or pain.

"They have no serious injuries," reported the nurse to the policewoman guarding Cromen.

"I feel fine," Nava coughed in reply.

Cromen nodded his head and smiled at Nava as a policewoman led him through an open portal, directly into the police station.

Nava raised her hand in surprise as if to signal "wait". But the portal closed, Cromen was gone, there was no goodbye. Feeling sad and worried, Nava wondered if she would ever see him again.

She called her mother, Myra, from the emergency waiting room and told her what had happened, leaving out the fact that her rescuer was Alton. Her mother was worried and stepped through her PersPort into the emergency room a few minutes later saying, "Your father will be here as soon as he can."

"Well, you look a mess, Nava. How do you feel? You weren't burned were you?" Myra asked, looking intently at her daughter and attempting to wipe a dark ash smear from Nava's cheek.

"No Mom, I'm okay," she said pushing her mother away gently. "They don't want me to leave until I see a doctor, but I feel fine, just a little tired and dirty." Her eyes still stung, she trembled slightly, but these details weren't shared with her mother.

The doctor checked Nava's vital signs and asked her how she felt. "Nava should be fine and is free to go," he told Myra.

Her father Landrow, called from work just as the doctor finished his exam. "You've had quite an adventure. I'm glad you're okay," He said to Nava, looking relieved.

"If I had a better ComPort, I would have been much safer," replied Nava, waving her ComPort for her father to see. "This thing nearly killed me."

"We'll talk about it later when I get home. See you then," Landrow smiled and rolled his eyes before his image disappeared.

The waiting room view screen covered the fire full time. Fire chief Benelo stated, "The good news is that, thanks to the efforts of everyone involved in firefighting and rescue efforts, there are no known injuries or homes destroyed. It is a clear case of arson, planned to take advantage of the extremely dry forest and strong east wind conditions for maximum destructive power. The ignition point was somewhere about kilometer 23 of the Filton pass trail. Anyone who was in the area early this morning is asked to please contact us with any information that you might have."

"We believe this to be the work of an Alton rebel group," chimed in Police Captain Stano. "We have one suspect in custody at this time, but the investigation is continuing. A reward has been posted for information that leads to the conviction of the arsonist. We will keep the public informed of any further developments."

"My goodness, whatever are they thinking? It was probably a couple of kids that lit something and tossed it through a home PersPort," remarked Myra before her portal opened in front of them. She stepped through the open portal and into their home with Nava close behind.

Cromen's experience was different. As soon as he arrived at the police station, he was handcuffed and frisked, all his possessions were taken before he was booked on suspicion of arson and thrown into a cold cell with various other Alton men all looking bewildered.

Several hours later, Cromen was brought into a small brightly lit interrogation room. "Why did you do it?" asked the detective.

"I didn't," responded Cromen flatly, hoping that he didn't sound confrontational.

"You were seen coming out of the burning forest. You're the only Alton seen anywhere near the fire. What were you doing there?"

"I was hiking and enjoying the beautiful forest. I didn't want it to burn."

"Why were you walking with the young Waru woman? Do you know her?"

"She found me during the fire and helped me escape," Cromen knew they wouldn't accept the idea of him helping a Waru.

They didn't use force but sent a variety of interrogators all asking the same questions.

"We'll go much easier on you if you confess to your crime," They offered numerous times.

Cromen knew he was innocent, they couldn't prove anything. He also knew the Waru didn't need proof to send an

Alton to prison. He did his best to maintain a calm friendly attitude.

Cromen left the police station through the police RingTech portal that opened in front of the Saint Carmen Altonville neighborhood gate. The Watchers were on duty, as always, observing people passing into and out of the Altonville gate. He walked through the gate and down the narrow street lined with flowering trees – gardens of flowers and vegetables surrounded most houses. The brick pavement seemed to flow through the neighborhood without corners or sharp turns. Homes had no fences, not in front, not behind, not between homes. Just gardens transitioning from one lot to the next, each one unique in style and character. People were everywhere enjoying the warm evening, in the gardens working, walking, riding bicycles, playing, and chatting with neighbors. These people of many cultures all worked, laughed, and played together, enjoying the beautiful evening.

Cromen's family home was made of off-white painted adobe with a roof of thatched palm, there were bright blue window frames and a cinnamon-colored door. It wasn't big but had a friendly well kept look. He stepped onto the low porch without seeing anyone and looked through the two small windows of the front door before entering. Cromen could see his parents standing in the living room embracing one another, their foreheads together, smiling and looking into each other's eyes. As he opened the door, they turned their smiles to him. The room was quiet, no view screen was playing. He felt good to be home and he smiled back at his parents.

Chapter 5 The United Worlds

Two hundred and twenty two human occupied worlds had been created by the United Worlds (UW) at the time of this story.

The UW Space Administration, formerly known as the National Air and Space Administration (NASA), created RingTech and first announced it to the world in the year 0 EE (2070 CE), following the first successful mission to another world.

The United States of America owned, controlled, and was responsible for RingTech. The good intentions of the United States towards all people of the world, prompted the sharing of RingTech, and the transfer of ownership and control to the United Nations.

The new RingTech department of the United Nations accelerated mass production of transportation and research portals while continuing space exploration and research for new uses for RingTech.

With the development of the redirect portal, planet terraforming became the largest government program in Earth history. As new planets became available and humans began moving out from Earth, the United Worlds Administration was created as a branch of the UN.

As planetary populations grew, the planetary governments became more important than the individual countries of Earth, and the United Worlds became the larger controlling government. The United Nations became Earth's representative to the United Worlds.

The primary goals of the United Worlds in populating new planets are:

1. Create healthy self sustaining colonies.
2. Reduce the population of Earth.
3. Preserve the ethnic and cultural heritage of the human race.
4. Preserve the biodiversity of all life.

To encourage healthy self sustaining colonies, the United Worlds manages RingTech for the benefit of all humanity, and to encourage advancement of civilization by promoting the Arcadian Path.

The United Worlds prioritizes the hopeful planet migrant applications based on need and ability to build a self sustaining colony. They work with the colonists to ensure a smooth transition to the new planet and to build self sufficiency. All major countries and religions of Earth now have a world or some part of a world for their own.

The United Worlds promotes peace and prosperity throughout the human occupied worlds by teaching the Arcadian Path. But some worlds, like Beryl, don't permit these teachings and don't allow an Arcadian Path teaching center on their world.

Beryl was the 137th planet made habitable during the great expansion of the 22nd and 23rd centuries CE. All immigrants to Beryl were members of the Waru Church of the Seven Apostles, hoping to create a home for their people that was free from outside influence.

Officially, the United Worlds governing board selected the Waru because they were a large unified group that had enough money, resources, and people to start a self reliant colony. Unofficially the United Worlds wanted them off the Earth because their religious activism was so disruptive to the advancement of civilization and teaching of the Arcadian Path.

The United Worlds was confident the Waru could quickly build and maintain a colony without much support. They were right, the Waru colony became self reliant in only 75 years. The UW was also right about the disruptive nature of the Waru, and their potential for causing problems.

Chapter 6 The Apostles

Four hundred years before Nava met Cromen and five years before RingTech was invented, the first of the Seven Apostles came to John Newton. The first Apostle, named Waru, gave scripture to John Newton in the early morning hours of January 11, 2065. She gave him scripture in the form of a computer text file.

John was only 32 years old at the time, but not a healthy young man, he suffered frequent bouts of depression with periods of agonizing migraine headaches. His head was throbbing with pain the night of January 10, as he worked doggedly on his theological research. He was absolutely certain that this research would relieve his suffering. If he could only find the key, John knew God would relieve his pain.

He had just laid his clouded aching head down on the desk when a soft knock on his front door startled him to attention. “Who the hell is knocking at two in the morning?” He said angrily, raising his head up from the desk. The door's view panel showed a small woman dressed in blue robes. “What do you want?” he asked in sleepy anger.

“Greetings. I am the Apostle Waru?” the stranger replied in a very serious voice. “I have what you are seeking.”

“What is it?” said John.

“It is what you seek.”

John didn't open the door. “What do you mean? How do you know what I'm looking for? Can you leave it on the steps?”

The apostle Waru placed something small on the step then stated, “We will return for it at the same time next week.” She then turned and quickly walked away without another word or glance. John watched through the door viewer as the apostle retreated, then he opened the door to find a small bright blue Memex cube.

"Some kind of joke," John muttered as he placed the cube on the computer memory reader. He found only one small text file which he opened.

Astonishment surged through him as he read what could only be the direct word of God. He could feel the truth of these words as if they connected directly to his soul. He saw it but couldn't believe it. Again and again he read the text, feeling sure that there was something wrong. His headache stopped completely, he felt unusually calm and awake.

"They were ordinary looking people wearing flowing colorful robes that seemed to glow," Newton said of the apostles. "Each Apostle stood quietly at his door and would not enter when I invited them in."

The apostles visited John once a week for 7 weeks, always on Monday morning at two AM, a different apostle and a different scripture text file each time they came. Waru, bringer of devotion was first, followed by Carmen, bringer of commitment, Timon, bringer of justice, Faro, bringer of honesty, Kento, bringer of truth, Karyl, bringer of chastity, and Thitis, bringer of forgiveness.

John's ailments disappeared, he didn't feel depressed, he had no more migraine headaches.

The apostles did not return to collect the last Memex cube, a cheap Memex 20-Terabyte cube like the ones they give out free for product promotion. That cube exists today, enshrined at the Seven Apostles of Scripture church headquarters located on Beryl. It is the last artifact known to have come directly from God.

John Newton became the first Profit of the Church of Seven Apostles which he created based on the Seven Holy Scriptures. Many people welcomed the news that there really is a God. They were excited to know that God had spoken to them in the form of scripture.

Chapter 7 The Gift

When Nava and her mom arrived home from the hospital, they opened the view screen to watch news of the fire. Nava was surprised to see Cromen on the screen in handcuffs at the police headquarters. “Look mom, there's Cromen, the guy who saved me.”

“Pause screen, back up five seconds,” Myra commanded the screen to get a better view. Cromen was unmistakable, his kinky brown hair standing out in the crowd.

“He saved you!” Myra exclaimed. “He's Alton. How do you know him?”

“Mom, I thought I was going to die. Seriously. I was scared to death and giving up hope when he found me and brought me to a safe place protected from the fire. And now, look, they're arresting him.”

“Maybe he started the fire and deserves to be arrested. Did he really save you?”

“Yes, the fire was very close, I was terrified and could hardly breath or see. I really thought I was going to die,” Nava became excited and trembled as she spoke. “They shouldn't arrest him, they should give him a reward. Isn't there something we can do?”

“Oh honey, he's Alton. The police might have other reasons to arrest him,” Myra paused a moment before continuing, “But if he saved your life, did he really save your life? My God Nava, we owe him a debt of thanks, something,” Myra paused again looking very serious. “We'll talk with your father when he gets home.”

“What if they hurt him? I should tell the police what happened.”

“Well, okay then! You're right. Lets give the police a call,” Myra stated firmly, and then “Call the police, non-emergency.”

A communication portal opened and the face of a young police woman appeared. “Greetings, police headquarters. How may I help you.”

“Hi, we have some information regarding an Alton man who was arrested in relation to today's fire.”

“Let me connect you to the officer handling that case,” said the police woman without changing her tone of voice or expression.

An older woman appeared after only a few moments, “This is inspector Gavin, who am I speaking with?”

“This is Myra Martin and my daughter Nava.”

“Good afternoon mam, I understand you have some information about the fire.”

“Yes, my daughter has told me that the Alton man you arrested was with her during the fire and that he saved her life.”

“Does your daughter know this man?”

“Only from today. She says that she was nearly engulfed in the fire when he found her and led her to safety.”

“How did he save her?”

“He led me to an old mine tunnel,” injected Nava. “We waited out the fire inside the tunnel.”

“That's interesting,” said the police woman. “He said just the opposite, that you rescued him. But it's not very important really, he's already been cleared and released. I'll make a note in the file and we'll contact you if more information is needed.”

“Can we get his contact information?,” asked Myra. “We would like to thank him personally.”

"Contact information is confidential, but this seems like an appropriate time to bend the rules a little. His name is Cromen Henderson and he lives at 23 Calle Cantil in the Altonville neighborhood. There is no phone number. I wouldn't go there without protection if I were you."

"Thank you for your help, we'll be careful."

Inspector Gavin's face disappeared and Myra turned to Nava, "Well, what do we do? Send him flowers and candy, or maybe a check. Let's wait and talk with your father. He should have a say in how to reward the man who saved your life."

"Croman Henderson," The name and address were firmly set in Nava's mind. She felt almost ecstatic knowing that he was free and that she had a way to contact him. Waiting for her father was slow and painful.

Landrow was late getting home and Nava bombarded him with questions immediately. He just listened without saying anything while fixing himself a snack.

"When should we visit and what should we bring?" he wondered aloud, sitting down and offering Nava a slice of cheese. "What do we do for the person that saved your life?"

They decided to visit Cromen on Saturday because Landrow had to work before then. "I want to have enough time to thank our hero properly."

They only had to wait two days before going to see Cromen, but to Nava those two days felt like two weeks. She had never been to Altonville before. It just wasn't done by the Waru. The only experience she had with the Alton were workers her parents had sponsored to do gardening and housework. They needed a sponsor to enter the Waru neighborhoods.

Nava dreamed of poor desperate Cromen, the man who had saved her life, living in poverty. She imagined small houses built of sticks and mud or with surplus material, she imagined the difficulty of living without water or electricity. And she cried about Cromen, this poor young man who had saved her life, living in misery.

Saturday mid-morning, Nava with her mom and dad stepped through the family PersPort portal to the entrance of Saint Carmen Altonville. Cromen greeted them with a big smile as they came through the gate, he offered his hand and introduced himself to Nava's parents.

Nava recognized him immediately but was surprised by the change in his appearance. The dirty young man in rough clothes that she had met in the fire was now beautiful and dazzling. Cromen's light tan clothes were of simple coarse material, decorated with buttons of orange Morganite gemstones. A braided cord-tie held his collar at the neck and was fastened by a one inch gemstone that was half ruby red and half emerald green.

Nava had heard of it, but she had never seen someone wearing gemstone jewelry before. She felt small and humble, mesmerized.

"We would be honored if you would have lunch with my family at our home," offered Cromen, bowing slightly. "It's not far. If that is okay?"

Myra looked at Landrow and they both smiled. "The honor would be ours. Thank you, Cromen," she said as they bowed in return.

Cromen led the way down a shady path through a grove of flowering trees. The houses looked small to Nava and close together. They were well cared for and blended into the forest and gardens that enveloped them. People outside were working in gardens, playing various games with discs and balls, and just walking and talking with others.

Nava was surprised to see her parents so obviously enjoying themselves. She had expected them to be nervous and worried, but they looked happier then she had seen them for some time.

Her father wouldn't tell her about the gift he planned for Cromen. “It better be something nice,” she told him again and again. But he only replied, “You'll like it. It will make you happy.” She saw nothing that her father brought with him, and it worried her a little.

Cromen's home looked very small to Nava as they approached. It was covered with flowering vines and shaded by large trees, one of which was completely covered by bright lemon yellow flowers. The house seemed to be a part of the garden and looked as if it had grown out of the ground like a mushroom sprouting up through the soil. Nava loved it and felt ashamed of her imagined image of the poor suffering Alton people.

Cromen's parents met them on the porch and had obviously dressed in preparation for the occasion. Their clothes were similar in material to those of Cromen and also adorned with bright gemstones. Inside, it was a well-kept comfortable home, much bigger than it looked from the outside. Friends and family were waiting to greet them. The warmth and friendliness of his family made Nava comfortable almost immediately. She enjoyed the conversation while sampling various fresh fruits and vegetables set out to snack on.

Cromen's Uncle Burt began playing light classical guitar music after introducing himself to everyone.

Now it was complete magic for Nava, the bright airy room filled with music and smiling friendly people gave her an emotional awakening. She recognized the beauty and special nature of the event and was smiling and enjoying every moment.

Cromen's happy face suddenly appeared in front of her and she hugged him without hesitation, not checking if her parents were watching. She felt embarrassed by her ignorant imagination of the Alton people, and looked into Cromen's friendly eyes with more love than she could ever remember feeling. Cromen saw the rising emotion in her face, took her hand and walked her out the side door into the garden.

They walked along holding hands through the flowers and vegetables and fruit trees. Nava was aware of the beautiful gardens around her but her mind was on Cromen. “I can't help it Cromen,” she said, looking at the bunches of ripe strawberries. “I love you and I don't even know who you are.”

“I accept your love and love you back,” replied Cromen, seeing the seriousness of her emotion. “It's okay. It's a good thing and I am happy to have whatever relationship we can share.”

They sat on a bench in the shade without talking, her emotional excitement made speaking difficult, she was sure she would say something stupid. Cromen saved her, “If you were Alton, or I were Waru, we could go on dates together and get to know each other better, but we are not and I worry about the problems our relationship could cause with the Waru Watchers.”

“You're so serious, Cromen. I don't care about the Watchers,” she stated in frustration.

“Oh Nava, you are beautiful and I would love to spend time with you, but you don't understand the system as I do. The Watchers may not be able to do much to you, but they can make life difficult for me and my people. They can cancel our work permits, they can throw us in jail, and they can physically harm us without any legal consequences. I appreciate and honor your love, but how can we spend time together without having problems?"

Nava understood that he was right, but she wanted to have Cromen in her life, wanted to know him more. "I know you're right. It makes me angry and sad but you're right and I don't want anything to hurt you," she dried her eyes and tried to smile without much success.

Seeing her struggle emotionally, Cromen said, "Come on, let's go play tag with the kids." There were always kids around playing and it wasn't hard to find a group to play with. The children all wanted to tag Cromen but he was fast and Nava was tagged first. She ran and laughed with the children until her eyes were dry and her face glowing with smile.

The meal was beginning as they reentered the house. Myra had observed Cromen and Nava's interaction in the garden and when their host seated Landrow between Cromen and Nava, she made Landrow change seats so that Nava and Cromen could sit together. Nava was amazed at this action and smiled big at her mother.

Cromen's father, James, stood and gave a blessing before they ate, "We are blessed this day with fine food provided by the hard work of many hands, and we are so happy to have new friends to sit at our table and share some of the delights of being human. Thank you universe for allowing us to live and appreciate life. Thank you for allowing us to understand who we are in this fantastic universe and for our ability appreciate the reality of being human," He than raised his glass and faced

Nava and her parents, "May you have a long and beautiful life."

The group all raised their glasses and drank in approval of these kind words.

Nava turned to Cromen. "I had a very different vision of how the Alton lived. I was expecting miserable living conditions with people suffering and unhappy. I'm glad to see how happy and healthy your people are."

Cromen gave her a curious smile, "It is a shame that our two cultures can't be more free in our interactions. We both have very good intentions and valuable knowledge to share."

Nava had never experienced a group of people that were so fun and easy to enjoy. She had such a good time that she was surprised by the meal winding down and dishes being cleared away.

Landrow stood up and looked around the room at the friendly faces before speaking. He asked Cromen to stand and the group quieted down quickly as Landrow looked at Cromen and began. "Without you Cromen, we would be burying our sweet daughter Nava today instead of enjoying the company of your beautiful family." Tears came to his eyes as he said this. "Nothing I can do could begin to show how much we appreciate what you have done for us. Maybe it was just a lucky coincidence that you were there, but you didn't leave her on the trail. You risked your life to bring her along with you to safety. By this action, you have made our lives so very much better and we would like to do something that could make your life better. So, I have purchased one RingTech PersPort, of the latest model, in your name to be owned by you and for use however you see fit,"

With these words, he pulled an envelope from his pocket, handed it to Cromen, and embraced him in a big hug.

The room went completely silent. Cromen looked shocked and worried for a moment, but then he smiled big, took a deep breath, and gave a strong hug in return. "Mr Martin, it seems too big a gift for action that anyone would do in the same circumstance," Cromen said smiling and shaking his head a little in disbelief.

"It is the least we can do," Landrow interrupted. "Your small action saved our daughter's life. We will always be in your debt, Cromen. Thank you."

Myra stood up, walked to Cromen and silently with tears in her eyes hugged Cromen, then said, "We love you Cromen, you will always be welcome in our home."

"A gift given from the heart with the best of intentions," replied Cromen, "cannot be refused. I accept it with great appreciation. It will be a big help for my people. I appreciate it and my people appreciate it. You are always welcome in our homes."

Everybody stood up clapping and cheering.

The floor was cleared for dancing and lively music brightened the room. Almost everyone joined hands and danced around a circle together for the first song and then broke up into groups and couples and individuals, each dancing in their own style. Nava had never really danced before, at least not with other people.

Landrow grabbed Nava after the group dance and asked: "How did you like the gift?" as they danced.

"It's wonderful Dad. You did just the right thing. You and Mom surprise me, like you knew just what would happen here. Did you arrange this ahead of time or something?"

"Your Mom and I both have some knowledge of the Alton culture and we knew exactly what would happen if we came here. We did let them know we were coming as a courtesy to them, but that was all. And it didn't matter if we had gifts or not. The Alton are extremely friendly people and this is how they treat guests."

"It's not what I expected, I'm a little overwhelmed. Do you like Cromen?"

"Yes," Landrow smiled, "I like him very much. But you know the risks for him of being friendly with you. So try not to get too involved."

Nava lost her smile, "I know Dad, I just wish it was different."

"The Watchers aren't here inside the Alton neighborhood," said Landrow, "and an Alton spy is highly unlikely, so enjoy and appreciate this opportunity. It is rare and special."

Nava with some sadness, understood and smiled. "I'll do my best to enjoy it."

Nava and Cromen danced together many times and were happy and light. When people got tired, the music changed to something more relaxing, and it was soon time to leave.

Myra and Landrow could have opened their personnel family portal and returned home immediately, but they chose to walk back to the Alton Gate through the beautiful forested neighborhood. There were lots of hugs and goodbyes on the porch before leaving with Cromen walking hand in hand to the gate with Nava. The night was still warm and the stars were clear and bright.

Before they could see the gate, Landrow stopped. "It's safer for Cromen if we say goodbye here out of view of the Watchers."

"Thank you," said Cromen, "You are right and considerate. I thank you for your generosity. It will not be forgotten," he hugged Myra and Landrow before turning to Nava. "I love you and appreciate your love, but there is great danger for us if we continue. I wish it were different."

Nava and her parents opened their personal portal and walked into their living room in silence.

Chapter 8 Eduard Alton

The day after they visited Cromen and his family, Nava's interest in the Alton people prompted her to ask her father, “Why are they called Alton?”

“Eduard Alton was the leader of their colony after the Waru forced them out of Waru society,” Landrow replied. “He created a colony almost completely governed by the Arcadian Path.”

“So that's where the Alton name came from, you sound like you admire him.”

“I do admire him,” Landrow replied. “He stood up for what he believed in the face of great social pressure against him. He fought for what he believed in.”

“Was he really Waru? They teach us that only members of the Waru faith were allowed to migrate to Beryl.”

“In the great emigration 200 years ago, there were many immigrants who were not strict followers of the Waru religion. People were looking for opportunity, a new life on another planet. Eduard Alton was one of those who was a little weak in his belief in the Waru faith.”

“He was an interesting character,” continued Landrow. “He was Waru but had been educated in public schools on Earth that included teaching the Arcadian Path.”

“They didn't teach that at my school.”

“No, you were educated in Waru schools that don't teach the Arcadian Path.”

“Why do you know all this? I've never heard any of it before.”

“My research for the university gives me access to historical documents that aren't available to the public. Want to hear more?”

“Sure.”

“Okay, here is what I can tell you about Eduard Alton.”

“He grew up in the Waru faith, attended church services regularly, and felt he belonged to the Waru culture. But he didn't believe that following the Arcadian Path was in conflict with the Waru religion. He didn't understand why something so helpful to people would be discouraged.”

“He arrived on Beryl in the second year of the big emigration and was a Miracle manager in the Department of Induction. He scheduled and managed angels that come through portals to provide help that might otherwise come from the government or hospitals.”

“There was even a “Win a Miracle' game show back then,” continued Landrow. “People prayed and sometimes their prayers were answered.”

“Ed liked being a Miracle worker, but could see that the people needed much more than fake angles coming to give them a gift.”

“With the rush and chaos of the ten year immigration, the housing and job situation was very bad. No one had gone hungry or been without shelter, but many people hadn't made the emotional transition to beryl very successfully. The difficulties of leaving your home planet and settling on a new one, were too much for some.”

“In the year EE 238 (2308 CE), after 8 years on Beryl, Eduard Alton created a website to find and meet other believers in the Arcadian Path. He wanted to find and connect with people on Beryl who were more like himself in their view of life."

"This action was liberating for Ed, but had the unfortunate side affect of attracting the Orthodox Waru attention."

"There are several things he wrote which I really like, 'Humans don't always make the best choices in life. Why should being human make you a sinner?' and 'What really makes a person good? It's not their beliefs or their culture or their money or their politics. No, it is their positive interaction with the people around them, and with the entire human society. It is the good that they do.'"

"That sounds like a good philosophy," Nava commented.

"He believed the Waru abstinence only policy and the lack of sex education left young adults unable to have a natural and safe sex life. Eduard Alton could see the effect of this policy in the large number of unplanned and under age pregnancies among the Waru. 'The vast majority of Waru are sexually frustrated,' Eduard wrote, 'they sacrifice their happiness in this life in the hope of going to Heaven in the next.'"

"He was critical of many of the rules about things the Waru call sin; dancing, self adornment, mixed swimming, alcohol. He advocated fun because it helps people be happy and healthy."

"The web page he created focused on the Arcadian Path. It asked that people with similar views contact him through the blog or email with their own ideas," he hadn't expected a lot of interest and he hadn't expected a negative reaction from the Orthodox Waru. But he got both."

"Some people were offended by his ideas. They reported him to the media as anti Waru. Eduard broke no law, but the media attention brought a flood of new participants to Eduard's website, both friendly and critical."

"There were no Watchers then, no one watching to see if you are being good Waru, no one monitoring your church attendance, no one watching who you visited."

"I don't think he intended to create a social movement. The thousands of people adding their support for Eduard Alton's ideas was probably a surprise to him."

"Some participants wanted radical change, Michael Doone was one of them. He joined Ed's website when it already had many thousands of members."

"Mr. Doone dominated the blog conversation with a message of hate and retribution for what he said were wrongs against humanity committed by the Waru. He claimed to be a faithful believer in the Arcadian Path, and that the tightly controlled Waru religious society violated every principle. Maybe he had a good point, but within Orthodox Waru society there were those who were greatly worried by the words of Michael Doone.

Chapter 9 Flush the Turds

Nava wanted to hear more, “Go on Dad. How is this Michael Doone involved with the separation of our society?”

“History is a little unclear, but Michael Doone came to Beryl in the first wave of immigration. There was some confusion about his name being connected to a bombing suspect in New York City, but the Orthodox Waru officials approved his passage.”

“The Orthodox Waru are a small minority of the Waru population,” continued Landrow. “But they exercise complete control of the church and the government of our planet. They hold the population to a very strict interpretation of the Seven Scriptures, but they are generous in their forgiveness. Michael Doone called it a never ending cycle of sin, guilt, and forgiveness. He said that normal human behavior should not be judged as sinful, but should be accepted if not appreciated, as part of being human.”

“The rising influence of Michael Doone caused enough concern among the Orthodox Waru that they began looking for ways to bring this unfaithful population under control.”

“On July 9, 2211 Michael Doone requested and was granted an audience with Waru Council of Elders right here in Saint Carmin. They permitted Mr. Doone 10 minutes to express his concerns.”

“Honorable Elders,” Mr. Doone began politely, “I am holding a partition signed by over two million citizens of Beryl. It reads as follows: 'We citizens of Beryl submit here, a list of suggestions with the intention of improving the society of

Beryl. We request they be considered by the council and be implemented to meet the needs of our people.

1. Encourage happiness and love in our society.

2. Treat each of us with respect.

3. Find a way to reduce fear among us. Living in fear devastates a person's production and creativity.

4. Provide sexual education in school so that our people can know how to behave safely when confronted with normal human desires."

"The council listened politely until John finished speaking. Without any discussion among the council members, the chairman rose and said, 'The council has heard you, Mr. Doone. We will consider your request.' They said nothing more."

"Further requests to address the Council of Elders were denied and months passed without a response from the council. There was no indication that they were actually considering his request."

"Michael Doone was certainly a man of action, not a man to be ignored," continued Landrow, a smile growing on his face. "He was very active on the Ed Alton website and wherever he could get his message across. But no word came from the council, as if they simply hoped that Michael Doone would go away."

"But it didn't end there. He didn't go away. One cool and drizzly morning two months after making his request, the Council of Elders was seated and called to order. The main business of the day was the case of two wealthy land owners who were fighting over mineral rights and border boundaries. The boundary between there land had never been properly surveyed and was not a concern until rich lithium deposits were discovered. Now they each claimed the mining rights to these deposits."

"About an hour after the hearing started people began arriving outside the chamber, popping through personal portals and gathering on the council chamber steps. By 9:30, there were more than 10,000 people chanting, "Happiness and Liberty for all." The noise could be heard inside the chamber and the proceedings were stopped. A civil protest was something new to Beryl."

"Police arrived and began grabbing protesters and pushing them through portals directly into jail cells. The protesters didn't resist the police or fight back, but instead they began rushing into any open police portal, some into jail cells, and some into the police station where the police had ported in from. Every single protester pushed to get in, pushed until the jail cells and offices were packed tight and no more could enter. It happened fast before the portals could close. Not all could get in and many waited for the police to find more space to put them. No more police portals opened and the remaining protesters chanted and mingled about for a time before going home."

"The city of Saint Carmin has a typical sewage processing system," continued Landrow. "A transfer facility receives sewage from each home or business via RingTech utility portal. The sewage is then pumped through another portal directly to a processing plant located on the East side of the Tikla mountains where it is processed for agricultural use."

"As the protesters outside dispersed, the council settled down and returned to the business of the day. As litigation of the land dispute restarted, a large utility portal opened in the general location of the front doors to the chamber. City sewage flowed into the chamber at a rate estimated at 4,000 liters per minute. Under considerable pressure, the sewage sprayed across the chamber to the far wall, covering everything and everyone with raw stinking filth. Council members pushed and shoved to get to the two small side doors, but much to late."

"The flow stopped with about 3 feet of sewage on the floor, sewage covered every single person and object in the room. The council members waded out of the chamber's front door with sewage in their nostrils, their hair, their mouth, and eyes. Stinking and dripping they walked out onto the front steps smearing city sewage all over the gleaming white marble.

Nava couldn't help laughing. "Are you kidding me, Dad?"

"No, this is the documented truth. A rain shower was ordered to begin the cleaning process and each dignified member of council undressed to nothing but their underwear there on the steps in the rain."

"How could this happen? Blocking technology is supposed to be perfect."

"And it is, but blocking fields only works when the system is energized. Someone somewhere had turned it off. And somehow at the same time another someone at the sewage plant redirected the main city sewage portal to flow into the Council Chamber."

"The offense to the Orthodox Waru was unbelievable, defiling high ranking members of the faith and nearly destroying their sacred chamber – It took 2 years before the chamber could be used again. The council knew full well that it could have been much worse. After all, the sewage flow had stopped in time. No one died."

"The Orthodox High Council had no alternative, the threat was too great. Something had to be done. Drastic measures were justified and supported by the common Waru faithful. The Directorate of Monitors was created to investigate and identify participants of this crime. This army of Monitors, what we now call 'Watchers' provided security for the temples and manpower to investigate crimes against the church."

"Did they ever catch the people who did this?" asked Nava.

"The conspirators who actually caused the sewage spill were never identified. Employees of the Sewage Transfer facility and the Portal Blocking Authority were highly scrutinized and many removed from their positions. Only the most devout Waru were allowed to remain in their jobs. But no, no one was ever charged with the crime."

"This is when the Waru forced the separation of the two societies. Every person that had ever joined or participated in the Ed Alton website was labeled as a traitor to Waru society. It was a time where neighbors accused each other of being followers of Alton. Families and friends of these suspects were put on the lists, along with every person who had not attended church regularly while on Beryl. These people were black listed, removed from their jobs, their RingTech portals confiscated, access to other portals denied."

"Sections of towns were divided off to create neighborhoods for the Alton people. The only work allowed the Alton were menial service and labor work. They were not allowed into Waru areas without a permit."

"There were six million people forced into these neighborhoods and in the years ahead millions more walked out on the Waru to live as an Alton."

"Waru were now required to attend church every Sunday and were visited by Watchers and punished financially if they missed too many church days."

"Didn't they punish Michael Doone?"

"Michael Doone and his hard core followers disappeared. No one knows how they escaped or where they went."

"So, that's the story of the Alton as I know it. Your mother and I have both done research on the Alton. As a cultural anthropologist, I don't get much opportunity to do direct field research of cultures other than Waru. The university and the Waru council are interested in understanding the Alton, mostly because they are viewed a threat to society. So I've learned a great deal about them. And your mom has worked on the psychological aspects of the Alton culture. We both see something good in these people. They seem so much happier and psychologically stronger than most of the Waru."

"What makes them so happy?"

"We're convinced that the teaching and practice of the Arcadian Path is the biggest positive influence on their society. They educate there children in how to have a happy contented life, how to be responsible for their own emotions."

"Why haven't you told me this before?"

"It might have alienated you from your own culture and friends."

"You don't have to worry about that, Dad. I'm already alienated and don't have any friends."

"I am sorry for that. But it's probably because your mom and I feel somewhat alienated from the Waru society ourselves."

"The other thing I need to say, is that your mother and I are not allowed to share this information. I think you're old enough now to respect the need for secrecy in this matter. The fact is that we have been trying to practice the Arcadian Path in our own lives for some years now."

"Dad, maybe it's time that you share the Arcadian Path with me."

"We'll get to that some day. But to add a little to the story, The Waru began to call the banished group Alton people. The Alton people embraced it and became proud of the name. There was a lot of depression and despair within them at first, but with time they developed a good system of government, and became a well functioning civilized society. They have a good education system that encourages the Arcadian Path as an active part of life no matter what your spiritual beliefs."

"Altons have no defined religion, but include people with many different religious beliefs, brought together by the shared repression they endure from the Waru and with their belief in the Arcadian path."

"How do they manage without RingTech?" asked Nava. "We depend on it for everything."

"Alton are allowed RingTech now, but the cost of a PersPort is more than most Alton earn in 10 years. The Alton use public transportation, bicycle, or walk mostly."

"It's hard to believe Dad," Nava responded sadly. "Why would the Orthodox Waru be worried about such nice people?"

"That dear Nava is a very complicated subject. We'll discuss it another time."

Chapter 10 The Mission

Nava was a naturally curious young woman, questioning everything, searching for her own version of what is right, not accepting anything unless it made sense to her. In her heart, she didn't fit in, anywhere.

Nava was excited and energized by the visit to Cromen's house and by the conversation with her father. Emboldened by this new knowledge of the Alton people, Nava's rebellious nature began to take control. After a week of thinking about it, she could wait no longer. She was determined to visit Cromen again.

The Watchers observed her enter the Altonville Gate but she didn't care. "The hell with them. What a cruel and stupid system they've created," she thought to herself as she passed through the gate.

Many Alton smiled and said hello as she walked along the shady path. She smiled and was happy to see Cromen's home again. His mother was in the front garden working on a strawberry patch. She greeted Nava with a hug and a smile. "Hello Nava, it's so nice to see you again. Would you like a strawberry?"

"Thank you mam," said Nava, enjoying the strawberry while exchanging pleasantries with Cromen's mom before asking, "Is Cromen home?"

"I think he's on the back porch playing with his crystals. You go on around and surprise him. He'll be happy to see you."

Nava walked around the house and found Cromen standing just outside the back porch holding a deep red crystal up to the sun, looking at it with such intensity that he didn't notice

Nava's approach. She stood and watched as he carefully studied the red gemstone, rotating it carefully in the sunlight.

Cromen was startled and almost dropped the crystal when he noticed Nava. A worried emotion crossed his face before he regained his composure. “Nava, how are you?” His intense and focused smile was mixed with questions that he didn't ask.

She knew what he was thinking. “I had to see you Cromen. You are the most wonderful man I've ever met. Maybe I am wrong, but I felt that you were...”

Nava hesitated and Cromen cut in. “Nava wait, there is something that I can't quite get clear in my mind. I feel such a strong connection to you after the fire that my mind is swirling with thoughts of you. I only know you a little but for some reason you have my heart. I worry though, about the danger for both of us. What isn't clear to me is what we can do.”

Their eyes connected and Nava moved closer. “I would never knowingly do anything to hurt you, Cromen. The only reason I've taken the risk of seeing you again is that I have an idea, a little crazy maybe.”

“Tell me Nava, I want to hear.”

“What do you think about joining the Waru religion?” Nava asked, then continued without waiting for his reply. “If you did, then we could see each other without worrying. You don't have to really believe everything, you just have to go along with the ritual. They're always desperate for converts.”

“It would be nice to see each other without fear. But I can't really change what I believe, it is who I am.”

“I don't want you to change, I just want to be with you. This is the only way I can think of that doesn't put us in danger.”

“Is it required that I pledge myself to the belief in the Waru faith?”

“There is nothing in the initiation that requires that. They only ask that you have an open heart and follow the Waru scripture.”

“What would I have to do?”

“Young Waru are expected to go on a mission to spread the scripture and bring converts to the Waru faith,” said Nava. “I've never gone on my mission and the church elders pressure me every week to make a commitment. The missions are all on other worlds which sounds interesting to me, but I feel conflicted about going because of my doubts about the Waru religion.”

“Okay, but how does the mission help us?” Cromen questioned.

“Be patient,” Nava smiled with some excitement. “The church has a program where anyone, including Alton, can become a member of the Waru church. It involves going on a mission as an apprentice to another Waru. There are no religious qualifications. We just submit our mission plan together. It's almost sure to be approved.”

“It's like a dream come true, Nava. A trip to another planet with the woman of my dreams. Will I need to cut my hair and wear different clothes?” Cromen asked.

“They will expect us to wear the conservative gray clothes of the Waru, but they won't ask you to cut your hair. Some of the apostles had long hair.”

“There is one other requirement. Because we're an unmarried couple, the Waru council requires that we submit a form of intent to marry. It's non binding but both of us must sign that we are interested in marriage and that we will not have sexual relations until we are married.”

"Hmm. I'm not sure how that might work out," Cromen said. "But it doesn't worry me as much as teaching a religion I don't know or believe in. As much as I like the idea of a God and protector, I can't believe the way that you do. To teach the Waru faith would feel like betraying my own beliefs. I would be deceiving people."

"I feel that way everyday, Cromen. I don't believe everything the Orthodox Waru teach. I have doubts about God. What will work for us? How can we do this without betraying ourselves?"

"It would be an opportunity to be together safely, and maybe have a great adventure," Cromen responded with a smile. "My imagination is running a little wild with the idea. It's exciting. Can we give the Waru scriptures a more tolerant face, focus on the good parts?"

"I have a hard time seeing the good parts," responded Nava. "What do you really believe about the Waru religion?

"People are all different and I respect the beliefs of others. I don't like to express my doubts about them."

"I think it's time you did," Nava replied firmly. "If we are going to spend time together, we should know each other. You won't offend me. My opinion of the Waru religion is probably worse than yours."

"The Waru are industrious and hard working people. And I like that they encourage free enterprise," Cromen offered.

"Come on Cromen, tell me what you really think. I know you well enough. You have a strong opinion about this."

"Okay!..," Cromen laughed with a curious smile before continuing. "The Waru have many problems. They don't understand what it means to be civilized. They're stuck with a primitive version of God. It's a bad religion because it causes unnecessary guilt and pain. I think your apostles and scriptures were the invention of a delusional schizophrenic, a man who so completely believed his delusion that he convinced millions of others that it was the truth."

"They're not my apostles, Cromen. And I am guilty of suspecting that you are right. I even doubt that the Profit John Newton believed in the scriptures himself."

"Don't feel guilty for having an open mind. It's something I liked about you when we first met. Your mind wants to know, you don't accept something without seeing the truth of it for yourself. Most Waru follow blindly, focused on pleasing God, they ignore their physical and true spiritual needs. They don't learn to love and forgive themselves because they think God controls their lives. Like sheep controlled by wolves, the Waru follow leaders who use fear and suffering to control the flock that feeds them. It's a very poor way to manage people, and the problems in your society are the result," Cromen paused and took a deep breath. "Is that enough?"

"I asked for it," Nava replied with a dazed smile. "It is a little shocking to hear stated those things that have been lurking, vague suspicions in my mind for so long. Thanks."

"Spreading the word of the Waru scriptures goes against what we both feel is right. We want to be honorable," Cromen mused thoughtfully. "Our personal integrity is one of the only things that we really have. Our character is what allows us to feel good about ourselves."

"I suppose you're right about our integrity, I never though of it in that way," Nava replied.

"Teaching the Arcadian Path might not live up to our mission agreement, but we would feel much better," Cromen offered.

"And I would like to learn more," replied Nava. "Could we find parts of the scriptures which agree with the Arcadian Path and only teach those parts?"

"Might work with a little modification. There are probably principles which don't conflict with Waru teaching," Cromen added. "But would we be teaching the Waru religion?"

"A version," replied Nava. "I am Waru. I understand the scriptures, and my views differ from the Orthodox Waru. It will be my version. It will be our version of the Waru religion."

"Maybe we can promote a better form of Waru religion," Cromen replied. "Sometimes I think the Orthodox Waru have lost faith in their own teachings, in desperation to hold the congregation together, they use force and manipulation to control society. This is just what alienates people and drives them away from the church. Do you know that Waru is the most common religion among the Alton?"

"Really, I thought that people who left the Waru were renouncing their faith."

"Maybe they are renouncing their faith in the Waru Church and its Orthodox clergy. But when they leave the Waru society, they rarely give up their faith in God or the teachings of the Waru scriptures."

"We should talk to these people," Nava replied. "It could help us to teach the Waru religion and the Arcadian Path together. What do you think their continued faith does for them?"

"There is something they like about being Waru. They feel comforted and protected by their belief in God. They believe in the goodness of God, the love of God. I can see how it might help someone feel good about life. But only if you can honestly believe. Which just doesn't work for me."

“Why can't you believe?”

“I don't know, maybe because my parents didn't teach me. Maybe my nature is to be more skeptical than other people.”

Their application for a one year mission was submitted that same week, it was accepted and approved by the Orthodox Waru Council of Elders. Their parents were happy with Nava and Cromen's decision. Mission training was a wonderful time for them, spending their days in class and evenings together talking about the Waru religion and the Arcadian Path, everyday falling ever deeper in love.

They received their mission destination assignment at the graduation ceremony after six weeks of training.

“Fomalhaut?” said Cromen. “I've heard the name, but don't know anything about it.”

Let's check,” said Nava. “WikiWorlds says Fomalhaut was the eighth planet to be terraformed. But the process of populating the planet was less organized than others. The United Worlds failed to provide a unified government sufficient to manage the diverse population. Now, with a population of 1.2 billion, the common human problems were crippling the welfare of many of these people.”

“It says that armed conflicts on Fomalhaut have broken out over borders disputes. Smaller ethnic groups are being abused by the more powerful and wealthy. Large areas of the richest lands are owned by a small number of wealthy families, while the workers are stuck in a life of poverty without opportunities for improvement. The prosperity that RingTech has brought to many has left a large population on Fomalhaut in deplorable conditions.”

“That doesn't sound good,” observed Cromen. “But maybe it makes fertile ground for Waru converts.”

Nava's mom, Myra, insisted on hosting a going away party. "It is against the rules, but we will open our portal to Cromen's family home. They are our family now and I want to share my home with them."

Landrow smiled, "Of course Myra, it is the right thing to do."

The two family homes were brought together as one through the RingTech PersPort of Nava's home. Going out the front door of one home led you in the front door of the other.

The party was filled with happy people, but restrained by nervous anticipation of Nava and Cromen impending departure. Everyone ate and laughed and danced, but with a certain subdued tension. Uncle Burt drank too much and started crying. Everyone hugged and said goodbye with tears in their eyes.

"I've never been here before," said Cromen the next morning, as he and Nava entered the United Worlds Off-World Transport station in Saint Carmen.

"Me too. It doesn't look like much," said Nava observing the unimpressive two story red brick building.

"Two for Fomalhaut," Cromen stated to onc of the wall mounted kiosks that lined all sides of the lobby. "Please show your I.D. to the screen," came the reply. A door adjoining the kiosk opened to a portal staging room where the technician helped them position their bags in front of the three meter portal ring.

"Ready to go?" asked the Technician.

"Ready," was Nava and Cromen's happy reply.

The portal opened and they stepped directly into the immigration office of planet Fomalhaut.

Nava and Cromen arrived in the capital city of New Singapore, Fomalhaut on a late winter day. A cold dusty wind greeted them as they stepped off the public transport and walked the few blocks to their apartment. The streets were crowded and homeless people begged on corners, mostly ignored by the passers bye.

"I thought things were bad on Beryl with the repression of the Alton," said Nava. "These people are suffering in a way I didn't know existed. I had imagined that your people were suffering because of our divided system, but not like this. It's horrible."

"This society has lost it's way," responded Cromen. "They need a lot more than we two lovers out for an adventure. They really need to revolutionize their way of living here."

The apartment was small by Beryl standards, even for the Alton. It was clean and comfortable with combined living room kitchen and one small separate bedroom. Nava laughed when she saw that there was only one bed, "That's a fairly clear signal that we're not expected to live up to the 'No Sex' agreement."

"Do you think they expect us to feel guilty and beg God for forgiveness? It smells like an evil plan to me," joked Cromen with a smile.

"An evil plan that I can appreciate," said Nava, pulling Cromen onto the bed with her.

"It is a beautiful plan. Their trap is our opportunity," he replied, taking Nava into his arms.

"Let's take advantage," were Nava's words just before they were overcome with wordless passion.

Chapter 11 Fomalhaut

Cromen rose early on their first morning. Realizing that there was no food or coffee in the apartment, he dressed quietly and slipped outside to a cool clear morning. He observed the old worn-out look of the buildings as he walked casually down the street in the fresh morning air. The neighborhood clearly spoke of prosperity past, the houses were run down, the streets were dirty. People watched him with suspicion. What had looked disappointing in last night's darkness looked worse in the bright morning light.

He entered the Dog-Patch cafe, a few blocks from their apartment. A tall woman with graying hair entered behind him and tugged on his shirt sleeve. When he turned to face her she pointed to his jeweled belt buckle and whispered in his ear, "You shouldn't wear that here."

Cromen searched her blue-gray eyes, surprised at the intense sincerity and concern. She shook her head seriously.

"Thank you," he whispered before she turned and left the cafe.

Cromen quickly pulled his shirt out to cover the brilliant blue and green tourmaline on the buckle. Theft is very rare among the Alton and the Waru don't permit jeweled adornments. His pretty gems had never been cause for worry before.

Cromen watched people more carefully as he carried coffee and pastries back to the apartment. Fewer people stared at him, but there was someone following him as he entered the apartment building.

Nava greeted him with a smile and a kiss, "Thanks Cromen, I was hoping that was where you went."

"I had a strange experience," he told her. "An old woman said that I shouldn't wear my gemstones. She implied that it was dangerous. She sounded serious. Do you think they're worth a lot here?"

"I don't know. We aren't allowed such pretty things," said Nava with worry on her face.

"The old lady's eyes had the look of terrible danger or death. It startled me. And I think someone followed me home," Cromen continued, glancing out the window at the street below. "I don't see anyone watching from the..."

A firm knock at the door interrupted Cromen and startled them both. "Who is it?" he queried.

"Inspector Kwong of the New Singapore police," came a friendly sounding reply. "I would appreciate a few words with you."

Cromen gave a little worried look at Nava who nodded a half-smile. He opened the door to see a tall well dressed Asian man holding his badge for Cromen to inspect. Cromen only looked in his eyes before offering his hand and inviting the man in. "Please come in, how may we help you?" he asked with concern clear on his face.

"You are new here aren't you?" asked inspector Kwong with a pleasant smile.

"We arrived last night."

"Where are you from?"

"We're from planet Beryl."

"Are you on a religious mission?"

"Yes, is that alright?"

"Sure, there is no problem with that. I have seen many missionaries from Beryl. I only came to explain a few things about Fomalhaut and New Singapore in particular."

"Is it my gems?" asked Cromen.

"In part. This is a much more dangerous place than your home-world. You shouldn't have anything of value on your person here, and those gems of yours have already been seen in the community. So your apartment isn't safe either."

"What should we do?"

"There is a commercial security vault close to the Dog Patch cafe. I want you to take everything you have of value and walk with me there. Wear some of your jewels in the open. Just one or two. You can check your things into a secure personal vault at the facility. People in the street will know that I advised you and that the jewels are no longer in your personal possession. You should be safe then."

"Are they really so valuable here?"

"One of those little shiny rocks of yours might be worth 10 years wages for me, and I make pretty good money. I'm no jeweler, but I am sure that I could be a rich man by selling those. There are people here who would happily kill you for any one of your stones."

"Who pays for them? Aren't they common here?"

"Very rare, very expensive. Only the wealthy posses such things."

As they walked to the security vault with inspector Kwong, Cromen noticed the same people watching them as in the morning. They watched as Cromen and Nava entered the vault company and watched as they came out without his jewel adornments.

"Glad I got to you before they did," inspector Kwong said, handing Cromen a business card and shaking his hand. "Have a good day. And be very careful."

Nava took Cromen's hand as they walked through the ugly streets back to the apartment, feeling worried and vulnerable in this new strange environment. No one followed them home.

"Why don't the Waru mine and sell the gems if they are so valuable?" Cromen asked. "They don't use them but they could make money with them."

"We are not allowed any personal adornment," said Nava. "And Beryl is a rich planet with many other resources to exploit. Maybe the Waru think that mining gems will cause too much temptation for the workers and have a corrupting influence."

They warmed the coffee and pastries, trying to relax and to enjoy their first morning on another planet, their first day living together.

At 1 pm they reported in at the Waru sanctuary for new arrival orientation. They were warned not to carry any valuables and were given an information manual with maps showing the dangerous or restricted areas to avoid. The last subject of discussion was the Arcadian Mind-Snake, which they should also avoid. They were directed to report for full Fomalhaut missionary orientation three days from now on Monday morning at 7:30 am.

"What is an Arcadian Mind-Snake?" Nava asked Cromen while walking home.

"I've read about them, but don't know much. They have some ability to alter your mood."

"Do they make you feel good? Do you eat them?"

"No, you don't eat them," Cromen smiled. "They emit some kind of electric waves or radio waves. I think they can make you feel good or bad."

"Do they live here?"

"They're from planet Arcadia. But some people keep them as therapy pets."

"Why should we avoid them?"

"I don't know what the danger could be. If they help people feel good then what's the harm?"

The full week of orientation meetings focused on exploiting the weakness of the culture to encourage conversion to the Waru faith. They learned how to present the Waru religion to the more desperate and needy as well as the wealthy citizens of Fomalhaut. Everyone has problems, problems that can only be solved with the right belief system, only with the right God, only with faith in and devotion to the Waru Scriptures.

The Waru sanctuary in New Singapore was a cathedral in the typical Waru style with a very tall central spire and seven smaller spires forming the perimeter, all glistening in gold and silver. After orientation, they met there at 7:30 am local time, 5 days a week, Tuesday through Saturday, to get instructions and materials for the day. Part of each day was spent going to appointments with people who had previously expressed an interest in the Waru faith. The remaining time, until 5:00 pm, they walked the neighborhoods passing out pamphlets and talking with people.

Nava was better at explaining the material, but Cromen had a way of making people comfortable with his friendly questions and very polite manors of interaction.

The work became routine and boring after about a week. They visited and presented religious information to people in the morning. Then they went door to door in the afternoon knocking and talking or just leaving pamphlets if no one was home. Their only relief from boredom were the interesting characters that they met.

Like the older lady who walked across the street, hobbled with her cane actually, to tell Cromen: "What a handsome young man you are. If I was younger, I'd pull you off the street and take you home."

Cromen smiled, thanked her earnestly, and offered her a Waru religious pamphlet. She laughed and said, "I thought you were too good to be true," before throwing the pamphlet to the ground and walking away.

"A skeptic," laughed Cromen, smiling. "A woman after my own heart."

"A hardcore sinner," Nava added laughing.

The old woman stopped and turned, looked at them both and said. "We're all born sinners, be proud of it."

"What sins should we be proud of?" Nava queried gently.

"Why your desire to feel good of course. The things that might make you feel good or help you to be happy. The desire for sexual stimulation and release is the most sinful in your religion. How can people ever be happy without satisfying their basic emotional needs?" the woman replied, looking at them severely.

"What about pregnancy and disease?" asked Nava.

"Religion won't protect you there," the woman said, shaking her head. "Only education, science, and medicine can solve that."

Nava nodded and took Cromen's hand before walking away. "Did you have useful sex education?"

"There were no demonstrations if that's what you mean," smiled Cromen.

"You know what I mean."

"There were lots of illustration about how sex physically works, every year from the beginning of school with a little more detail each year. In high school, they taught us about the psychological effects of our physical desires and sexual activities. They taught us how to avoid disease or unwanted pregnancy. They taught us that an active sex life is very healthy both physically and mentally. Life is not easy, sex can help you feel love and reduce the negative effect of the many stresses in life."

"In my school, they only taught abstinence and the consequences of committing this horrible sin. They made us recite the Seventh Sacred Promise every day at school. Let me recite it for you," smiled Nava.

"I will have no sexual activities nor desire sex, except for the purpose of procreation. I will not have sexual activity with a partner other than my spouse. I am forbidden to have or desire immoral sexual activity, specifically: adultery, fornication, pornography, homosexuality, transexuality, sodomy, masturbation, group sex, rape, incest, pedophilia, and bestiality."

"Wow, that's some list," replied Cromen. "It makes me horny just hearing it. And they make you memorize and recite it every day?"

"Every day they remind us of what we're missing," Nava joked. "Tempting your imagination daily."

"You're not ashamed of making love with me," Cromen responded, looking at her with a surprised smile. "I don't see guilt on your face."

"My parents talk about it as something good. They told me enough to understand how to deal with this part of my life in a healthy way. Most kids don't have parents like mine, many feel guilty about their sexual desires, they even feel guilty about masturbating."

"Wow, that's no way to live. But it explains some of the unhappiness I see in the Waru people."

My parents are better than most," Nava offered, "they seem to have a sex life and are affectionate with each other."

"Good for them," smiled Cromen. "My parents often say love-making keeps their relationship happy and healthy. I think they do it a lot."

“I hope so,” Nava laughed. "It's really sad that people fear something so natural and good for you, We're not primitive animals. We can be emotionally fulfilled without harming anyone. Why does the church impose such a horrible policy?"

"It was logical in the distant past," replied Cromen, "when there was no way to control diseases or prevent pregnancy. Sick people and children without good parents would be a burden on society. It was a way to protect the community."

"But why now?" Nava asked. "We have medicine. We have birth control. And we understand the negative emotional effects of repressing our desires."

"Control?" offered Cromen. "They want you to feel guilty. They want you to seek forgiveness from God. It's how they keep you dependent on the church." Cromen paused and laughed "They want you to be a sinner."

"Then sinners we will be," said Nava with a big smile, taking Cromen's hand and pulling him closer.

Cromen thought about real sin, the sin of hurting yourself or others. He stopped, looked into her light brown eyes, pulled her close, and kissed her lips tenderly, before saying, "Love is never a sin."

Chapter 12 Mind Control

Living together was frustrating at times for Nava and Cromen. They had arguments and unhappy moments, but love held them together and seemed to grow with the passing of each new difficulty. They were happy together, each encouraging the other to love themselves and feel good about life.

The warming weather brought green growth and the bloom of spring. The ugly gray streets were transformed slowly by advancing green foliage, creeping everywhere, covering the trash and dirt, shading the streets, and bringing a fresh feel to the city.

Nava and Cromen talked about philosophy and religion together constantly during their daily work routine. It was their job after all, and they both felt a passion to understand and help each other. The people they met seemed friendlier and happier, like the green growth of spring had invaded them with some calming magic spell.

In late spring, they were given a new region farther from the city, a wealthy neighborhood of big houses and pretty gardens. There were no appointments here, just door-to-door house visits. The people were unfriendly, no one talked with them or invited them inside their home. So they were surprised in the late morning by the warm greeting they received on the porch of a smaller house with pretty gardens.

"Good morning," smiled the small middle-aged man, offering his hand to shake. "You look like you're on a mission. I'm Greyson. Welcome to our home. Please sit down and rest awhile."

Cromen and Nava thanked Greyson and sat down together in a wooden porch swing. They had hardly settled when the front door opened and a thin woman with graying hair came out carrying a tray of ice tea and cookies. "Hi, I'm Daria. You look like you might need a little refreshment."

"Thank you," they said in unison. "You are very kind," smiled Nava. "May I help you?"

"Just sit and relax," Daria replied with a smile. "Where are you from?"

"We're from planet Beryl," said Cromen. "Thank you for your generosity. You're the first friendly people we've met in this neighborhood."

"Don't judge them too harshly," Greyson replied. "They're all caught up in the rat race, the fight for success, they don't have time to spend meeting people and enjoying life. Try to forgive them, they have not found a better way."

"How do you stay so happy living among them? You seem out of place," stated Nava.

"They're not bad people, they just don't know what's important in life," answered Greyson. "We try to live with another philosophy."

"I'm interested to hear about your philosophy," Nava responded seriously. "Our official mission is to spread the word of the Waru scriptures, but we're both open-minded people eager to learn."

"It is the most simple that there is," Greyson responded. "We follow the Arcadian Path. Have you heard of this?"

"I have lived by the Arcadian Path my whole life," said Cromen. "Nava is just learning."

"But you're teaching Waru religion. How does that work for you?" asked Daria.

"It's educational," smiled Cromen. "We're working it out."

"We have something else that helps us appreciate life. " Daria offered. "Are you familiar with the Arcadian Mind-Snake?"

"Only a little. The Waru warned us to avoid them," Cromen replied.

"Well, they can hurt you if they feel bad, but for us, the benefit they provided is worth the effort of keeping them happy."

"How do they help? It's some kind of mind control, isn't it? Do you have them here?"

"Yes, we maintain a small colony to give us an emotional boost. Life is difficult and it's nice to have something which makes it feel better. We also supply them to people who wish to live with the positive influence that the Mind-Snakes can provide. Would you like to see them?" Daria offered.

Cromen gave Nava a questioning look and she responded with a smiling nod.

Daria led them through a neat and clean but simple house to a door near the back. Greyson asked them to wait outside the door as he opened it and stepped through.

"He's feeding them," said Daria. "The happier they are the better the effect they have."

A couple of minutes passed before the door opened again. "Please step into the vestibule," requested Greyson, directing them through the door into a small windowless room. He closed the door behind them.

"The room they live in is enclosed in a net of copper wire which isolates the outside world from the emotional emanations the Snakes create. So you can't feel them when you're outside their enclosure. They're eating happily right now and when I open this inner door you will feel them. It will be surprising at first. Shocking maybe. Just try to relax, focus on your breathing. You can leave at any time if you feel overwhelmed."

Greyson opened the door just a crack. Nava and Cromen both jerked physically and looked at each other, tears came to Nava's eyes as she took a deep breath and moved into Cromen's arms.

"I didn't know that I could feel this good," smiled Cromen, gasping a little and looking sort of crazed. Nava only beamed a smile in reply as Greyson opened the door fully and invited them inside.

A chest-high glass wall formed this side of a large enclosure and a small staircase led to a platform at the top edge of the wall. Rich soil filled the space on the other side of the glass and gave a clean earthy smell to the room. Green plant matter could be seen on the surface and something was actively moving under the plants pulling them down and eating them.

Greyson smiled, "We shouldn't stay long. It's your first time," encouraging Nava and Cromen to leave the room. He closed the door, and lead them back to the front porch. Cromen and Nava both looked out of breath, a little dazed, but happy and smiling fiercely.

Nava's smile glowed, her eyes sparkled.

"How could this be bad for you?" Cromen asked of himself and the world.

"It is somewhat psychologically addictive," answered Daria. "The more time you spend with them the less overwhelming the effect. Visiting them every day for a few minutes seems to be about right for us."

"I still feel really good," said Nava, "like I'm a little drunk or stoned or something. Does it last long?"

"The first contact will last a few hours to a few days, but longer exposure will change the way you feel forever. It is as though you learn how to feel good, as though your brain learns to act differently."

"Why would anyone be afraid of them?" asked Cromen, "They're like a shortcut to enlightenment, a direct path to nirvana."

"When the snakes are unhappy the effect is horribly painful and can cause psychological damage," said Daria. "You must take good care of them and not do anything to irritate them."

"They can open doors to your happy emotions, but they don't help you feel good about who you are," added Greyson. "They are only one tool in the struggle for happiness. A tool that you need to use wisely."

"To have a good civilized society, we each need to be civilized. We must care about other people, all other people. Just because you feel great doesn't make you a good person," continued Greyson. "Why should a person care about others when they have everything they need to feel happy? Some people isolate themselves with their Mind-Snakes and live like hermits. After several years of regular constant exposure, your brain eventually adjusts and you no longer feel the effect."

"Some people go mad after long exposure," Daria added. "The snakes can be helpful if used properly. As Greyson said, it's just one tool in your struggle for a happy contented life."

"Follow the Arcadian Path if you want to be happy," Greyson suggested as Nava and Cromen stepped off the porch and down the front walkway.

"Be good to yourselves," added Daria. "And come visit us anytime you like."

"You know Daria, Mae might like to meet those two," Greyson said as he watched Nava and Cromen walking away. "Remind me when we see her again."

"Wow, what nice people," Nava commented with a smile as they walked down the sidewalk.

"I wish more people were like them," Cromen replied. "I'd like to be like them."

"Me too," Nava agreed, still smiling and excited.

On arriving home that afternoon, they looked up Arcadian Mind-Snake. Cromen read: "The Arcadian Mind-Snakes are highly regulated because they can invade people's minds at a distance. If kept properly, Mind-Snakes emanate an almost euphoric feeling for anyone close enough to feel it. They are used for many things. They can help people feel better about life, reduce depression, relieve the suffering of grief, and sooth a person at the time of death. But when the Mind-Snakes are not maintained well, the emotion that they project can be anything from painful depression to panic and terror."

"I'd like to have them someday," said Cromen. "They can help bring happiness to everyone."

Nava laughed, "I think the Waru all need the Mind-Snakes to counteract the constant negative buzz of the Waru media on Beryl. The news they present only causes anxiety and worry. Over and over again, they harp on the same fearful messages."

"As I said, the Orthodox Waru want you to be afraid."

Chapter 13 Change your Mind

It was a warm clear blue Saturday morning with a few puffy clouds passing by, a nice day. Nava and Cromen arrived quite happily and on time for the second of 5 morning appointments. They were greeted at the door and invited into the large beautiful home by a tallish middle-aged woman with dark skin and long wavy black hair. She wore blue pants held by a silver belt, and a white blouse, practical and elegant, tight enough to show her lean healthy body.

She brought them into the library, asked them to sit at a large wooden table, and introduced herself only as Mae. After exchanging pleasantries and offering coffee and snacks, she started the conversation very seriously: "I brought you here for a reason. I have some friends that I believe you met, Daria and Greyson."

"Yes, they seem like very nice people," answered Nava.

"They are good people," stated Mae. "They told me you are preaching not only Waru religion but also the Arcadian Path. Is that true?"

"Yes, we've been teaching the Arcadian Path to those who seem interested," replied Cromen while giving Nava a worried look.

"That's a pretty big challenge. I don't immediately see how the two are compatible. Why would you teach them both?"

"I'm not from a Waru background," said Cromen, "and I've studied the Arcadian Path throughout my life. It would be hard for me to preach the Waru religion which I don't know well and don't agree with."

"And I am Waru," said Nava, "but not very satisfied with many of their teachings. We really came on this mission as a way to be together. We are doing the best we can to preach Waru without feeling guilty," Nava finished with an uncertain smile

"Most missionaries from Beryl are religious fanatics. They actually think that they are helping people with their Waru philosophy," said Mae giving a critical laugh.

"I think they mean well," said Cromen.

"I know they do, but they are closed-minded and ignorant of reality."

"Their reality is based on blind religious belief, it has no basis in factual information," Cromen replied.

"Exactly," said Mae. "And whatever they believe, be it fact or fiction, is none of our business. Only their actions. When they harm other people the United Worlds feels compelled to help."

"Are the Waru hurting anyone?" Nava asked.

"If I show you how the Waru are causing chaos on this world, would you consider another kind of Mission? A mission that could save millions of lives," Mae queried.

"Who are you and why should we believe you?" asked Cromen. "Is it dangerous?

"I am with the United Worlds Intelligence Agency. Here's my identification," Mae said as she held up an ID chip that projected a hologram with her image with United Worlds Intelligence Agency markings.

"Where's your name?" Nava asked.

"It's too dangerous to show my name. You can see my protected image and the I.D. Number. Take the identification number and check with the agency if you are skeptical."

Cromen wrote down the ID number.

"How could we help you?"

"The Waru have missions on most of the inhabited worlds. But missionaries, like you, are only one part of their mission plan. Upfront, the Waru mission is one of spreading the Waru faith and bringing converts to their congregation. This is how they explain their presence throughout the United Worlds planets. On the face of it, there is no reason for the United Worlds to be concerned."

"But unfortunately there is a hidden part of their missions, hidden from all but the most trusted members. The Orthodox Waru are spreading chaos wherever they can. The purpose of this chaos is to scare people, make life harder for the common people. They use deception, propaganda, and technology to destabilizes economies, create famine and cause wars to divide people. These actions drive people to religion, drive them straight into the waiting arms of the Waru."

"The only weapon we have against them is our ability to reveal the truth of their activities. By exposing the leaders, the UW hopes to end this destabilizing force, make human society safer and more healthy for all."

"We need someone to help us get evidence and expose the criminal actions of the Orthodox Waru," she said with a questioning gaze.

"What can we do to help?" asked Nava, a little worried, "You're telling us things we've never heard before and asking us to spy on people you say are dangerous. We don't know important people or anyone involved in these activities."

"You may not know who you think you know," stated Mae. "I'm only asking if you are open to the idea of helping. Your position as missionaries puts you near certain people. We would like you to observe them and report what you see. That's all. For now, I only ask that you think about it. I'll contact you in a few days for your decision, and instructions if you decide to help," Mae stood and offered her hand. "It was very nice to meet you."

As they left the house and walked down the street, Nava said to Cromen, "That was a little strange. She thinks that the Orthodox Waru are trying to take over the universe. Could she is right?"

"She said the Orthodox Waru are deliberately hurting people, causing war and famine. If true, I want to help," replied Cromen. "Do you believe her?"

"I found her believable in general," said Nava as they walked along. "But, I wonder if there are things she's not telling us."

"I bet the house doesn't belong to her," said Cromen. "I wonder if the owners even know she was there."

"I found her very believable," replied Nava. "But we should check her credentials."

"I felt that we could trust her, too," replied Cromen. "But let's check her credentials when we get home. Right now we have just enough time to make our next appointment."

"I don't want to believe her. I want some proof before I do something that might be risky. If they are so sure, then why don't they arrest these people?" Nava asked as they walked down the street.

"It just feels like something the Orthodox Waru would do," replied Cromen. "I want to help if I really can. But you're right, we should ask for some evidence before we get involved."

Three days later, on the last appointment of the morning, they arrived at a small middle-class home that badly needed painting. The yard was a mess, overgrown with weeds, kids' toys were scattered around. When they approached the front door, it opened and Mae stood just inside. "Greetings Nava. Greetings Cromen. Please come in and relax. How are you doing?"

"We're doing pretty good," replied Nava for them both. "And you?"

"Life's always a challenge, but I guess I like it that way. I'm good," responded Mae.

"You have a different house," observed Nava.

"Yes, I'm borrowing it for a short time. I don't have a choice. Security Control knows when and where it will be safest to meet with you. Have you considered my proposal?" she asked.

"Your I.D. checked out okay," said Cromen. "But I think we're both hesitant of getting involved with something potentially dangerous. If you could show us evidence, we might feel more compelled to help."

Mae relaxed and smiled. "I have various video images showing the director of your sanctuary with several others," she replied. "They have been dressing sometimes as Zedori and sometimes as Tequin and attacking restaurants and business of the other group. These two groups, Zedori and Tequin, make up sixty percent of the population on Fomalhaut and they are on the brink of war. Each retaliates for the attack on their people and it just escalates from there."

"Do you mean the Orthodox Waru are deliberately causing the one group to think the other group has attacked them?" asked Cromen.

Mae pulled a small VisiPort device from her pocket and opened a holographic projection video. A dozen men dressed in traditional Zedori clothes could be seen walking past the camera, each face was clearly visible. Deacon Stuart and several other high-ranking sanctuary leaders were unmistakable. The camera followed them a short distance when they turned and each threw a small package into a restaurant. They ran back past the video recorder as shock waves rocked the camera and the restaurant exploded in flame. The faces weren't as clear in the second video, but the identity was without question. Different clothes, different place, but the same action of throwing bombs into a restaurant and running away.

"Well, that's pretty clear," Cromen stated with anger in his voice and shock on his face. "Why haven't you arrested them?"

"This is happening on several of the United Worlds' planets. These people throwing the bombs are only low-level operatives. If we stop them, others will take their place almost immediately. We need to get evidence on the higher-level organizers," replied Mae.

"Is this where we come in?" asked Nava with concern.

"Yes," said Mae. "We need to find out who is giving the directions. We need to identify the leaders and stop them from causing more harm. You will be in danger if they catch you spying, but we'll do everything we can to protect you."

Nava and Cromen looked into each other's faces for a moment before nodding and turning to Mae. "We will help," said Nava with a hesitant smile.

"When you are inside the Sanctuary," said Mae, "We would like you to use a MicroPort recording device to record activities of the leaders. The MicroPort can open a tiny portal allowing audio and video to be recorded."

"The problem," replied Cromen, "is that we're not inside the sanctuary for much time each day, and rarely have private moments where we could monitor something."

"You can set the MicroPort in a safe location inside the sanctuary," said Mae. "Set it to record activity in the room you think important conversations would take place. Retrieve it every day if you can and check what has been recorded. Then bring it outside the sanctuary. Once outside the sanctuary blocking field, it will automatically upload the files to the United Worlds Security hub. The information will then be available to people working the case."

The recording device looked like a metal bank card with a name that was unfamiliar to Nava or Cromen. They set it to monitor the main conference room and left it under a stack of books in the briefing room.

They checked the spy device each morning for a week before finding something interesting. The video showed Elder Smith with six high-level sanctuary Deacons walking through an open portal into a large office or conference room.

The video showed the group returning 2 hours later, through a portal that opened near the center of the room. Elder Smith walked through followed by the six Deacons. People were standing in groups talking in a room on the other side of the portal. As the last deacon passed through, a large heavy-set man presented himself before the portal and called to Elder Smith, "Dan, You're doing great work. I'm confident you can pull this off. I expect some exciting news very soon. Good luck. And be careful, the United Worlds may be watching."

"Thank you, your holiness," responded Elder Smith. "You can count on us."

The portal closed and Elder Smith turned to the Deacons. "Let's make it quick. See you at the staging site at 8:30. Don't be late."

"I can't believe it," stated Nava to Cromen. "That was the Apostle Carlyle. How can he be involved in something so horrible? Maybe there's something else they're planning?"

"They're hiding something. Why else would he be worried about the United Worlds watching?" responded Cromen while gathering their daily supplies. "Let's take this outside so the information can be transmitted."

The streets were almost deserted as Cromen and Nava drove to their assigned area for the day. Groups of people gathered on the corners, wearing traditional Zedori clothes. They looked at Nava and Cromen with suspicion as they drove past.

"My God, they have swords and pistols. Something's going on," said Nava turning on the radio. "Where are the police?"

Cromen searched for and found the morning news broadcast.

.... "Another attack last night on the Zedori neighborhood has killed at least 12 and injured dozens more. This is the fourth bombing this month and has escalated tension between the Zedori and the Tequin. The police are advising people to stay indoors today and wait for further instructions. The latest bombing appears to be retaliation by Tequin for the bombing last week of a mid-town Zedori restaurant. Talks are ongoing between leaders of the two groups, each group blames the other for the escalation of violence. Small conflicts have broken out in neighborhoods all over the city. Officials have implemented a 10 person limit to any gatherings and a curfew of 10 pm is in effect until further notice."

"How could we not know this was happening?" quipped Cromen. "We've been living in our own little world, not paying attention to the society around us. I have read about bombings but didn't realize the magnitude of the problem."

"It's like the media's been downplaying this whole story. Now it's exploding and everyone is surprised," replied Nava. "What are we going to do?"

"We're very busy today, twelve appointments, even some in the early afternoon," answered Cromen. "Should we talk to the sanctuary about the safety of continuing our work today?"

"They didn't tell us anything out of the ordinary this morning. Maybe we should call so they know we're worried. They might wonder if we don't call," replied Nava, taping her ComPort.

"Sanctuary," she said and a few moments later a portal opened in front of her, with the floating head of Deacon Stuart on the other side.

"Greetings Nava," he said. "how may I be of assistance?"

"We just heard about the police order and there are violent-looking people on the street. Should we work today?" asked Nava with a worried voice.

"The area you're working in today shouldn't be affected by these violent people," the Deacon replied. "Just stay away from groups and you should be fine. Your job is important and the people need you more than ever today. Be careful and call back if you have any problems."

"The people need us more than ever today," Cromen exclaimed after the ComPort closed. "He said it like today is a perfect day to be out recruiting converts. Like we shouldn't miss this great opportunity."

"He probably sees it that way," replied Nava with an angry scowl. "Why doesn't Mae expose them and stop this?"

"Mae's only an operative like you and me," responded Cromen. "Hundreds, thousands, even millions of lives could be at stake, and the United Worlds can't save them all. What a terrible responsibility her agency has."

"I'm worried. This isn't part of the adventure I envisioned for us. Will Mae protect us? Can she get us out of the Sanctuary if we get caught? Can we just go home now and forget about these otherworldly problems?"

"Mae said we could stop if it became too dangerous for us. But how do we know when? It all feels dangerous to me now," replied Cromen. "Like we're trapped in a demented cat and mouse game. And we're the mice."

"More like tigers hunting blindfolded lambs," replied Nava. "I really want to go home, but not to the same situation."

"We have the crystals," responded Cromen. "We could go anywhere. Let's give it another day or two."

"Okay, but let's be ready to leave in a hurry."

The next few days passed without significant problems. The streets were calmer, Nava and Cromen had begun to relax and forget about the danger they felt earlier.

Mae was waiting for them on their second appointment of the morning. She greeted them in a small second-floor apartment. The meeting was short.

"Good work, your new evidence is very helpful," she said, "but it's not enough for us to go after the Waru High Council. It implicates one of the seven Apostles. But we need to know if direction comes from the Profit or is Apostle Carlyle working on his own. We need something more."

"It is beginning to feel dangerous," said Cromen. "Can you protect us from these people if they discover we're spying?

"The United Worlds will do everything we can to ensure your safety," replied Mae. "I will personally protect you if I can. But you can stop anytime if you feel too threatened."

"I think we're okay for now," Nava said, looking hesitantly at Cromen.

"Thank you," said Mae. "Keep up the good work. Be proud of what you are doing. I'll see you soon."

Nava and Cromen checked the MicroPort recorder the next day after the regular morning meeting. In a small private room off the lecture hall, they viewed the MicroPort recording. The Apostle Carlyle was standing on the other side of an open portal in the same room as before. "This will be the last one for the time being," he said clearly to Elder Smith and the group of Deacon's walking through the portal. "Let's reap what we have sown for a while. Keep your recruiters busy."

Two other Apostles were standing with Profit Hendon in the background. "Don't worry about a thing, we'll get you out if there is any trouble," assured the Profit.

Nava and Cromen were intently focused on the MicroPort viewer. As Cromen turned it off an arm reached around him and tried to grab the MicroPort. The device fell to the floor and the man crushed it with his foot. It was Deacon Stuart. Cromen shoved him to the ground and grabbed the damaged MicroPort from the floor.

"Give me that. What are you doing?" yelled the Deacon.

Without hesitation, Cromen grabbed Nava by the arm and they ran. Two other deacons observed the commotion and chased them to the front door.

"Get them," yelled Deacon Stuart. "Don't let them escape."

They reached the door. Deacons were grabbing at their clothing as they opened the door and struggled through. The hands released and the pursuit stopped immediately as they passed through to the outside.

Nava looked behind as they reached the car and got in, "I don't see anyone following."

"They'll follow somehow. Should we go to the apartment or is it too risky?"

"If we hurry, maybe the apartment is okay right now. But then what. Where are we safe? I wish we had a way to contact Mae."

"Let's get our stuff and try to contact someone at the United Worlds," replied Cromen. "The MicroPort may still be readable and it holds the evidence that Mae needs. These people need to be stopped," stated Cromen in nervous anger.

"They scare the shit out of me, Cromen. Let's not waste time getting our stuff. What do we need from the apartment?"

"You're right, there's nothing there that we can't replace. And the apartment is the only place they know to look for us. We'll stop at the vault for our gems and then head to the nearest off-world Transport Station."

"Maybe we can get to the United Worlds office here on Fomalhaut?" interrupted Nava. "Or, better yet, let's go see Greyson and Daria. They might have a way to contact Mae."

"Good Idea. But let's pick up the gems first, money might be useful in escaping these people."

Chapter 14 A Really Bad Mood

No one was on the porch as they approached the house, but Daria met them at the door, invited them in, hugged them both, and asked how they were.

Before they could answer, she looked at them closely and asked, "Is everything alright?"

"We were hoping that you could help us contact Mae," said Nava, looking intently into Daria's eyes, revealing fully her desperation.

Daria hesitated, looking back at them curiously, "Let me get Greyson," her serious look changing to a sweet devious smile.

"Greyson," she called, then said to Cromen and Nava. "I don't think we have a way to contact Mae. She just pops in when she wants our help with something. Is there anything we can help you with?"

"I appreciate your generosity, but there's something we need to give directly to her," replied Nava.

"Good morning," smiled Greyson on entering the room. "Nice to see you again."

"They have something they need to give to Mae," cut in Daria, "and they were hoping we could help them contact her."

"I guess it's part of Mae's personal protection strategy. We've never had a way to contact her. When she wants something she arrives where we are. Can we help you?" responded Greyson.

"What would be the fastest way to get something important to her," Cromen responded. "It's an emergency. The information we have puts us in danger. And I am sorry, but we have brought this danger to your house."

"Don't worry about us, we can take care of ourselves," said Daria with a devious smile. "Do you think your pursuers might be coming here?"

"They could," replied Cromen.

"We need an action plan, Greyson." Daria announced with excitement clear in her face.

"I'll get the shields," said Greyson turning quickly away.

"You can use our PersPort," offered Daria. "Where would you like to go? The United Worlds Fomalhaut headquarters might be a good start. Or you could go to an off-world Transport site and pick another planet. We've had to do that before," Daria smiled in memory despite the tense moment.

"The deacons are sure to be watching all these places," said Cromen. "The local UW headquarters probably has Waru spies. The UW headquarters on Utopia would be safer. Maybe we should go there."

"My first priority is to get away from the Orthodox Waru here on Fomalhaut," said Nava. "Then we can focus on finding Mae or her organization."

"Here, put this on if we have any trouble," Greyson said upon returning. He handed them each a flexible copper wire mesh hood. "Now, have we decided on a plan?"

"Almost," said Cromen. "We need money to travel with. We don't have enough credit, but we have these." Cromen took a lumpy rolled clothe from his pocket and unrolled it on the table.

Greyson and Daria looked with wonder at the brilliantly colored gems visible in small hand-sewn pockets. Carefully, Daria removed a vibrant pink gem as big as her thumb. She held it up to the light and looked through the flawless glowing stone. "I like this one," she swooned, looking as though she was under a magic spell.

"It's a Morganite," offered Cromen, "the same mineral as emerald and aquamarine, but a different color."

"I'll give you 2 million credits," offered Greyson. "Not a unit more."

"Two million credits," exclaimed Cromen with gaping eyes. “That's too much.”

"I know a good deal when I see it. It's worth twice what I offer. And if I had the money I would gladly pay it. Because Daria likes it. What do you say, is it a deal?" asked Greyson.

Cromen smiled and put out his hand. "It's a deal."

"Bank Charles," exclaimed Greyson. A portal opened and he talked directly to a teller machine. "Withdraw two million credits and make two cards of one million credits, one each for these two people." Then turning to Nava and Cromen he said, "Show your identification."

Daria had been monitoring the front window. "Put on your hoods, they have arrived," she exclaimed while putting on her copper wire mesh hood and hurrying toward the back of the house.

Nava and Cromen each presented their ID for scanning and then put on their copper wire hoods. As the machine issued a card in each of their names, there was a loud knock on the front door.

"I'm coming," called Daria loudly to her three hooded friends in the living room, and the three Deacons waiting outside the door.

"I'll set the portal for the New Singapore off-world Transport station," said Greyson calmly.

Daria entered the room hooded, wearing heavy black gloves, and holding an Arcadian Mind-Snake wiggling violently in her grasp. "They hate this," she said to Cromen and Nava as she approached the front door. "And those boys outside are going to hate it too." You could hear the smile in Daria's voice.

The Waru Deacons stopped knocking on the door. The knocking was replaced by other sounds, banging on the porch floor, moaning noises, sounds of agony.

"You should hurry. I don't want to hurt the poor fellas too much," Daria said sympathetically.

"The port's opening now," said Greyson. "Good luck. And get rid of anything they gave you that might hold a tracking device. Hurry!"

Nava and Cromen said "Thank you," as they quickly stepped through the portal.

"Such nice young people," Daria said to Greyson. "I hate to see them in trouble. And we started it by giving them to Mae. They may need our help in the future."

"I think you're right," Greyson responded. "And I'd like to see these nasty Orthodox Waru brought to justice. Let's keep an eye on Nava and Cromen."

The Off-World Transport lobby looked angry and disturbed. People were staring at Nava and Cromen. There were babies crying and parents fighting, people were weeping and moaning.

Nava pulled off her hood while Cromen stood looking at the destination boards. "I'm glad we had the hoods on. I wonder if these people know they just had a blast from the Mind-Snake," he whispered, removing his own hood.

"Where do we go?" Nava asked, looking thoughtfully at the boards. "Can we go to the UW headquarters on Utopia?"

"Let's try it," replied Cromen, as he held his ID up to the reader on the floating ticket kiosk and said, "Utopia."

"You do not have authorization for this destination," replied the machine. "Requests for authorization can be submitted through your local United Worlds office."

"I think someone's watching us," said Nava. "Let's go anywhere fast."

"Two tickets to Shangri-la, please," Cromen whispered to the kiosk.

The machine issued 2 small cards. "Go to station eight, your RingTech Off-World port access will be available in 10 minutes at station eight."

As they walked to station eight a man on one side and a woman on the other began walking towards them.

"Come on," said Cromen, taking Nava by the hand and moving faster towards the station. The followers held back when they entered the station 8 staging area.

"Give me your phone," Nava demanded quietly. "Greyson said to ditch anything the Waru gave us."

She found a place to sit down close to a family with a lot of bags. The family entered the off-world transfer chamber before Nava and Cromen.

"That family has new phones," Nava said quietly to Cromen, grinning slyly.

The RingTech supervising technician called them up, took their tickets, and opened a security door, allowing them to enter the transfer chamber.

"Can people in the lobby tell where we are going?" Nava asked the technician nervously as they entered.

"Your destination is completely confidential," replied the technician. "I don't know where you are going. The kiosk does not repeat your destination out loud and nothing on the ticket indicates the destination. I just insert your ticket and the machine sets the location. Even the other side of the portal is designed so it can't be identified from here. Only you and the machine know your destination. It's very confidential by design."

"Are you ready to go?" he smiled.

"Yes, thank you," said Nava.

"Good luck," replied the Tech as Nava and Cromen stepped through the portal from Fomalhaut onto planet Shangri-la.

Chapter 15 John Behan

Our story needs to go back now, back to a time before Beryl was inhabited by humans, back 208 years before our story begins, to the year 226 EE, back to the time when the United Worlds was deciding which, if any, of the newly terraformed planets would be given to the Waru Church of the Seven Apostles.

On this particular day, the United Worlds was holding a parade to celebrate the selection of planet Shangri-la as the new home of the Arcadian Path Society, a non-profit organization with billions of members. The United Worlds was confident that the Arcadian Path Society could establish a successful colony and that it would be an example of good governance.

The Arcadian Path Society was selected for planet Shangri-la over the protests of the Waru Church of Seven Apostles. The Waru were outraged at their rejection and public criticism of their church by the United Worlds. Many Waru protesters stood among the large crowd watching the parade celebrating the Arcadian Path Society's new home.

John Behan watched the parade from a third-floor hotel window. John was one of the many faithful Waru angered by the selection of the Arcadian Path for planet Shangri-la. He looked out the hotel window and smiled at the beautiful sunny fall day and the thousands of spectators lining the New York City parade route. A holographic King Kong swung from the top of the Empire State Building with biplanes circling above. Green Dragons swooped on crowds of people screaming and laughing below. Confetti swirled about the marching bands and flamboyant floats parading down the wide avenue.

"Damn these irreligious idiots," John grumbled, watching the floats and bands pass by. "How can they deny the one true God?"

John looked on at the parade, checking his watch regularly in nervous anticipation. Three small explosions heard in the street below brought a smile to his face. He watched as people in the street began to move in his direction. There were more explosions closer to him and people began to panic, running away from the sound. People screaming and running from the crowd behind, pushed into the crowd in front of them. Three more explosions drove the panicked crowd into an uncontrollable stampede. John grinned with childish excitement. His fifteen small explosive devices worked perfectly. They couldn't do much physical harm, but they were very loud.

He waited several hours for the chaos to reside before returning home on the subway crowded with parade watchers. "Did you hear about the little girl?" asked a passenger.

"No," John replied. "What little girl?"

"A little girl was crushed to death in the stampede of people," replied the passenger.

"How terrible," John said in nervous reply. He was shocked. He hated these people, their blasphemy of everything sacred and holy. But he hadn't meant to hurt or kill anyone. He felt bad for the little girl but still felt justified in his actions.

John began to worry about being caught. "I could go to jail for life," he told himself. But several days passed in normal routine, attending classes at the university, church on Sunday, and working part-time as a legal aid intern. With each passing day, he grew more confident of escaping detection.

On arriving home from work a week after the parade, a deacon of his church was waiting outside John's home. He knew the man well and greeted him. "Good afternoon Deacon Elwood," extending his hand, trying to look as calm as possible.

"Good afternoon, John," replied the deacon in a friendly manner. "I'm here to escort you to an urgent meeting with the Elder council. Please come without delay," said the Deacon directing John to the waiting car.

"A meeting with the council? Why would they want to talk with me?"

"There is nothing to worry about. I assure you," replied the Deacon earnestly. "Please come."

John got into the front seat beside Deacon Elwood driving.

"Where are we going?" asked John.

"The New York City Temple," replied the deacon. "To the regional administration headquarters."

"What do they want with me?"

"You'll have to wait," the Deacon replied. "I know as little as you."

On arrival at the gleaming silver, seven-sided, seventy eight story temple, John was brought in by a side entrance. A private elevator took them up to the 68th floor and they entered a large, opulent wood-paneled office that looked out across the city.

Two men and a woman stood across a heavy wooden table. John recognized them as church elders.

"Welcome John Behan," said the woman in the center. "Please come in and sit down. I am Elder Jane. This is Elder Higgins and Elder White."

John bowed slightly to each and sat in the chair indicated across the table from them.

"We have noticed you," said Elder Jane. "You're a very devout Waru, intelligent, and hard-working."

"Thank you, your eminence," said John with a slight bow of his head. "I have tried to be good." He was beginning to relax.

"Then why did you set off those explosions," Elder Jane asked abruptly.

John hesitated, wondering how they could know. "I didn't mean to hurt anybody," he said. "I just wanted to scare them a little."

"What you did is a serious crime, John. What were you thinking? Why did you do it?"

"I hate these people," replied John nervously. "Ignoring God, Living a life of sin, pretending that God does not even exist. I think they should be punished for their crimes against God."

"And you are right to think so," responded Elder Jane firmly. "But it's criminal and dangerous to do something like you did, dangerous for you and dangerous for the Church."

"I feel sorry about the little girl," replied John nervously.

"We know you do," said the Elder. "And we hate to see your life ruined for this little prank. It would be terrible to have you imprisoned for so many years."

"Will you turn me into the police?" asked John, hopeless despair creeping into his emotions.

"Legally we are bound by the laws of this country to report what we know of this crime to the authorities," said Elder Higgins.

The extended silence was torture. John sat silently, accepting his fate, his despair turning to dark ugly resignation.

"We know you are a good faithful Waru and we recognize your intellect and talent," said Elder Higgins, after John had suffered long enough. "Your academic achievements in political science and law are impressive and would be extremely useful to the Church of Seven Apostles."

"We like your spirit," stated Elder Jane directly. "It would be tragic to loose you to this screwed-up political system."

John's emotions perked up a little on hearing some softening in the Elder's tone of voice. "What am I here for?" he thought to himself. "Why haven't they already reported me?" John waited, unsure if he should ask.

"It's not all negative," Elder White spoke for the first time, his tone was friendly. "As a result of your violent action, there have been more than 1,000 additional converts to the Waru Church this week."

"The police suspect the Waru in general, but they don't have any evidence connecting you to the crime," said Elder Jane. "And we don't want to give the United Worlds another reason to persecute the Waru church, do we, John?"

"No Mam, we don't want that," agreed John, in troubled confusion.

"A Waru terror attack that killed a four-year-old girl would be very bad press." Elder Jane paused briefly, knitted her brow, and with squinting serious eyes focused directly on John, she continued: "So, the council has decided to offer you protection from prosecution."

"Protection?" John replied, too overwhelmed to say more.

"Yes, John," continued Elder Jane. "We will shield you from prosecution, but there are conditions, John."

"Conditions, what conditions?" John replied, feeling relieved, beginning to relax. "I'd do almost anything to stay out of jail."

"Would you accept a position within the Orthodox church government?" asked Elder Higgins.

"You mean work for the church directly, become orthodox?" asked John. "Doing what?"

"We're offering you an Orthodox position as an Intelligence Coordinator," replied Elder Jane with a friendly smile. "We do a lot of data gathering and analysis. With your education and unrestrained devotion to God, we think you would fit in nicely."

Facing life in prison only moments before, now liberated and offered a dreamed of opportunity, John sat in stunned silence, letting his emotions settle. An Orthodox position in the church was only offered to the select few. He was overwhelmed.

"You won't enter at the bottom," continued Elder Jane after letting John adjust his mind. "Because of your education, faithful church attendance, and clearly demonstrated power of devotion, you will enter official service as a Deacon First Class, with all the privileges and benefits that go with that rank and title. If you accept our offer, you will be initiated next Wednesday at 3 pm. What do you say?"

John's eyes widened and his smile grew as he listened to these words. "Yes," he exclaimed, beaming. "Nothing would make me happier."

And thus began the career of John Behan, considered to be the most creative and influential member in the history of the Orthodox Waru Church of Seven Apostles.

Chapter 16 Shangri-la

The sweet aroma of Jasmine and honeysuckle greeted Cromen and Nava as they stepped out of the nondescript arrivals chamber. A pristine tropical paradise came into view when they entered the Off-Worlds transport station lobby on Shangri-la.

"Welcome," said a tall slender Asian woman stepping forward to greet them. She wore an honest friendly smile and comfortable light brown linen clothes that looked casually official. "Welcome," she repeated, "Welcome to Shangri-la."

Nava and Cromen just smiled in return, still stunned by the excitement of the previous few minutes. Their frantic escape from the Waru caused nervous, fear-driven, adrenaline to surge through their veins. Cromen felt Nava trembling as she pulled him close. Only minutes before, Daria had confronted the Waru deacons with a wiggling unhappy Arcadian Mind-Snake.

"Thank you," Cromen responded. After taking a deep breath. "We are very tired and hungry. Could you direct us to someplace relaxing? We would like to rest."

"I recommend the Royal Palace of Aeon," replied the woman as she presented a holographic projection of beautiful white sand beaches with turquoise water, palm trees, and waterfalls.

"That's perfect," said Cromen, hardly glancing at it. "Thank you."

The woman tapped a few buttons on her ComPort and a portal opened into the lobby of the Royal Palace Hotel. Cromen and Nava stepped through after thanking her.

A long wide porch, with large bamboo timbers holding a palm thatch roof, served as the hotel lobby of the Aeon Royal Palace. Smooth dark teak wood shined on the floor. Sand spread out from the lobby steps to meet a calm turquoise sea, dotted with islands stretching into the distant horizon. Large shade trees cast deep shadows across the sand and framed the ocean view from the lobby.

"Welcome, Ms. Martin and Mr. Henderson. Welcome to the Aeon Royal Palace Hotel. My name is Bree," said the young red-haired woman. "Your cabana is ready and waiting for you, please follow me."

Bree led the way through lush flower-filled gardens lining the grassy path to their cabana. Stepping up onto a low porch Bree opened the Rosewood door and invited them in.

"Please let me know if there is anything we can do to make your stay with us more enjoyable."

"Thank you," said Cromen. "We are rather hungry."

"There is fruit and nuts here in your room," she said with a glowing smile that made the simple snack sound delicious. "And our restaurant is open for seaside dining or room service. It's a very good restaurant. Your room is equipped with UniPort and a PersPort so you can eat at or order from any restaurant on the planet."

"Everything is keyed to your ID," she continued. "The door only opens for you and only you two have UniPort access while you stay in this cabana. Present your ID and give a few verbal commands, the UniPort computer will then know your voice and won't need your ID in the future."

She showed them how to access the UniPort that provided communication, internet, and portal control. "This is how you access the UniPort bank box," she continued. "It opens a small portal so you can place your valuables directly into a secure bank box."

"Don't hesitate to contact us if you have any problems or questions. Enjoy your stay," smiled Bree as she stepped out and closed the door behind her.

Nava and Cromen stood silently waiting for their emotions to catch up with them. The adrenaline still pulsing through their bodies, Nava moved into Cromen's arms and they held each other quietly for several minutes. "I'm scared," said Nava, pulling Cromen onto the bed and beginning to cry. They cried together for what seemed like hours, finally letting go of each other and some of the nervous tension which had gripped them.

"What do we have to eat?" asked Cromen, kissing Nava and getting up from the bed. "Wow, look at these figs," he said, selecting two fat amber figs and handing one to Nava.

"I'm scared, Cromen," said Nava looking at the fig. "What are we going to do? We can't go home, we're being chased by murderers. I really want to get rid of this MicroPort thing."

"Let's see what we can do," said Cromen, munching on the fig. "UniPort, call UW Headquarters."

"Good afternoon, United Worlds Shangri-la, how may I help you?" came a pleasant voice through the portal.

"Hi, Good afternoon," Nava began. "We need to contact someone in the UW security division. We only know her as Mae and we don't know how to contact her. It's very important."

"I'll connect you to our Security Department. Have a great day," came the reply.

Nava repeated her words to a man at the local UW Security Department. The man wanted to know more than Nava would tell. But he eventually connected her to the United Worlds Security Headquarters on Utopia. The agent on Utopia only asked for their first names and the planet involved, then said pleasantly, "Mae will contact you," before he abruptly closed the connection.

"Mae will contact us," exclaimed Nava, hugging Cromen with an excited smile. "Now I'm hungry, let's eat."

Nava and Cromen ordered grilled salmon and wine from the hotel restaurant delivered to the room and sat nibbling snacks. They were talking and laughing nervously about skinny Daria holding the wiggling Mind-Snake, when a bell rang and a pleasant voice said, "Your meal service is ready. May we enter?"

"Yes, please come in," said Cromen.

The waiter pushed a service cart through a delivery portal that opened near the front door. He arranged the table and told them, "Push this button on the cart when you are finished. A portal will open in front of the cart and you can push it through. Enjoy your meal."

Cromen and Nava were enjoying the salmon with Brussels Sprouts and Brown rice when they heard Mae's voice. "May I open portal?"

"Yes, please," replied Nava with some excitement.

Mae's tired face looked out at them through the open portal, Yawning like she just woke up. "Greetings. How are you? Have you been injured?"

"Just scared," replied Nava.

"I'm happy to see you're safe and I will personally do everything I can to protect you."

"We appreciated everything you can do for us," replied Cromen.

"You seem to have attracted the attention of the radical Orthodox Waru. They're looking for you all over the place, particularly on planet Lithia. Were you there or did they lose your trail?"

"I dropped the ComPort phones that the Waru Deacons gave us into another traveler's bag at the Off-World transport station," said Nava. "They must have gone to Lithia."

"Smart girl," Mae smiled. "Good job. Do you still have the MicroPort? I'd like to get technicians working on it immediately."

"I'll get is right away," said Cromen followed by, "Open vault."

The vault portal opened in front of him. Cromen retrieved the MicroPort card and handed it to Mae.

"It has been smashed badly," said Mae, looking at the little card as she handed it to someone through an open portal next to her. "But I've seen worse that still had a good memory. Let's hope."

"I think you found a great place to stay for a while," Mae continued. "I've credited your accounts with enough funds to cover your inconvenience and to keep you comfortable where you are. You've been a great help and the United Worlds will protect you, but you must follow my instructions exactly."

"Do not make any off-world contact. We'll let your family know that you're alright. Stay there on Shangri-la. It is about as safe a place as any and traveling to another world could expose you. And try to relax and enjoy yourselves. You've had a traumatic experience. It's probably safe to go out, find something therapeutic, have some fun."

"I'll contact you as soon as I have more information. Do you have any questions for me?"

"Are we really safe here?" asked Nava.

"I am confident that only you and I know where you are. So, I think you are pretty safe for now."

Nava gave a hesitant smile in reply.

"Don't worry, you're okay. Relax, have some fun. I'll contact you in a day or two," said Mae before closing the port.

Nava and Cromen looked at each other, the nervous tension that knotted their stomach began to relax. The feeling of safety and the removal of the MicroPort burden rapidly improved their mood.

"There's still light outside, let's go for a walk," suggested Cromen.

The late afternoon sun cast coconut tree shadows on the sand as they walked barefoot along the beach. Warm turquoise water splashed at their feet from an occasional small wave. In silence, they walked the long white strand of beach, enjoying the beauty of the place. Huge snow-covered mountains could be seen rising from the distant hills, dense forests covered all but the high peaks. The ocean was dotted with small islands between where they walked and a larger island on the horizon.

"Wow," observed Cromen, "I had no idea it was so beautiful."

"Everywhere you look, there is something amazing," replied Nava. "How'd you pick this planet?"

"It's the first place I thought of when we needed a planet quickly. I've read about it because it's the center of Arcadian Path education and research. Shangri-la was developed with the intention of creating the most perfect society. All the people living on this planet follow the Arcadian Path."

"Anyone can come here, anyone," he continued. "They want Shangri-la to be an example of a truly civilized human society.

People of all kinds live here and they all care about the well-being of the others. It takes happy healthy people with the right intentions to make a healthy society. These are people of the highest moral character, they truly understand what it means to be a good civilized person."

"I don't like to think of my people as uncivilized," said Nava, "But the contrast between Shangri-la and Beryl is too much. It seems to me that the Orthodox Waru don't want a good society. The more I see of other people and places, the more I want to rebel against my church."

"And so you should," Cromen replied. "Don't we each need to discover who we are and what feels right to us? And as long as your idea of reality doesn't hurt other people, it is as good as anyone else's."

"Mormon, Waru, Mennonite, all have small colonies on Shangri-la," Cromen continued. "They worship as they like but include the Arcadian Path in their system of beliefs."

"Is there a cultural center or museum here? I want to learn more," asked Nava directing them back toward the hotel.

"There must be something like that. Let's go for a swim," Cromen suggested, feeling the warm clear water with his feet.

"I'd like that. Is it safe?" asked Nava.

"I don't think they have dangerous animals or biting insects on this world. Let's go get something to wear and ask in the lobby about dangers in the water."

"The only concern is the coral, it's beautiful but sharp," said the lobby attendant. "Don't try to walk on it without shoes. But the bottom is sandy without coral for about 50 meters from the beach. There are swimsuits and snorkeling gear in your cabana. Just be careful of the coral."

"Oooh, this is amazing," said Nava, floating in the warm clear turquoise water wearing a simple one-piece suit. "I could float here forever."

"Amazing!" said Cromen standing up and smiling at Nava. "You look amazing in that suit."

"It's more revealing than I would have selected. But it fits perfectly. Do you think they guessed our sizes?" asked Nava.

"Well, mine's is a little tight in the crotch. I'm suspicious that they did guess our sizes correctly and had some ulterior motives in selecting revealing suits," Cromen joked with a smile. "I don't mind."

"Your showing," laughed Nava, looking at the bulge in his swimsuit.

They played and kissed and frolicked with each other in the warm relaxing water as sunset came and went.

"We should go to our room," suggested Nava, holding Cromen tight against her body, excited by his warm and roving hands.

"It's very private here in the dark," responded Cromen with a soft smile.

"We need the bed for what I want," replied Nava, smiling devilishly, her own hands roving about Cromen's sensitive areas.

Chirping birds and light rain dripping from trees and roof woke them in the morning.

"Cromen, you're rich," said Nava, looking up from her pillow and thinking about his gemstones with a dreamy half-awake smile.

"We're rich, Nava," replied Cromen. "With the money from Mae and our gemstones, we could live here on Utopia. Let's enjoy today. Try to stay low-key, but let's do something fun."

"Computer," said Nava, "what are the most beautiful and exciting things to do on this planet?"

"Many say that the most beautiful thing to do on Shangri-la is the drive from Punta Uva to the summit of Mount Peace. The route passes through seven different ecological zones from tropical hillsides covered with flowering trees, through temperate zones where wildflowers line the roadside, through conifer forests and cloud forests, to the snow-covered rocky summit which is often above the clouds and presents an incredible view of Mount Miles and the Finerty Range. The route was constructed and is maintained for the best view possible. It takes 2 hours to cover the 83 kilometers one-way and there is car portal access at both ends."

"That sounds pretty good," said Cromen. "What do you think?"

"A relaxing drive sounds good to me," replied Nava, "Maybe tomorrow we'll feel more like excitement."

"Computer, car rental, luxury."

A big list of images appeared on the room's wall screen.

"What do you think of that one?" asked Nava, pointing to a classic-style sedan.

"Makes me happy. Should we get it?" replied Cromen.

"Computer, we want to rent that car in one hour. At this time we want to order breakfast," commanded Nava.

Small fillets of Yellow Tail, wheels of sweet potato fried in olive oil, hot spicy carrots, and delicious fresh roasted coffee were delivered on the porch. Nava and Cromen relaxed and enjoyed their breakfast in this beautiful place, recovering slowly from their traumatic experience of the day before.

The car was waiting for them when they arrived in the rental agency lobby. The agent had set their destination before they arrived.

I was a dark green 1941 Cadillac 2 door coupe on the outside, with lots of shiny chrome. But inside, there were no front seats or control panel, a large luxuriant leather tuck and roll sofa wrapped around the back. Every comfort you might want for a 2-hour drive was available on request. The top was Flexglass which could darken to match the car or lighten to become nearly invisible.

They got in, coffee in hand, and sat back on the couch. "Ask the computer for anything you like," instructed the rental agent. "Have a good trip."

An AutoPort opened in front of them and the car drove through onto a light-colored road surface overlooking a rocky coastal shoreline. There were no markings or signs anywhere to be seen. The road color varied and blended into the landscape it traveled through.

"Punta Uva, known for secluded beaches, snorkeling, and fishing," said the car as the road wound along steep cliffs overlooking the coastline of tropical beaches and rocky points.

"What a view. Let's stop!" exclaimed Nava.

The car pulled in at the next viewpoint. "This is Point Hullot," said the car. "The large distant island is named Nice Island, the islands in between are the Paradise Archipelago."

"That's kind of funny. What island are we on?" asked Nava.

"You are on the continent of Nirvana," responded the car. "the largest of four continents. There are 17,534 habitable islands on Shangri-la."

They kicked back on the sofa and watched the magnificent scenery flow by as the car drove on. From lush jungle up through a temperate forest of Oak and Maple, on through conifer forests, the car climbed. Finally rising above the tree line near four thousand meters elevation.

"Mount Peace summit," said the car on reaching their destination. "This breathtaking view is of Mount Miles and the Finerty Range, a mountain range comparable with the Himalaya mountains on Earth."

"It's freezing out here," Nava exclaimed, following Cromen out of the car at the summit.

"I can hardly breath," replied Cromen. "There's not much oxygen."

The jagged snow-capped mountain peaks rose up, and away into the distance. "Mount Miles is out there someplace," Cromen commented. "Named for the creator of the Arcadian Path. Let's get back to the warm car."

"I think I can see Mount Miles better when my eyes thaw out," agreed Nava.

"It's comfortable here on the couch," Cromen observed after reentering the car. "Let's find a place to park and enjoy the view from the car for a while."

The car maneuvered to give them the best view of the mountain peaks.

"It's mesmerizing," Nava said after some minutes staring silently at the magnificent scene. "But I'm getting hungry. Let's go back and get lunch at the palace."

"Sounds good to me," answered Cromen. "Car, take us back."

After passing through the AutoPort at over 4000 meters and arriving back at the rental car agency near sea level, the cabin remained sealed for a few minutes to allow the cabin pressure to equalize with outside pressure.

After eating lunch, swimming, and laying on the sandy beach quietly for some time, Nava took a deep relaxing breath saying, "I'm beginning to like this place."

"Me too. After yesterday, this feels like a miracle."

"What's next on our agenda?" asked Nava.

"We've had the most beautiful," responded Cromen. "Should we try the most exciting?"

"I'm more interested in learning about the Arcadian Path. Can we do exciting tomorrow?" said Nava.

"Computer, we want an introduction to the Arcadian path."

"The Arcadian Path University headquarters are located here on Shangri-la." responded the computer. "The museum and cultural center offers a variety of classes that cover basic Arcadian Path concepts. The University offers programs leading to the highest academic degrees and leads the Galaxy in Arcadian Path research and education."

"Interested?" asked Cromen.

"Yeah, I'd like to see the University and learn a little more. But only if you want," she responded.

"Let's go," replied Cromen. "I want to see what the masters have to say. It is my culture after all."

Chapter 17 Arcadian Path

Cromen looked down from the welcome center porch overlooking the campus. “It's enormous,” he exclaimed “As big as any city I've seen.”

“And it's beautiful,” responded Nava, looking out on the vast campus of large buildings and towers standing out from the trees and gardens. The architecture varied, with clusters of Mediterranean, Tibetan, and Japanese style buildings visible nearby.

An older man with a red brown ponytail and freckled face approached them casually, offered a friendly smile and a hand to shake. “Greetings, I'm Beldon. Welcome to the Shangri-la Arcadian Path University. May I help you find what you seek?”

“Greetings, and thank you,” replied Cromen, “We're interested in introductory information about the Arcadian Path.”

“The museum's interactive Omni Sphere Format has a great Arcadian Path introduction that provides history and basic concepts in a visual format. It takes about an hour. More advanced classes are available, but I recommend the museum first if you're just beginning your journey on the Arcadian Path.”

“That sounds perfect,” said Nava with a smile. “I can't wait to get started. Where do we go?”

“Right this way,” said Beldon, leading them to a PersPort kiosk where he said, “Arcadian Path introduction” to the computer.

“May you have a great day and a happy life,” Beldon offered with a smile as they stepped through the portal and entered the museum.

The Omni Sphere was a small room with only a dozen chairs, lined up in three rows facing the same direction. The lights dimmed as soon as Nava and Cromen sat down.

The dome enclosed them in a sphere of image and sound. Holographic images moved in and out of the wall from the beautiful green pastoral setting beyond. The scene surrounded them with nature, snow capped mountain peaks, forests and green grassy meadows, streams and lakes. Birds fluttered and gave song to the panorama, animals moved among the bushes cautiously. A nearly naked family of humans walked along a trail near the lake.

"Arcadia," came a woman's voice filled with love. "A place of bountiful natural splendor and harmony, the perfect place for human existence."

A large tiger jumped over Nava's shoulder, raced through the tall grass meadow and grabbed a small screaming child. It walked more casually back through Nava and Cromen's viewing space, with the child in it's mouth dripping blood along the floor.

"Arcadia is a beautiful dream," continued the narrator. "But reality can never be perfect."

The scene changed to a large twenty first century city. Automobile traffic passed in front of them and pedestrians filled the sidewalk wearing face masks covering mouth and nose. Homeless people slept on the sidewalk.

"What is civilization?"

"It brings you groceries, provides a safe place to live in a community with others. The better a civilization provides those necessities, the healthier and happier are the people."

The scene changed again, Nava and Cromen were sitting in a beautiful green meadow filled with wildflowers. Buildings and homes formed a small community on a river, mountain peaks decorated the distance. Music could be heard, there were people dancing in the town square. They all looked healthy and happy.

"The Arcadian Path provides a vision of a perfect civilization, a path to a fulfilling life for all. It shows us a better way to treat ourselves and each other."

"The three foundations of the Arcadian Path are the Goals of Civilization, the Principle of Humanity, and Scientific Spirituality."

"The Goals of Civilization – There are eight goals that provide a vision of a perfect civilization."

Freedom – All people have freedom to live their lives as they wish as long as they do not hurt other people. People are more creative and productive when freedom is unrestricted.

Harmony – No one lives in fear of another. All people of all cultures, ages, races, countries, religions, sexes or sexual orientations, and physical characteristics are respected equally. Diversity is not only respected but is appreciated. Harmony sets people free to appreciate life.

Value – Hard work, innovation, and creativity add great value to society and should be appreciated and rewarded fairly.

Opportunity – All people have opportunities for improving their lives and living conditions. Without opportunity, people have no hope, no dreams, no inspiration, their creativity is lost.

Harmony with Nature – The healthy natural environment is what allows us to live.

Education – Everyone has access to a reality based education uncorrupted by government, religion, or private interests. Education gives each person the knowledge and ability that they need to succeed in pursuing their version of happiness.

Peace – Governments are at peace with each other and their primary work is to improve the lives of their citizens.

Justice – Laws are just and applied equally to all people. People cannot live in harmony if treated differently.

"I have never heard them all together before," Nava told Cromen. "They make sense, but how does a person use them?"

"It is what you should expect of yourself and your society," Cromen replied. "Believing in them forms your value system and shapes how you behave with others."

"The Principle of Humanity," continued the narrator after their conversation. "The first responsibility of every human being is to love themselves and be happy. The second responsibility is to love other people and to wish them happiness."

"Following the Principle of Humanity is not simple and requires education and training provided by Scientific Spirituality."

"Scientific Spirituality - A field of science that helps everyone follow the Arcadian Path and live by the Principle of Humanity. Modern medicine can cure almost all physical problems with the human body. Scientific Spirituality uses science to cure the mind.

The latest scientific information from the fields of human evolutionary development, psychology, religion, biology, sociology, biochemistry, and neuroscience, are united with a database of psychoanalytic research that includes four hundred years of data collected from billions of individuals throughout the United Worlds. Live updates to the database come from real time data with the case information for active current Scientific Spirituality system users."

"So Scientific Spirituality can make me happy with my life." Nava said to Cromen as they walked out of the museum.

"It gives you the ability to help yourself," replied Cromen. "It's you that does the work."

Chapter 18 Trouble in Paradise

Nava and Cromen returned to the hotel laughing and happy in love. Their first full day on Shangri-la had been beautiful and enlightening. Mae, waiting in their room, brought them immediately back to reality.

"Greetings. Have you had a nice day?" Mae asked.

"It's been great," said Nava smiling.

"Well, I'm happy for that. I've come in person because of the serious nature of what I have to ask you. The MicroPort you gave me is completely unreadable."

"I need to know everything that you saw and heard on the MicroPort video. Please tell me every detail."

"It was only about 2 minutes," began Cromen. "A portal opened to the same room as before. The Apostle Carlyle was standing on the other side of the portal. He said something like, 'This is the last one for now,' speaking to Elder Smith and a group of Deacon's who were walking through the portal into the Fomalhaut Sanctuary conference room."

"What did he say next Nava? It was something like 'We'll take the benefits for a while and let things cool off a bit.'"

"Yes, that's about right, then he said to 'Keep your recruiters busy.'"

"Two other Apostles," Nava continued, "were standing with Profit Hendon in the background. I'm not sure which ones. The Profit Hendon said clearly to Elder Smith, "Don't worry about anything, we'll protect you if there is trouble."

"That was it."

"This is the first evidence we have seen that the Profit is directly involved. It's exactly what we needed."

"The Waru think you have the MicroPort and that it holds incriminating information. And they know you've seen the information. You are the only witnesses to the Profit's criminal activities."

"I believe Shangri-la is safe for you. But we can put you into a protection facility, comfortable but confined, if you wish."

"I would rather stay here for now," Nava stated hesitantly. Cromen nodded agreement.

"For your current safety, I'm giving you each a modified security ComPort," said Mae, handing them each a ComPort. "Pushing this button will immediately open a portal to a randomly selected business on the far side of the planet. It will appear to the business owner that you have arrived to shop. It also broadcasts an alert message to me and I'll take what action I can. Only use them if necessary."

"If they catch you, tell them the MicroPort is in a vault on Beryl. It's the only place the Profit and Apostles might act openly. We'll know where to find you. They won't harm you until they have that chip, but they may resort to torture if you don't deliver."

"I am sure this is difficult for you. Try to relax if you can. I'll talk with you soon," Mae finished, stepping through an open portal, turning and raising a hand in serious farewell.

"I'm scared. Maybe we should go to their special security facility," said Nava.

"Maybe you're right. It's hard to know how much danger we're in," replied Cromen.

After breakfast the next morning they went for a walk on the beach.

"I didn't sleep very well," said Cromen. "I couldn't stop thinking about what we've seen and the danger we're in."

"I want to go to the protection facility," Nava said. "I think you should too."

"We'll contact Mae when we get back."

They walked along the beach hand in hand, but finding it difficult to enjoy the natural beauty surrounding them.

A portal opened suddenly in front of them and two Deacons stepped out holding stun guns. Nava quickly pushed the button on her security ComPort and a portal opened beside her, she and Cromen ran through the portal and into a clothing store. One of the pursuers jumped through the portal before it closed. He stood behind them, his weapon in hand. Several shoppers and attendants observed them enter and saw the weapon.

An alarm button was pressed bringing two police officers only seconds later. The Deacon backed off, shook his head, opened a portal and made his escape.

A UW Intelligence Agent arrived as soon as the Deacon disappeared. He showed his United Worlds badge and introduced himself as agent Franklin. "You're still in danger, follow me," he said, directing Nava and Cromen, back through his open portal.

The portal closed as soon as they stepped through and the agent directed them down a corridor and into a large office. There were three others in the room. Nava recognized Deacon Stuart, gave a startled "Oh," and pressed the ComPort button. She stepped through quickly but Cromen was in the firm grip of the Deacons and she closed her portal before a Deacon could follow.

A legitimate Intelligence officer arrived quickly at the department store where he found Nava trembling and angry. Mae arrived a few minutes later.

"They seem to know where you are before we do," Mae observed. "Like they can track the ComPort I gave you. That's not possible unless there's a spy at the highest level of our intelligence department. Let's go Nava, I'll take you someplace safer," said Mae, opening a port next to her and beckoning Nava to follow.

"What about Cromen?" Nava asked in nervous anger.

"We know he's here on planet Shangri-la right now," continued Mae, closing the portal after they entered a nice casual looking office. "And we have the off-world portals carefully watched. We'll find him."

"I'm going to make your ID show up in another place," added Mae, "if you don't mind. We'll see if there's a reaction. Use you as bait, even if you're not there."

"I would do anything to get Cromen back," said Nava, still very angry. "Where are we?"

"Sweetheart, you are on the crown jewel of the United Worlds, the planet Utopia, headquarters of the United Worlds. This is my home office. You can stay with me for a while, if that's okay? There is a spare bedroom."

"That sounds good Mae. It's a nice place, not much like you first described to me."

"I think you are safer here for the time being. There is plenty to do. Try not to worry, Cromen's a strong, smart man. We have a good chance of getting him back."

"How did we get here?" asked Nava. "I thought PersPorts were only capable of on-world porting."

"That's only a setting in the BroadPort network system. My PersPort is authorized for off-world travel."

Nava explored her new home the next day while Mae was out, but found it difficult to keep Cromen out of her mind.

"How are you doing there?" asked Mae over ComPort from her office.

"I feel safe here," replied Nava, "but I'm worried about Cromen."

"I wish that I had some news for you," said Mae. "I don't think he's in danger right now. But his ComPort has disappeared from our tracking system. Either they destroyed the ComPort or they are outside the BroadPort network system."

"But," Mae continued, "we did have some luck with your ID location ploy. We had our top-secret database show your ID at the off-world transport station on planet Britannia. And again, when you checked into a hotel there. Ten minutes after you checked in, a man opened a portal in your room where we were waiting, and he was captured. He hasn't and probably won't give us any useful information, but the fact that he ported into your hotel using an unregistered ComPort tells us plenty. The ComPort he used was not manufactured by RingTech. We've never seen that before. Someone has duplicated RingTech technology and is making bootleg portal equipment."

"And how did they find you and Cromen on Shangri-la?" continued Mae. "So few people had access to that information. I'm worried about everyone working around me. Someone very close to me is a spy."

Chapter 19 Return to Beryl

Cromen struggled with his Waru captors and activated his security ComPort but he could not brake free to pass through the open portal. They forced him to the floor and put him in hand cuffs, searched him thoroughly, and removed the security ComPort.

It was a dim cold room where they brought him and locked his handcuffs to a heavy metal desk. Only two questions were asked: “Where is the MicroPort, and what did you see?”

“I didn't see anything,” replied Cromen. “It was blank.”

They didn't like his answer. “You're lying. Tell us the truth now or you'll regret it. What did you see and where is the MicroPort?”

They didn't explain the devise as they stripped Cromen naked and strapped him to a wooden table, but he understood what it was when they attached an electrical wire to his big toe and another wire fixed securely to his testicles. At the first application, Cromen gasped and shook, he wiggled and moaned with pain as the electrical current twisted his muscles and made his balls feel like they were being crushed with a three-pound hammer blow.

“No real damage yet,” smiled the Deacon after turning off the current, “That's just a light sample of what's to come. Answer the questions.”

“I don't know anything,” Cromen demanded moments before his world exploded with unbearable pain.

Cromen didn't last very long, trembling violently and sweating from the throbbing pain, he gave in and told them where the MicroPort was located. He told them what he saw on the video and gave them the location of the security vault on Beryl. He told them that the vault could only be opened by using his own DNA and hand print.

"Okay," the lead interrogator said to the others. "We need him to get the MicroPort. Make him comfortable while we prepare for Beryl. I'd like to leave within the hour."

"My god," thought Cromen to himself. "Make me comfortable they say." His groin still driving terrible waves of pain throughout his body. The guards watched in amusement as Cromen struggled painfully to put on his clothes.

He was taken to a small room and given food and water. "I wasn't really hungry anyway," thought Cromen, aching badly and looking at the bologna sandwich on white bread, and the small bowl of macaroni and cheese they had given him. But after some consideration he changed his mind and decided, "I should eat. I don't know what's coming next and I need to keep my energy up." Cromen sat cold and shaking, quietly suffering his pain, eating angrily.

He thought about the Off-World transport facility and wondered how they would manage to get him through such a public place without being noticed. Would they drug him and put him into a suitcase? Or simply hold some weapon on him and tell the transport officials that he was a prisoner. Cromen knew Mae's people would be watching the off-world transport station and there could a chance to escape. He thought about how to bring attention to himself when they were in the off world transit station. "I will struggle and scream if I can," he told himself.

Three agents entered the room together and found him moaning and holding his groin. Unlocking his restraint to the table, the lead agent said, "Come on, get up now, it's time to go," and roughly pulled him out the door.

Cromen groaned and moaned as he got to his feet. "This is it," he thought to himself. "Be ready to fight."

The agents surrounded him before opening a portal and walking him through. This room looked a lot like the room he had just left. "Welcome to Beryl," an agent said, as he chained Cromen to another table.

Cromen slumped down in his chair, all hope of escape at the Off-Worlds transport station disappeared in an instant. "What's next?" He thought in misery. He knew they would come soon to bring him to the security vault.

Slowly recovering from the pain in his groin, he began thinking again, "How did we get here without going to the Off-Worlds Transit station? Mae and the United Worlds won't know that I left Shangri-la, they won't know that I'm on Beryl. But Mae should be watching the security vault," he thought with a little more hope. "Opportunities will come."

"What do you mean we can't go yet?" Cromen heard the guards speaking. "If the vault company doesn't open for a few hours, we'll put him in general lockup until then."

The guards led him painfully down a long plain corridor and into what looked like a police holding area. They opened one of the cell doors and placed him inside after taking off his hand cuffs.

As he shuffled towards an empty chair, a scrawny old man looked at him and said, "You're not from here are you?"

"I don't think so?" replied Cromen, gently sitting down in the chair.

"If you get out of here, look on Ariel."

"Why should I look on Ariel? For what?" asked Cromen, knowing Ariel was a wild and forbidden continent, thinking the man must be a little crazy.

"The secrets," replied the old man. "That's where they hide everything, that's where they control everything."

"How do you know this?" asked Cromen with increasing interest.

"I've worked here on Ariel all my life," the man continued. "I know too much. That's why I'm going to Hell."

"Why Hell, are you sick and dying? Don't you have any hope of something better?"

"No, no, I'm not dying. I'm going to the planet named Hell. Maybe you haven't heard of it. That's where the Orthodox Waru send people for punishment."

"Where are we now?"

"Ariel of course, this is where they bring all the prisoners. You'll go to Hell too, when they finish with you."

"I don't think I'll be going to Hell," said Cromen painfully to the old man, "When they get what they want from me they'll kill me because of what I saw. And they'll be finished with me soon."

"Why would they kill you? You're young and strong, you'll go to hell and be forced to work. No one comes back from Hell. You might as well be dead to the outside worlds. Killing for no reason is not their style. Don't worry too much, it won't help anything."

Cromen sat in nervous pain talking with the old man in the holding cell until guards opened the cell and took him out.

"Good luck, I'll see you in Hell," said the old man.

The Secure Vault was his last hope of escaping his captors and staying alive. He knew they would kill him if they had the MicroPort or they knew that it was blank.

They ported directly into the small lobby of the vault company, a dozen doors stationed around the side walls had portal control terminals beside each door. Cromen provided his identification and security code to a terminal. The door opened automatically, permitting entry to a small room with table and chairs, Closing of the heavy door energized the security access interface panel, set seamlessly in the table top. Cromen placed his right hand on the hand reader which measured his temperature and pulse, scanned his entire hand print, and obtained a DNA sample.

There was a pause. The guard nervously handled his ComPort.

They both knew, that if Cromen's biometric data matched the data on file, a portal would open to the private vault. If it didn't match, a security official would talk with them very soon.

Cromen and the guard looked at each other, felt the tension in the other's eyes.

The portal opened to the relief of both and they could see the broken MicroPort inside. The guard reached in, picked up the MicroPort and slumped back into his chair unconscious.

Almost immediately the door opened and two United Worlds Intelligence officers entered, first searching and handcuffing the Deacon and then freeing Cromen. "Are you okay, Mr Henderson? You look a little tired."

"I'm okay now," answered Cromen. "I am so glad to see you that I can hardly feel the pain in my balls."

"Ouch!" said one of the agents. "That sounds painful, let's get you to a hospital right away."

"I need to tell Mae something," said Cromen to the agents before stepping into a hospital emergency room with one of them. "Tell her to look on Ariel. I think there is something important on Ariel."

“I'll make sure she gets your message,” said one of the agents as the portal closed behind them.

“I've been shocked in the testicles and still have great pain,” Cromen told the nurse as she approached, not wanting to give much detail.

“I'm agent Phil,” said a short slender man entering the room. He showed his badge to the nurse and said, “I'm here for Cromen's protection.”

“Let's have the doctor look at you right away. Follow me please,” said the nurse leading them through an open portal into an exam room.

The portal closed behind them and the nurse gave Cromen an exam gown.

“Put this on and the doctor will see you in a few minutes,” said the nurse, opening a door and stepping out.

“You won't need to do that,” said Agent Phil as Cromen began removing his shoes.

Cromen looked up to see an open portal and two men stepping into the exam room. They quickly grabbed him, covered his mouth, and forced him back through the portal. It closed and Cromen was standing back in the isolation room.

Chapter 20 Discoveries

Mae rushed through an open portal in to Nava's room, looking angry and frustrated. “We had him Nava, but lost him again.”

“Oh shit, Mae,” replied Nava. “Is their any hope for Cromen?”

“I think he is okay for now, they'll keep him alive to keep you quiet. He is in danger, Nava. I wish I had better news.”

“Just sitting around waiting is killing me,” replied Nava. “I want to do something.”

“I have a proposal for you,” said Mae. “How would you feel about working with me for a while? You would be close to me where I can protect you. We know there are spies, I can't trust anyone else with your safety.”

“If you think I am safer, I'd like to stay with you. Do you mean going with you everywhere?”

“Yes, pretty much.”

I won't slow you down, will I?”

“I think you can keep up,” said Mae, “and you may be of some help.”

“During the few moments we had Cromen in our hands,” Mae continued, “he told our agents that we should look on Ariel, there is something on Ariel. Apparently he saw or heard something about Ariel. How would you feel about going with me to investigate? It could be dangerous, but less dangerous than sitting in one place where someone might locate you.”

“I'm all yours Mae,” Nava said, feeling excitement pushing aside her worried tension.

“How fast can you be ready?”

"If I leave everything here, I can go right now," replied Nava. "If I take everything, I'm ready to go immediately," she smiled, feeling a little better, knowing that they were doing something.

"This is the RingTech Remote Integrated Data Collection System," said Mae, leading Nava into an intelligence collection and analysis laboratory. "RIDCS for short, is a computer controlled network of portals that use the most advanced sensing technology to provide images and video recording far beyond ordinary sensor portal capabilities."

"I probably can't imagine," replied Nava, feeling a little intimidated by the high level intelligence equipment.

"What do you know about Ariel?" Mae asked, sitting with Nava at a RIDCS console.

"Only what they teach us in school. It's the smallest continent on Beryl and is protected as a wild nature preserve. No one lives there. Only university research teams are permitted access."

"Isn't that a little out of character for the Waru?" Mae asked, "Why would they want to protect a natural area? The whole planet was created solely for human benefit, there is no natural or endangered habitat to protect. The Waru seem to exploit the rest of Beryl efficiently. Why don't they use Ariel?"

"I never thought of it before," Nava replied. "What are they preserving it for?"

Mae brought an image of the planet Beryl onto the large wall monitor. Ariel was in the center.

"This is an aerial view looking down at the continent," said Mae. "The whole continent is blocked from portal access, so we can't use a portal to go directly to the continent. However, we can look at it from outside the blocking field."

“It just looks like forest,” observed Nava.

“SatPort sensor shows no large structures anywhere on the surface. Imaging shows no significant ground disturbance anywhere.”

“Could there be something underground?” asked Nava.

“Good question. If there is a facility, it is underground, below the reach of LIDAR. We'll look deeper underground next. The blocking field that surrounds Ariel prevents us from using an external portal to look and explore underground, but we have a way around that. I've ordered an exploration probe dropped from a portal above the blocking field. It will take a few minutes for it to fall through the blocking field, land, and initialize.”

“What amazing things you can do, Mae,” Nava observed, sitting at Mae's shoulder, following her moves on the large computer interface panel.

“The probe is down and initializing now,” replied Mae with a smile after waiting several minutes. “We've got full control from here now, so lets begins sweeping,” Mae added while showing Nava how to control the probe. “I'll set it to automatically identify voids in the rock. It's a big area and will take some time. Let's go have some lunch.”

“It's nice to see your head focused on the solution, Nava. And not trapped dwelling on your fear,” Mae offered as they ate together in the secure facility's cafeteria.

“Your job is so interesting and exciting,” Nava replied across the table. “But it's dangerous. How do you do it?”

“It is difficult at times,” replied Mae, “but I like what I do and I feel good about doing something important. Scientific Spirituality helps me control my fears and maintain control of my actions.”

“How does that help?” asked Nava.

“It improves my ability to focus on the moment, gives me tools so I am ready for anything. It helps build your confidence by training, practice, and meditation. You gain better control of your emotions. It helps you shape yourself into who you want to be, it helps you love yourself and be happier.”

“It sounds so positive. I want to know more.”

“I'm always happy to share,” said Mae, “But right now we should get back to the lab and see how our scan is doing.”

“It's finding underground structures,” observed Mae, stepping into the laboratory and looking at the big screen. An underground labyrinth of tunnels and chambers was visible on the display.

“It's like an ant colony on an enormous scale. It's huge,” exclaimed Nava, “How could it be there?”

“It must have taken a hundred years to construct,” replied Mae, shaking her head with confused excitement. “It's astounding and clearly above my decision level. Jack, our department head, needs to see this. We can't continue without advising him of what we've found.”

Jack stepped into the room through a portal a few minutes after Mae called him. Slim, muscular, and energetic, Jack smiled his magic smile and introduced himself to Nava. “I'm Happy to meet you Nava,” he said, offering his hand to shake. “Thank you for having the courage to work with us. Your bravery has opened our eyes to something very dangerous and we are in your debt.”

“Nice to meet you, Sir. I just want to get Cromen back and feel safe again. I am frightened for myself and Cromen,” responded Nava, feeling somewhat intimidated by the energy and intensity of Jack's presence.

“Nava,” he replied, taking her hand and looking into her eyes with sincere compassion. “We will do everything in our power to bring Cromen home safe.”

“Thank you,” said Nava, feeling relief in knowing that this powerful intelligent person was in charge. Everything about him felt of real honesty and genuine concern.

“What do you have, Mae?” he said, squeezing and releasing Nava's hand nicely and turning to Mae.

“There is a very large underground facility on the continent of Ariel on the planet Beryl,” she reported. “We don't know what it is, but believe it to be connected with the Orthodox Waru secret society that's been causing problems on Fomalhaut and other planets.”

“It is big,” commented Jack, looking at the wall monitor with keen interest. “There must be thousands of people in that place. Are they aware we're looking at them?”

“I don't think so,” responded Mae. “Our high speed scan shouldn't be detectable.”

“We need to see what's going on in there,” stated Jack, intensely scrutinizing the monitor, as if he could see something more than was on the screen. “Don't use any scanning techniques that might tip them off. I want you to go in there and get more information, do it soon. Good work Mae. I'll talk with you two in a few hours,” He smiled a more concerned smile as he nodded to Nava and Mae before stepping through his reopened portal.

“Am I going with with you Mae?” asked Nava. “I feel safer with you, than remaining here. And I want to help fix things if I can.”

“We have an hour or two to prepare. You can think about it. We'll clear it with Jack after we see Smitty.”

"Who's Smitty?" asked Nava as Mae opened a portal.

"Here she is over there," replied Mae leading Nava through a portal and into a large office workshop with a dozen or more people at computers and workbenches.

A muscular black woman sitting at a high workbench turned to see who was porting in. "Oh, it's you Mae. I was expecting Jack, but I'm always expecting Jack. That man has way too much energy. Who's your friend?" she said with a friendly smile.

"This is Nava," Mae responded to Smitty.

"And this is Graphene Smith," Mae said to Nava. "She makes things that keep us safe."

"Smitty to you, Nava. Nice to meet you," said Smitty extending a hand and a friendly smile.

Nava shook the hand, feeling impressed by the Smitty's powerful energy. "It's very nice to meet you," replied Nava, finding it easy to smile back.

"Nava needs protection and I'd like her to get a few things," Mae said to Smitty. "First, I would like her fitted with armor and your latest cloak prototype if possible."

"I can give her a cloaking belt like yours," replied Smitty. "But these are the only two in existence for now. We'll begin mass production in a few weeks."

"Come with me," directed Smitty, walking to a glass booth against the near wall. "Step inside and stand still for a few moments," Smitty said to Nava, opening the glass door.

Nava stepped into the booth and Smitty closed the door behind her. After only a second or two and Smitty opened the door, "That's got your measurements okay. Let's get your belt."

Smitty turned to a panel and pushed a few buttons to open a small portal. The belt she removed from the portal was about three centimeters wide and made of a silvery metallic material.

"This looks a lot like yours," Nava said to Mae. "I always thought it was a beautiful belt."

"Thanks, I like it. And now you have one of your own," replied Mae with a smile. "Function doesn't need to be ugly."

"It needs to look good so you can wear it all the time without being conspicuous," said Smitty. "There's a button on the bottom of the buckle," she continued, showing Nava how to turn it on and off. "Here, put it on and buckle up. We'll give it a test."

Smitty stepped back and picked up something from the table.

"Ready?" she said smiling, after Nava had buckled the belt. Smitty threw something directly at Nava. The small bean bag bounced off Nava's chest and fell to the floor.

Nava gave a startled laugh saying, "Is that what's supposed to happen?"

"I don't think it's turned on," replied Smitty. "Check it out."

"Oh, I see," said Nava, fumbling with the buckle. "I've got it now."

Smitty threw the bean bag again and Nava reached out to catch it this time. But the bean bag disappeared in front of Nava and she heard it hit the wall behind her.

"How did it do that?" said Nava, looking surprised.

"Very advanced phased array sensors and a high speed quantum processor on the belt detect physical objects moving toward you. The sensor and processors are so fast that they can activate the protection system in time to open a portal to let the object pass to the space behind you. Now come over here and look into the mirror."

Nava looked at herself in the mirror and saw nothing unusual. She thought that the silver belt looked great.

"Now push the top button the belt," directed Smitty.

Nava looked at the belt buckle and then pressed a small flat button and looked up at Smitty and Mae.

"You've got it now," said Smitty. "It's working perfectly. Look in the mirror."

Nava turned and looked. She couldn't find herself in the mirror. "I am here? I can see you and I can see my body when I look directly at myself. But I'm not in the mirror," Nava said with a surprised smile spreading across her face.

"You are invisible to us," said Smitty. "In this mode, the belt activates an extremely fast portal system that opens and closes portals all around your body, rapidly and at all angles. It works so fast that all we can see is the space behind you. No matter what angle we look, we only see the other side of the portal. The cloaking mode takes more power, so if you leave it in the cloaking mode all the time, you'll need to charge it up every day or two. The buttons will get warm when you need to charge."

"You are invisible but not invulnerable," continued Smitty. "Neither mode will protect you from fire, flood, poison gas, or anything liquid or gaseous in the space around you. Gases and liquids are slow to penetrate the shield and that gives you time to activate an escape portal and step out of danger. Just squeeze both buttons at the same time and an escape portal opens to a friendly and safe location."

"Like the security ComPort that Mae gave me before. How does it find a safe location," asked Nava.

"They work on the same system. The belt maintains BroadPort system connectivity while it's energized," said Smitty, "and it provides position information to our Central Protection system. The system maintains a selection of safe portal locations and provides that information to your belt, so it's ready to immediately open a portal to safety from wherever you are."

"Wow!" exclaimed Nava, "Imagine all the things you could do with this."

"Remember, people can hear you and smell you," said Smitty. "So don't get too close. Use it with care and it will keep you safe."

"What else do you need, Mae?"

"She needs a ComPort with off-world capabilities."

Smitty got the ComPort and demonstrated the operational functions to Nava.

"I knew he'd follow you here sometime," Smitty said to Nava and Mae upon seeing Jack step in through an open portal.

"Did you break another ComPort, Jack?" asked Smitty with a smile, knowing he was here for Mae.

"You always give me the broken ones," Jack replied with a questioning smile.

"We need to talk, Mae. If you are done here, could you step into my office?" Jack said to Mae and Nava with a much more serious tone.

To Nava, Jacks office first felt like a cave in the side of a cliff with large view windows looking out across a stunning mountainous landscape. It took her a moment, but Nava soon realized that the windows were portals and the solid rock walls were real. They were enclosed in solid rock someplace inside Utopia.

"Come in and find a chair. There's water on the table if you would like," offered Jack.

"A picture is developing," he said in a serious voice, "of a large organization which has stolen RingTech's most advanced technology. To do this they must have infiltrated every corner of the United Worlds organization with spies. This is the most serious threat to the United Worlds in our entire history of existence."

"On the surface, the Waru are a religious organization with an aggressive recruiting program. At a deeper level, the Orthodox members of the Waru church are directing enormous spying operations and stealing our latest technology. Terrorizing citizens to gain Waru converts is trivial compared to what we are now finding."

"I've seen their negative side," Nava answered. "But it is still hard to believe my church would do this?"

"What's the motive behind this perversion of their religious teachings?" Jack asked without expecting reply. "I've received permission and resources to go into Ariel big, with tens of thousand of troops. It will be very strong response but must be a complete surprise. It will take two days for us to prepare. In the meantime, I want you, Mae, to sneak into the facility and do what you can to prevent the destruction of their records. It's critical that we learn everything we can about the organization."

"I'm currently guarding Nava and think it is best for her safety that she stay with me. She is all geared up and willing to accompany me into Ariel. She even has one of Smitty's new cloaks. May we have your permission?" asked Mae.

“Nava,” said the director looking carefully into Nava's face. “Do you understand the danger and are you willing to work with Mae on this project?”

“I'm scared but want to help. Yes, I want to go,” stated Nava.

“Thank you Nava, you are brave and honorable. You may go with Mae, but be careful.”

“When can you leave?” asked Jack looking at them seriously.

Chapter 21 Gone to Hell

"How's that Scientific Spirituality working for you now? You lousy Alton," said the Deacon standing guard over Cromen. "You people are all the same. You think you can escape God's wrath by your silly little meditation exercises. God is all seeing and knows of your fornication and devil worship. You'll have no peace until you beg forgiveness from the one true God."

Cromen sat quietly through the Deacon's tirade, feeling the weight and pain of his confinement. He knew better than to argue philosophy with the angry guard. Cromen had no wish to discover the limits of their brutality. The pain of his throbbing testicles told him to keep quiet.

"Time to go," said another deacon coming through the door. The two deacons unlocked Cromen from the desk and stood him up, handcuffed behind his back. One deacon held his arms from behind.

"It's been so nice to have you here," said the other deacon, stepping in front of Cromen and smiling as he swung a powerful right fist into Cromen's abdomen. "Just a friendly reminder of how much fun it's been."

Cromen doubled over and gasped in pain as the guards laughed and pushed him out the door.

"Come on, get your ass moving," said a guard, as they hustled Cromen down the corridor and into a side room. The large ring and control terminal made it obvious where they were.

The portal operator looked at them, "The destination's set for Hell induction center. Are you ready to go?"

"Open the port," said one of the guards. "Let's send him to Hell where he belongs."

The portal opened to a very similar portal control room with two uniformed guards. They stepped through the portal, exchanged a few pleasantries with the guards on this side before taking Cromen by the arms and leading him back through the portal.

"Welcome to Hell," said one of the guards as the portal closed behind them. "I Hope you have a long and painful stay."

They both laughed before one turned to the portal operator and said, "He belongs to Red Devil 9."

The operator took a minute before the portal opened to another similar looking portal room. "Red Devil 9" was spelled out in large red letters on one wall. The guards marched Cromen through the portal, down a hall and into a well lit room where they strapped him firmly to a table, flat on his back. They put a gag in his mouth, then strapped his right arm to a side board. A shiny mechanical device slide automatically from the end of the board over his hand, stopping at his middle forearm. The laser tattoo felt like fire on Cromen's skin, but took less than a minute to complete.

With an effort, Cromen could just see his number as the machine finished, it almost glowed in bright red, "RD9B11702".

He was unstrapped and walked back to the transportation room where they entered another corridor. The walls were blank and there were no doors on either side. At the end of the corridor was a large heavy metal door which the guards activated. The door made several mechanical clicking and whirring sounds before it slid quickly to the side giving passage to a chamber with another heavy metal door on the far end. The last door didn't open until the door behind was closed.

Fragrant humid air greeted Cromen when the guards opened the last door. They led Cromen outside onto a veranda under a roof of large timber bamboo and thatched palm. A few simple tables and chairs sat on the gray slate floor. The veranda occupied a flat step or shelf cut from the side of a volcanic rock hillside. Cromen could see an ocean through breaks in the trees.

The guards led Cromen a few meters from the door, where he could see the door was set in the solid basalt rock of the hillside. As they removed Cromen's handcuffs one guard told Cromen, “You're not our concern anymore. May you be of value here in hell.” They turned and reentered the chamber door.

“Greetings,” an old man in blue coveralls said as he approached Cromen. “My name's Albert, I'm the resource representative here for your induction,” he said while extending a friendly hand.

“Thank you,” responded Cromen, shaking Albert's hand.

“You look to be in pain, brother. Do you need help?”

“I have pain but it only needs time to heal,” replied Cromen. “It's nice to see a friendly face.”

“We're all brothers,” said Albert, managing a little twinkle in his soft smile. “We are all brothers. And everyone needs time to heal.”

“Thank you,” replied Cromen. “This is not what I expected of Hell.”

“This place you have come to is like other human places, only the rules are a little different,” Albert continued. “Everything here is about value to your owner. You and I are owned by the Red Devil Corporation. You exist for their pleasure or profit."

"Is there no way to appeal this injustice?" asked Cromen.

"Put it out of your head," replied Albert firmly. "You are here to stay. Make the best of it. You're young and healthy, you can make a good life here if you provide good value to your master."

Cromen's head was throbbing with the horror of his situation.

Albert saw the frustration growing on Cromen's face. "I wish I could be more encouraging. I know it's a hard thing to accept, but no one here wants you to suffer. We want you to be happy here in Hell. Everyone provides their best value when they are healthy and happy."

As he listened, Cromen's anger grew. He felt like strangling the man and was breathing hard trying to control himself.

Albert got down on one knee, looked up at Cromen briefly before speaking softly but clearly, "I am not your enemy, I am your friend. I can't change your situation, but maybe I can help you adjust to it. I've been here a long time. I've seen many thousands pass through that door. Don't hurt yourself. You may not like it but you are safe here."

Cromen sat down and breathed deeply several times. "I apologize for my anger. Right now all I can think of is how to escape. I can't stay here."

"Everyone wants to go back," said Albert, "But no one does. Come on, let's go down into town and get you a place to live. It's a walk of a few hundred meters to the town below. Can you walk okay?"

"Yes, if we go a little slow."

Albert talked as they walked down a wide well kept grassy path. “You'll need testing to determine where to place you, so the Masters get the most value. In hell your value is everything, doesn't matter what you have done before unless it has value to your owner. Doesn't matter what you know unless it adds value. Doesn't matter what you can do unless it adds value.”

Cromen could see through the lush vegetation a small city spreading out like a fan radiating from the end of the path. The sound of footsteps from behind made Cromen nervous and he looked back.

“Don't worry,” said Albert, “they're only workers returning home. Most of the city passes through that door to work each day. This group must be on early shift just getting off.”

Cromen walked slowly due to his pain. The group of workers caught up to them, giving cheerful greetings as they passed.

“The dark blue jump suits of factory workers,” commented Albert.

“Where do they work?” asked Cromen.

“I don't know. Even they don't know,” replied Albert. “They just go in the door to work and come out the door to go home. That simple. As long as you work good everything is easy. Life can be good here in Hell.”

“But you're all slaves, how can you be happy like that?” asked Cromen.

“Everyone is a slave in some way. Right now you're a slave to your emotional attachments, laboring over your desire to escape and to be where you were before. Wanting what we don't have is a strong human characteristic that enslaves us, and being a slave to yourself can be hard. Relax, let your master have some of that responsibility. Enjoy what you can here. Red Devil is a very good master. You could have done much worse."

"Maybe you're right," conceded Cromen hesitantly. He heard the logic and wisdom in Albert's words, but was horrified by their truth.

"I wish I had another option to offer you, brother," continued Albert. "But true freedom only comes in death. As long as you live, you are a slave to your own human character and people are often bad masters of themselves, for some it is worse than being enslaved by another."

The grassy path became narrower as they entered the city. At times crowded with people coming and going, the way was lined with small shops and restaurants; owners out front beckoning passers by to enter. The buildings on either side were made of wooden poles and mud plaster, all the same brown dirt color, irregular shaped, with sloppy thatched roofs. Most were single story with shared walls between buildings. Narrow side streets branched off either side at irregular intervals.

"Has anyone ever escaped?" asked Cromen.

"They have tried," said Albert. "But the only way out of hell is through an off-world portal like the one you came through. And those portals sit inside that second door in the tunnel. The work transport ring is inside the first door which opens regularly to transport workers. But the inner door never opens unless the outer door is closed."

"Have people tried to escape through the door?" Cromen continued.

"Yes, people have tried to attack or open the inner door," said Albert. "Sometimes it's well planned, sometimes just an explosion of rage. The result is always the same. The guards simply close the outer door and open the work transport portal to the vacuum of space. No one ever comes back from attacking the inner door."

Albert led them down a winding side path lined with brown mud plaster walls, and opened a blue wooden door. Cromen followed him into a small courtyard. A narrow covered porch ran across the opposite side, a meter wide just high enough to sit on. The wall behind the porch had numbered doors every few meters.

"Good Afternoon, Anne, Robert," said Albert to a man and woman sitting on the porch. Their feet hung over the edge touching the grassy courtyard. "This is our new guest, Cromen."

Anne and Robert nodded in dreary reply.

"They're new arrivals, too," Albert told Cromen. "Your room is over here," he continued, stepping onto the porch and opening a blue door marked with a red 6.

The wooden floor squeaked under foot as Cromen walked into the small room. A bed filled the back third of the space and several large pillows lay on the woven palm leaf floor mat, a high window above the bed was open allowing air to flow easily through.

"There is community food service," said Albert, "three times a day, seven am, one pm, and seven pm."

Walking out of the room, Albert pointed to a wooden barrel, "That's your drinking water in the barrel, it's a rainwater system. And come over here, let me show you the toilet."

Cromen followed Albert to one end of the porch and into the last door. A raised flat platform with a hole to sit over is all there was in the room. It smelled terrible. “How does it work?” he asked

“There are workers who come once a week to dip it out,” said Albert. “They fertilizer the land so the fruits and vegetable grow better. So don't put anything but body waste in there. The workers will make you take it out again.”

Albert then directed Cromen off the porch and to a small walled off area made of wood and woven natural fiber. “This is the bathing area,” he said opening the door, “There are buckets and sponges and soap. You have to draw your own water. Please keep it clean.”

It was a bare four sided room, open to the sky above. Cromen admired the floor's large flat slabs of slate loosely laid on fine river gravel.

“It's simple, but I guess it works,” commented Cromen.

“I'll meet you tomorrow morning for breakfast and we'll get you tested,” Albert said. “You have everything you need here to survive. My advice to you, Cromen, is to go out and explore the place, meet people. We're all in the same situation. Try to appreciate what you do have instead of worrying about what you don't have.”

“You shouldn't have any problem finding the dinning hall and community center,” Albert said with a smile, shaking Cromen's hand before passing through the courtyard door.

Cromen turned to Anne and Robert. “May I ask how long you've been here?” inquired Cromen.

“This is our second day,” replied Anne, with hopeless despair clear in her voice. Robert looked on without interest, depression gripping his mind in darkness.

Cromen sat down on the porch nearby feeling about how Robert looked.

"I just want to leave, man," said Robert after a few minutes

"Me too," replied Cromen. "I don't care how good they make it for me. I'm nobodies slave. I've got to get out of here."

Chapter 22 Ariel

"It is a few hours before dawn on Ariel and there is no moon, so you should be hard to see," Smitty told Mae and Nava as they climbed down into a small dark boat floating in shallow water, a large portal ring was visible in front of the boat. "We picked this spot because the sea is calm and the blocking field boundary is not far from shore. We will be about two kilometers from the beach," said Smitty. "Are you ready to go?"

"As ready as possible," smiled Mae. "Thanks for everything, Smitty. Let's go."

"Hold on now," Smitty replied, "you might get splashed when we open the portal and door. Good luck."

The lights turned out and the portal opened in front of them to show a mildly turbulent sea surface. Waves splashed in through the portal and disturbed the water where the small dark craft held Mae and Nava waiting anxiously. Mae guided the boat through the open portal and into the sea, accelerating as they cleared the portal. A tracking beacon dropped earlier from a portal above the blocking field, now guided them toward a beach where the small craft could land.

"We should be passing through the blocking field about now," said Mae, after a few minutes. "I don't think we've attracted any attention."

The acoustically dampened electric motor drove them silently through the dark night unseen, water splashing against the hull was the only sound.

As Nava watched the approaching coastline with her infrared glasses, her thoughts turned to Cromen, her feelings turned to worry. But as frightened as she felt, she was doing the right thing. Maybe for the first time in her life, she knew what was right. She felt an overwhelming intention to fight for what she believed.

Nava felt excited, crazy, scared, nervous, ready for anything. She looked over at Mae, her flat gray hooded jumpsuit wasn't tight but fit every curve of Mae's strong lean body perfectly. Guessing Mae to be over 50, Nava admired her for her good health and beautiful spirit. She smiled in admiration, wishing to be like her.

Mae steered the boat up onto a small sandy beach and engaged the wheeled propulsion to drive them into the thick forest. "This should do," Mae said after finding a clearing in the forest that was hidden from view. "It'll be light soon. Let's set up the portal ring and have a little snack before we go exploring. I'll go cover our tracks."

Nava set up the folding PersPort, as she had been trained the day before. When Mae returned the two-meter tall circular metal ring stood supported by a lightweight graphite frame.

"Are we ready to go?" asked Mae returning from her task.

"Just making the last connections now."

Nava and Mae relaxed together eating energy bars, drinking strong coffee, and listening to the sound of the jungle, just awakening around them to the brightening predawn sky. Birds sang in greeting of the day while Mae set the destination on the PersPort control panel.

She did a high-speed image capture through the port at a speed too fast for the human eye to see. "It looks clear. We're going in cloaked," said Mae. "Energize your belt."

Nava pressed the upper button on her silver belt. "I think I'm ready," She said, looking at Mae and only seeing the small faint light in the infrared frequency. The antenna-like fiber extended outside her cloak to allow Nava to see her location using infrared glasses.

They were completely invisible to normal vision as they walked together through the portal into the secret underground facility. It looked like a subway transit station, empty of people, dirty and unused. Mae checked around the station and walked up to a destination map on the wall where she took a high-definition photo of the map.

"It's just what I was hoping for. We have a map that identifies the spaces from our scan. Now we can put names to those spaces to help decide where to go."

"Why did you pick this spot?" asked Nava.

"All the long tunnels in this underground facility meet here. So I made a guess," replied Mae looking at the board. "They probably use only portals to travel around the facility now, and abandon this old transport system. Glad it's still here."

"I see administration listed here," said Nava pointing to a large rectangle labeled Admin.

"I'm tempted to check in on Research and Development or Manufacturing," said Mae. "But let's do administration first, it shouldn't take much time. Shall we?"

"Let's go," Nava agreed, nodding her head.

People were coming and going, but no one noticed as Mae and Nava stepped through a portal into a corner of the admin facility. Long rows of cubicles with desks filled the enormous central floor of the facility, private offices lined the walls.

"All we need is an empty cubicle with a computer," said Mae. "Let's find the restrooms."

They stood watching for people leaving their desks and coming towards them. Soon they saw a heavy-set middle-aged man get up and walk in their direction. They gave him a wide berth as they passed on their way to his desk.

Mae found an open data port on the back of the computer and plugged in an interface module. "That should do it. Let's go visit something more interesting. Let the hackers back at headquarters do their work."

Nava followed Mae's little green light into an empty back corner and waited until Mae opened another portal.

The next space they entered was very different, with bright lights and a high ceiling, heavy equipment was placed orderly around the room and various machine noises emanated from the busy people at every work station. The space was clean and well ventilated.

Mae began walking through the facility, recording video of every machine. "It looks like there building RingTech portals and control systems," she whispered to Nava. "You take video down that row and I'll do this one. Record anything and everything."

Nava crossed to the far side and began recording all that she saw. She rejoined Mae when she reached the end of the row.

"Let's go see R&D next," Mae said, leading the way to a hidden corner of the workshop. She energized the portal and Nava followed her through to another large workshop with hundreds of machines and workbenches. The equipment was clustered into groups where engineers and scientists in white smocks moved about drinking coffee, talking with each other, and looking at their work.

"Meet you at the other end," said Mae. "Try to get an image of every workbench and machine."

Nava worked her way to the far side of the room, staying as far from people as possible, but getting close enough for good video images. It was more than an hour before she reached the other end of the workshop. Mae was waiting for her.

"I was able to install a tap on a computer in here also. It may be a separate network," Mae whispered to Nava. "I think we've got everything we need. Let's get going."

Mae led the way to a secluded corner where she opened a portal. They stepped through into the hot shady jungle clearing next to their amphibious vehicle.

We'll leave as soon as it gets dark," said Mae. "Let's pack everything up and get some rest before nightfall."

There were no biting insects, as the Bioengineers had not included them in the seeding of planet Beryl. But there were lots of annoying flies thirsting for the salty sweat of their skin.

"I wish we could go for a swim," said Nava, resting in the shade.

"Why not," replied Mae. "We'll go cloaked, it should be pretty safe."

Nava eagerly stripped naked and fastened her silver belt around her bare waist. As they left their jungle shelter and stepped onto the small sandy beach, a beautiful rocky coastline came into view on the left side, the right side being blocked by trees and a rocky outcrop.

"I'm sure they have a surveillance system, but it shouldn't pick us up as long as we're cloaked," Mae commented to Nava as they walked across the beach.

Nava followed Mae's footprints into the water. She floated there on her back, relaxing and gazing up at the blue sky. "I can't believe we did it," she said to Mae.

"You're a brave girl," Mae replied. "You did a great job and should be proud of yourself."

"I was scared, but it actually felt pretty safe. I never really felt threatened."

"Equipment and planning," replied Mae. "That's what kept us safe. We didn't need to take much risk."

"You're amazing," Nava said, smiling at Mae. "I wish I was more like you."

"Be careful what you wish for, Nava," responded Mae. "Your dreams could come true."

"Then I'll wish for Cromen to be safe and come back to me soon," said Nava in a more serious tone of voice.

"The cloak is like SPF 1000 sun protection," said Mae. "We could hang out all day in the sun and never get a tan."

Nava lay on the soft white sand. "I can't feel the sun, but the sand is hot," she said laying back and letting the warmth penetrate her body.

Mae joined her on the sand saying, "Ooh, this is nice."

The day passed calmly and Mae and Nava returned safely to Smitty's workshop laboratory the same way they came – small boat until they were outside the blocking field, then through an open portal into the workshop.

"Nice work Mae," said Jack waiting with Smitty to greet them. "How did Nava work out?"

"She was a big help. And," replied Mae, "I think she liked it."

Nava smiled nervously, "It was exciting."

"Well thanks for your good work, Nava. It is appreciated at the highest levels," Jack responded with a firm direct smile.

"Mae, I would like to talk with you two in my office for a few minutes before you head home," he said, leading them through his open portal.

"We've been downloading data as fast as we can from your data taps on their computer network. Teams of analysts are digging in. What we've found so far is startling," Jack said firmly. "These people, the Orthodox Waru, have every bit of technology that we have and have had it for hundreds of years. They receive every new advanced piece of equipment as quick as we make it."

"What is their Research and Development doing, if they get the benefit of ours?" asked Mae.

"They appear to be working on modifications to portal control systems," Jack replied. "But we haven't had enough time to understand it all yet."

"We're hoping to find a list of their spies within our organization. We'll keep looking."

"The United Worlds is going to raid the Ariel facility in force as soon as possible, but we must assume that our rapid preparation will be noticed by their spies. They will know we're coming and will be making their own preparations. I want you and Nava to accompany the intelligence agents in charge of the attack. You may be of some use to them."

"Is there any word of Cromen?" asked Nava.

"We believe he was at the Ariel facility before being rescued at the vault. But we don't know where he was taken after he was recaptured at the hospital," answered Jack. "We hope to learn more from tomorrow's raid. Get some rest now. The attack starts tomorrow at midnight."

It was late afternoon when the two arrived in Mae's apartment. They were tired and went early to bed. A ComPort call request woke them at three am. "It's Jack," Mae exclaimed loudly while picking up the ComPort from her bedside.

"Can't you give a girl some rest?" she stated sleepily.

"Sorry Mae, I gave you as much time as I could," replied Jack. "The attack has been moved up. We need you here as soon as you can make it."

The control room was a busy place, but not crowded, when Nava and Mae entered. General Green, the Space Marine liaison to the intelligence service welcomed them and asked that they sit to the side unless called upon. Control consoles and computers lined the sides of the room, large view screens covered the walls, one large RingTech Portal was mounted on the front wall with various monitors screens above and to the sides.

"Drop the redirect portals," commanded the general. "Ready the troops, the doors open in ten minutes."

"We're a little late to the game," whispered Mae into Nava's ear.

Redirect portals and control technicians were dropped from above the blocking field. Parachutes brought them gently to the ground inside Ariel's blocking field, where the technician quickly had them operational and connected to the agency's encrypted BroadPort network. The portal operators established connectivity with the command center and opened portals between the Ariel facility and a point just inside Ariel's blocking field. The troops standing at an open portal just outside the blocking field began jumping across the open space, out one portal and into another, directly into the underground facility.

Troops began reporting back to control after only a few seconds. "The lights are out and there is no power in the space," came comments from a team in the R&D area. "We haven't seen any people yet."

Then from several different locations, "It's a trap!" "Lava coming in!" "Pull back now!"

"What the hell is happening down there?" yelled general Green.

"The chambers are filling with molten lava, sir," was the communication officer's reply. "They must have opened redirect portals to a magma chamber deep underground."

"Retreat! Retreat! Retreat!" the general exclaimed loudly. "Are we getting out okay? Is anybody trapped?"

"No reports of serious injury, Sir," came the reply. "They say the magma isn't moving fast. But it is filling every chamber of the facility. There won't be anything left for us to look at."

"It's a good thing you got in there yesterday," said the General, turning to Mae and Nava. "At least we have something to work with."

Chapter 23 The Profit

The Grand Temple of Saint Newton, in Saint Carmin City, is the largest cathedral that ever existed. Seven Silver Apostles top the seven gleaming spires equally spaced defining the outer wall, an eighth spire rises at the center. This central spire, which they say represents God himself, rises high above the seven outer spires. A brilliant silver ball decorates the top of this central tower, long silver spikes radiate from it like beams of light. The Grand Temple is said to be visible from over one hundred kilometers distance.

Colonnades of white marble support the complex fan vaulted ceiling of silver and dark blue. The dais of the Seven Apostles occupies the center of the cathedral and rises forty meters above the black marble floor. Its presence dominates the cathedral from every point within. Seven Apostle thrones sit thirty meters up, evenly spaced around dais forming a seven fluted column. An eighth chair, the Profit throne, sits at the center ten meters above the seven.

Vapor rose and swirled around the column, enveloping the eight thrones. Thunder reverberated throughout the cathedral and the vapor dissipated to reveal the Profit and Seven Apostles standing before their thrones.

The Seven Apostles wore brightly colored, extravagantly decorated robes and matching pointy hats. Each elaborately decorated throne faced outward, looking down on part of the surrounding congregation. The Profit throne graced the top of the tower, light radiated from a silver ball set above his throne. The rays of light shifted and changed color reflecting the mood of the Profit. This entire tower of thrones rotated slowly, providing an equal view of the Profit and Apostles to all worshipers.

The congregation, seated on hard wooden benches stretched out into the distance. Twenty-five thousand worshipers attended the sermon in person. Millions more attended via a ComPort sermon app. The sermon app opens a tiny portal to allow a person to view and hear the sermon. The viewers show up in the temple as millions of tiny dots of light floating in the air surrounding the dais just outside the blocking field.

"Only through the worship of God does a person deserve respect. Fear the wrath of God," exclaimed the Profit. "Abstinence, hard work, and the love of God provide the only path to heaven. Sin is responsible for all our problems. Ethical living and confession of sin is your only way to salvation, your only path to heaven."

"Only true believers have value to God. Only true believers deserve the blessings and opportunities God gives."

"Be suspicious of non-believers, they are a sinful temptation, nothing more. The Alton people are poor ignorant children, unable to see the truth. These Alton people are an example of those who do not follow the Seven Scriptures."

"Pleasure seekers, abandoning God, the Alton live shallow lives of self-gratification and sensual pleasure. Their parties, dancing, gambling, drinking, and smoking cannabis will condemn them to Hell eternal. But worst of all, these Alton people consider sex to be a good and healthy practice."

"Not only are they sinners of the worst kind, but they have helped the United Worlds to attack our planet, attack our religious authority. They helped the United Worlds invade our sacred continent of Ariel. Yes, the United Worlds have attacked and destroyed our research station on Ariel."

"They will feel the wrath of God. They will suffer for their actions. They will burn for their sins. They will suffer burning excruciating unbearable pain in Hell for all eternity."

The Profit stood a moment with raised arms then exclaimed sternly, "Repent your sins."

Clouds of vapor enveloped the dais. It stopped rotating and the profit light went dark.

Fifteen minutes of silent prayer following the sermon was mandatory and strictly enforced. The little lights surrounding the central dais blinked out after exactly fifteen minutes. The crowd stood up from the hard wooden benches and left as quickly as they could.

Profit Charles Henden was the twenty-fifth profit in direct line of descent from the original profit John Newton. It was the seventeenth year of his lifetime appointment. All of the Apostles who had appointed him still held their position at the Council of Seven Apostles. Profit Henden had selected his cousin Merriam to replace him in the position he vacated as Apostle.

At the end of the sermon, Profit Henden returned to the Profit's council chamber. The seven apostles were seated around an eight-sided table. The profit stepped up and sat in his large leather chair, which sat a meter above the others.

He Looked down on the Seven Apostles, "Is everybody ready? I'd like to make this quick if we can."

Seeing agreement around the table he began, "Let's start with you, Apostle Smater. What is the current status of Ariel?"

"Yes your Godliness," replied the short chubby apostle. "As you all know there was an intrusion at the Ariel facility. The

United Worlds was able to install a bug and had limited access to our computer systems for about 2 hours. Rogers, in the United Worlds intelligence department, reported this intrusion and their plan to capture our people and facility. We began feeding them bogus data as soon as we found the bugs and are working to determine what information they were able to obtain before we made the switch."

"And the attack," asked the profit, "have they attacked?"

"Yes, your Godliness. We thought we had two days, but they came a day early with a large military force."

"It's sad to see it go," said the Profit. "The Ariel facility was the creative vision of the great Profit John Behan in the early days here on Beryl. It has played such an important part in developing our technologies for expansion and self-preservation. But it has lost much of its importance and the work can be taken up again at newer and better facilities on Eden."

"Was the evacuation plan successful?" asked the Profit.

"Yes, your Godliness. The evacuation plan was executed perfectly and the facility flooded with magma. Our people inside the United Worlds warned us in time to execute our plan before the Space Marines arrived."

"Was anyone hurt or any sensitive information lost?" asked the Profit.

"The evacuation went smoothly and was completed only a few minutes before the Space Marines arrived. None of our people were injured. The chambers were flooding with magma as the United Worlds entered, they found nothing of use."

"We can't ignore this violation," replied Profit Hendon. "We'll give them something to think about. Execute the bombardment plan, immediately. That should confuse the

United Worlds and provide our followers the justification for leaving the United Worlds. It is long overdue. We will force the United Worlds to stay out of our business."

"Yes, your Godliness. It will be done."

"Next, I want an 'Ultimatum Statement' delivered to the United Worlds immediately after the magma bombardments Blame them for the unjustifiable attack on defenseless Beryl. Hold the United Worlds fully responsible for the atrocious devastation. We will issue our declaration of independence along with an ultimatum. Demand an end to United Worlds spying on the Waru, and threaten them with consequences if they continue their interference with the Waru people."

"Yes your Godliness, it will be done."

"How is our little sister, the Reformed Church of the Seven Apostles doing?" Profit Hendon asked. "Are we still protected?"

"The United Worlds did not get anything from Ariel that would identify our intelligence officers."

"That's good, keep it that way."

“Let's move on to our weekly reports," said the Profit, looking disturbed. "How is business on Hell this week?"

"Growing," Apostle Mark said, happy to be giving good news. "Profits for the week show a twenty-three percent annualized rate of return. That's up three percent over last week and seven percent over this same weekly rate this time last year. The number of workers on Hell has increased by twelve percent over last year."

"Good work, Mark," replied Profit Hendon. "Keep it up."

"Apostle Johnson. Your Heaven report please."

"Heaven has been flat this past week, but up thirteen percent for the year and three percent higher for the month compared to last year."

"It's good to see improvement," said the Profit, "What can we do to keep the profit flowing?"

"Our biggest increase in retirement to Heaven has come from planet Fomalhaut. The social disruption campaign has frightened many into seeking a comfortable and safe escape from the tensions of their lives. I think we are on the right path here and would ask for more action. Keep it up."

"It does seem to be working well," smiled the Profit, "but it requires a certain amount of tact. This brings us to your department Apostle Merriam. How are we doing with social disruption?"

"It seems to be working perfectly," she replied. "We've seen five percent growth in Waru converts in the past year in addition to the retirements going to Heaven as mentioned by Apostle Johnson."

"Good Job Merriam."

"Internal affairs, are the people sinning enough? Are the people repentant, apostle Carlyle?"

"Sinning is up four percent over last week," replied Apostle Carlyle. "But repentance continues to decline."

"Why the problem with repentance?" Asked the Profit. "Why don't they feel guilty?"

"It is the Alton, your godliness," replied Apostle Carlyle. "They aren't suffering enough, and the Waru congregation is tempted by the Alton's pagan pleasure-seeking attitude."

"We need to do something about these Alton," replied the Profit. "There may be an opportunity soon to get rid of them once and for all."

"Sum things up for us Apostle Chevsky," commanded the Profit. "How are our commercial enterprises doing around the United Worlds?"

"Our siphoning of .01% on all bank transactions has grown by 4% in the last year, roughly reflecting the growth of human population in the United Worlds."

"We expect that leaving the UW will result in an improvement in our bottom line."

"What about our Missionary work?

"Our missions are stronger than ever on the primary mission planets. We should be effective in maintaining recruitment and retirement with very little change from the present. To sum it up, everything is going well. Your brilliant plan is working perfectly."

Chapter 24 Work

Cromen awoke at dawn on his first morning in Hell. The sun was only beginning to brighten the sky as he visited the toilet and bathhouse. He slipped out of the front door silently, before the others awoke, to get a look at this place they call Hell. Sleepy shopkeepers were out front cleaning their entry area, getting their shops ready for the day. A few early morning workers in jumpsuits walked up the wide grassy path toward the door to their workplace.

People were friendly but seemed to carry some mental burden. Greetings were restrained as though they were unsure of their feelings. As if they couldn't allow themselves to really feel cheerful. Or maybe they were just sleepy.

"The well-organized community and the small houses remind me a little of home," thought Cromen. "Everyone has a place in the society, everyone has food and shelter and a healthy secure environment to live in. It would be perfect except the people have no freedom, no opportunity, no control of their lives. They've lost their spirit and passion for life."

The houses were spaced farther apart as Cromen walked out from the town center, but there were no gardeners, no vegetable fields, no one working the land surrounding the town. "Where are the workers that Albert spoke of?" Cromen wondered. "Or do they just spread the human waste from the latrine around the forest?"

The countryside was lush and green with jungle and grassland intermixed. Cromen was surprised when he realized that all the trees and bushes were some kind of fruit; mango, avocado, jack fruit, orange, banana, lychee, papaya, – he couldn't see a tree or bush that didn't carry some kind of food.

There were birds moving through the trees but not eating fruit, they were all insect eaters or pollinators. And the insects, he thought, were probably all pollinators also. Like other man-made worlds, there were no biting insects, no rats or mice, no animals eating fruit on the trees. The weeds were mostly edible vegetables. The non-food plants all provided something useful to sustain human life; nitrogen-fixing plants that enriched the soil, grass for the animals to eat and nest in, and large timber bamboo the people use for building.

"The planet was designed and created to nourish and provide for people," Cromen thought to himself. "An entire planetary ecosystem completely designed to feed and provide for humans."

Chickens and turkeys were everywhere in the town and forest. He saw people searching through the tall grass collecting eggs and saw goats, sheep, and cattle roaming and grazing freely on the thick grass.

Coconut and Sea Grape lined the white sandy beach where Cromen observed several small fishing boats pulled up on shore. People were holding one end of a long net, the other end was being rowed ashore by a small boat a short distance down the beach. Fish were jumping inside the net enclosure. Other men and women brought dipping nets and began taking large fish from the water and putting them in baskets. When the baskets were full the net was released, freeing the remaining fish back into the sea.

A group of small wild pigs crossed his path on the way back into town, Cromen smiled, laughed out loud, and said, "The entire planet's an enormous self-sustaining supermarket. Free food everywhere you look."

It was a few minutes before seven when Cromen arrived back at his room. "Good morning," said Albert sitting on the porch, "I thought I would stop by before breakfast to see how you were doing."

"I'm okay," answered Cromen. "I've been out for a walk. It's an interesting planet you have. Some would call it paradise."

"Some," replied Albert, seriously. "But it's too early to talk philosophy, lets go get some breakfast."

"It's so easy to live off the land here," said Cromen. "Why do people go to work at all?"

"If people don't work, then the master takes them to therapy. It's one of the few times that the Red Devil masters come out of the outer door. They come out in force with stun guns and take people who aren't working, ten, twenty, thirty, sometimes more. They take the people to therapy."

"What do they do to them?" asked Cromen, following Albert's through the now busy street.

"No one knows for sure," replied Albert. "They return a few days later, normal but ready, happy even, to work. We suspect hypnotism because the people don't remember anything that happened to them."

"I don't think I want to find out," Cromen said with a twisted face. "What's the point of rebelling? You might as well just go to work."

"You're beginning to catch on," smiled Albert, leading them up a short rock staircase to a large open cafeteria. "Grab a tray," he said, picking up a tray and getting into the food-service line.

"The masters provide us with simple hand tools only, shovels, rakes, axes, knives, pots and pans, and utensils for cooking and eating. As much as we want of this kind of thing.

But that is all they give to us, that and the clothes we wear. No machinery or electricity to run it, no gas or the equipment that uses it. Beyond these tools, we have only the things we can make from nature with our own hands and bodies."

"They allow 20% of the working-age population to stay at home to provide food and shelter for the workers. It turns out most people would rather go to work than to stay back and gather and prepare food. So there is a rotating schedule for many of the food worker positions. We all take a turn."

"There is almost no crime here," Albert continued. "The masters maintain very strict control. They're watching us all the time. They know when someone commits a crime. That's the other time they come out of the portal, to take away criminals. And those people don't come back."

About thirty tables with chairs filled most of the large covered patio, it was open on three sides with the kitchen and serving line filling one end. Men and women all wore the same style jumpsuit, but in a half dozen different colors.

Cromen smiled when he saw the serving table covered with many of the fruits and vegetables he had seen growing wild during his morning walk. He took some fruit and a piece of grilled mackerel.

Albert found a table looking out onto a grassy park that might be the town square. The large shade trees were mature mango, avocado, guava, and jack fruit. A small wooden gazebo stood near the center, chicken and turkeys roamed freely.

"I don't see many children," Cromen observed.

"They eat at 7:30," replied Albert. "To give the adults time to eat and get to work."

"Is there a school? The children I do see are wearing coveralls. Do they work?"

Albert looked at him with a questioning smile. "Inside that door in the hillside," he responded. "Red Devil educates everyone here. Education helps our children to be good workers. An educated worker provides more value."

"Are the children slaves?" Cromen asked.

"Yes, children that are born here will become working slaves when they are old enough." replied Albert. "There are some children that are fifth or sixth generation slaves. They don't know another way of life and make the best workers."

"Do you have doctors?" asked Cromen.

"The Red Devil takes care of that too. If you have a medical problem, go to the door and they will let you in and take care of you. Anytime, night or day. They take care of our bodies. We take care of our spirit."

"It's such a perfectly organized society, but the people don't seem particularly happy," observed Cromen. "In fact, many look depressed."

"People have a safe healthy life here. But without freedom and opportunity, they have no dreams. They only care about doing sufficient work to keep the masters happy. Without dreams and some degree of hope that your dreams could come true, the human spirit is lost."

"How do you live here, Albert, without being depressed?"

"You are alive, you have the ability to enjoy the things you do have. You choose to suffer, you choose to be depressed."

"The Arcadian Path suggests that the individual has a responsibility to learn to live happily," responded Cromen. "People need to take control of their lives. The need to learn to appreciate existence and the beautiful life all around them."

"Those are wonderful ideas, Cromen. And I hope they work for you. But without freedom, there are no dreams or opportunities, without freedom it is difficult to appreciate life and be happy."

"I can understand their depression," Cromen answered. "And I don't want to stay here."

Adult workers began leaving the nearly full cafeteria around 7:30 as children began entering.

"Let's make room for the others," said Albert when they had finished eating.

Cromen followed Albert out of the cafeteria, through town, and up the grassy path to the door in the hillside. There were many people standing under the veranda chatting and waiting their turn for the door. People with yellow coveralls were lined up and entering the outer door. The line stopped several times as quotas were met at one destination and another destination for yellow workers was selected.

"You'll go in after yellow," instructed Albert, walking to the end of the yellow line. "You'll go in alone and it might take several hours. Answer all their questions and do everything they ask of you and it will go faster."

"Where can I find you when I am finished?"

"It's always easy to find me at mealtimes," Albert replied. "Or ask around the community center. I'm usually close by."

When the yellow jumpsuits had all entered, Albert stood before the closed door and said, "Testing B11702". Cromen looked at his red tattoo and recognized his number. "Go on in," instructed Albert when the door opened.

A portal opened just inside the outer door and Cromen walked into a small examination room. The room was divided in half by a clear glass wall. His side had only a body scanning machine and an exercise machine.

"Remove your clothes and lay down on the scanning table," directed a heavyset woman on the other side of the glass. She wore a white lab coat with a bright red RD embroidered on the left chest.

Cromen removed his clothes and lay down on the scanning table which then slid automatically through a scanning ring. The woman sat down at a small table, energized the desk monitor, and began asking questions. The questions made no sense to Cromen.

"Why aren't you married? At twenty-seven most people are married."

"I guess I haven't found the right woman."

"Are you homosexual?"

"No."

"Have you ever acted?"

"No. Only play-acting with kids."

Do you sing or dance?

"Not very well."

"Do you play a musical instrument?"

"I always wanted to but I don't seem to stick with it."

"Do you have any special talent?"

"Not yet, nothing that I know of."

The machine took blood samples and hair samples. While still naked, he was directed to the exercise machine and asked to perform several exercises which measured his strength and endurance.

The woman attendant watched Cromen's body carefully the whole time he was naked.

"We may have other work for you soon," she informed Cromen, "but for now you will work in light industry. Here is your uniform,"

A light blue cotton jumpsuit appeared on the scanning table. "Get dressed and leave your old clothes here," she directed.

The jumpsuit fit perfectly as did the underwear, socks, and comfortable sneakers. As soon as he was dressed, the portal opened and he walked back out to the warm sunny afternoon at Red Devil Nine. The veranda was almost empty as Cromen walked off and headed down the path to town. He found Albert sitting at a table in the community center.

"How did it go?" queried Albert.

"Fine, I guess. I'll work in light industry for now. They said they might have other work for me soon."

"Really," responded Albert with disappointment. "I was afraid they might do that to you. They only say that when they're considering you for personal service or entertainment work. And you're an awful nice-looking young fellow. Just the type."

"Personal services, what does that mean?" asked Cromen.

"Some rich lady might pay to have you as a companion," answered Albert. "That might be the best value you could provide to Red Devil 9."

"You mean a male concubine?" returned Cromen, knitting his brow and twisting his head, trying to come to terms with this possibility. "They can't force me to do that, can they?"

"They tend to handle it delicately," said Albert, sidestepping the question. "Everyone involved wants it to work out. Try to think of it as a friendly relationship where you provide a service."

"But what about Nava, I'd feel like I was betraying her," said Cromen, feeling depressed.

"I am sorry Cromen, but you'll never see her again. Believe me, it's better for you to just move on and make the best of the life you're offered here. They'll prepare you and you'll go on a date with the lady and see if the relationship works. If yes, good for you both. If it doesn't work out, you simply return to light industrial work. You keep her happy and you won't come back here. It sounds like Heaven to many of us."

Cromen was dazed, understanding better now the pain in these people's eyes, understanding how hard Hell could be on a person. No choice, no opportunity, no plans or dreams. His mind was searching, searching desperately for a way out of Hell. In this place, there was no hope for escape, no hope of seeing Nava again. Maybe in another place there would be some opportunity.

"The only reason I'd consider this at all is that there may be possibilities for escape."

"Well," said Albert, a little disappointed in Cromen's focus on escaping Hell. "Dream what you like. Just be at the door tomorrow morning ready for work."

"What if I run?" asked Cromen, feeling desperate. "I can live off the land."

"You'd get bored pretty quick," Albert replied. "And they would catch you and send you to therapy."

Cromen head was throbbing. "Don't you want to leave this place? Can't you all just rush the door or something?"

"If a portal opened right here, right now to some other place, every man, woman, and child would run as fast as they could to get through. No one wants to be here, Cromen. But if we're stuck here, we need to make the best of it and not destroy ourselves worrying about things we can't change."

Cromen couldn't remember ever feeling so depressed. He got up listlessly, walked out of the community building, and wandered through the streets aimlessly. Eventually, he found himself sitting on the sandy beach in the shade. His mind swirled with the erotic fantasy of some unknown woman who wants him for his body, smashing against his love of Nava and his desire to be faithful. His mind screaming with the desire to be free of this place.

Taking several deep breaths, Cromen began to meditate. It had been a long time but he knew the process. For almost an hour his mind drifted from the focused silence of meditation to the explosion of anger and panic that came with enslavement. After some time he felt calmer but still lost. He couldn't decide what to do.

Cromen was at the community center for breakfast the next morning and sat with the others in light blue coveralls. They walked up the hill to the door together and he listlessly followed them through.

"You'll work with me until you catch on. There's not much to it," said one of the blue-uniformed workers.

Cromen followed him down a long row of weaving machines producing cloth. There were hundreds of machines creating fabric in a wide variety of colors and patterns.

"We have three jobs here," said the worker, "reload the machines before they are empty, remove the fabric when it's finished, and clear jammed machine when something goes wrong."

Cromen caught on quickly and spent the day on his own going from machine to machine. His heavy heart rebelling, making each action he took an angry forced event. "It is Hell," he thought to himself.

Near the end of his work shift that day, Cromen was brought into another office.

"You have been selected by Miss Janet Crawford as a potential companion," an attendant said flatly across the glass wall. "Here she is in her home," he continued while showing holographic video and still images of a middle-aged woman, tall, dark, pretty, a little heavy. The photos showed her in a variety of clothes, some elegant, some sexy and very revealing.

Cromen looked at the attractive woman who had chosen him. She wasn't young but was quite sexy, and she wanted him physically. His building erection made him feel like a dog, but he couldn't help it.

"She'd like a date with you tomorrow afternoon to get to know you. Will you accept this date?"

"Yes," responded Cromen nervously, but without hesitation.

"Come to the door tomorrow at 1 PM."

"Don't fight it, man," said Albert, seeing the lost look on Cromen's face. "You will only make things harder. A bad situation doesn't justify self-destruction. Get a grip. Maybe it's bad, but don't let anger consume you. Relax and enjoy the opportunity."

Cromen knew the words were true, but they only made him more angry. He returned to his room and sat on the porch, his mind throbbing with frustration and anger.

"This may be an opportunity to escape from Hell," thought Cromen to himself. "If this is the only way to get out, so be it."

Chapter 25 Heaven

While Cromen was getting acquainted with Hell, Nava and Mae were still on Utopia recovering from their adventure on Ariel.

"I don't think the Orthodox Waru are worried about you and Cromen anymore," said Mae. "They have bigger problems than you two. It may not be safe to go home yet, but at least they aren't focused on you anymore."

"That's a relief. But what about Cromen, is there any news?"

"Nothing yet," Mae replied. "But it's time to go see Jack. Maybe he knows something."

Jack looked excited when they came in. "They've terraformed their own planet," he said in amazement. "We've found an unrecorded world which the Orthodox Waru are using."

"What's there?" Mae asked in surprise.

"SpyPort shows a planet with a good healthy atmosphere and a moderate population. It's not blocked and we don't see any evidence of military installations. We'd like to know what's going on there but we need more information before we show up in force."

"Are you asking us to take a look?" asked Mae.

"Well," Jack looked from Mae to Nava. "You two are good together. What do you say, Nava? Would you like to explore an unknown world?"

Nava nodded her head. "Okay," with something of a timid smile.

"Thank you," replied Jack to Nava, knowing Mae couldn't resist the opportunity. "Talk to Smitty and do whatever else you need. I'd like you to leave as soon as you are ready."

"Have you heard anything about Cromen?" asked Nava.

"Nothing yet. But there's still a mountain of Ariel information to sort through. I'm sure we'll find him soon."

It took Smitty only a few minutes to examine and calibrate their equipment. "Everything's charged up and functioning properly. We've placed a redirect portal on the surface. It's paired with your ComPorts and loaded with the latest version of SpyPort. If you're ready to go, I'll get Jack down here."

"We've had a snack and a bathroom break," Mae said. "Are you ready Nava?"

"An unknown world," she replied, smiling nervously. "I can't wait."

Jack walked in from his office portal. "We can put you in wherever you would like. I suggest a city."

"The bigger the better," replied Mae.

"We've picked a spot that looks hidden behind buildings. Are you ready to go?"

"Let's go," said Mae taking a deep breath.

"Ready," said Nava with an excited tension on her face.

"Jack, you never told us the name of this planet," queried Mae.

"Heaven," Jack replied. "They call it Heaven."

"Let's cloak," Mae said to Nava, before fooling with her belt and vanishing.

"I've always wanted to go to Heaven," Nava said with a smile as they walked through the open portal into a tree-shaded space between buildings. Robotic gardeners cutting grass and trimming hedges ignored the invisible visitors.

A white street came into view as they walked around the building corner. The white brick pavement stretched into the distance with gleaming white buildings decorating either side as far as the eye could see.

"What do you think of this place," Mae wondered out loud, pausing to examine this strange new world.

As they watched, a portal opened about a block up the street and a large limousine drove out. The beautiful opulent automobile pulled up to the curb and stopped in front of the building near Nava and Mae.

"What a car," observed Nava. "I've never seen anything so extravagant. Is this a bank or something?"

"I don't know. It doesn't have any signs to indicate a business," answered Mae, leading them to the street to get a better look.

Mae and Nava watched the golden front doors of the building open and a red carpet roll automatically down the white marble stairs, ending at the curbside door of the limousine. A fat man of late middle age stepped out the door wearing a white tuxedo, a top hat, and a young blond woman on his arm. She was about his height and very sexy in dress and physique. They stood together arm in arm, looking out between white marble columns at the people who had gathered along each side of the red carpet. The people were excited, they cheered and clapped. The white tuxedo puffed out his chest and smiled as he walked down the white marble stairs with his lady on his arm. They both waved and smiled at the enthusiastic crowd.

"They're holograms," said Nava, trying to hold back her laughter. "It's a phony cheering section."

"Very sophisticated holograms," Mae observed. "I've never seen holograms look so real."

The crowd oohed and aahed in appreciation of the couple as the holographic chauffeur opened the car door and bowed to the white tuxedo entering the limousine. People waved goodbye as the limousine pulled away, then they vanished as it drove through an open portal up the street. The red carpet hologram rolled automatically up the stairs and put itself away.

"She was phony too, a very sophisticated hologram," said Mae, looking somewhat bewildered. "Is this the kind of research and development they were doing on Ariel?"

"Was the whole scene staged for the stuffed tuxedo?" Nava laughed. "It's one of the funniest things I've ever seen, like a ridiculous little play they put on for us."

"Let's hope it's not for us. It must have been for the man. He was the only real person there. There was no one else watching."

"What terrible vanity," said Nava. "He didn't even look like he enjoyed it. He only permitted the praise."

"Let's try to find some clothes of the local fashion so we can walk around uncloaked and maybe talk to people," said Mae, taking out the SpyPort and searching the buildings nearby.

"Do we really need to uncloak and talk with people?" asked Nava. "Maybe we should go into one of those bigger buildings down the street and see what's there?"

"Not very fashions conscious, are you," smiled Mae. "But you're probably right, let's go."

They ported into a vacant room halfway up one of the biggest buildings. It was a bedroom fitted lavishly in blue and gold. A large tapestry of men and women dancing naked among the flowers of a pastoral forest glen hung on one wall. Everywhere was luxury and extravagance.

"Someone's residence," observed Nava, glancing about.

"This isn't what we want. Let's look for some kind of government or administration building," Mae stated, sitting down on a couch. "But it's a nice place to work for a few minutes. Hope the owner doesn't pop in."

"Nothing's blocked here," said Mae, after looking at the SpyPort a few minutes. "They don't have blocking fields around any of the buildings. Don't they have anything to hide? Look around for any clothes we might wear."

While Mae worked with her SpyPort, Nava explored the room. Inside the closet she found men's clothes and a thin flesh-colored jumpsuit of a strange soft material, it felt like skin.

"What's this?" she asked, holding up the garment for Mae to see.

"What, don't you have those on Beryl?" Mae asked in surprise. "It's a sinsi-suit, an erotic stimulation suit that works with holographic sex programs."

"Ew, and I'm touching it," Nava held it away from her with two fingers. "That's creepy. Do they come in men's and women's?"

"No, they're all the same. To reverse the sex of the suit, you simply turn it inside out," Mae replied. "What"s the brand?

"It says, SimSex," Nava replied, putting the suit very carefully back into the closet.

"It's a good brand," Mae said with a smile. "One of the best. Mines a Sexodyne. It works better for me, feels like the real thing."

"Not you Mae?" said Nava, grinning in surprise.

"Don't knock it until you've tried it," responded Mae. "Doctors say sex is good for you, very good for you, and I really like it. Clears, or maybe it resets my mind. Makes life feel more exciting and beautiful, helps me feel better about everything."

"You make it sound so natural and healthy.

"Human sexuality should be treated as a divine gift. There is no shame or guilt in sex if it harms no one. Why shouldn't we seek pleasure in our lives? Pleasure is a source of joy, directly linked to your happiness and well-being."

"The Waru only teach about the problems sex causes and the sin of it in God's eyes. Like all pleasure, sex is a sin."

"I don't want to argue religion," said Mae. "I only offer my own experience."

Nava just smiled back.

"I've found something more interesting," said Mae, showing Nava the SpyPort images of a large elegant ballroom. Revelers filled the dance floor in front of the bandstand where a holographic big band played lively but antiquated music.

The people were dressed extravagantly, mostly couples. Each couple had one young beautiful partner, the other partner older and not so beautiful. The couples sat side by side at dinner tables, the older partner eating and drinking freely, the younger partner giving affectionate attention to their companion. There were also older married couples sitting together, each with their fantasy partner on the other side giving them attention.

"They're all wearing Sinsi-Suits under their clothes," observed Mae. "Their holographic partners feel real to them. They can see them, feel them, interact as though the holograms were real people."

"Wow, what a party," Nava said while watching the scene over Mae's shoulder. "Can we get in?"

"It's too crowded for our cloaks. Look at this. A heavyset older woman is lying on the floor, drunk or dead."

They watched as a portal opened next to the woman, robotic arms came through and lifted the woman gently off the floor then retreated back through the portal. Her young handsome man followed close beside her.

"It does look fun," said Mae. "But I don't think we'll learn anything useful from these people. I'll keep looking."

While Mae searched for something more useful, Nava used her SpyPort to watch the party. She watched handsome and voluptuous robotic waiters and waitresses roam the hall, serving food and drink, collecting dirty dishes. Each uniformed in the most suggestive and revealing costumes, all of them flirting with the clients. And the clients showed their appreciation by fondling and groping the robots freely.

"It looks fun, but the people don't look very happy," Nava stated. "Oh, look, that lady who passed out is back and she looks fresh and lively. What did they do to her?"

"She doesn't look sober, but she looks energetic and excited. What did they give her?" replied Mae.

As they watched, the woman walked with her man into one of the darker back corners of the hall and found a large sofa. She pulled down her panties, revealing the skin-colored Sinsi-Suit underneath, and lay back on the couch with her legs wide.

"We shouldn't watch this," said Nava, holding the SpyPort steady on the scene.

"That's enough. I have better things to do," said Mae, returning to her search.

"Okay. You're right," said Nava, flushed and excited, turning the SpyPort away from the couple. "Oh my goodness. Mae, you have to see this."

Mae looked at Nava's SpyPort to see a full-fledged orgy happening on sofas and chairs and rugs in one back corner of the ballroom.

"Enough," cried Mae with an excited laugh after watching the scene for several minutes. "I can't take any more. Watch something else. Look for something useful," she continued, after recovering herself. "I can't find anything but homes, restaurants, shops, and resorts. No schools or hospitals, no government buildings of any kind. No offices or factories, no grocery stores. So many spas and ballrooms, all filled to capacity. Every restaurant I've found has entertainment and dancing. Plenty of luxury resorts on beautiful beaches, half the people young and beautiful, the other half not so much. It's the same scene everywhere. Maybe this is a resort area and I should expand my search."

"I get the feeling that all these people do is parade around in their vanity all day," commented Nava. "They party all night and have sex with their favorite holographic partner or partners whenever they feel like it."

"Party till you drop and then party some more. It sounds fun to me," said Mae with a funny smile. "But too much will make you sick."

"It probably gets boring after a while," Nava added. "They look like they're in a frantic hurry to find something. Like they have no idea how to really feel happy. Are they addicted to self-indulgence, and feeling guilty for their sin?"

"Guilt for having a good time," Mae answered. "What a crazy way to live. Their natural human desire for adventure, excitement, and sexual pleasure on one side, pulling against their religious beliefs on the other."

"Too bad they can't just relax and enjoy it," responded Nava. "It feels all wrong."

"I have found something, I think," said Mae. "Not sure what it is. Come look. There are hundreds or thousands of identical large industrial buildings. They're located in an isolated area well away from the cities. Let's see what's inside."

Nava watched over Mae's shoulder, as she guided the SpyPort inside a large building with rows of computer racks running down one side. "Those look like quantum computers and servers. The latest PortNet G-90 technology," observed Mae. "They probably provide portal control and holographic image interaction with the SinsiSuits."

"The other side of the room is filled with rows of tightly spaced redirect portal rings standing perpendicular to the wall," Mae continued. "The rings are so tightly spaced that they look like a long tube running the full length of the wall."

"Let's go look," said Nava. "I don't see anyone there. Maybe we can tap into the computer system."

Mae opened a portal with her ComPort and they entered the building.

"What are all the portal rings for?" Nava asked. "There are thousands of them."

"Imagine the millions of people and things that use portals every day. They need many millions of portals to satisfy the demand."

"How do they work? They are so close together that they can't open here."

"No, these are redirect portals that have two portal rings connected. They open a portal from one place to another without the portal ring being physically located at either location."

"Like the planet atmosphere portals?"

"That's right."

A virtual interface terminal popped up as Mae approached the computer racks. Terminals popped up at the end of every computer rack as they walked by. Mae located a computer network router mounted near the end of a rack then inserted a small device into a Universal Quantum port of the router. A green light glowed on the little device indicating an active connection to the United Worlds intelligence service.

"That should make Jack happy," said Mae. "It connects through the probe Jack sent down. I hope he gets lots of data. Let's take a look at the virtual terminal. They aren't password-protected, like they don't expect anyone to come here but technicians."

"Why have terminals here at all?" asked Nava. "Why not do everything remotely?"

"I think this is all standard off-the-shelf equipment," Mae replied, "They come with virtual terminals. Maybe no one ever does come here. Let's see what we can find."

"Search for heaven retirement," suggested Mae. "This place looks like it is mostly retirees."

Nava found another terminal and they both started browsing. "Here's something that might be good," offered Nava after a little searching. "Listen to this."

"Heaven, where your trouble-free life begins. Heaven, where every wish is delivered, every dream comes true, every worry taken care of for you."

"You're going to heaven someday. Why wait for it? Go to Heaven while you can still enjoy it."

"Do you still dream of the young women or men that refused you in your youth? You can have them in Heaven."

"Are you joking?" exclaimed Mae. "That's a sales pitch for this place."

"Excitement and pleasure uninterrupted," Nava continued with a growing smile.

"Live a life of beautiful beaches, luxurious casino resorts, and pleasure unending. Your religious commitments have been satisfied, your bonds are broken. Indulge your every fantasy. No guilt, no worry, no stress, no limits."

"Live as you've never lived before. Live the life you deserve. Make Heaven your last and greatest adventure."

"Sounds pretty sweet," Mae said. "It's a good sales pitch. Do they deliver?"

"Here's the small print," Nava continued.

"Heaven has been officially blessed by the Orthodox Waru Council of Seven Apostles for your pleasure and indulgence. Gambling, drinking, sex, debauchery, extravagance, luxury, perversion, and drugs are all sanctioned in Heaven. You have been preapproved for one of 5 luxury levels (see attached award letter) based on your net worth."

"And a note," continued Nava.

"If information about Heaven is shared with anyone, this offer will be rescinded."

"These are all rich Waru who've completely abandon their previous lives," said Mae. "Coming here is the reward for their success. They buy-in at the luxury level they can afford. And I'm guessing Heaven takes every penny they have."

"I don't think these people live long here," added Nava. "Do they know that they're coming here to indulge themselves to death?"

"Search for Cromen," suggested Mae.

"Good idea, let's see," replied Nava, typing in "Cromen Henderson," and watching the display. "Here he is," she exclaimed, surprised and excited. "Could there be more than one Cromen Henderson?"

"What does it say?" responded Mae.

"It says that he has been condemned to Hell for crimes against God. That must be him. What does it mean?" asked Nava "Is he alive?"

"It says that his current location is Red Devil 9," offered Mae, looking over her shoulder. "So, I think he's alive."

"What's Red Devil 9?" exclaimed Nava in frustration. "And where is it?"

Chapter 26 Miss Janet

"I've got to make it good," Cromen said to himself as he walked up the grassy path to the work portal on the hillside. He arrived early for his one PM appointment with Miss Janet Crawford.

"She's got to keep me," he thought. "She is using me, why shouldn't I use her. She could be my way out of Hell."

There were only a few people on the veranda when Cromen arrived. He was admitted as soon as he announced himself outside the door. The outer door opened and he walked through an open portal into a large dressing room with two robo-attendants. The attendants removed his clothes and Cromen stood patiently while they quickly trimmed his body hair. He was seated to trim his head hair, then shaved, followed by a manicure and pedicure. He was gently scrubbed in a hot soapy shower, both patted and blown dry, rubbed with body lotion, perfumed, and dressed.

Cromen felt good, laughed for the first time in days. "What kind of person wants so much help taking a shower?" he thought to himself. "I did enjoy it though."

He smiled at his image in the mirror. "I'll try to enjoy everything that happens here including Miss Janet. I have no choice, I have no guilt."

His blue denim pants, held by a brown leather belt, just touched the comfortable brown leather shoes. A red cotton polo shirt showed off his physique. He admired himself in the mirror and flexed his muscles a little.

A chime sounded after a few idle minutes and a portal opened nearby. Cromen stepped through without waiting to be directed. Soft music played as he advanced into the room, natural light entered through very tall picture windows that formed a triangle tapering upward from the black marble floor to the apex of the ceiling. Small flowering trees in large colorful planters shaded the patio around a fountain splashed indoor swimming pool which decorated the sunny side of the room. A large Jacuzzi was visible on the other side of the window from the pool.

"Cromen, I think you're pretty cute and hope we can get along," Miss Janet said coldly, entering the room and walking around him slowly.

Cromen relaxed, took a deep breath, and tried to give a muscular pose.

She smiled in appreciation. "I have only two rules. Live by these rules and we'll get along just fine. Number one is: always follow my directions exactly. Number two is: don't ask questions."

"Yes mam," replied Cromen. "Your rules are my rules and I will obey them."

"Good, I just wanted to make that clear. Come Cromen, let's have a little snack," she said, directing him to an elegantly prepared lunch of lightly smoked salmon and fresh raspberries.

They sat on the veranda overlooking the sea and coastline. "You have such a beautiful home," offered Cromen, trying to make casual conversation.

"Thank you, it is nice, but it gets lonely when no one else is here."

"Such a beautiful woman should have many admirers."

Miss Janet smiled. "Thank you. I'm too busy for complicated relationships. That's what you're for, Cromen. Do you think you can make me feel good when I want it?"

"I will do my best," he replied with a devilish grin calculated to show his physical interest.

"Shall we enjoy the Jacuzzi?" she offered, her eyes not hiding her intentions.

"Yes ,Mam," Cromen replied. "Where is my suit?"

"You won't need one," Janet said as her gown slipped off her shoulders revealing a small white bikini."

"Wow, you look amazing," Cromen said with passion while removing his clothes.

"Thank you, I love your strong young body," Miss Janet replied casually.

Cromen didn't wait for Janet to make the first move. He wanted to make it as good as he could for her. They began in the Jacuzzi and finished on the garden couch, but it wasn't really over. Janet kept Cromen overnight, he was just what she wanted.

"I'm a working girl, Cromen," she told him the next morning. "I won't be here most of the time. You're free to roam around and enjoy my estate. There are beautiful places to swim and hike. Explore all you like, get some exercise, and don't get bored."

"It is such a beautiful place. I'm sure I can find something to enjoy."

"I would like that," she replied sternly. "And it would be best for you. Relax, enjoy yourself and we won't have any problems."

Cromen explored the house thoroughly as soon as she left. There were no portals or portal controls anywhere open to him, no computer, no ComPort. "How does she control the portal system?" he asked himself. "Is everything controlled by her voice? A portal is the only way out of this. I will find a way out, and by force if necessary."

The beach was beautiful soft white sand, the sea sparkling clear and comfortably warm. Cromen swam a little and then ran down the beach running and running, until the white sand was broken by a small rocky peninsula jutting out from the jungle into the water. An overgrown trail through the vegetation led Cromen to a rocky overlook with a 10-meter drop off to the water below. He could see a path leading down to the beach on the other side, but he decided to sit on the rocks and meditate for a while.

The dark serpentine rock was flat and smooth, with a comfortable area to sit. As he crossed his legs in preparation to meditate, the zoom of a brightly colored hummingbird speeding past his right ear caught his attention. Turning to watch it hover on a flowering bush near a large mango tree, he noticed names in the bark of the tree, men's and women's names. Some were very old and almost covered by bark growth, others looked very fresh.

"They're like me," he thought to himself. "People trapped in this perverted world without hope."

He looked for and found a piece of sharp rock, and without knowing exactly why, Cromen carved his own name there in the tree bark with the others.

"Where did all these people go?" Cromen thought to himself. "Does she just rent them for a time and send them back to Hell when she's finished with them? Or is there something worse? Did they meet their end here in some terrible way?"

Janet returned in the late afternoon and spent an hour talking on the ComPort. Cromen overheard the other person repeatedly call her Sister Janet. "Make it happen or I'll have your nuts in a jar," Miss Janet yelled angrily before closing the portal.

She raged around the house, very agitated. "Come with me."

With an angry gaze, she directed Cromen to a locked room he hadn't been in before. "Take off your clothes," she demanded.

Cromen stripped quickly, observing what he first thought was an exercise room, but then recognized it as more of a torture chamber.

"I didn't agree to this," said Cromen beginning to panic as she strapped his ankles to the floor and then his wrists to straps from above, one at a time until he was in a standing spread-eagle position. "This wasn't part of the deal," he said with rising fear.

"There is no deal!" she exclaimed in her most irritating voice. "You are mine for whatever I want."

That terribly angry voice grated on Cromen nerves. "Who is she to hold such power over me," he wondered. "How could a modern society allow such a person to exist?"

She didn't hurt him much, her sadistic actions redirected her anger into a sexual frenzy that lasted late into the night, leaving her exhausted. She wasn't there when Cromen got up in the morning.

The next day passed more calmly in a comfortable routine, robots cleaning and dressing him, Cromen acting the affectionate puppy when she was home, and swimming and exploring when she was away.

"We're throwing a little party tonight, Cromen," she said on coming home that day. "You'll need to be on your best behavior."

"Yes, Miss Janet. You can count on me."

"I'd like you to wear this," Miss Janet told him, coming forward and buckling a silver collar around his neck. "You won't be on the leash the whole time," she added with a devious smile.

"There are special party rules," she continued seriously in her irritating command voice. "You are only permitted to talk with people if they talk to you first or if I direct you. You will go with and obey anyone that I give you to. You already know the rest, obey my commands, and don't ask questions of anyone."

"You have my word," Cromen said, bowing with a smile.

Cromen counted fourteen couples, but couldn't be sure. Each couple arrived like Cromen and Janet, held together with a leash. Older men or women each holding a chain with a beautiful young woman or man attached. He could feel the sexual tension in the house and found it nearly as terrifying as miss Janet with her whip. He soon realized that this was a kind of swinger party, where they swing, not with each other, but with each other's pets. Cromen knew he would have to perform.

"I'm a sex slave," hc thought to himself with growing awareness of the women that were watching him intently. They felt more like adversaries to him than potential lovers.

A well-built blond woman tugged at her companion's chain and approached Miss Janet. She was quite attractive physically. Her eyes looked much older than her face or body, and her eyes were looking at Cromen. "Relax, breath, pose casually to give her a good view," thought Cromen to himself. "I am only here to please. And I want to keep Miss Janet happy."

"Good evening Miss Janet. I like your man. He looks fresh."

"Hello, Phyllis. Yes, I've only had him for a few days now. He's been a good performer, so far."

"What a perfect muscular young body," said Miss Phyllis, looking at Cromen with hungry eyes.

She had a jabbing demanding attitude. To Cromen she felt like a boxer in a lady suit, but he couldn't help notice her beautiful full breasts and buttocks. The coldness of her eyes and speech made him cringe at the thought, but he knew his place and smiled in response to her gaze.

"I have a few things to talk over with Miss Phyllis," said Miss Janet to Cromen. "You sit here and talk with Pablo while we chat."

Their leashes were released and Pablo and Cromen sat down on the cushioned wicker couch.

"I guess we're allowed to talk. I'm Cromen," he said, offering a hand to shake.

"Pablo," replied the tall slender young man, shaking Cromen's hand without interest. "They are watching, so talk low and without emotion."

"How long have you been with Miss Phyllis?" asked Cromen in a whisper.

"About 5 months now," Pablo spoke softly in reply. "You're new."

"Yes, I've been here less than a week. Did you come from Hell?" Cromen asked.

"All the pets come from Hell," replied Pablo, as though everyone knows that.

"Who are these people?"

"Shhhhh. They're all Elders of the Orthodox Waru religion," whispered Pablo. "We're not supposed to know that. So be careful."

Pablo could read the surprise on Cromen's face. "Laugh like we're talking about sex or something. Don't look too serious."

Cromen took a breath, smiled, and then laughed a little out loud. Pablo laughed and nodded in reply.

The women heard them laugh and looked up from their somewhat heated negotiations, both scowled at the men before returning to their conversation.

"Tell them we were talking about sex. They will ask."

"Do you know where we are, Pablo?"

"I think we are on a planet called Eden," he replied. "I think all the Elders live here."

"I've never heard of it," Cromen said with a fake smile, trying to contain the emotional impact of what Pablo told him. He took a deep breath. "Where do we go when we leave here?"

"No one knows. I think some go back to Hell. We only see each other at these parties. You're here at one party and someone else is with Miss Janet at the next party. She changes pets often."

"How many elders are there in the church?" asked Cromen.

"I would guess hundreds of thousands. I wonder if they all have pets?"

"This must be a crazy renegade group," Cromen stated. "How could a church allow their ministers to enslave people for their personal benefit and sexual pleasure?"

"I can't imagine the church permits this behavior," replied Pablo with a handsome and obviously much-practiced smile.

"I couldn't have imagined a church that enslaves people in Hell either," said Cromen. "But here we are."

Miss Janet and Miss Phyllis finished their conversation and returned to Cromen and Pablo.

"You be good to Miss Phyllis," said Miss Janet, handing Cromen's leash to Miss Phyllis.

"And you take good care of my Pablo," Miss Phyllis said with suspicion. "I need him back in good condition."

Miss Janet laughed and led Pablo away to visit with other guests.

"Let's eat," Miss Phyllis commanded, leading Cromen to the buffet table. She ate a big steak with mashed potatoes and gravy. Cromen had a few pieces of sushi and some vegetables.

"You need to eat more than that to keep your strength up," said Miss Phyllis returning to the table for pie and ice cream.

Cromen thought she seemed nervous or frightened and he didn't like the amount of scotch whiskey she was drinking. They meandered from group to group. The conversation was always about the pets, what they found attractive about one or another and how well the different pets performed their service. Stories were told of past pets, remembered for some remarkable physical feature or ability, bringing smiles and dreamy looks for some and hilarious laughter for others.

Cromen felt sick and angry. He wanted to physically beat them all. It was like a dog show but for pet humans, the owners judging the other person's pet on the sexual potential. Cromen practiced his best smile and waited his time.

The party began to break up after about three hours. It had been enough time to eat, share a few stories, and exchange bed-mates. Miss Phyllis drunkenly thanked her hostess and grabbed a plate of chicken wings to bring home. She opened a portal and lead Cromen directly into her bedroom chamber.

"Undress," she commanded, sitting on the bedside with the plate of chicken wings on her lap.

"I don't want to do this," thought Cromen to himself as he removed his shoes. "I am a pawn in some strange game where I don't know the rules or the stakes. But her body looks great," he thought while removing his shirt.

He smiled, taking off his pants and thinking, "I have no alternative but to play my part and hope for a way to escape."

As he approached Miss Phyllis, still sitting on the bedside, she coughed and looked surprised. The plate of wings dropped to the floor and she began choking. Her hands reached for her throat, her eyes bulged, she began jerking violently. Cromen grabbed her, turned her around, and gave a quick squeeze to her lower abdomen, hoping to dislodge whatever was stuck in her throat. Nothing happened. As she lost consciousness a portal opened next to her, a robo-nurse lifted Miss Phyllis from the floor and retreated back through the portal. Cromen lunged beneath the mechanical arms and passed through the portal before it closed.

The robo-nurse placed Miss Phyllis on an examination table while Cromen crouched under the table trying to be quiet and stay out of the way. The robot ignored his presence. One side of the room was open and he could see other examination rooms across a corridor. Cromen found a simple belt buckle on his collar that was easily undone and removed it from his neck. He Crawled carefully from under the table and stepped naked into the corridor. The robo-nurse acted like he wasn't there.

The corridor ran some distance in each direction, terminating at another corridor lined with examination rooms. Cromen walked cautiously along the corridor, feeling vulnerable in his nakedness. He glanced into each room he passed until finding a man's clothes hanging on the wall beside an examination table. He quickly dressed in the expensive clothing that was a bit too large, then he began exploring.

Passing several side corridors, he turned right at the end, thinking it was the outer wall of the building. He followed the corridor and was rewarded by finding what he hoped was a door to the outside. There were no handles to pull or knobs to turn. Just a flat metal door. It didn't move when he pushed, and he pushed as hard as he could. It wouldn't open for him.

Cromen examined the wall, floor, and ceiling for a control panel or switch. There was nothing. As he was considering options and thinking about looking somewhere else, Cromen noticed letters scratched on the door. It was crude, not easy to see, he could just make it out, B E L T.

"Belt," he said aloud. "I get it. I need one of their belts."

Cromen hurried from examination room to examination room until he found a belt on the floor, one of the control belts the masters always wore.

"There must have been others like me who came this way." Cromen thought to himself, feeling hopeful for the first time, hopeful that he might actually escape his captivity. The door slid open automatically as he approached and Cromen stepped cautiously through to find light rain falling in the warm fragrant air. The doors slid shut behind him as he walked out.

Chapter 27 Ordainment of John Behan

In the year 226 EE (2296 CE), 208 years before Cromen met Nava, John Behan was ordained as Deacon First Class in the Orthodox Church of the Seven Apostles. This was during the middle of the Great Expansion, at a time when the United Worlds was evaluating organizations for immigration to the new worlds that were becoming available through the UW planet terraforming program. It was a time before RingTech was available to the general public, before blocking fields had been developed, a time when RingTech was more tightly regulated by the United Worlds.

All major countries of the Earth had their own new planet, all major religions had a new planet. Everybody wanted one, every organization, tribe, ethnic group, religion, culture, political party, sports league, and special interest club wanted a planet of their own. Applicants were evaluated and ranked according to their size and potential to develop a successful self-reliant colony on another world. The group's acceptance of the Arcadian Path philosophy was an important consideration to the United Worlds in their ranking of the potential candidates.

The Waru Church of Seven Apostles had applied many times for a world of their own, but other racial, religious, and political groups were competing for these same worlds. The Waru had sufficient population and wealth, but other applicants had much better acceptance of the Arcadian Path. This is all that held the Waru back, this was the deciding factor in the rejection of their applications.

This is how John Behan justified bombing the New York City parade. The United Worlds had rejected the Waru application for another world. "A world which the Waru deserved," thought John.

They had given the planet to a smaller group only because that group was dedicated to the Arcadian Path.

The episode of bombing the parade and the Elders inviting him to join the Orthodox Waru had elevated John's spirits greatly. But waiting for his ordainment ceremony was difficult. John spent little time outside and watched his windows constantly, fearful the police might arrive and destroy his new opportunity. The days before ordainment passed slowly.

John arrived 30 minutes early for his ordainment appointment. At 3 pm he was admitted into a large office where Elder Jane welcomed him from her seat in a large ornate chair three steps up on a raised platform. A silver carpet ran down the stairs, then a few meters onto the floor in front. The Banner of the Seven Apostles hung behind her. Six Elders stood three to each side of Elder Jane to witness John's ordainment.

She directed him to stand in front of her without speaking to him. "Kneel," was her first word to him.

John knelt where Elder Jane indicated on the carpet in front of her.

"John Behan, you will affirm your devotion to the Orthodox Church of the Seven Apostles by your commitment to the eight Sacred Promises. They are slightly different than the seven Sacred Promises of the non-Orthodox Waru."

John nodded his head affirmatively.

"John Behan, do you swear to be faithful to the one true God, and to the word of God as revealed to you by the Profit and Seven Apostles?"

"I do so swear," he replied, thinking there was nothing new in that promise.

"Do you swear to respect and obey the authority of the Orthodox Waru Clergy?"

"I do swear."

"Do you swear that you will not commit Murder or Rape unless so directed or permitted by the Orthodox Waru Clergy?"

"Yes, I swear," replied John, noticing that permission for murder and rape was not in the seven normal Sacred Promises used by the non orthodox Waru.

"Do you swear that you will not take the property of others, not steal or cheat people of their money or property, including but not limited to embezzlement, fraud, tax evasion, robbery, and vandalism; unless so directed or permitted by the Orthodox Waru Clergy."

"I do so swear," said John, wondering when they give permission for these things.

"Do you swear that you will not lie or intentionally deceive another by speaking a falsehood, unless so directed or permitted by the Orthodox Waru Clergy?"

"I do so swear."

"There are three promises for which violation is unforgivable," she continued. "Violate these promises and you will be sent directly to Hell. As church leaders, we have an image to maintain and we have secrets to protect."

"I understand," John stated with a nod, wondering what was coming next.

"Do you swear, under the penalty of going to Hell, that you will never allow a layperson to catch you sinning in any form?"

"I do swear," replied John, unsure of the significance of the question.

"Do you swear, under the penalty of going to Hell, that you will never tell a layperson anything about the Governance of the Church of the Seven Apostles, how we are organized, or anything about our church administration?"

"I do so swear," replied John, curiosity knitting his brow.

"John Behan, do you swear, under the penalty of going to Hell, that you will never divulge the existence of, or any information contained in the 8th Sacred Scripture, to any layperson, or to divulge information regarding your specific sin level to any church official below you."

John looked puzzled. Elder Jane nodded at him with a friendly smile.

"I do so swear," he replied with a hesitant look.

"Rise Deacon First Class John Behan. Welcome to the holy circle of the Orthodox Church of Seven Apostles," Elder Jane said smiling.

John stood up. All the officials present came forward and embraced him saying, "Welcome, Brother John," and, "Good to have you, Brother."

"We need to explain a few things about the organization," said Elder Jane after the welcoming had died down.

John focused on Elder Jane, giving his full attention.

"You are now a member of the Holy Circle, an Orthodox member of the Church of the Seven Apostles. As a trusted confidante, secrets will be revealed to you, surprising, if not shocking secrets. What I tell you is the truth, truth which will both enrich and complicate your life."

Elder Jane paused a moment and looked seriously into John's eyes before continuing.

"God did not stop speaking to the Profit John Newton after the 7th scripture. There was an 8th and final Apostle who brought Sacred Scripture. The 8th scripture defines the church hierarchy and administrative organization, and it defines the level of sin each of us is permitted. As an Orthodox member of the Church of Seven Apostles, you have earned the right to forgiveness eternal for your sins. But only for those sins permitted to your rank of Deacon First Class."

John looked at her with surprise and skepticism, feeling guilty for some of his past behavior. Sure, he masturbated sometimes, and rarely even made love with a woman. Who didn't?

"May I read the 8th Scripture?" asked John.

"You may read the sections applicable to a Deacon First class or below," replied Elder Jane. "The 8th Scripture is divided by organizational level. Each level has different sin permissions. You are only permitted to know the details of your sin level and that of the levels below you."

"As a Deacon first class, almost any sin you commit which doesn't harm another church member or official is acceptable behavior."

"The 8th Scripture also defines your salary as a percentage of church revenue based on the number of Deacons. You won't need to worry about money," she concluded.

"It feels like a dream. I need to rethink my entire existence. But I like it," John smiled. "It is enlightening ... and exciting."

"It is good that you see it that way," smiled the Elder. "We're all happy to have you. Elder White is your direct supervisor, he'll explain your duties and get you settled in. Again, welcome to the fold."

"It's about control," Elder White said while directing John to his new office. "It is our responsibility to provide the control that they lack."

"Are the rules of sin only tools to control the people?"

"It is one method of control," replied Elder White. "It's for their own good. Without this control, our society would deteriorate into bedlam."

John's elevation from faithful Waru layperson into the holy circle of the Orthodox Waru brought a whole new world of opportunity, professional and personal.

John had ideas, ideas the Orthodox Waru leaders liked.

He was instrumental in increasing the number of Waru Deacons and Elders spying at the highest levels of the United Worlds Government. "The more spies we have inside the United Worlds government, the better protected we are from unjustified persecution," he argued.

It wasn't hard to get Elder White to appreciate and support John's plan, but it wasn't easy to accomplish.

The United Worlds had become increasingly hesitant to hire or promote Waru employees due to the Waru objection to the Arcadian Path.

John solved this problem by creating the Reformed Church of the Seven Apostles (RCSA). The "Reformers" claimed to embrace the Arcadian Path, while still holding faith in the teaching of the Seven Scriptures. John had the Reformers condemned publicly by the church and expelled from the normal Waru Church of the Seven Apostles.

The Reformers blended in and became trusted members of the United Worlds society. In a few years, the Reformers rose in positions of authority as engineers, scientists, and administrators. Reformers became the largest single religious group employed by the United Worlds government, and every one was a spy.

The Waru had another significant problem at this time as is illustrated by this news article from that period.

"Apostle indicted on child molestation charges," read the headline. "Apostle Carl Johnson of the Waru Church of the Seven Apostles was arrested today as he left the Church of Seven Apostles temple in New York City at 3:45 pm local time. Police would only say that the victim was underage. The arraignment hearing is scheduled for tomorrow at 10.00 AM."

"Elder Nemin," continued the announcement, "the Church of Seven Apostles communications director, issued a brief statement. 'The accusations against Apostle Johnson are completely false,' he stated, 'and have no basis in fact. These trumped-up charges are the latest example of the United Worlds smear campaign to discredit the truth of God.' Elder Nemin did not answer questions from the press."

"The charges against Apostle Johnson follow on the heels of last week's accusation, by a Brooklyn high school junior, that he was paid to have sex with an elder of the church. Charges have not yet been filed in that case."

"This latest incident brings the number of sex abuse cases attributed to members of the Waru church to 167 for the year to date. The church paid out over 700 million dollars in sexual harassment settlements and lawyers fees last year. They continue to claim the accusations are entirely false, driven by 'greedy lawyers taking advantage of the rich and generous church.'"

Following the successful creation of the Reformed Church of the Seven Apostles, John was promoted to Elder Third Class and made Director of the Ministry of Public Perception. He established the Trusted Network News Service, determined to change public opinion of the Waru. Propaganda techniques copied from Nazi Germany and other popular fascist organizations were used extensively.

"Blame some other group for the offense you commit. Repeat the lie often enough and people will believe it," instructed Elder Behan to his staff. "Repeat your fabricated story to the public audience, repeat it over and over again. The more they hear it, the more believable the story becomes. And the truth is never as important as what the people believe."

Throughout the world, road signs, internet advertisements, radio, television, everywhere you looked were the Waru messages: "The United Worlds is lying about Waru sexual abuse; The United Worlds is trying to force the Arcadian Path on the Waru People; The United Worlds denies the existence of God; The United Worlds is forcing your children to learn the Arcadian Path religion; The United Worlds has denied the Waru a planet because of their religious beliefs."

John also increased Waru demonstrations at schools, boards of education, and government offices, to keep the unhappy Waru visible to the public.

The United Worlds General Council did eventually choose the Waru to colonize planet Beryl. There was no question that the Waru had the people and resources to build a self-sustaining colony on a new planet. But the United Worlds was concerned about the kind of life people would have under Orthodox Waru leadership. One United Worlds Council member admitted off the record that, "It was better to put these people on another planet than to keep them on Earth. They are just too disruptive to society. Let them live by themselves if they can't live with others. But we won't permit them to rename that planet. It was not created for them or their religion."

For his success in obtaining planet Beryl for the Waru, John Behan was promoted to Elder First Class and made director of the Ministry of Intelligence only two years after ordainment.

"We need a secret facility," John declared forcefully of the Apostles during the initial planning meetings for relocating to Beryl. "I want the continent of Ariel dedicated exclusively to secret research and intelligence work. We need a place well hidden from the prying eyes of the United Worlds and the Waru masses."

As director of Intelligence, John improved and increased the systematic theft of United Worlds' property and technology. And more importantly, John proposed stealing planets from the United Worlds. "We have people at all levels of government. We can control and hide anything."

The Council of Seven liked John's idea and within 3 years of moving to Beryl, terraforming began secretly on Planet Eden. The groundwork was soon laid for three other planets, all hidden by the network of Reformers spying within the United Worlds government.

The early years were a time of chaos on Beryl, with millions of homes, offices, and factories being constructed to care for the 157 million Waru that made the transfer from Earth to Beryl. Some of the less faithful Waru were agitating for a more compassionate society that included the Arcadian Path.

The Profit and Apostles looked to Elder John Behan for ideas to solve the problem created by this vocal group of unfaithful Waru.

"Eduard Alton's Arcadian Path website is bringing together many thousands of unfaithful Waru," the Profit told John. "It's disrupting our faithful congregation. Can we do something to bring these people back to the faith?"

"I don't think we can change their minds," John told him. "These people are already corrupted. The only way to stop their corrupting influence is to separate them from society."

"How can we justify removing them from society?" asked an Apostle. "The common Waru would be shocked."

"You're right," was John's reply. "The faithful Waru congregation needs a justification. Something that makes removing the unfaithful agitators appear logical and necessary."

"See what you can do about it, John," replied the Profit. "We trust your ability to make it work."

John's plan was simple. Create a blasphemous atrocity and blame the members of Eduard Alton's Arcadian Path website.

Under the name of "Robert Doone," John personally infiltrated Eduard Alton's website. His blog writings openly criticized the Waru church for violating the Arcadian Path and advocated for change. These actions gained him the support of thousands of angry unfaithful Waru.

With the full approval of the Profit and Seven Apostles, John ordered and managed the flooding of the Saint Carmen Elder Council Chamber with city sewage. The Orthodox Waru destroyed their own sacred council chamber and covered many respected Elders in excrement for the good of the Orthodox Waru church.

And it worked.

Blame was quickly directed at Eduard Alton and the people using his website, and the faithful Waru believed the story. It must have been those unfaithful Eduard Alton people who violated their sacred Council Chamber with excrement. Who else would do such a thing?

Removal of the Alton people from Waru society was carried out according to plan without disrupting the faithful Waru. An army of Watchers was created to ensure the Alton would no longer interfere with Waru society.

So impressed was the Profit Arnold that he encouraged John Behan to marry his daughter Phyllis. This marriage gave John the family connection needed for his eventual promotion to Apostle.

Chapter 28 Eden

"Call Jack," Mae said to her ComPort. There was a long pause before Jack's face appeared through a floating portal window.

"Hello, Mae. We found the spies," exclaimed Jack with excitement, "And I am happy to say that you and I aren't on the list."

"Is Smitty okay?" Mae asked with concern.

"Yes, Smitty is okay. But Bob Johnson and Phil Slater are on the list. Spies are all around us. It was hidden in plain sight in our own UW Intel admin database. Have you ever heard of the Reformed Church of the Seven Apostles?"

Jack continued after seeing blank looks from both Mae and Nava. "It's a sect that split from the Waru church hundreds of years ago. They have a website, you can check it out. The interesting thing about this religious group is their membership list, it is made up entirely of employees in the United Worlds government. There are several million members, and every one of them is spying on our government for the Orthodox Waru."

"We didn't recognize it as a list of spies until we correlated the membership with UW employees."

"It was right in front of us. Every person on the membership list works for the UW government in some form or other, including people working directly with me," said Jack, "and you, Mae."

"It's a relief," Mae confided, "to know who we can and can't trust."

"Jack, we have found Heaven to be a very interesting place," offered Mae. "The planet seems to be a retirement home for the wealthy Waru, but it's not a healthy setup. It looks like the Orthodox Waru take all the retiree's money and then encourage them to indulge themselves to death. It's all parties, rich food, drugs, and sex until they drop dead. Drugs are used to prop the people up so they can indulge some more."

"Everything we learn about these Orthodox Waru is baffling," replied Jack. "Your data tap is flowing full force. We're pulling data faster than we can analyze it. Hopefully, we will find some answers about this organization. Have you seen any indication of military defense?"

"It's a big planet," replied Mae. "But not only haven't we seen any military, but there don't seem to be any real people monitoring anything. The large industrial buildings have no people working or guarding them. There are large complexes, thousands and thousands of them, identical industrial buildings full of portals and computer systems with no one there. We haven't seen a single real person other than the retirees."

"Doesn't look like they're worried about visitors," replied Jack. "Is there anything more you can do there?"

"Maybe, but first Jack, we have found a planet called Eden. It appears to be a planet for the pleasure of the Orthodox Waru only. Heaven is for the common Waru lay people to retire and Eden is for the Orthodox leaders of the church. And Jack, we have found something strange and interesting: the Orthodox Waru are allowed to sin."

"What do you mean?"

"I mean that there is a double standard. Nava found an 8th scripture cited in the information about Eden resorts. It allows the Orthodox Waru to sin without guilt. All those sins that are forbidden the common Waru laypeople are not forbidden the clergy."

"An 8th scripture, what kind of sense does that make?" stated Jack, shaking his head like there was something loose inside. "This religion just gets weirder and weirder. So what about this planet Eden? Is there any reason to go there?"

"We're not sure. It looks fun to me, but unless we can find the location in their database, we have no way to get there."

"Jack, one of the things we found most interesting is a general guide to the separate resort levels on Eden. The rules for each level are based on the 8th scripture."

"What do you have?" Jack said with interest.

"Eden resorts are described as Exclusive Pleasure Palaces available only to the Orthodox Waru. The place they go for fun. Like a big exclusive casino resort for the entire Orthodox Waru organization. But without the unruly masses of common Waru," said Mae with a smile. "Let me read you a little from these brochures."

"There is a different brochure for each level, Novice, Pastor, Deacon, and Elder. The difference between the brochures appears to be only the level of sin permitted."

"Based on the level of sin?" Jack asked in amazement.

"Yes," continued Mae, smiling to herself. "The Orthodox Waru are permitted to sin based on their rank within the church. Listen to this."

"Level 1 – Novice sins permitted: Masturbation, pornography, alcohol, gambling."

"Are you joking with me, Mae? I'm too busy for this kind of thing," Jack interjected.

"It looks real to me, Jack. Listen to this for the Novices."

"Watch biblical classics on live view portal in the privacy of your room. Get as close as you like."

"Watch Eve seduce Adam, see the original sin in vivid live action detail."

"Watch Tamar, dressed as a prostitute, seduce her father-in-law, Judah."

"Watch Esther the beautiful slave girl show her talent in the performance that made her a queen, an amazing classic sex scene, not to be missed."

"Indulge your thirst with unlimited alcoholic beverages in every form known to man."

"Games that never stop. Whatever and whenever you like to play."

"Are you sure you're not making this up?" Jack asked again seriously.

"No, it's real and it only gets better. Level 2, the Pastor level adds the following sins: SinsiSuit sex, real sex with one opposite-sex partner at a time, without oral stimulation, and cannabis."

"Create your own fantasy sex experience," it says. "Enjoy it with the partner of your dreams. Holographic SinsiSuits provide the ultimate experience, often better than real sex. Bring your own SinsiSuit or one can be provided for you. (SinsiSuit Level four or higher Quantum Holographic interface required for optimal performance)."

"Hook up with hundreds of prospects, each one looking for the same thing you are. Just don't use your mouth."

"There is no finer bud anywhere in the galaxy than you will find in Eden."

"I'm having a hard time with this, Mae, it's like these people have embraced and institutionalized the behavior which they define and preach as immoral."

"I wonder if they feel guilty," asked Nava.

Mae continued, "Level 3, the Deacon level adds the following sins: masochism, adultery, fornication, sex with anyone (18 or older) including oral stimulation, anal sex, homosexual sex, sex with more than one partner, opium, cocaine."

"Thou may covet thy neighbor's wife. Do you lust after women or men with the desire for immoral sex? Those desires are a gift from God that should not be ignored. Enjoy it every way you like it."

"Indulge your Masochistic urges – Feel the pain, intensify your pleasure. Available in SinsiSuit and live-action."

"Everything goes, amazing venues filled with people looking for the same thing you are. Enjoy sex however you like it, whenever you like it. Partners as young as 18 are looking for you."

"24 hours a day Orgies! Drop-in and enjoy the fun. There's a party and you are always invited."

"Opium dens to help you relax. Cocaine for your energetic pleasure."

Jack was silent.

"And next," Mae continued. "Level 4, the Elder level adds the following sins: sadism, consensual sex with persons under eighteen years of age, extortion, bribery, and slavery."

"Masochists are lined up begging for your personal attention."

"Children under eighteen available, but you must bribe them. (age of children and the bribe needed may vary)."

"That is the strangest thing I have ever heard," said Jack, beginning to smile, still suspicious that Mae was joking. "Do they enjoy it less when it's not considered a sin? What do you think is the punishment for sinning above your level? Is there more?"

"That's all we have right now," Mae smiled. "They don't show anything about Apostles or Profits. But what more could they be permitted."

"Are you ready to come home?" asked Jack.

"I feel pretty safe here right now," replied Mae. "I'd like another day or two to get a better look. If that's okay with you?"

"I trust your judgment, Mae. Let me know if you need anything from me. Is there more? I've got to run."

"No, that's all we have to report," replied Mae. "Talk with you soon."

"Good luck. Keep me informed," Jack said before closing the ComPort portal.

"This is a good private spot to use for exploring the planet and the computer systems," said Mae with a smile. "Let's see what we can find."

"Should I try to access my email?" Nava asked.

"Yeah, give yours a try," said Mae. "Mine is only working through our probe. My email on this computer doesn't connect to the right routers, or something."

"Could we hack into somebody else's account?" asked Nava, "We have a lot of control from these terminals."

"We seem to have administrative rights," added Mae. "Try the Profits email."

"Maybe send the 8th Scripture our to the world directly from him," suggested Nava.

"Ooh, That would be a nice surprise," smiled Mae. "See what you can do with that while I search for other ways to control or disrupt their systems."

"I found it, it's simple," offered Nava after a time of intense scrutiny of the email settings. "I can log in to the Profit's emails account. Should I send the eighth scripture to only the Waru groups, or to the world? The world group includes many millions of email addresses outside the Waru church."

"Good work, Nava," Mae said with a smile. "Send it to everyone you can.

"Should I send the email now?" asked Nava. "We've been here playing with their system long enough."

"Yes," replied Mae, "Go ahead and send the email. Send it to everybody. The more the merrier."

"There it goes, the eighth Waru Scripture is on the way," said Nava with a big smile. "That will surprise a lot of people. They won't believe it."

"See if your email account works. Send an email to your parents if you can," said Mae. "They'll be worried about you. Then we'll move to another location."

"It looks like my email went through to my mom." said Nava after a few minutes.

"They might come looking for us when they see the eighth scripture has been revealed," commented Mae. "Let's find another location similar to this one and get something to eat on the way. It could be a long night."

"Their buffets look good? Can we maneuver around the real people," asked Nava.

"I think we can. The holograms and robots shouldn't mind," replied Mae.

Chapter 29 Raining Molten Magma

"Good morning. This is Jami Rogers with the United World's Public News Service."

"There are reports this morning of a major attack on the world of Beryl. No one has claimed responsibility for the attack. Here is our reporter on the scene."

"Good morning, this is Amy Sniderfield, in Behan City, Beryl. Worshipers had just finished prayers and were retiring when the sky burst open. The video you are watching is from a hotel rooftop looking across the city. In the distance, you can see bright flaming blobs of molten magma raining down through the atmosphere impacting on the outskirts of the city. Explosions rock the image as the shock waves from the magma impact reached the recorder. You can hear loud rumbling vibrations as the flaming terror moved west, raining down on city, town, and field, smashing and crashing down on the helpless people below."

"As you can see, there has been an enormous loss of human life, large sections of the city have been buried under the molten rock and shock waves have devastated an area around the impact sites. The Profit Hendon called for calm and said that he will personally ensure the people responsible are caught and brought to justice."

"Thank you, Amy," Rogers said, taking up the story again. "UW RingTech engineers say it would require a large redirect portal with the safety features disabled. Either someone has built their own portal system or someone inside the UW RingTech Portal Administration is collaborating with the perpetrators."

"United Worlds President Angela Congo said that medical assistance and disaster recovery aid is already on the scene and more assistance is on the way. She has requested an audience with Beryl's ambassador to discuss the attack on Beryl."

"Stay tuned to the UW Public News Service to get up-to-date information as this tragic story unfolds."

Jack turned off the view screen and turned to President Congo sitting in his office. "That's all the information we have right now. We don't know any more than the news outlets."

"Did they attack themselves?" asked the President. "What kind of strategy is that?"

"If they want popular support for leaving the UW," speculated Jack, "this might do it for them. They have issued a statement blaming the UW for the attack and declaring independence."

"But their own people," replied Madam President. "It's hard to believe this of anyone."

"We've had a lot of surprises from the Orthodox Waru recently," Jack replied.

"We can't wait for more surprises like this," President Congo stated firmly to Jack. "Their ambassador is stalling. We need to stop them before more innocent people are killed."

"The only opportunity to capture the Profit and Apostles is during a sermon," replied Jack. "They appear in public during their daily sermons, perched way up on an enormous pulpit thirty and forty meters above the floor. A blocking field envelopes the central pulpit for twenty meters around."

"Do whatever you need to Jack," the President replied. "We must get this stopped."

"We could open a redirect portal big enough to drop the entire blocked area around their throne tower into the vacuum of space, but that might be too shocking for the general public. And there would be civilian casualties."

"I am open to that option," she replied, "but only as a last resort. What else can you do?"

"The next sermon is tomorrow at 10 am local time," Jack replied. "The Profit and Apostles should be there on the pulpit. A well-timed assault may work by dropping through the blocking field from above. But my confidence in success is low. They probably have quick escape portals ready at the push of a button. But we will try."

"We need to do something," President Congo replied. "Have you had any luck finding where they live?"

"Nothing yet, we suspect they live on another secret world, planet Eden, which we are just beginning to investigate. Our agents on planet Heaven have given us access to Heaven's information servers. We hope to know more, very soon."

"Two planets, Jack?"

"Yes, mam."

"Give me regular updates," the president commanded nicely as she opened a portal and left Jack to his planning.

The Space Marine Special Operations Team-1 staging and action zone was inside a large industrial building. Multiple overhead cranes provided flexibility in mission configuration.

Today the floor was configured with one portal ring flat in the center of the floor, seven identical portal rings formed a circle around the center. The positions were calculated carefully to ensure each portal opened directly above the Profit or one of the Apostles. Eight ropes hung to the floor from a frame three meters above. The extra rope was coiled neatly on the floor beside each one of the eight portal rings.

Large view screens showed multiple images inside the cathedral. One from directly above the pulpit, and three looking at the pulpit from different audience viewpoints.

They should arrive soon," Jack announced, watching the clock carefully. "It's ten now, they usually arrive within a couple of minutes. Here they come."

Clouds of mist seen on the view panels enveloped the entire forty-meter pulpit structure. Lights flashed and the mist faded revealing the Profit in full regalia standing with raised arms looking out on the congregation. Finely dressed Apostles with arms raised stood on each of the seven platforms projecting from the tower ten meters below the Profit.

"We go in three minutes," ordered the Marine Captain. "Give them a little time to get comfortable."

"I bring the most serious news," began the Profit. "Our God has been attacked again by the United Worlds. Our planet and our people have been attacked. Will this persecution of the true people of God ever stop?" raged the Profit, his mood light beaming blood-red rays out from atop his throne.

'Ready," commanded the captain, waiting for the Profit's next sentence to begin.

"Good and faithful Waru," the Profit continued.

"Go," ordered the Captain.

Eight portals opened simultaneously, Marines jumped through and swiftly slid down their ropes towards the Profit and seven Apostles. Halfway down, the Profit heard them and pushed his escape button. Clouds of vapor enveloped the marines sliding down from above. The Profit and seven

Apostles were gone before a single marine set foot on the pulpit. Jack had failed.

An announcement was made by the Orthodox Waru council the following morning. "Good and faithful Waru. Due to the Alton people's continued assistance of the United Worlds' effort to undermine our sovereignty, Profit Hendon has ordered all people of the Altonville communities to be relocated."

Chapter 30 Another World

It was late at night when Cromen followed Miss Phyllis through the emergency hospital portal, but it felt like mid-day here as he looked out across the concrete pavement. Rows of enormous single-story buildings blocked his view in every direction. Each building is identical to the other, huge light brown rectangular featureless blocks. No windows, no roof overhang, no pipes or fixtures, only the one small door interrupted the plain smooth walls everywhere.

Cromen looked around and walked back to the door he'd come out of. It opened, he looked down the corridor of emergency rooms, then stepped back outside again. "Just checking," he said to himself.

A Large arrow was scratched clearly in the paint of the metal door. "Follow or not follow?" Cromen thought to himself. "It's crude, not made by any official. If there is someone else here, I might as well find out who they are."

Seeing nothing more interesting than the arrow on the door, Cromen started cautiously jogging in the direction the arrow pointed. He didn't know where he was or what might come next, but Cromen had never felt more relieved in his life. The desperation of his enslavement being slowly replaced by crazy unrealistic hope brightening the darker corners of his mind.

Crude arrows were scratched into every door he came to. Buildings were more run down as he progressed through the seemingly endless maze of concrete buildings. Walls were crumbling, small bushes sprouted from cracks in the pavement. Up seventeen rows of buildings and down thirteen he followed the arrows until he came to a door without an arrow. There was a five-pointed star scratched in its surface.

Cromen looked at the door and hesitated. "I've come this far, I can't back out now," he thought out loud, deciding to face whoever had led him here, rather than hide without knowing.

The door opened automatically as he approached holding the control belt in his hand. The exam rooms he saw were a little different from the ones he had entered with Miss Phyllis. It was quiet and only partially lit. Dirty dishes were stacked neatly along the wall. There was complete silence. "Hello," he said loudly with a clear and friendly voice, "I come in peace. Is anybody here?"

"What? Who's there?" came a surprised reply.

"I followed your arrows," said Cromen.

A slender man with very dark skin and kinky black hair walked out of an examination room, then stopped and looked at Cromen.

"Where did you come from?" asked the man, looking suspiciously at Cromen's expensive clothes that didn't fit.

"I was a slave on Hell," Cromen replied. "I escaped by following my master through an emergency hospital portal. Then I followed the door arrows and found myself here."

Well," said the man with a softening face, beginning to smile. "Come on in. My name's David."

Cromen extended his hand, "I'm Cromen, and I'm very happy to meet you, David."

"You're a happy surprise for me, too," David replied, clasping Cromen hand, the smile growing on his face. "I haven't seen or talked with anyone for several weeks."

"How did you come here?"

"Like you, I jumped into an emergency hospital portal."

"Is there anyone else here?" Cromen queried.

"Not that I know of."

"Won't they come after me?"

"Why do they care about you?" asked David. "Are you so important?"

"I was a slave on loan to this lady, Miss Phyllis. She choked and I followed her through the emergency hospital portal. I think she died."

"So, Miss Phyllis croaks of natural causes and you disappear," David responded, "They don't know what happened to you, maybe she ported you someplace or you drowned trying to escape. There are plenty more pets where you came from. They won't give you a second thought."

"Well, okay," said Cromen. "Maybe you're right, they haven't followed you."

"No, I think you're safe here for the time being. Who knows what the future might bring."

Cromen relaxed and felt a little better. "How do you live here? You can't just go into a hospital room and ask for Salmon Patties, can you?" He asked with a smile.

"It was hard at first, I almost starved to death," David said with a serious look, "I learned to sneak into the recovery wards where they give people actual food. But now I have it delivered."

"Have it delivered?" queried Cromen smiling. "Then maybe I can have Salmon Patties?"

"Sure, whatever you like," responded David. "Come on, we'll go over to the computer center and order up. I'm kind of hungry myself."

David led the way.

"You appear to live in an abandoned hospital. Are there no computer terminals here?" Cromen asked.

"None that work for me, I think the only computer interface in this old hospital building is through the robotic doctors or nurses. I never could figure out how to get one of them to place an order for me. I even tried acting like a patient but they ignored me. Like they're set to only work on their assigned patients."

"Why is your building vacant?" asked Cromen as they walked along between the buildings.

"It's old and deteriorating. The equipment is more advanced in the new hospitals. I think they built a new one then abandoned this one. Maybe it's easier to build a new one than refurbish the old."

"I saw a building under construction on my way here," replied Cromen. "It appeared to be growing by itself. There were no workers or equipment visible."

"It's a 3-D printer that has a portal around the print head and it prints through the portal. Who knows where the machine is located. Probably near the source of the material."

David led the way into a building that looked just like all the others. There was an arrow scratched on the door and the letter "C" scratched below it. Inside were rows and rows of computer racks.

David led them to the end of one rack and a holographic terminal appeared. "I've created a shortcut here, do you see," David pointed out the button labeled "Food."

"It took nearly a week to find how to get food sent to the building where I'm living," remarked David. "I must have sent food to a thousand different places before I discovered the right room number."

Cromen watched intently as David navigated to the menu and searched on Salmon Patties.

"Anything you would like with that?" asked David.

"How about Brussels Sprouts in garlic sauce and a piece of pecan pie."

"You got it. That sounds good to me. I'll double the order."

"Something to drink?"

"Just water," responded Cromen.

"I feel like celebrating. How about a bottle of Glen Locklan whiskey."

"You can order whiskey?" Cromen asked in surprise.

"It's on the menu, so yes, we can order whiskey."

"I'll set the delivery time for ten minutes from now and we are ready to go."

The food was waiting on the side table when they arrived back at David's living quarters.

"You have it pretty good here," said Cromen, enjoying his meal and feeling better than he had for some time.

"Things have improved," David replied with a smile, raising his glass in a toast to Cromen. "I spent my first few nights hiding from the robot nurses and stealing bags of liquid nutrients from the patients. It may be nutritious, but the stuff tastes horrible and hunger drove out to explore."

"Have you tried anything else?" asked Cromen. "Do you think we can open a portal and get ourselves out of here?"

"I think it's possible," David replied. "I had to take care of food and shelter first. But lately, I've been trying to learn how to operate the transportation portal control system. I have access to the system, but I'm confused about the controls."

"How did you direct food here?" asked Cromen.

"That was through a hospital patient care system. It has a patient interface for ordering. I only had to provide a room number."

"Can you select a destination from a map on the portal control system?" asked Cromen.

"It's there, but I can't identify the locations. The only worlds available are Beryl, Hell, Heaven, and Eden. We're on Eden, and I'm not going back to hell. If I show up on Beryl, I would be returned to Hell. I've never heard of Heaven before."

"Well, that's weird. I've never heard of it either. Is there some way to send a message?"

"I've tried," David replied, "but it doesn't find the email addresses that I use. Like it only connects to these five worlds."

"About half of these buildings are dedicated to transport redirect portals," David said as they sat enjoying their food and drink. "There must be millions of portal rings. But we can only open portals on or between these four worlds."

"Who owns this place?" Cromen asked thoughtfully. "Is it all part of the Waru church?

"I'd say yes," replied David. "It looks to me like they've created their own secret worlds, separate from the United Worlds."

"It seems impossible," Cromen responded, feeling a little dizzy with the realization of what brought him to this place. "Do we have access to other information?"

"I haven't found anything to be blocked from this terminal yet, but I haven't probed around for much except food and portal control."

"Can you search for a person?" asked Cromen. "Search on me, Cromen Henderson."

David found a search engine and typed in Cromen's name. "Hey, here you are," said David after a few moments. "it says you are condemned to Hell for actions against the Waru people."

"Nothing more?" Cromen asked.

"It says that you are the property of the Red Devil Corporation, assigned to the RD9 colony. That's all."

"Search on Nava Martin," said Cromen. "Just in case."

"Girlfriend?" queried David, typing in the name. "Here she is. It says that she is wanted for Crimes against God. Whatever that means. So I am guessing she's your partner in crime."

"My girlfriend, yes. But we committed no crime. Does it tell you where she is?"

"Reported to have been involved with the raid on Ariel. Whereabouts are unknown. It lists you and someone named Mae as accomplices."

"They don't have her," Cromen exclaimed with relief. "That's good, even if I don't know where she is."

"What about this raid on Ariel?" Cromen asked. "Do you have access to news or information? Have you looked for news from around the United Worlds?"

"So far I've only found the official Orthodox Waru news feed," answered David. "So the news is very biased, but let's have a look."

"Holy shit!" exclaimed David after some time searching. "Look at this, it says that the United Worlds has violated the sovereign territory of Beryl by attacking a small research facility on the continent of Ariel. No one was injured but the facility was completely destroyed in the attack."

"Mae got my message," Cromen thought to himself with satisfaction. "That's no research facility," he said "It's where they took me before sending me to Hell."

"Me too. There is something more. It says that the United Worlds has attacked the world of Beryl by sending molten magma raining down onto a large inhabited area. Thousands of people have been killed. The United Worlds has denied responsibility and has falsely accused the Orthodox Waru of committing this horrible act. Due to the escalating violence of the United Worlds toward the Waru church, the high council is declaring independence from the United Worlds and is doing everything possible to protect the people of Beryl from further aggressive action."

"What areas were destroyed?" Cromen asked, gripped with fear for his family on Beryl.

"It says that the magma destroyed the Altonville neighborhood on the outskirts of Behan City and one-quarter of the city itself. An estimated one hundred and fifty thousand people have been killed."

"My family is okay," said Cromen sadly. "I can't believe the cruelty these Orthodox Waru commit in the name of God. We've got to stop them," he continued with angry tears running down his cheeks.

"I'm with you on that. We'll do everything we can. You look tired, Cromen. The Glen Locklan is working its magic. Have another shot and then let's find you a bed."

"I am tired," Cromen replied, feeling the whiskey. "It was late night when I jumped through the emergency portal."

"And you've been here all day," replied David

The hospital bed was comfortable. Despite the excitement of the day and the tragic news, Cromen's exhaustion and the whiskey brought sleep quickly. A deeper sleep than he had for many days – deep, but troubled by dreams of terror and torture.

"Where do you come from, David?" Cromen asked the next morning while they were investigating the portal control system.

"I'm from the planet Alkebulon. The population is mostly of African descent, like me."

"How did you turn up in hell?"

"I met and fell in love with a Waru missionary woman, Gala. She abandon her mission to live with me, and we were happy together for several months. Then the Watchers came one night and grabbed us from our bed. They sent us to hell without any trial or anything. I don't even know what law we broke. We did nothing illegal. Sometimes I suspect that one of the Deacons was interested in Gala and did this to us out of jealous rage."

"Do you know where she is now?"

"The computer says that she's still there on Hell, at the Black Cat 17 colony."

Cromen thought of his own experience with the leash around his neck and he knew how painful that image of Gala must be for David.

"I've been trying to find a way to rescue Gala. Even if I could only bring her here, it would be better than Hell," said David, with hopeless determination in his eyes. "Gala is young and beautiful. I can't stand the idea of her being someone's personal pet."

"Look, there is more news."

"The United Worlds has directly attacked the Waru high Council today in another violation of United Worlds Sovereignty laws. Their violent effort to detain our holy leadership is an act of War."

"This attack comes just hours after the United Worlds attacked Beryl with molten magma. Their attempt to blame the Waru for these attacks is a clear demonstration of failed United Worlds policy."

"What can we do?" Cromen exclaimed in frustration. "Should we go to Beryl?"

"I don't want to leave without trying to get Gala," replied David.

"I'll do whatever I can to help you. We should make Gala our first priority."

Chapter 31 Revelation

Most Waru stayed home the day after the Magma bombing, watching the daily sermon via portal. Nava's parents watched from their home.

"What's going on?" exclaimed Landrow as the Space Marines descended towards the Profit and Apostles. "They're attacking the Profit."

Myra watched by his side as the Space Marines failed in their attempt to capture the Profit. "What do you make of that?" she asked the air. "Is someone going to drop molten magma on us next?"

"I don't think we're getting the full story," Landrow replied. "I wish we knew what was really going on."

Later that afternoon Nava's parents received another surprise, "Look at this, Honey," Myra said to her husband, "We've received an email directly from the Profit. It's a copy of what is described as the eighth Waru scripture."

"Really, how could there be an eighth scripture," questioned Landrow. "Is it some new revelation?"

"The date says 2052, the same year as the seven scriptures." replied Myra. "It is mostly organization and administration plans for the Orthodox Waru church, but part of it sounds crazy."

"It can't be real," stated Landrow, looking very suspicious. "Are you sure it's from the Profit?"

"It's the same email address as always. And listen to this, the Orthodox are permitted to sin," Myra smiled in disbelief, "Authorization to sin is permitted based on the rank within the church. Common Waru lay members have no permission to sin, while the Orthodox Waru are permitted some level of sin.

There are even detailed lists of sins permitted for each level, from Novice to Pastor to Deacon to Elder to Apostle to Profit. They are all listed. At each rank and step, they receive increasing authority to sin. The Profit has no restrictions on sin whatsoever."

"You're making this up," smiled Landrow, coming to Myra's side and looking at the screen. "Let me see."

"Well, if it's made up, they did a great job copying the style," replied Myra. "And how did they send it from the Profits email address?"

"It is just ludicrous," Landrow exclaimed, looking seriously at the document. "Somebody's joke. They made it up and hacked the Profit's email account. It can't be real."

"If it's a Joke, I don't think it's funny," said Myra. "It would explain too much about the Orthodox. Like why they don't live among us?"

"My God, how could the church permit Elders to have sex with children?" said Landrow after reading the passages Myra pointed out to him. "I can't believe it."

"Everything forbidden to us is acceptable for them," said Myra. "I've always been suspicious of these mysterious church leaders, but I never suspected this."

"Hey, look. We have an email from Nava too," said Myra with excited surprise.

"What does she say? Read it to me."

"Hi, Mom and Dad. I am safe and well, don't worry about me. No time to talk. Just wanted to say that the 8th scripture is real. I hope to be home soon. Lots of love, Nava."

"What has she gotten herself into?" Myra asked, looking worried and angry. "She runs off on a mission with Cromen and then they disappear. United Worlds agents tell us not to worry, that she's safe. And now she is involved with the revelation of this crazy 8th scripture."

"Who was the Profit's email addressed to?" asked Landrow.

"It looks like the normal distribution to all church members," said Myra turning on the view screen to check the news.

"Good evening, this is the Trusted News Network with Chet Chesterfield coming to you live from the Grand Temple of the Church of the Seven Apostles, with the latest breaking news from around the universe today. We bring you all the news that you should hear."

"The 8th scripture you may have received in your email is a hoax perpetrated by an Alton rebel group. The high council has declared it blasphemy. If you received an email, containing the eighth scripture, you are ordered to delete it, and any copies you have of this false document. The continued possession or distribution of this false and unholy eighth scripture is forbidden. Violators of this edict will be punished and excommunicated."

"Let's go see Cromen's parents," said Landrow. "I hear that some of the Alton have access to the United Worlds public news service."

"Okay, let's go."

Myra and Landrow were met by Cromen's parents on the front porch with a warm and welcome greeting.

"Have you heard anything about Nava and Cromen?" they asked.

"We received an email from Nava today," said Myra. "It was short and said she was okay. But she said nothing about Cromen. Have you heard anything?"

"Not a thing," said Cromen's mom Ginger. "The United Worlds has told us that they're safe. They seem to have gotten into some kind of trouble. It's good to hear that Nava is okay."

"They are strong and resourceful young adults," said Landrow, seeing the concern in her eyes. "I shouldn't worry too much."

"We've come hoping that you have access to unfiltered United Worlds news," said Myra. "We only have the official church news. You know, 'All the news we can't trust.'"

"We do have a way, but of course it's illegal," said Cromen's dad, James. "What are you looking for?"

"We've received information that there is an eighth Waru Scripture," said Myra. "But the High Council denies that it is true."

"An eighth scripture. That sounds interesting," said James. "I need to go through a proxy server, but it's not too hard. Let's take a look."

After a few minutes, James reached the United Worlds news service website.

"There is surprising news today of an 8th Waru scripture. This information comes directly from the United Worlds Intelligence Service and they say that it appears to be legitimate. The scripture is being analyzed and the text has not been released to the general public as of yet."

"In another surprising Waru related story, a Waru subcult has been discovered spying on the United Worlds. The Reformed Church of the Seven Scriptures is a Waru religious splinter sect that has been identified as a major spy ring. Authorities revealed today that the group appears to only exist as a spying operation for the Orthodox Waru. They have infiltrated every branch and department of the United Worlds government and have been spying since before planet terraforming was possible. We don't know at this time what purpose the Waru have for spying on the United Worlds. Further information is sure to follow."

"Well, what do you think it means?" asked James.

"Is the Waru religion only a corrupt institution, organized for the pleasure and profit of the Orthodox Waru?" asked Myra. "I'm about finished with them."

"Don't judge them too harshly," said Ginger. "They are human I think. Under their clothes, they're naked like everyone else."

"But they're claiming that the 8th scripture is a hoax and they're blaming an Alton rebel group," said Myra. "I'm worried they will do something to your people in retribution."

"Alton rebel group?" questioned James in reply. "There is no Alton rebel group."

"The Waru are using you as scapegoats," said Landrow. "Blaming you for their crimes. The worse the situation is for the Orthodox Waru, the more they will blame the Alton."

"What more can they do to us?" replied James. "Would they physically attack us?"

"I think they might," said Landrow. "You are welcome at our house until things cool down."

"Thank you, but we'll stay here for now with our people," said Ginger. "Hiding wouldn't help anything."

"You're probably right," said Landrow. "I'll talk with a group of university professor associates of mine. You might be surprised how many Waru will stand up for the Alton. Many recognize the treatment of the Alton as unjust and inhumane. And with these new revelations, there will be a flood of supporters protecting you. I will see to it."

"Thank you Landrow," said James. "We appreciate your concern. It is very good of you. But please don't get yourselves hurt in this mess."

Chapter 32 Cromen and David Rescue Gala

"I've got it," stated David with some excitement. "The problem is that we are not on Eden or Hell. We are on Heaven. It was here all the time, I just didn't see the obvious."

"You mean that the hospital emergency portal brought us from Eden to Heaven?"

"That's exactly what I am saying."

"Then maybe we can rescue Gala," said Cromen, thinking how he would feel if Nava were in Hell, and thinking that action might help with David's desperation. "Let's get to work on it."

"Now that I know where we are, I can open a portal from here to almost anywhere on the four worlds," said David. "Both the starting point and the destination can be selected from a map or satellite view."

"We can't wear these clothes if we open a portal to Black Cat 17 and search for Gala," David offered. "We would cause a lot of excitement and bring the attention of the masters."

"I can probably get a jumpsuit from Albert, at Red Devil nine," Cromen suggested. "I can go late at night so I'm not observed by others."

"Okay, I can zoom in on RD-9 here on the map. Where do you need to go?"

"There, zoom in on that area. That's the courtyard of the place where he lives, set it right there."

"It's set. I'll reopen the same portal in ten minutes. Are you ready?"

"I'm ready," replied Cromen.

He walked through the open portal into the dark courtyard and stepped up onto the empty porch. He found Albert's door and tapped lightly.

"Who's there?" asked Albert, startled by the late-night visitor.

"Cromen," he whispered.

The door opened after a short pause and Albert looked in wonder at Cromen standing in the dark wearing loose-fitting street clothes. "What are you doing here?"

"Albert, I need your help."

"How did you get here? I never thought I'd see you again."

"It's a long story. And I don't have time now."

"You found a way out?" Albert asked in an excited voice. "Take me with you."

"I need a jumpsuit, Albert. We'll come back for you as soon as we can. We need you here for now. A portal will open for you and all the slaves sometime in the next day or two."

"I have a few spare suits here," said Albert, retreating into his room and quickly returning with a stack of jumpsuits in various colors.

"May I take two?

"Of course, take all you want."

"We'll open the portal for you as soon as we can. Be ready."

"Try to open the portal in the evening when we're all here," requested Albert.

"If we can," said Cromen seriously, as the portal opened there in the courtyard next to them.

"We'll be ready," replied Albert, excitement creeping into his sleepy mind. He watched with a growing smile as Cromen stepped through the portal.

"Mission accomplished," said Cromen to David when he arrived back at the portal control point. "Now it's your turn to play. Do you know where to go?"

"I can't find the person in charge at night, I don't know who they are or where they live," said David while putting on a blue jumpsuit. "But it's daytime at Black Cat 17. If we open a portal near the community center in daylight, it might cause some excitement."

"Let's open the portal in the park area outside the Community Center and only very briefly. It opens, you jump through and I close it immediately, only a couple of seconds. Maybe no one will notice."

"That sounds good. I want thirty minutes. If I'm not there when you open the portal, close it after five seconds and open again five minutes later," David said to Cromen with excitement. "I'm ready."

"Good luck," Cromen replied as he opened the portal.

David stepped through and the portal closed quickly behind him. His arrival hadn't drawn attention and he walked casually across the grass and up the community center steps. Glancing around the nearly empty dining area, he observed one table where a tall black woman sat talking with several other people.

Her eyes fixed on David as he approached and she stood up from the table to meet him, guiding him away from the group.

"Who are you, and how did you get here?" she said with a questioning gaze.

"My name's David. I'm looking for Gala."

"Why should I trust you?"

David pulled up his sleeve to reveal the tattoo given to him when he arrived in Hell.

"That doesn't prove anything, it could be faked. Why shouldn't I turn you in to the masters? You could be their agent, how else could you get here?"

"Gala knows me."

"So you know Gala?" said the coordinator, looking suspiciously at David. "Let's go ask her."

David only nodded and followed, feeling surprised that his search for Gala could go so easily.

"I'm Lorna," said the woman as they walked through the village streets.

"We may be able to open a portal for you all in the next day or two," David said as they walked the narrow streets.

"Are you serious about a portal opening for us?"

"Yes mam," replied David, "I believe we will make it happen. Keep it secret but be ready."

Lorna stopped before a door and said: "Gala's been through a lot, and has just recently come back to us. You be good to her."

Lorna opened the door and stepped into a small courtyard, Gala was sitting on the porch looking miserable. She said hello to Lorna and didn't seem to notice David until he spoke.

"Gala."

She closed her eyes and shook her head, not believing what she saw. Knowing it to be impossible.

"Gala," he repeated. "It's me, David. I'm here to take you away."

"It can't be," she said, opening her eyes and looking up at him. An instant later she was in his arms and they were crying together happily.

"Come my love we need to hurry."

Lorna led the way back to the community center, forgotten where her doubts, her mind now filled with the possibility of freedom.

"We're here sweetheart," said David when they arrived at the designated location. "A portal will open here soon."

"Thank you," David said to Lorna while they waited for the portal to open. "We'll open a portal for you near the community center. Be ready."

Oh, we'll be ready," Lorna replied. "Don't you worry about that?"

The portal opened and David and Gala walked through. Gala smiled hello to Cromen and sat down quickly, overcome by the rapid change of events in her life. David brought some water and sat down beside her.

Chapter 33 Buffet

"My stomach is growling," Nava told Mae. "We haven't eaten since we arrived. Find us a good buffet to raid."

"This one looks good," Mae replied after a little searching, "and not a big crowd. We'll have to go in cloaked," Mae stated. "Our jumpsuits wouldn't fit into the high-class party atmosphere."

"Everything looks incredible," whispered Nava, looking down a long serving table after they arrived at the buffet. "But I suppose that we should load up on stuff that will last. We may not get another chance for a while."

"Grab anything that's not too messy or perishable, and fits inside your cloak," Mae quietly replied, starting down one side of the table.

"Meet you at the other end," whispered Nava, starting down the other side.

Mae opened a portal to another building similar to the last and Nava followed her through. They were still sitting on the floor enjoying their stolen feast when Jack called.

"Mae, something significant has happened which you need to know," he stated seriously. "Last night planet Beryl was attacked with a bombardment of molten magma. Thousands of innocent people have been killed. It appears the Orthodox Waru attacked there own people."

"How could they Jack? Their own people?" Mae replied in confused frustration.

"And that's not all," Jack continued seriously. "The Orthodox Waru are blaming the United Worlds for the attack. They have declared independence, siting this attack as justification. This is probably their motive for the attack. They need their people to be afraid of the United Worlds. They need the common Waru to want independence."

"The Orthodox Waru do something terrible and blame the United Worlds so that their people will support leaving the UW. Do I understand this correctly Jack? And can they actually secede from the United Worlds?"

"You have it right Mae. They're trying to scare their own people into supporting secession from the UW. They can secede if the majority of their people support it. The United Worlds can conduct an unbiased election and let the people of Beryl decide with their vote. But the leaders of Beryl haven't asked for this."

"We attempted to arrest the Profit and Apostles for this crime. But they escaped and we don't know where they are," continued Jack. "The Orthodox Waru have issued an ultimatum. If we don't meet their demands, they threaten to destroy all the UW planets."

"What area was attacked?" asked Nava unable to hold back her concern. "Was it Carmen city?"

"It was a smaller city called Behan city," Jack replied. "The attack was centered on the Alton neighborhood. Sorry I can't tell you more."

"Can they actually harm the United Worlds?" Mae asked.

"I suspect they can," Jack replied. "They have already demonstrated their ability and willingness for destruction."

"Is there anything we can do?" asked Mae.

"Continue your investigation of Heaven, you might find something useful and it's good to have someone behind the lines. Check in more often if you can. You should have my email with the Orthodox Waru declaration of independence and demand. I don't have much time right now. Keep in touch.

Talk with Smitty if I'm not available. I've got to run. Good luck." Jack's face disappeared as soon as he had given his directions.

"Well, he cut that short," observed Mae. "They must be going crazy at Headquarters with so much happening in the last few days."

"Check your email, Mae. I want to know about this declaration of independence."

"It's short," began Mae, looking at her email, "The Church of the Seven Apostles has suffered greatly from the United Worlds' interference in our sacred religious affairs, and from their relentless oppression of our religious beliefs. The Church of the Seven Apostles has a God-given right to religious liberty, and it is no longer possible to have religious freedom as a member of the United Worlds. Therefore, the Profit and Seven Apostles of the Orthodox Church of the Seven Apostles do hereby declare our independence and sovereignty from the United Worlds Administration, from this day forward."

"It will be considered an act of war if the United Worlds fails to respect the sovereignty of the Church of the Seven Apostles. God will punish the United Worlds severely for any further aggression."

"If Beryl has declared independence," observed Nava. "Does that mean I'm not a member of the United Worlds anymore?"

"Not yet, I hope," Mae replied, continuing her search.

"I've found what looks like a master control for all the transportation portals of the Orthodox Waru," she said. "It includes portals reserved for only the Profit and seven Apostles. The controls are similar to the United Worlds BroadPort portal control system, but they call it GodPort.

Their system has many more options than the standard RingTech control system."

"Really, GodPort," Nava said with a grin. "Sounds like a joke. Could we use it to send the Profit someplace unpleasant?"

"I wish it was that simple. If we open the Profit's portal to someplace, he probably wouldn't walk through."

"Locate an escape destination," suggested Nava. "We need to be ready to go."

"Good idea, you're thinking like a spy now. I've found several buildings that look like this one," replied Mae. "We can move fast if we need to."

"Look at this," continued Mae. "They have a place called Purgatory."

"What kind of place would they name Purgatory?" asked Nava. "It doesn't sound like fun to me."

"It shows up as a moon of Eden on their portal destination map," Mae answered. "But only accessible through a dedicated Profit and Apostle portal system."

"I'd like to know what it is," replied Nava. "But let's not go unless we have to."

"Agreed," answered Mae. "I suspect it's some kind of war room or command and control center. It could be a stronghold where they go when they are feeling vulnerable or are under attack."

"Shh," whispered Mae, "Did I hear footsteps?"

"We should go," said Nava.

Mae opened a portal and Nava and Mae stepped through. It was not what they expected. The room looked identical to the building they just left, rows of transport rings occupying one side of the building and rows of computer equipment racks filing the other. But there was the smell of food cooking and there was music coming from somewhere not too far away. Mae put a finger to her lips indicating silence. Nava had already turned on her cloak and disappeared.

"Let's see who's here," whispered an invisible Mae. "It doesn't sound threatening at the moment."

As Nava and Mae advanced toward the music, they began to hear soft voices. The rows of equipment stopped about five meters from the end of the building and there was a large open space between the equipment and the wall. Furniture, couches, tables, chairs, and a kitchen were set up making a comfortable living space. Several people sat at a table eating, others stood in front of a large view screen.

"Let's go out of sight to uncloak," said Mae. "We don't want to surprise them."

"Who do you think they are?" asked Nava quietly. "This doesn't look like anything sanctioned by the rulers of Heaven."

"No, I suspect that they are renegades," said Mae. "A small group of people that escaped from their retirement and now scavenge off the retirement facilities. They look healthier than the others we've seen."

"Greetings," Mae exclaimed clearly as they stepped from behind the computer rack into view of the people. "We come in peace."

"Who are you?" came the reply from a slender woman with long silvery hair.

"I'm Mae, and this is Nava. We're from the United Worlds government. We're here to investigate potential corruption within the Orthodox Waru church. You need not worry about our presence. We will not harm you or cause you to be harmed."

Mae paused to observe the effect of her words. "We are looking for information," she continued, speaking to the group of now frozen people, every single eye fixed intently on Mae. "I am sorry to disturb your dinner. Would you permit us to come in and talk with you?"

"Please do come in. You are welcome here. And we have plenty of food to share if you're hungry."

"Thank you," Nava replied with a smile. "We would be delighted."

"I'm Gloria," said the woman, "Come in and make yourselves at home," she continued in a warm grandmotherly voice.

"Why are you here?" asked Mae. "You're the only people we've seen outside the retirement facilities."

"You mean the death camps?" smiled a short muscular man walking over and putting his arm around Gloria. "We are the lucky few that escaped."

"This is Jim," Gloria said smiling and giving him a kiss.

"Has anyone come looking for you?" asked Nava.

"These buildings are all run remotely," said Jim. "Even equipment replacement is done through service portals. No one ever comes here."

"They think we are dead," offered Gloria with a funny smile. "Our old homes have new occupants. Heaven has forgotten us."

"You're doing okay here," said Mae. "You look so much healthier than the others out there enjoying the Heaven retirement system."

"We've escaped the pleasure trap," Gloria replied. "And we've created a much happier retirement here on the fringe of Heaven."

"I like to think of us as survivors," Jim added. "The few who took our lives back from the evil power of the Orthodox Waru."

"Where do you come from?" asked Mae. "How did you get here?"

"We are from planets all over the United Worlds," Jim replied. "Mostly worlds with problems."

"The Waru have a great sales program for Heaven retirement," Gloria added. "It looks fabulous when they tell you about it."

"It is a lot of fun at first," Jim continued. "Party, party, party, like you're a teenager running wild without limits."

"But there is nothing healthy about Heaven," said Gloria. "No exercise programs, no learning programs, no focus at all on your health and well-being. They want you to party yourself to an early death."

"As fast as possible," added Jim. "Heaven's a profitable scam. You give up all your money for a promised life of eternal pleasure. But the sooner you die, the better for them."

"It was fun for a time," Gloria reminisced with a dreamy smile. "The fantasy lovers and orgies could be so exciting. Wake up every day with your dream lover, go swimming, dancing, have an elegant dinner, and then have amazing sex with your fantasy lover and or others. Oh, it had its moments. But I can't do that all the time and there is nothing much else to do."

"They give you all kinds of drugs," Jim added with a smile. "I've never had such a hard erection in my life."

"You do pretty good without those drugs," smiled Gloria.

"If you're tired, they give you something to liven you up," Jim continued, "If you can't sleep, there's a drug for that. If you feel depressed, there's a drug to pep you up."

"And sex, sex, sex, what an erotic dream it was," Jim went on with a reminiscent smile. "But after a while, it just felt cold. I was never so bored and unhappy in my life. It was a miracle when I met Gloria. I needed a person in my life, a real relationship. I needed someone I could love."

"We tried to live together in the retirement facilities without participating in the fantasy it provides," said Gloria. "But it was disturbing to live in that strange erotic dream world. The distraction is hard on a real relationship. So we found another place to live."

"We live well here," Jim said. "We have portal control and can go to the beach or a wild party if we want to. Food and creature comforts are a portal step away. But we like the privacy of living in this place where we're not bombarded with fantasy."

"The private mansion they give you is really a giant hospital room, where you are under constant monitoring and observation," added Gloria.

The group of four couples had gathered around and behind Gloria and Jim, watching and listening to the exchange of words.

"From what we've seen of the retirement facilities, you're lucky to have escaped with your lives," said Mae. "I am happy to see you doing well here and I can assure you that the United Worlds will correct this situation in time. But you will need to be patient, we are the first United Worlds investigators to come to Heaven and observe the situation here. We were sent to investigate potential criminal activities conducted in the name of the Orthodox Waru. If you have special knowledge that might help in our investigation, please let us know."

"I am an expert on the BroadPort portal control system, if that is helpful to you," said a woman from the group. "My name is Florence. My company built and maintained many of these systems for the United Worlds."

"Thank you Florence," said Mae. "Your knowledge could be very helpful. Does anyone else have special skills with computer or portal systems?"

No one else spoke up.

"If you have portal control, why haven't you sent yourselves home?" asked Nava.

"None of us have much to go home to," said Gloria. "We gave up everything we own for retirement here on Heaven. And we feel fairly happy and secure here."

"If we start messing with the off-world transport system," said Florence, "we might draw the attention of the Watchers."

"Would you be willing to take that risk for us?" asked Mae of the group. "The United Worlds will correct your situation and restore your previous finances if I am successful here. I guarantee it."

"Our little group has grown accustomed to each other," said Gloria with a smile. "We like living together. But we could all live together in a much better place. I know this group well enough to say we are behind you with all our support."

The people standing behind Gloria nodded and smiled in affirmation. "Yes. Here, here. We're all yours." Were stated by the group in enthusiastic support.

"All right then," smiled Mae. "I am honored to work with you. Thank you."

"We don't know yet how the Orthodox Waru will react when they discover that the United Worlds knows about their hidden planets and illicit activities," Mae added.

"The United Worlds has no record of this world being created, yet here it is," she continued, looking seriously at the group. "Apparently, they've been spying and stealing technology and resources from before terraforming first began. The United Worlds has been infiltrated with spies from the time of its creation, from the time that the first RingTech portal was created. They built these hidden worlds using United Worlds technology and resources, but without the knowledge or approval of the United Worlds government."

"How many hidden worlds do the Waru have?" asked Jim.

"Right now we believe that there are two," replied Mae. "But there could be more."

"There are at least four," offered Florence. "I've looked at their portal control system. And these four worlds are on a different portal control system than the other worlds. These four worlds are on the GodPort system which is isolated from the United Worlds BroadPort system. I wondered why they were different. Now I understand."

"You see four worlds?" asked Mae. "What are the names."

"Heaven, where we are," said Florence. "Then there is Hell, Eden, and Zion. The planet Beryl is also connected to the GodPort System."

"We've never heard of Hell or Zion before. What do you know about them?"

"I know that Hell has regular traffic with Beryl," Florence replied. "Zion can only be accessed through a dedicated system all its own."

"Is there a way to put all four worlds onto the BroadPort system?" asked Mae.

"The Waru portal control system allows the worlds to be connected or disconnected," replied Florence. "The United

Worlds' portal control system doesn't have that feature, they are always connected to BroadPort."

"I can change settings for all the worlds but Zion, where access is more restricted. For the others worlds, I can change settings to permit both BroadPort and GodPort connections," Florence answered. "But I'm a little worried about getting the attention of the Waru Watchers."

"We may ask you to do that at some point in time," replied Mae. "But only if and when we need it."

"Can you show us how to control the system in case we need to?" asked Nava. "I am not very familiar with portal control systems."

"Yes, I would be happy to give you some instruction," replied Florence directing Nava to the end of one of the computer racks. "The user interface is not difficult to understand. Let us put the portal activity on the big display so everyone can watch."

Florence used the holographic virtual terminal to first show the five Waru worlds. "Each of the five worlds is represented by a point with a name beside it. The yellow lines you see connecting the worlds represent the portal openings between those worlds. You can zoom in to see details of that traffic, how much, what size, where exactly it is coming from, and where exactly it is going. You can see here," Florence pointed to a planet with very few lines connecting to other planets, "the dedicated Profit portal system that only allows the Profit and Apostles to access Purgatory. "

"If they have a dedicated portal system, can we monitor the movement of the Profit and Apostles?"

"Yes, we should be able to," Florence replied. "There is an e-log showing the date, time, and connection locations."

"When was the last opening?

"Approximately two hours ago," Florence responded after finding the portal log. "It opened from Purgatory to Eden. I can't tell who used the portal."

"Can we go to Purgatory?" Mae asked.

"With a push of a button," Florence smiled, "I can put you on Purgatory. But you will be going in blind. We don't know what's there."

"Can you stop the traffic?" asked Nava.

"It's simple on this Waru system," replied Florence. "The traffic you see here represents portal openings between these worlds that have already happened. I can connect, disconnect, or change the GodPort and BroadPort connection for each world. "

"Did you say you have the ability to change between the two portal control systems from here, right now?" asked Mae.

"Yes," Florence continued. "It can be done through the user interface. I have administrative rights."

"Look what they are showing on the small screen," broke in Nava. "it's news from Beryl."

Everyone turned their attention to a smaller screen nearby.

"Good morning, this is the Trusted News Network with Chet Chesterfield coming to you live from the Grand Temple of the Church of the Seven Apostles, with the latest breaking news from around the universe today. We bring you all the news that you should hear."

"The United Worlds BroadPort system has failed," Chet announced with a smile. "Without the use of their only portal tracking system, the United Worlds has lost virtually all transportation capability, communications, electricity, and water and sewer services. They have only manual control of their portals and there is no word as to when the BroadPort control system will be restored."

"This crippling event is a direct result of the poor engineering and maintenance typical of the Arcadian Path philosophy of happiness first and responsibility second. Fortunately for the people of Beryl, we of the Church of the Seven Apostles have a more reliable system that is undisturbed by the turbulent events in those United Worlds of sin. You can have full confidence that your GodPort system will continue to provide all the services you need."

"Due to the ongoing aggression of the United Worlds towards the Church of the Seven Apostles and the world of Beryl, the Profit has chosen at this time to seek a path to separation and independence from the United Worlds."

"Can you check the system, Florence?"

"Yes, here is the BroadPort map," she said, pushing a virtual button.

The display showed the hundreds of dots representing the 218 worlds of the United Worlds. There were no yellow lines connecting these worlds spread across the Milky Way galaxy.

"This is strange," Florence stated. "I switched to the BroadPort system monitor screen and it shows no traffic between planets. There must be something wrong."

Mae took out her Com Port. "Call Smitty," she commanded.

There was only silence as Mae looked at her ComPort. "It says that I have no connection."

"I think the United Worlds worlds really have been disconnected from the BroadPort system," said Florence.

"How can that be?" Mae exclaimed, "People need that system to survive. They won't have electricity or water, or a functioning sewage system," Mae continued, anger spreading across her face. "They won't have food. Work will stop everywhere. Society will collapse."

"Can you turn them back on?" Mae asked Florence. "Most of the people on these worlds are completely dependent on RingTech to survive."

"It is only a setting," Florence said, looking at the system settings. It will take time to reconnect all the worlds, and we might draw the attention of the Watchers."

"Please, start immediately with Utopia," said Mae. "We'll find a way to deal with any Watchers that might come to visit."

Florence reconnected Utopia to the BroadPort system with Mae and Nava watching. Mae called Jack as soon as the connection was made.

"I've been stuck in my office of cold dark rock for the past 30 minutes," said Jack, "I am only now hearing reports that RingTech has failed on all the worlds."

"Not failed Jack, disconnected," Mae said, grabbing Jack's attention. "We reconnected you from here. It seems the Orthodox Waru added switches into the BroadPort system. They can turn them on and off. We have access to their system from here and are reconnecting the other worlds as we speak."

"Florence," Mae said turning towards her. "Can you give administrative rights to Jack?"

"I think so, I'll need to add Utopia to the GodPort system. Give me a couple of minutes."

"Jack, there are two other secret worlds, Zion only allows access by the Profit and Apostles. The other world, Hell, we don't know anything about."

"How many worlds beyond these," Jack exclaimed, incredulous. "My God, where does it end? What is Zion, Mae? Is it a military stronghold for the rulers of this empire?"

"My guess, from looking at the other worlds, is that Zion is a world for only the Profit and Apostle families. We can't go there directly. The only access is through Purgatory, Eden's largest moon. Only portals dedicated for the Profit and Apostles have access to Purgatory."

"Can you get there?

"Yes, we can. Florence, my Chief Technical Officer," Mae smiled, "says she can do it for us. We're monitoring the Profit portal. Should we follow him if we can?"

"I leave that decision up to you," directed Jack. "It sounds risky, but could be crucial to preventing further destruction from this group."

"Florence is connecting Utopia to the hidden worlds through the GodPort system. You should have access to our location very soon."

"I'll be ready to follow you when I can," Jack replied.

While they talked a man wearing a red jumpsuit walked in. "I was a slave of the Orthodox Waru in Hell. Please protect me," he stated clearly.

Gloria approached the man, "Come in," she said. "We will do what we can. How did you get here?"

"There's an open portal outside," the man replied. "I don't want to go back to Hell."

"Jack, something else is happening," Mae reported, following Gloria to the door which was propped open. She looked outside a few moments. "Someone has opened a portal, Jack. There are hundreds of people arriving here all wearing colored jumpsuits. They say they were slaves of the Orthodox Waru on the planet Hell."

"Slaves from Hell?" Jack asked. "Are they causing any problems?"

"No problem so far. They're walking around asking for help."

"The profit portal just opened to Purgatory," Florence cut in.

"Everything's happening at once here Jack. The Profit just went to Purgatory. I'm going after him. Are you with me Nava?"

"I'm safer with you than on my own," Nava replied nervously.

"Good luck and be careful," Jack replied. "I'll follow as soon as I can."

"Ready Nava?" Mae smiled on observing Nava's affirmative head nod.

"I'll go in uncloaked, you follow me but fully cloaked," Mae ordered.

Nava nodded acceptance and disappeared.

"When Jack arrives," Mae said to Florence, "have him follow us to Purgatory. And keep reconnecting worlds when you can. Okay Florence, open the door to Purgatory."

"I'll do all I can," said Florence. "Opening portal now."

Mae stepped through the open portal into a large busy room. Monitors filled the walls, scores of technicians worked intently at computer desks which filled the floor. The Profit and seven Apostles stood nearby with their attention focused on the wall monitors.

No one noticed Mae at first, standing there alone in the busy command post. "Gentlemen," Mae exclaimed loudly, the stun gun in her hand pointed at the Profit. "Don't move or I'll shoot the Profit."

Everyone looked at her in surprise, except the Profit who quickly stepped through a portal which opened close him. The

Apostles rushed toward the open portal but were too late to pass through.

I'll shoot the next person that moves," said Mae, holding her weapon on the group of now frozen Apostles.

Apostle Carlyle turned in expectation of a portal opening. Mae shot him before they both realized that there was no open portal. He slumped to the floor unconscious. "Leave him where he is," ordered Mae. "No one move or I'll shoot you too."

"Everyone move away from the control consoles, keep your hands where I can see them," she ordered, pointing her weapon around the room. "Sit on the floor and be quiet."

Chairs scraped and knocked as the technicians all moved onto the floor.

Mae had only a few minutes to wait before Jack stepped lively through an open portal followed by a dozen Space Marines ready for action.

"Nava, are you here?" Mae asked the room, now filled with Space Marines, Apostles, and technicians.

"Jack, I think Nava followed the Profit through his portal to Zion."

"Can we follow?" he asked in reply,

"It didn't work for our stunned Apostle Carlyle there on the floor. He was expecting a portal to open and I shot him when he began to move. But no portal opened. I assume he was trying to get to Zion."

"What do we need to do to get that portal open?" Jack commanded of the room.

"Let's get Florence in here," stated Mae. "She knows these systems better than we do."

Florence entered and looked at the system. "The positioning system is disconnected from the other end. We can't open a portal until that system is reconnected. We have no position information on Zion."

"Mae, there has been another attack by the Profit. He has opened the atmosphere control portals of Utopia to the vacuum of space. It is locked in place, sucking the atmosphere from the planet. They threaten to do the same on all the UW planets if we don't stop our attacks."

"This is crazy, Jack," Mae stated in surprise. "Do they actually have the power to destroy us all?"

"This is a very grave threat. Our space exploration ships are moving into position to destroy the terraform rings if necessary. If we don't get control or destroy this ring within a week, we'll be forced to evacuate Utopia. And if the Waru are able to stop BroadPort again, we won't be able to evacuate the planet. Billions of lives are at risk."

"President Congo asked me to come personally to lead the effort to capture the Profit. She sends her thanks for the important work you and Nava are doing."

"Nice of her to think of us," Mae responded.

"She's handling this crisis well," Jack replied. "Removal of the Waru Reformer spies from our ranks left us short of staff to work all these problems. Madam President directed me to put most of my people to work restoring Utopia's atmosphere ring. But she authorized us to draw on the Space Marines to support our work here. They are a good team, as good as it gets."

Chapter 34 Zion

Nava remained cloaked as she followed Mae through the portal to Purgatory. She took a few steps into an open space near the Profit and Apostles.

"Gentlemen, don't move or I shoot the Profit," Mae announced to the control room.

The Profit immediately opened a portal but Nava was between the portal and the Profit. As he lunged toward the open portal, Nava tried to avoid contact and stepped through the portal before him. She had nowhere else to go.

The portal closed immediately after Nava and the Profit passed through. A single technician occupied the small Zion control room. "Disable the positioning system immediately," ordered the Profit. "Don't let anyone pass without my personnel authorization."

"Yes your Godliness," replied the technician as he turned off the positioning system.

Nava moved toward the control panel and observed the technician flip two switches. But in her effort to avoid contact with the passing Profit, she bumped a small table causing it to move slightly. Nava uttered a slight "Uhg!" in surprise,

"There is someone here," said the technician. "It's some kind of invisibility cloak or something."

"You're Crazy. There's nobody here but you and I," replied the Profit, looking around the space.

"Keep the portal system disconnected. Let no one pass without my direct permission. Zion is closed until further notice," he concluded while using a ComPort to open a portal and leave the control room.

Nava moved to a corner of the room and froze, hoping the attendant would forget about her.

"Is there someone here?" the technician said out loud, walking around the room, carefully reaching out his arms and sweeping each corner. Nava moved silently to the far side of the room but he was sweeping toward her. She was losing hope of escaping his search when a side door opened and another technician walked in.

"Lunchtime," he said. Leaving the door open and setting down a tray on the control desk. Nava moved quickly past him and out the door before waiting to see what happened. She heard the first technician say, "I could swear there was someone in here with me, using some kind of invisibility cloak or something."

"Never heard of one of those," replied the other technician. "Don't let them eat your lunch," he smiled before leaving.

Nava walk quickly along a short corridor passing several closed doors before entering a large lobby with chairs and a reception desk. "It looks like the transportation lobby is closed for lunch," she thought when she saw no one was there. She opened the front door, walked out, and heard the door click shut behind her.

Bright daylight warmed the humid noonday air which greeted her. A strong pleasing floral fragrance was contaminated by something else, like garbage, like excrement.

After hurrying across the porch and down a short flight of steps, she looked back at the featureless gray building. "Transport" was the only identifying mark on the building. "How will I get back inside?" she thought to herself. "I've got to turn on that system or I'll never find Cromen, or get home. I'll give them a little time to finish searching. Maybe it will open after lunch."

Ragged-looking people sat on porches of small broken-down houses that lined both sides of the dirty street. Young children ran naked through the neighborhood. Trash, garbage, and junk lay everywhere around the houses and streets. Chickens, goats, and pigs roamed freely. Excrement decorated the roadside.

Nava strode down the middle of the street observing all she could see. Larger and better houses on the hill above caught her attention. She turned on a side street that followed a small bubbling stream uphill toward the nicer houses. Avocado and Guava littered the forest road, fruit hung heavy on the trees and bushes all around. Naked people swam in the deeper pools of the stream and sunbathed on the large boulders.

A young woman, laughing and screaming playfully, ran naked from the forest onto the road in front of Nava. The woman paused briefly to look back at her naked pursuer. She screamed and smiled on seeing him, and continued across the road into the forest. Across the road he hurried, an excited smile on his hairy face, intent on catching the women luring him on, beckoning him to satisfy their desire.

The nicer homes were fenced and walled. She could see flower gardens and swimming pools. "This looks nice," she thought, "but what a difference from the people down below."

Nava walked back down the hill thinking about how to get through the locked door. There were people on the porch of the building when she returned, people with clothes on, obviously waiting for the door to open.

Nava didn't wait long. A woman appeared on the inside of the transportation lobby door. The people outside pushed and crowded together as a woman on the inside opened the door and stood to the side. Each person struggled to get through the door before the other. Nava waited for the crowd to clear before entering. The noisy people crushed up against the service counter as Nava walked invisibly and silently past them, down the corridor and into the control room she had come from.

A single woman technician sat in the control room watching a small view screen, she looked up as the door closed and then looked back at her screen without reaction. Nava moved quietly to the control panel.

The technician was surprised when the Nava flipped the two switches and the equipment hummed to life. "That's weird," she exclaimed, getting up from her chair and walking toward the control panel.

Nava moved a chair into her path and was preparing to fight.

"What the hell?" exclaimed the terrified technician, "there are ghosts in here." She ran from the room and Nava locked the door behind her.

"Come on Mae," Nava pleaded aloud, as someone pounded on the door. She put her back against it when she heard keys rattling on the other side but she couldn't hold them. The door was slowly being pushed open. Nava released it quickly while throwing chairs and tables into the path of the technicians entering, attempting to delay their advance toward the control panel. Six or eight technicians and police pushed timidly into the room. "I told you there was someone here," exclaimed the first technician swinging a long pole. Another technician threw a fire extinguisher. Both objects passed through Nava's cloak without touching her.

As the attackers advanced, and Nava backed up against the control panel preparing for a fight, a portal opened amid the crowd of technicians and police, Mae and Jack, followed by agents and Space Marines flooded into the room and quickly took control of the surprised attackers.

Nava uncloaked and gave Mae a big hug, letting go of the terror of the last few minutes. "I am so glad to see you, Mae."

"Me too," Mae said with a big smile. "We didn't know where you were or how to find you. This planet's well hidden. Are you alright?"

"I'm nervous, but okay," Nava replied. "It's been scary but interesting."

Under Jack's direction, agents began scanning the surrounding area with SpyPorts. "Have you been outside?" Jack asked Nava. "Where are we?"

"I think it's some kind of public portal transportation facility. Outside is mostly houses and forest," said Nava, "But it's a little weird," she added with a curious smile.

Jack's men quickly explored and took control of the building. The only resistance encountered was a cup thrown when they interrupted a romantic encounter in a small back office. The cup bounced harmlessly against the wall.

"Set up the command post in the lobby area," Jack commanded. "Everything can be done from here. Set a one hundred-meter defense perimeter around the building. I want direct portal access established between here and Utopia. Can Florence help with that, Mae?" Jack asked before continuing his instructions. "Let's get more SpyPorts set up over here."

Mae understood Jack's question as a command and immediately returned to Purgatory to get Florence.

Agents continued to pour in through open portals, pulling larger portable RingTech systems on dollies and carts. Ten minutes after arrival the lobby was an organized command center.

"Search for military installations. Watch for equipment or troops approaching our position," Jack calmly directed, knowing full well that each of these men was already actively working on exactly what he told them to do.

"We have more control from here," commented Florence, arriving with Mae and examining the Zion portal control system. "A little more seems to be revealed with each step toward Zion. We should be able to get Utopia connected from here."

"This can't be the only way in," Jack said to Florence. "They must have a back door. How are they being supplied?"

"This portal control route map shows connections that are not on the other control systems," observed Florence. "There are several connection paths between Zion and Beryl."

"Please continue investigating, Florence," Jack requested, "You're a big help."

"There's no evidence of military presence," stated an agent to Jack. "No bases, no fortifications, no weaponry anywhere."

"They're overconfident in the secrecy of this place," Jack replied. "Do we know where the Profit is?"

"We've located his estate," replied an agent. "There's a portal blocking field around the house. We have no way verify that he's inside."

"Team 1 ready," commanded Jack. "Let's go knock on his door and see who's home."

"Standing at the ready, sir," came the reply.

"Open a portal as close as you can to the house," Jack ordered.

"This should do it," responded the portal engineer. "The house is about 200 meters straight down the path you see here."

"Team 1, let's go," Jack said, stepping through the portal into the tropical jungle. "Mae, Nava follow us cloaked."

Two squads of Space Marines followed Jack and many agents through the portal. Mae and Nava followed unseen but close behind.

"Don't the marines have cloaks?" Nava asked Mae.

"No, the cloak is a very new technology," replied Mae. "Smitty helped develop it. You and I have the latest prototype models."

A dark blue house was visible at a distance down the forest path. The large central spire rose above the seven smaller spires which marked the corners of the seven-sided house. Large gardens and verandas decorate the gardens all around the house. The palatial home sat on a small bluff overlooking a long stretch of white sand beach lined with palm trees. The Turquoise sea extended to the horizon, broken only by a few small islands.

"We see no guards," said the marine captain.

Nava could see the team members advancing in front. Some marines fanned out into the jungle and two held back to watch the rear.

"Hold," came a command from a point man. "Franklin just disappeared Sir. He stepped into a portal trap."

A scream was heard from above, followed by a crashing thump in the jungle nearby. "The trap must have opened a portal to some point above us," observed the marine captain.

"They're bombing us with our own men," replied Jack. "We need to find these traps before we lose anyone else."

"They're redirect portals, sir," the marine captain replied. "Not physically here."

"Can we find and destroy the sensors?" asked Jack.

"Our scanners didn't pick them up. They're probably MicroPort infrared sensors that aren't actually here either," replied the captain. "They don't emit energy. We don't have a way to locate them."

"It will take a lot of time to clear a path. What prevents us from opening portals from just inside this blocking field," Jack observed. "Bring portable PersPorts and set them up just inside. Maybe we can bypass the jungle path."

Another scream and crash was heard in the jungle nearby.

"Everyone retrace your steps carefully and return to our starting point," ordered the captain.

Two portable PersPorts arrived as the Marines gathered outside the blocking field. "Set them up just inside the field. Prepare to open portals near the house," the captain commanded.

"There is another blocking field closer to the house," stated the portal operator after setting up and energizing the PersPort inside the outer blocking field. "We can open a portal about halfway to the house. No closer."

"It feels like a trap to me," Jack commented. "Send in two marines, keep the portal open."

The portal opened and two marines stepped through onto the jungle path.

"I am approaching the blocking field now, sir" reported one marine.

"He disappeared," stated the other marine. "I think he walked through a portal."

"I'm on the other side of the house from you," stated the first marine. "As I approached the blocking field, a portal must have opened. It looked like the same jungle and I walked through it before realizing what it was. I am retracing my steps."

"He's back, sir," stated the other marine.

"Smoke and mirrors," Jack said. "They don't want a fight. They're trying to scare us away. How do we get through this thing?

"We can kill a redirect portal while it's open, sir," offered the captain. "An ax blow across the edge of the open redirect portal will destroy the ring. If we kill a couple of rings we should be able to get past that second blocking field."

"Let's try it," Jack ordered.

Two broken axes lay beside the path as Jack and the marines crossed the blocking field and proceeded cautiously toward the house.

The Profit sat in a throne-like lounge chair, as marines advanced onto the large veranda, He gazed out across the swimming pool to the beach beyond. Beautiful young women swam in the pool and exercised nearby. One young woman rubbed his back while two sat beside him, one on each side.

"They don't live there," explained the Profit to the marines as they approached. He looked surprised, but calm. "They only come when I call them. I like to see them work out."

"Hold!" commanded the marine captain of his team.

"He's here sir. You better come up."

Jack walked onto the wide patio near the captain's position, about ten meters from Profit Hendon. The women all moved away from the Profit.

"I'm not sure he's thinking clearly, sir," the captain told Jack. "He doesn't understand the situation."

"I maintain respectability here," Profit Hendon told Jack. "I am the Profit, my moral standards are the highest."

"Yes, your Godliness," said Jack moving a few steps closer to the Profit. "Do you know who we are and why we're here?"

"You have no right to be here. Who invited you? I am the authority here, and my authority comes directly from God. The eighth scripture gives me complete authority," stated Profit Hendon confidently. "God has commanded me to control the unholy and imperfect masses."

"Please come with us your Godliness?" Jack requested, hoping they wouldn't need to use force.

"This is God's territory," replied the Profit, standing up and puffing out his chest.

"We have a warrant for your arrest," Jack offered. "Please come."

"My actions are justified by the 8th scripture," the Profit continued defiantly. "God chose me."

"Of course your Godliness," Jack said as he signaled the captain to move in. "We just want to talk, everything is okay."

As the Marines came up to Jack's position, the Profit pulled something from his pocket. "You'll never see," he exclaimed ust before a portal opened and he stepped through. Jack and the Marines were too late to reached him. The portal closed and he was gone.

"Damn that slippery devil, we should have stunned the guy on first sight," Jack raged at himself. "Where did he go? Mae, see if Florence can help us again."

"I'm on it."

"He's on Beryl," Florence exclaimed from the Zion control room. "I have disconnected the portal control device he was using from the system. He can't open another portal with it. He went to the Grand Temple of Saint Carmen on Beryl."

"Can you take us there?" Jack asked. "Team-1, are you ready to move."

"Team-1 ready, sir."

"I can put you inside the Temple whenever you want," Florence smiled.

"Are you coming, Nava?" Jack asked.

"Return to Beryl to catch the evil Profit?" Nava's nervous laugh and smile gave the answer.

"Florence, open the portal please," Jack requested. "Let's go."

Chapter 35 Emancipation

"Where do we put the people from Hell?" asked David. "We can't send them to a place without facilities. They need food and shelter."

"We could bring them here," said Cromen. "They could take over the abandon buildings and order food like we do."

"Do we have space for all of the people from Hell?"

"There are enormous hotel resorts on Eden," Gala volunteered. "I've seen a couple."

"How do we find them? Do you know where they are?"

"Eden is the only name I've heard. Let's see what we can find in the system," Gala replied as she began searching on the computer. David and Cromen joined in the search.

"There are thousands of resort hotels," said Cromen after some investigation, "We could send different Hell communities to different resorts."

"There are millions of people on Hell," stated David, "I don't think these hotels will hold them all."

"And I don't think anyone from Hell will mind sharing a room," Gala offered with a smile.

"There's almost no limit to the number of portals we can open," said David, "What about this world?"

"Let's see what we can find on Heaven," replied Cromen, "we should spread them out. We can use the resorts on Eden and whatever we find here on Heaven."

"When we start flooding Heaven and Eden with people from Hell," said David, "somebody is going to react in a big way. We might have Watchers crawling all over the place."

"Should we fill all the building here with people?" asked Cromen, "Then it'll be more difficult for the Watchers to find anyone who is controlling the portals. They'll be overwhelmed."

"And we're dressed in coveralls like all the other ex-slaves," Gala observed. "They won't know who to take."

"We could train the ex-slaves to work the portal system," David suggested. "It's simple to learn. There could be hundreds or thousands of people opening portals from all over these buildings. That would make it happen faster and be more difficult for the Watchers to stop. Teach all the ex-slaves to use the portal system."

"You boys are going to bring havoc," Gala said with a smile. "Bring on the chaos. It's time. If we start with a few, we can train them to be trainers. I wanna get these bastards. It's payback time."

"I like the plan," Cromen said, smiling back at them. "How about bringing a group to train first, then we can open all the portals at once."

"We'll bring them from the night side of Hell," David offered. "They won't be missed until they don't show up for the morning work detail."

"It should be bedtime at Red Devil 9 right now. What are we waiting for?" beamed Cromen, excited by the newfound sense of control, eager to strike a blow against the Orthodox Waru who had imprisoned him.

"Just put them everywhere, Casinos, hospitals, resorts, Leave the portals open," suggested David.

"We can't just open portal," Gala added. "We should send a message with them. Have them say, 'We were slaves of the Orthodox Waru on Hell. Please protect us.'"

"I like it

"Hey guys," Gala said, looking at the streaming Waru news channel. "The Waru news says something about a failed attack on the Profit in the Grand Temple on Beryl. The Orthodox Waru blame the Alton people for working with the United Worlds. Now the Alton are being removed from planet Beryl for crimes against God. Aren't you Alton?" she said, looking at Cromen.

"Yes, they are my people," responded Cromen, intense anger gripping his face, "let me see that. It says that all Alton people will line up at noon for relocation. Those not complying with the order will be forcefully captured and punished before being sent to Hell."

"This is today, only a couple of hours from now. It changes everything," Cromen said with focused anger while moving to a control terminal. "We should flood Beryl with the ex-slaves from Hell. The Orthodox Waru may be strong, but we've got an army behind us ready to go. Ex-slaves from Hell flooding into their cathedrals should get some attention and complicate any plans the Orthodox Waru might have. My people will welcome the ex-slaves."

"Okay let's open a portal to Red Devil 9 and get some people here to train," David suggested, "It shouldn't take long. Bring a lot of them. Fill the whole damn place around the building. That will confuse anyone that comes looking for us."

"I'll go talk with Albert," Cromen said. "I'm sure he'll help coordinate the slaves we send to Beryl."

"I'll concentrate on training the ex-slaves and selecting destinations on Beryl," replied Gala, excitement flooding her face. "I know this portal control system and the layout of Beryl. I just wish I could see their ugly Orthodox Waru faces when they're surrounded by ex-slaves from Hell."

Chapter 36 Battle of Beryl

Unseen speakers blared through small portals opened in the air around St. Carmen Altonville. "All Alton people are directed to surrender for relocation today at 12 o'clock noon. Those who surrender peacefully will be treated with respect and dignity. Those that resist will be subject to more aggressive actions." The speakers blared all morning. Thousands of Watchers in riot gear, with stun guns and wooden clubs, assembled outside every Alton neighborhood on Beryl.

At 11 am, Cromen's mother Ginger led a group of Alton women out the front gate, bringing water and snacks to the Watchers. "Please don't hurt the children," they asked politely of the Watchers.

At 12 noon, there were no Alton people lined up for relocation, not one anywhere. The order was given for troops to enter Altonville and capture the Alton.

As the Watchers marched in military formation toward the gate, portals opened in front of the advancing troops. People came through the portals, Waru laypeople, not just one or two, but thousands and thousands of common Waru. They arrived through their PersPorts directly in the path of the Watchers, blocking their advance.

The Watcher Army hesitated, stopped. "Forward," came the blaring command encouraging the Watchers to push into the crowd. They met resistance from Waru protesters, who passively blocked the path and gave way very slowly. As the number of protesters grew, a powerful pushing match ensued.

The Watchers began using portals to bypass the crowd, appearing inside the Alton gate, leaving some to deal with the protesters outside. The Waru protesters also changed tactics, appearing inside the gate, appearing all around the neighborhood.

The Alton people gathered in the town square when the attack began. They were photographed sitting passively under the trees, so that none could be shown guilty of protesting.

The Watchers pushed on through the rebellious Waru until they found the Alton and began pushing them through open portals. Waru rebels crowded in among the Alton and were pushed through the open portals along with the Alton. As many protesters as they took away, more arrived, it was as if the entire Waru congregation were revolting against the Orthodox Waru Watchers.

But the Watchers continued their task of removing the Alton, herding them in groups and ones and twos through the open portals.

At about one PM, other people began to arrive, people in colored jumpsuits. Thousands streamed in through multiple open portals. Each of the new arrivals repeated, "We were slaves of the Orthodox Waru on Hell. Please protect us."

The slaves from Hell didn't know what the fighting was about, but they recognized the Watchers. Some ex-slaves blended in with the passive Alton. Others were ready to fight and joined with the WARU protesters protecting the Alton, blocking the Watchers from reaching the Alton. Their number of ex-slaves soon became overpowering and the Watchers had to fall back.

The commander of the Watcher Army recognized the truth of these new arrivals. "If someone's releasing slaves from Hell, then we have bigger things to worry about than the Alton."

"Fall back," he ordered. "Regroup at the gate."

Altonville was full of people, the remaining Alton, the Waru rebel supporters, and thousands of ex-slaves from Hell. There was a great sigh of relief as the Watchers retreated. It was short-lived. Nearly one-third of all Alton had been removed, families had been torn apart. The remaining Alton were frightened and worried.

Ex-slaves continued to stream in from portals opened throughout Altonville.

"Do you have a leader?" James asked of the ex-slaves. "Is someone in charge?" He continued to ask until directed to an older man in light blue coveralls.

"Are you in charge of these people?" James asked the man.

"Well," said he, "they often listen to what I have to say, but nobody is in charge of this group. A guy named Cromen opened the portals for us. My name is Albert. What can I do for you?"

"Cromen?" exclaimed James. "A young man with kinky brown hair?"

"Yeah, that's him," replied Albert. "He sent this group of slaves to protect his home. Do you know him?"

"He's my son. Where is he?"

"He's on another planet where he is controlling all these portals," answered Albert with a smile. "You have a fine boy."

"There is something big happening at the Temple," Landrow said on approaching James and Albert. "We should bring everyone we can. The Waru protesters are opening portals right now and moving that way."

"Red Devil Nine," Albert exclaimed loudly. "Red Devil Nine. Follow me."

Men and women in jumpsuits congregated around Albert. Landrow led the Waru rebels and the ex-slaves through a portal that he opened in Landrow's living room. The group crowded in and filled the space. "Okay," stated Landrow, "I'm opening outside one of the seven entrances of the Grand Temple of Saint Carmin."

Landrow, James, Albert, and the ex-slaves poured out of the living room and into the crowd gathered outside the temple. Watchers guarded the seven entrances to the temple. Thousands of Waru rebels and ex-slaves surrounded each door, holding their distance from the Watchers. Ex-slaves and rebels continued streaming in through portals all around.

"What should we do?" Albert asked James and Landrow. "We might be able to overpower the Watchers at the doors, but nobody wants to get zapped with those stun guns they carry."

"There is no one controlling this mob," James replied, watching the increasing numbers and the slow surge toward the doors. "We can't stop it. They may rush the doors at any moment, but there will be a lot of injuries."

"The Waru protesters are holding back and watching their ComPorts," Landrow observed while walking toward a Waru protester. "What is everyone looking at?" he asked.

"The Profit is inside the temple on his dais surrounded by Space Marines. They're trying to capture him again. And the Marines are themselves surrounded by Watchers," replied the Waru woman.

Landrow opened the sermon attendance app on his ComPort which allowed him to look inside the temple.

At this time on planet Heaven, Cromen, David, and Gala were supervising the liberated slaves who filled the building they were in. Ex-slaves were at the control of hundreds of terminals in dozens of buildings. Smiling with excitement and focused intently on opening portals from Hell to Heaven,

Eden, and every temple or Altonville town square on planet Beryl. The joy of liberation glowed on their faces, they worked with excited passion to free their brother slaves.

"I think it's running itself pretty well," Cromen said smiling with satisfaction. "I want to go home and see if I can help."

"I'm with you," said David. "If Gala agrees."

"It's my home too. Are you asking if I want to go home and kick some Orthodox Waru butt?" Gala smiled. "There is nothing, absolutely nothing, anywhere on any planet, that would make me happier."

Cromen led David and Gala through an open portal into the community center of Cromen's hometown, Altonville St. Carmin. It was crowded with Alton, Waru rebels, and ex-slaves. Groups were gathered around Waru rebels, watching their ComPorts.

"Have you seen my parents?" Cromen asked of a family neighbor he recognized.

"When did you get back Cromen," the woman replied in surprise, "It's nice to see you."

"Thank you. I just arrived."

"Your father went to the temple with some of the men," she continued. "Something big is happening."

"And my mom?"

"She's around here someplace. I saw her over by the gazebo with a Waru friend."

Cromen surprised his mom as she and Myra were focused intently on Myra's ComPort. He approached quietly from behind and said softly "Mom."

Ginger froze and turned slowly, smiled and trembled, her eyes teared. "Cromen!" she exclaimed throwing her arms around him. "I've been worried about you. Are you alright?"

"Yes mom, I'm great."

"Someone said you brought all these ex-slaves here."

"I had a part. This is David and Gala, we three released the slaves."

"Good job," injected Myra. "Do you know where Nava is?"

"No," Cromen replied. "It's been weeks since we got separated."

"She was okay a couple of days ago," Myra added.

"We should go help your father," interrupted Ginger on seeing the worried mood holding both Cromen and Myra. "He's at the Temple with Landrow."

"I can get us there, but we need to go through our home and from there to the temple" stated Myra, watching her ComPort, looking angry and ready for action.

"I have a better way," Cromen stated, give me two minutes. "The portal should still be open."

Cromen ran back to find the portal he arrived from still open. He ran through the portal into the computer facility on Heaven and took control of a terminal. "Open a portal between every Altonville town square and the Grand Temple of Saint Carmin," he told the group of excited ex-slaves working at terminals all around him.

Cromen opened a new portal from his own town square to the temple and ran back through the portal the way he came. People were already beginning to walk through the newly opened portal to the temple.

"Mom, we can all go through here," Cromen said when he returned to the group.

"There are some people looking for you Cromen," Ginger told her son. "An older couple carrying suitcases."

"No," exclaimed Cromen in happy surprise. "It can't be Daria and Greyson. How could they be here."

Cromen found them standing together near the portal that led to the temple. "What are you doing here?" Cromen asked, giving them both an emotional hug.

"We were worried about you," replied Greyson.

"And we need a little excitement," added Daria. "This is just the kind of thing we specialize in. Mae tipped us off this morning by email that we might be useful."

"We're all going to the temple," Cromen told them. "The United Worlds Space Marines are trying to capture the Profit. It might get dangerous."

"That's why we're here," said Daria with a sweet grandmotherly smile.

"Well then," said Ginger, "what are we waiting here for?"

The crowd of angry Waru rebels and ex-slaves surrounded the temple. Cromen could see dozens of portals open with ex-slaves in coveralls streaming through.

"My ComPort shows Landrow to be outside the southwest door," said Myra directing them through the crowd and around the building.

James was watching Landrow's ComPort as they approached, Cromen grabbed his father, turn him around, and gave him a firm hug, "Dad," was all he said.

"Cromen," came James' heartfelt reply.

"Something is happening," exclaimed Landrow, with his gaze fixed on his ComPort. "There's been fighting between the Marines and the Waru. But now it looks like the Marines are preparing to capture the Profit."

Albert found Cromen, "The people from Hell are itching for a fight. They are moving forward without any control. And it looks like the Watchers are bringing bigger weapons?"

"Try to hold back the ex-slaves," Cromen asked Albert. "We have our own secret weapon and I don't want our people getting hurt."

Albert smiled and ran to the front of the surging ex-slaves, talking to individuals and spreading the word to stand back from the door.

"Landrow, can you open a portal close to the door?" Cromen asked.

"Yes, with our home PersPort," Landrow replied. "We have to go to our home first. From there we can do it. But who wants to step through a portal into the midst of all the Watchers guarding the door?"

"I think we can manage," stated Greyson. "Just get us close to those doors. We'll take care of the guards."

Landrow looked at Daria and Greyson with surprise.

"They can do it," Cromen added, laughing with tears running down his face.

Landrow opened the portal and walked into his living room with Daria and Greyson, Myra, and Cromen with his parents.

Greyson handed a copper mesh hood to each of them. "Put them on," he stated firmly. "When you have your hoods on and the portal destination is set, Daria and I will open our boxes. Open the portal as soon as we have the Mind-Snakes in our hands."

With copper mesh hoods to protect them from the angry Mind-Snake's debilitating radiation, Daria and Greyson opened their boxes. "They don't like to be touched," Daria said, reaching in with long gloved hands. "It's best to hold them with both hands. But oh how they hate it. Are you ready Greyson?"

"Yes dear," replied Greyson with an excited smile. "Let's go open the temple door for these nice people."

With wriggling Mind-Snake and a glow of maniacal excitement, Daria drew a deep breath. "Open the portal please Landrow. This shouldn't take long."

Albert was watching from outside the temple as Daria and Greyson stepped into the middle of the Watcher guards at the door. The Mind-Snakes held out high in front of them were wiggling violently. The Watchers fell immediately to the ground, shaking in pain.

At Daria's direction, Cromen brought the two cages to secure the Mind-Snakes. As soon as the Mind-Snakes were locked inside Cromen signaled to Albert and the crowd surged toward the doors and flooded inside the temple.

Chapter 37 The Whole World is Watching.

"Shields up," Jack commanded immediately as he entered the Grand Temple with Mae, Nava, and the team of space marines. The temple was teaming with Watchers, thousands of Watchers.

"Defensive positions. Let's get more Marines in here," Jack ordered.

The Watcher commander was busy coordinating the transfer of troops coming from Eden. They had to be organized and sent through portals to areas of Beryl that needed them most.

Thousands of Watchers in riot gear were arriving through some portals and being directed into other portals. The disorganized chaotic movement of troops reflected the obvious lack of preparation among the low-level Watcher conscripts. The majority of Watchers were not professionals, they had been forced into service only the day before, had never seen combat, or even used a stun gun. Many didn't even know what the fight was about. They had not trained together, didn't know who their commander was, and were terrified.

In the enormous poorly lit cathedral the appearance of thirty marines among the chaos was not noticed by the Watchers. They didn't notice the Space Marines for several minutes.

"Watchers attack," ordered a frightened commander when he became aware of the marines.

Many Watcher troops did not yet know of the Marine presence. Thinking the order to attack could only mean attack through the portals standing open, hundreds of Watchers streamed out of the temple before the command could be clarified.

As the watchers became aware of the marines they hesitantly surrounded Jack's team, at a distance, not advancing. The Watchers were prepared with wooden clubs and stun guns in anticipation of facing weaponless Alton people. They hadn't anticipated Space Marines.

"Flash-fire level one on my command," ordered the Marine Captain. "Fire."

A burst of bright solar heat exploded in front of the Watchers. It was only a tenth of a second burst of solar heat, but they all moved back.

"Attack," screamed the inexperienced Watcher commander. "Attack, attack, attack."

"Fire," commanded the marine captain. "Fire at will." He stated as the Watchers began advancing towards the Marines.

Hundreds of small solar flashes brightened the room. Hundreds of Watchers lay moaning on the floor. The microsecond burst of near-solar intensity knocked them to the floor, almost bringing them to their senses. This shock of superior firepower and the increasing number of Marines stabilized the situation for the moment. The Watchers held back.

"Let's try to get the Profit while they hesitate," Jack ordered.

"We're ready to open portals above the blocking field and drop in on his position?" replied the captain.

"Are these all ViewPorts?" Jack asked, observing many thousands of floating dots just outside the blocking field.

"Yes," Nava replied, "each one is a person watching from home or on their ComPort. That's how most Waru attend church services."

"Not much we can do about that," Jack commented. "Maybe it is better if they're watching."

"You have no right here," yelled the Profit from above, surprising the Watchers who had been unaware of his presence. "Go out from God's house."

"Prepare to drop on him," ordered Jack. "Let's set up a portal ring inside the blocked area. Maybe we can open on his platform. We'll try to reach him from above and the side."

"Yes, sir," the captain replied, immediately directing his marines to action.

The Profits light came on, radiating orange shimmering light from his position above his throne.

"You have no right to be here," screamed the Profit. The orange light turned red at his burst of his anger, flooding the cathedral with crimson. "Do not approach the dais. I will destroy all your foolish pagan worlds. Heretics and blasphemers all. You will burn in hell for eternity," the Profit raged, the red glow pulsed, and the dais began to rotate.

"I was chosen by God," screamed the Profit frantically on observing Marines coming down from above him. "The eighth scripture gives me authority, I alone above all others. You will all be destroyed. All your worlds, all your kind, you and your Arcadian Path foolishness. I will destroy you all."

The Marines below surrounding the central dais were at a standoff with the Watchers that encircled them. Millions of tiny dots floated in the air surrounded the dais. Millions of common Waru watched as marines approached their Profit's position from above. They watched as he climbed onto the railing forty meters above the temple floor.

"Stop, don't come any closer," the Profit threatened, balancing on the parapet. "God will strike you dead

"Hold off," Jack ordered the captain, "we can't stun him there."

"We're holding on your orders sir," came the captain's reply.

"Would you be able to open a portal directly in front of him and either pull him through or jump in and tackle him on the floor?" Jack asked of the captain.

"The rotating dais makes it difficult to hold a portal open in front of him. I'll put my best portal operator on it," the captain responded. "We need to time the opening perfectly. But it may be our best option."

"It's the only option and we're out of time. Make it happen. Now," Jack ordered.

From the millions of dots of light surrounding the Profit, the audience watched the portal open. The marines timed their jump precisely, already being in motion before the portal opened. The audience saw the marines come through the portal just out of reach of the Profit. It had opened a split second too early, the marines fell to the platform floor behind the railing without touching the Profit.

"You have no right. The eighth scripture protects me," screamed the desperate Profit, turning to see the marines gain their footing and move toward him, his face wild with fear and anger. The radiant light shifted from red to yellow and orange and to red again, reflecting the Profit's terror.

The people at home saw it, everyone watching saw it. The Profit twisted slightly and lost his balance. He teetered momentarily on one foot waving his arms to gain control. The marines lunging hands reached only air. The Profit tumbled over the edge crying in terror. "Nooooo."

The scream stopped when he hit an Apostle platform ten meters below. The scream stopped but the Profit continued downward, bouncing off the Apostle platform, tumbling silently another thirty meters to the cathedral floor. The dull "thwack" of his body echoed through the silent cathedral. The Profit light stopped radiating from the Profit chair forty meters up on the dais. Silence invaded the temple.

A marine corpsman ran forward, knelt over the Profit's body. "He's dead," the woman said rising, looking down at the mangled bloody body.

"Attack!" broke the silence. The Commander of the Watchers reacted unwisely, with rage and anger on seeing his beloved profit lying dead on the floor. "Attack, attack."

The Watchers advanced cautiously toward the Marines they encircled. "Flash-fire level three on my mark," ordered the Marine commander, pausing a moment. "Fire."

A burst of intense light knocked the first line of Watchers to the floor in pain and fright.

"Attack!" screamed the Watcher commander.

"Ready, flash fire level five on my mark," ordered the Marine commander.

"Fire." pause, "Fire." pause, "Fire," ordered the Marine captain, pausing long enough for the first line of Watchers to fall before firing on the next line.

As the marines held off the attacking watchers, Cromen and Albert with the Red Devil 9 ex-slaves flooded through the large temple doors.

The Watchers froze for a moment, now being trapped between the marines they surrounded at the center of the circle and the ex-slaves and Waru rebels who surrounded them.

"What is happening?" Jack exclaimed. "People are coming in from outside. Whose side are they on?"

"Florence told me that people are coming from planet Hell," said Mae. "They're arriving all over Beryl by the thousands."

"Do we have communications with Florence?" Jack asked Mae.

"I have communication with her now," replied Mae. "She says there is a lot of portal traffic from Eden to Beryl, bringing more Orthodox Waru watchers."

"Can she shut them down?" asked Jack.

"I hear you, Jack," Florence's floating head responded on Mae's ComPort. "I can shut down the portals from Eden. Should I also stop the flow from Hell?" Florence asked.

"No," replied Jack, as he observed fighting between the arrivals from Hell and the Watchers. "I think the people from Hell are helping. That gives me an idea."

The Watchers were caught between the ex-slaves on the outside and the Space Marines at the center. They hesitated and moved back despite the screaming attack order. Fighting with the ex-slaves was escalating and hundreds of Watchers lay in pain on the floor as portals opened among them. A panicked retreat began with Watchers that could still move, pushing and shoving to get through the open portals. The ex-slaves pursued and harassed them as they made their escape.

"Let them go," Jack ordered.

"Why did they open portals while their commander was still ordering attack?" asked the Marine captain after the last Watcher that could walk had exited the temple.

"I didn't hear a retreat order," Mae commented as she and Nava uncloaked.

"They didn't open the portals," replied Jack, smiling at Mae. "Florence opened those portals. She opened them directly to Hell."

"Florence you're amazing!" exclaimed Nava.

"I don't remember when I've had so much fun," Florence responded. "There is something deeply satisfying about sending all those damn Watchers to Hell."

"President Congo is calling," Jack cut in. "She has been closely following our progress."

"Hello, Jack. Congratulations on getting the Profit," began President Angela Congo. "I have another small crisis to tell you about. Just when we think we've stopped these renegades, they spring another surprise."

"What is it Madam President?" Jack asked.

"The atmosphere rings on all of the United World's planets have been sabotaged. All of them, they have all shut down."

"I have someone here that is pretty good with the Orthodox Waru secret portal control systems," said Jack. “I think she can do something.”

"Yes, have her look at it," replied the President. "But we don't think it's a problem with system settings this time, it looks like a virus has corrupted the control interface on each ring. The only way to fix it may be to go physically to each of the 436 rings and replace the interface module. But we should be able to fix them remotely."

"Are there any worlds in danger?" asked Jack.

"They should all be fine," she replied. "Fortunately the United Worlds can fix this. It's just such a nuisance. Have we seen the last of these pranks, Jack? What else is coming?"

"I wish I knew Madam President," Jack replied. "The remainder of the high-level Orthodox Waru are isolated on their secret planets. Florence tells me she has complete control of their portal systems and has isolated each world so they don't have off-world transport."

"If we control their portal access," observed President Congo. "It should be only a matter of time before we have them under control."

"There is someone outside claiming to be Nava's parents," the marine captain reported to Jack.

"I apologize for the interruption Madam President," said Jack.

"Not at all, Jack. I'd like to meet them," replied President Congo.

"Let them through, captain. I'm pretty sure Nava won't mind," Jack said grinning while turning to see Nava smile.

Nava with a beaming smile hurried through the crowd of ex-slaves and wounded Waru to meet her parents coming through the door. Grabbing them one in each arm, she kissed and hugged them. "I love you guys," her eyes full of tears, her smile full of happiness.

Cromen had followed Myra and Landrow with his own parents. He stood smiling humbly trying to hold back his excitement, waiting for Nava to see him.

"Cromen," Nava exclaimed on seeing him, rushing to smother him in kisses. "I've never been so happy. It's over, it is over. We're home. Come on," she said to the group after gaining a little composure. "I want you to meet Mae and Jack."

"Your daughter has been a tremendous help," Jack said to Myra and Landrow. "You should be very proud."

"Tremendous help is putting it mildly," Mae added. "She found and exposed the eighth scripture. And Nava's bravery and quick thinking are what allowed us to find the Profit and follow him here."

"I'd like to meet them, Jack," President Congo cut in politely.

"Excuse me Madam President," Jack replied. "This is Nava Martin and her parents Myra and Landrow. And this is Cromen Henderson with his parents, Ginger and James."

"What strong and beautiful spirits your children have," President Congo said to the parents. "The United Worlds is forever in their debt. We are all very proud of them. Thank you, Nava and Cromen for risking your lives to make our worlds a better place for all. You are greatly appreciated. I am sorry I don't have time to visit with you now, but I invite you all to Utopia for a celebration in honor of Nava and Cromen. Jack will arrange things. Thank you all."

Everyone smiled and thanked the President before she closed her portal.

"Let us hope," Jack said looking seriously at the people around him, "that we have witnessed the last act of this tragedy."

"This whole event is on the news," Landrow commented. "I think the people of Beryl are beginning to see the truth about this horrible corrupt Orthodox Waru organization."

"Well Mae," Jack said, "I think it's time for us to go. We have about a million things to do."

"Don't we always?" replied Mae.

Chapter 38 The Cleanup

President Angela Congo addressed the special session of the United Worlds on Sunday 26 June, 436 EE.

"The violent attack on the United Worlds has ended. The Orthodox Waru are no longer a threat to our peaceful society. Brave people have protected our modern civilization from the violent organized corruption of the Orthodox Waru. The corruption they legitimized by a belief that God chose them above all others to rule. How could something so morally corrupt exist for so long?"

"The Orthodox Waru have violated every Goal of Civilization. Not once or twice, but every minute of every hour of every day for more than 400 years. This organization has murdered thousands of there own innocent followers and has enslaved millions more. They attempted to destroy the United Worlds."

"Let me make it very clear," she stated strongly, "the Waru are a complete and separate organization and religion from the Orthodox Waru. No one should criticize the good Waru people or their faith in God. They played an important role in defeating the Orthodox Waru and deserve the full support and respect of all the United Worlds. The Waru are free to live by their religious belief in any form they wish, as long as their actions do not harm other people."

"It is not what a person believes or how they live that makes them a good person, it is their behavior toward others. Only by good actions can a person have respect for themselves and be of value to others."

"It was only by the actions of good people that the United Worlds avoided further tragedy, loss of life, and destruction,"

President Congo looked at the group in the front row. "Please stand."

"Jack, Mae, Nava, Cromen, David, Gala, and Florence," she went on, smiling at the group standing in front of her. "All the people of the United Worlds owe each of you, and the many others that helped you, a debt of thanks for your heroic actions that prevented a much more significant disaster."

The audience stood clapping in appreciation. Pride filled the faces of Nava and Cromen's parents as they looked at the couple standing together. Nava saw tears on Cromen's face and her eyes began to water.

"Thank you," said Madam President. "We will never forget what you have done for us. Please be seated."

"Just when we begin to think the human race has become civilized," she continued, "someone proves us wrong. They show us the uncivilized side of human nature. They show us that side which the Arcadian Path helps us to manage in a healthy way."

"The behavior of the Orthodox Waru might have been standard church practices during the middle ages and the inquisition, but it is unacceptable in our modern enlightened society. They have violated the trust of their followers, and used their religious influence to deceive and manipulate. They took their pleasure from abusing others. The Orthodox Waru have violated every law of civilization, every law that protects us from the negative behavior of others."

"The Orthodox Waru will not be permitted to continue their violence. Those not prosecuted for crimes against civilization will be monitored to ensure they do not pose a danger to the people around them."

"The United Worlds will create an interim government until Planet Beryl creates a new government of their own. A government which will actually improve the lives of all their people."

"Those liberated from Hell and the retirees on Heaven will have our full support. The United Worlds will help them recover from their trauma and to find a good life in society."

"Members of the Reformed Church of Seven Apostles will be punished for crimes of espionage and robbery. But most will continue working for the United Worlds. They will explain the details of their spying and stealing operations."

"There is only one true sin – irresponsible behavior that hurts yourself or others. Becoming responsible is a lifelong journey each of us takes by ourselves. And it is a difficult journey, a journey best taken with a guide. The Arcadian Path is that guide. The guide to a fulfilling life. The guide to a better civilization."

Chapter 39 The Wedding

Double rainbows embraced the tropical garden of the Aeon Royal Palace on planet Shangri-la. Cromen's uncle Burt played classical guitar in the shade of a yellow flowering Primavera tree. Yellow flowers covered the grass where Nava and Cromen stood beside David and Gala for a simple but beautiful double marriage ceremony. President Angela Congo presided.

The wedding dinner on the large veranda was a casual affair with a few speeches and many toasts. The tragedies they had overcome together bonded them in joy and appreciation of life. They talked like old friends catching up after a long separation.

"What progress has been made with the Orthodox Waru?" Cromen asked of Jack.

"Eden is under control and we are prosecuting the worst offenders. But Zion is another matter. You may know that the Profit is always chosen from among the direct descendants of John Newton or John Behan. We've discovered a strong genetic tendency for schizophrenia in these families. With so much inbreeding over the last 400 years and the lack of mental health support, schizophrenia has become widespread among the population of Zion."

"The society there is completely disorganized, very few people are educated and many are homeless, living off the land and what they can gather. It will take time to fix the mental health issues of the millions of Profit's descendants living on Planet Zion."

"Are you staying here for your honeymoon?" Jack asked Nava and Cromen.

"Yes, we plan to relax and see some more of Shangri-la," responded Nava, "David and Gala are planning to spend some time here also before they return to David's homeworld Alkebulan."

"What's Alkebulan like?" asked Mae. "I've never been there."

"We are from the continent of Africa on old Earth," replied David. "The plant and animal life all comes from Africa. There are large wildlife protection zones where animals like giraffes, elephants, and zebra roam freely. We even have islands where we keep lions and other dangerous animals. And the people are the friendliest anywhere."

"It sounds beautiful," Mae replied. "I'd like to see it someday."

"David and I plan to live there," Gala added. "We'll stay on Shangri-la for a time after our honeymoon to study the Arcadian Path before we go home. Cromen got us interested and Nava wants to stay to take classes with us."

"Good for you," Mae said with a smile. "Nothing could be better."

"What about you Mae?" Nava asked with interest and concern. "I miss you."

"I miss you, too," she replied. "Jack is forcing me to take two months off."

"What will you do with your time off?"

"I'm going to Earth," Mae replied. "I've always wanted to see the birthplace of man. I hear it is very beautiful. After that, I'm sure Jack has something for me to do."

"I also have something for Nava and Cromen to do," added Jack. "You have worked with courage and intelligence throughout this ordeal. There is a place for you in our organization. When you're ready, give me a call."

"Thanks for the offer, Jack," replied Cromen. "But that life might be too exciting for us."

"We'll keep it in mind," Nava replied. "But after some studying here, Cromen and I are going to mine gemstones and mineral specimens on Beryl."

"That sounds beautiful," commented Florence who had been listening in. "What an exciting thing to do."

"What will you and the other refugees from Heaven do now?" Nava asked Florence.

"There is some very nice land available on Hell," Florence responded "But to tell the truth, our little group of friends were pretty happy on Heaven. So we're planning to share one of the mansions there and continue enjoying the facilities, but on our own terms."

"How is the colony of Mind-Snakes doing?" Daria asked Cromen.

"They are very happy," Cromen replied. "My parents are caring for them. The colony is growing and we are already providing free five-minute sessions all over Beryl. They are helping to make people feel the beauty of life."

Daria hugged him and smiled.

"Where will you and the ex-slaves from Hell live?" Cromen asked Albert when he approached.

"Hell is called Liberty now," Albert replied with a happy smile. "I'll soon own some of the land I was enslaved on; a beachfront paradise."

"How is Planet Beryl doing?" Albert asked of Nava's father

"It is coming to life," Landrow replied cheerfully. "I've never felt so optimistic about our future. The people of Beryl are waking up from a 400 year Orthodox Waru nightmare."

"It's about time," exclaimed Nava, smiling and holding Cromen close at her side.

"We're building an Arcadian Path University extension," added Cromen. "And a new government modeled on the Goals of Civilization. Beryl is becoming the paradise it should be."

* * *

And so the awakening of Beryl began. The true character of the Orthodox Waru was revealed, the weight of repression was lifted. The people of Beryl are waking from 400 years of abuse. Waking to a world no longer controlled by fear and guilt, they are waking to the beautiful reality of existence. The people of Beryl are embracing the Arcadian Path, learning to face the future without fear.

Beryl today is a thriving prosperous planet with a civilized society that has learned to appreciate the gift of life, a society guided by truth, compassion, and love. Beryl has become a truly civilized world guided by the Arcadian Path.

END

Appendix 1 The Arcadian Path Philosophy

The Arcadian Path is a philosophy designed to build a society that supports the individual, a society where every individual can learn to live a happy productive life. It shows us a better way to treat ourselves and each other.

The three foundations of the Arcadian Path are the Goals of Civilization, the Principle of Humanity, and Scientific Spirituality.

<u>The Goals of Civilization</u>

The eight goals provide a vision of a perfect civilization.

<u>Freedom</u> – All people have the freedom to live their lives as they wish as long as they do not hurt other people. People are more creative and productive when freedom is unrestricted.

<u>Harmony</u> – No one lives in fear of another. All people of all cultures, ages, races, countries, religions, sexes or sexual orientations, physical characteristics (and...?) are respected equally. Diversity is not only respected but is appreciated. Harmony sets people free to appreciate life.

<u>Value</u> – Hard work, innovation, and creativity add great value to society and should be appreciated and rewarded fairly.

<u>Opportunity</u> – All people have opportunities for improving their lives and living conditions. Without opportunity, people have no hope, no dreams, no inspiration, their creativity is lost.

<u>Harmony with Nature</u> – The healthy natural environment is what allows us to live.

Education – Everyone has access to good education uncorrupted by government, religion, or private interests. Education gives each person the knowledge and ability that they need to succeed in pursuing their version of happiness.

Peace – Governments are at peace with each other and their primary work is to improve the lives of their citizens.

Justice – Laws are just and applied equally to all people. People cannot live in harmony if treated differently.

The Principle of Humanity

The first responsibility of every human being is to love themselves and be happy. The second responsibility is to love other people and to wish them happiness.

Following the Principle of Humanity can be improved by education and training provided by Scientific Spirituality.

Scientific Spirituality

A field of science that helps everyone follow the Arcadian Path and live by the Principle of Humanity. Modern medicine can cure almost all physical problems with the human body. Scientific Spirituality uses science to cure the mind.

The latest scientific information from the fields of human evolutionary development, psychology, religion, biology, sociology, biochemistry, and neuroscience, are united with a database of psychoanalytic research that includes four hundred years of data collected from billions of individuals throughout the United Worlds. Live updates to the database come from real-time data with the case information for active current Scientific Spirituality system users.

Science shows us the true beauty of the universe and what it means to be human, reveals our complex evolutionary nature, and explains our complicated emotions. Scientific Spirituality shows us how to feel the beauty of being human.

About the Author

After 30 years as a US Navy Physicist, Jeff is dreaming of a more positive purpose to his life. He is dreaming of a world that does not need warships.

Jeff Taylor is a baby boomer, hippy dropout, and anti-war protester, who was forced into the US Army during the Vietnam conflict. He is a free-thinking humanist, physicist, geologist, skeptic, father, grandfather, and husband. He loves to hike in the mountains, swim in the ocean, dance in the moonlight, and make love with his wife, Elvira.

He believes that the scientific knowledge of who we are in this universe is the most beautiful enlightening information in existence and that scientific knowledge will show humanity the path to a better world civilization.

Jeff appreciates his front-row seat on the Universe, and hopes that you appreciate yours.

If you enjoyed reading The Arcadian Path, you might also like to read "Another Path" which contains the third story in the United Worlds History Series; "The Arcadian Path" and "Beryl Awakening." Available on Amazon.

If you are interested the Arcadian Path philosophy, visit www.arcadianpath.com

www.ingramcontent.com/pod-product-compliance
Lightning Source LLC
LaVergne TN
LVHW010556100826
845148LV00014B/2740

* 9 7 8 0 5 7 8 3 0 2 9 5 9 *